Honor & Glory

Kim Murphy

Library of Congress Cataloging-in-Publication Data

Murphy, Kim.
    Honor & glory / Kim Murphy.
         p. cm.
    1. Virginia–History–Civil War, 1861-1865–Fiction. 2. Fredericksburg (Va.)–Fiction. I. Title: Honor and glory. II. Title.
    PS3613.U745H66 2004
    813'.6–dc22
                                                    2003016034

For My Parents,
who gave me the love for books, and General A.P. Hill
and Elizabeth Van Lew.

Chapter One

Fredericksburg, Virginia
December 18, 1862

METAL POUNDED ON PARTLY frozen earth. Picks and shovels tapped and scraped—hundreds of them chipping away precious red clay in the brisk winter air.

Alice McGuire looked to the heights. Grim reality replaced any thought of war's glory.

Men in blue woolen overcoats carried white flags of truce while Confederate soldiers looked on. Many Rebels also wore blue. Beside shallow trenches, pale corpses glistened in the sunlight. Hundreds upon hundreds of bodies stacked on top of one another—mostly naked. The picks and shovels were digging mass graves.

Queasy to the pit of her stomach, Alice clamped a hand over her mouth.

A strong hand grasped her arm and led her away from the ghastly scene. "The boys came down during the night," Colonel William Jackson said in his thick Charleston accent. "Many had no shoes. They took advantage of those who no longer needed them."

Wheezing, Alice halted in the middle of the road to catch her breath. She sank, but the colonel caught her in his arms. All of those lives—gone. Most of them had been mere boys—even younger than herself. How many mamas, wives, and sweethearts grieved over such a senseless waste?

The colonel's coal-black eyes shimmered as he kept a firm grip on her arm until her wobbly knees steadied. She pressed a hand to her temple and waited for the lightheaded feeling to pass. "I had no idea..."

"No one ever does until they've witnessed it firsthand."

Less than a fortnight ago, she had danced long into the night. The officers, so proud and brave, had been especially handsome in their gray uniforms trimmed with gold embroidered braids. Most of them, including the colonel, had asked her for the honor of a dance, which she gave cheerfully to the men marching off to an unknown fate. How could such carefree times have turned to total devastation? "But you've witnessed it many times."

Beside the carriage, her sister, Amanda waited. "We came to see the house," she reminded them, pursing her lips.

The colonel helped the women into the buggy before mounting his blue-roan gelding. He led the way through a side street. Charred houses had collapsed in ruins. Buildings fortunate enough to remain standing had entire sides blown away. Rickety wagons creaked along the muddy road as a few brave neighbors and shopkeepers sifted through rubble. Unlike other mornings, no greetings were exchanged.

A dying fire burst a plume of smoke in a final frenzy. Sputtering back a cough, Alice drew her cloak around her. Nothing seemed real. At least the sun had spread a little warmth to the wintery air. Unable to rid her mind of the lifeless bodies on the hillside, she shivered. Many of the wounded would have frozen to death with their final cries for home going unheard.

As they rounded the corner, the colonel's dark eyes flickered strength once more. From his tall, straight figure in the saddle to the sword at his side, he represented courage. The defense of Fredericksburg hadn't been his first battle.

They neared the house, and Amanda halted the buggy out front. The picket fence was splintered and rails were missing. Red bricks crumbled onto the street. One chimney had been blown to bits. Windows were shattered and shutters sagged. A hole from a shell had pierced the porch rail cleanly through.

A seventy-year-old oak had crushed the edge of the porch. From a thick branch, a swing once hung with a seat made of fine hickory. Papa had cut it specially for her before he died. Alice had insisted on bringing it from the farm when she and Mama had moved to town.

Why was she thinking of childish things? "I suppose it could have been worse," she said in a non-blinking daze.

Amanda gave her a reassuring hug. "We might be able to salvage something inside."

Wishful thinking—Amanda always had a bright way of looking at things. Yet, engaged to a Yankee, her sister was unlikely to come right out and admit that bluecoats were responsible for ransacking the town. "I fancy we should consider ourselves lucky that we have a house with a roof."

Amanda exchanged a nervous glance with her. For days, she had waited at the farm for news of her fiancé. While Sam Prescott had survived, his brother hadn't been so lucky. Like so many others, he was making the final journey home in a pine coffin. Doubtful that either man was involved in the looting, Alice said a silent prayer. Let her find it in her heart to forgive the enemy. On the heights at the edge of town, they had paid dearly.

Colonel Jackson helped her from the carriage. Face-to-face with him, she found renewed strength in his presence. In the thick of the fighting with so many dead, his life had been spared. "Thank you, Colonel."

Nodding a welcome, he extended a hand for Amanda.

Where the picket fence once stood, Alice raised her skirt and stepped over rubble. Near the steps, shredded linen waved in striped strips from Mama's favorite chair. Numb and shocked by the sights, she passed through the splintered door. In the parlor the sofa had been overturned, and shattered glass from goblets and china spread across the wood floor. Past the stairs and through the hall to the kitchen, the breakfast table was missing and the tinware, dented.

The door flapped back and forth in icy wind gusts, and the air was dreadfully cold. A shapeless blue form lodged in the frame kept it from closing. A Yankee must have dropped his bag of stolen goods on the way out. Another wintry blast swept through the kitchen.

Tightening her cloak, Alice scurried to the door. She reached for the knob, and her hand froze in midair.

Sightless eyes stared up at her. The misshapen blue figure was a dead Yankee.

Paralyzed, she screamed.

Move . . . She stumbled back a few steps.

But the eyes—dead and unseeing—kept looking her direction.

She screamed again.

Footsteps rushed toward her. Colonel Jackson burst into the kitchen with his pistol drawn.

Alice pointed to the body. "A Yankee!"

He bent over the blue form and holstered the gun. "He won't be giving you any trouble." Calm and collected, he straightened. "I'll take care of him."

Her fear faded. "Mama and I are in your debt."

The colonel thrust his hands under the frozen corpse's arms and dragged the body from the doorstep.

Amanda entered the kitchen and hugged her.

Dead—all of those Yankees frozen to death on the hillside. "It was a dead Yankee," Alice said. "Colonel Jackson is seeing to him."

"You and Mama will stay with me until you're on your feet again. Now let's see if there's anything we can salvage."

Taking a deep breath, Alice went into the dining room.

Chairs were smashed, and Mama's rose pattern china shattered.

Bending down, she sifted through chair legs, assorted broken wood, and glass to retrieve a fork from the debris. The looters had missed a silver fork. One silver fork and no table left to use it on. Alice dropped the fork to the floor and stood. "I must find a broom and clean up this mess. Amanda, where's the broom?"

Amanda's arms went around her. "We're not going to clean today."

In the parlor a broken picture frame lay next to the overturned sofa. The oil canvas had been cut from it. Worthless—the frame was absolutely worthless without the painting.

Alice made a fist. "Damn them! Damn them to hell. And you're just as bad—being engaged to one."

Amanda's eyes brimmed with tears and her skirt flew behind her as she retreated from the room, passing Colonel Jackson on the way out. With his hat in hand, he watched Amanda leave.

"She took offense because I damned the Yankee bastards," Alice said, "...*all* of them."

"No wonder she got riled."

"Don't tell me you're defending the filthy scalawags?"

"Defend the Yanks? Hardly—but I can separate the *bastards* from the rest."

Whether his comment was mocking her swearing or not, she couldn't be certain. "I'm delighted you can make that sort of distinction."

"Alice, if it brings you comfort, many who were responsible are lying on the hillside."

Dead—like the Yankee she had discovered inside the back door. "No, it doesn't give me comfort, but what shall we do? Amanda may be willing to take us in, but she'll be marrying Major Prescott soon. Even with his support, she can't afford to keep us for the remainder of the war."

With the mention of Amanda's upcoming wedding, his eyes fixed on the wall behind her. According to the rumors about town, he had courted Amanda, or some Yankee woman, depending on the source. No matter which account was true, it was obvious, he was fond of Amanda—maybe even loved her. Some versions of the story even proclaimed the baby that Amanda carried might actually be his.

"Colonel?"

He blinked. "Many families have gone to Richmond."

Richmond? The thought of Mama and her alone in an overcrowded city searching for a rented room and a way to sustain themselves frightened her. "Abandon our home for good?"

Amanda's face was pinched with anxiety when she rejoined them. "I apologize for running out. This is a difficult time for all of us, but I won't hear of my family becoming refugees. As long as I have a roof over my head, we shall find a way."

"Forgive me, Amanda," Alice stated, "if I don't believe the Lord will provide."

Amanda raised a finger in protest.

"Ladies..." The colonel held up a hand. "Quarrels won't resolve anything. There's enough of that already." He faced Amanda. "I can raise funds in exchange for—medicine, clothing..."

"Wil Jackson..." Amanda shook her head furiously. "I can't believe you're even suggesting such a thing. I won't smuggle supplies again."

"You saw the boys. Have you ever been in freezing weather with only threadbare clothing?"

"No, I haven't, but I can't do it."

"I have boys dying. The Yankees know you. They won't suspect—"

"I said no. I meant it."

As the colonel fell silent, Alice suspected he was a man unaccustomed to taking "no" for an answer. Only desperation would have driven him to plead.

"I'll do it," Alice said, breaking the stalemate.

Amanda and the colonel looked in her direction.

A year ago she had offered similar services and been rejected. Times were harder now, and she and Mama needed the money. "I will get the supplies," she repeated.

"It's too dangerous," Amanda argued. The colonel studied her as if considering the proposition. "Wil, please don't agree to this. We're friends."

"You protect her too much." In resignation, Wil slipped his hat on his head and turned. "But I will abide by your wishes."

"On second thought," Amanda said, "we should get a start on cleaning this mess. I'll fetch the broom."

Ignoring Amanda, Alice followed the colonel outside. "Colonel . . . Wil . . ." In the nine years she had known him, it was the first time she had resorted to his given name. "I know how to get the supplies that you require."

By the spot on the porch where a shell had pierced the rail, he came to a halt. "Amanda's right. It's too dangerous."

"You say that because I'm her younger sister." In the war with the Mexicans, he had taken a bullet intended for Amanda's now-dead husband and almost died. He had been very young at the time—even younger than she was now. "How old were you when you saw your first battle?"

He smiled in understanding. "That doesn't change matters."

"I know how to get the supplies," she demanded.

"Miss McGuire . . ."

"Alice."

"Alice," he agreed. "It was a foolish notion proposed in haste. The war has changed since Amanda smuggled supplies. I won't endanger your life."

Alice sensed someone watching them and glanced over her shoulder. With the broom in hand, Amanda stood in the doorway. Apparently satisfied by Wil's answer, she retreated inside.

As Wil strode to his horse, his sword clanked and his spurs jingled.

Alice caught up with him by the roan gelding's side. "Take a look around you, Colonel. All that Mama and I had was here. As I recall, you paid Amanda in gold."

He untied the gelding from one of the few standing trees. "I have given Amanda my word."

"What's more important? Your word in haste to Amanda, or our sick and wounded soldiers in need of medicine? How many will die if we don't get it to them?" Despair was etched in his face. Sympathy—she had struck a chord. "Wil, at least give me a chance."

A slight grin appeared on his lips. "You are very persuasive, Alice. Exactly how do you intend on securing the supplies?"

"Amanda visits the wounded in the Yankee hospitals. I can accompany her and gather supplies a little at a time."

"The Yankees regard such acquisitions as stealing."

Stealing—such an ugly word. His message was clear. She would be imprisoned if caught. But overnight, her world had vanished. How had she remained sheltered from the war for so long? The bodies on the heights had opened her eyes.

Suddenly, she saw Amanda in a new light. Only three years separated them, and, brave throughout the war, her sister had kept hope alive. Material goods might have disappeared, but Alice was no longer fearful of facing the unknown. "The Yankees have forced us to take desperate measures."

"They have indeed." He lifted her hand to his lips and kissed it. "I look forward to doing business with you."

His gaze met hers, and Alice shivered. His stare was no longer the sort a man would give a little girl.

The day after Christmas, Wil forded the Rappahannock River into Yankee territory. Although it was the holiday season, the Yanks were restless, and he remained on his guard. Fortunately, he encountered none.

The whitewash of Amanda's farmhouse came into view, and he reined his horse toward it. He brought the roan to a halt in the farm-yard. After he dismounted, Amanda's free servant, Ezra, led the horse away.

Before he knocked, Alice opened the door to greet him. "I'm glad you could come, Colonel."

Her auburn hair was coiled in ringlets and her smile—radiant. Her new demeanor hadn't been the result of battle fatigue. The girl had blossomed into a woman.

"Mama is helping Amanda. There are no Yankees except for Sam," she said in reference to Amanda's fiancé.

He bowed slightly. "I thank you for not taking the liberty of inviting a whole slew of Yanks."

"Amanda knew you wouldn't attend if she had." She hung his hat and overcoat on a peg inside the door and led the way to the parlor.

A woman in mourning black sat on the tapestry sofa—a Yankee widow. Normally such a meeting would be a disquieting situation, but Holly Prescott had her own agenda. Her presence only meant one thing—she wanted money.

"Mrs. Prescott," Alice said, introducing them, "I would like you to meet Colonel William Jackson. Colonel, Mrs. Charles Prescott."

"Ma'am."

Holly held up her hand. He obliged by kissing it.

She withdrew her hand, and a sly spark entered her eyes. "Colonel, I believe we've met before."

She didn't waste time. "As I recall, at the general's reception three years ago. I couldn't forget such a charming..." He nearly choked on the word. "... *lady*."

Shoving out her chin, she spread her fan and waved it in his face. "You must be thinking of someone else. My recollection is of a more recent nature."

So she wasn't playing the part of grieving widow. "Where would I have met a Yankee officer's wife?"

Her eyes seethed, and she snapped the fan shut.

"Let me extend my sympathy for your husband's passing," he said.

Holly raised her hand slightly, then lowered it to her lap. If Alice hadn't been present, she undoubtedly would have slapped him. "Your condolences are held in their proper regard," she replied in a clipped manner.

Alice forced a smile. "Perhaps I should fetch some tea."

"That would be most kind of you." Holly tugged on the pearl beads around her neck, and Alice made a hasty retreat to the kitchen. Holly shook a fist. "How dare you, Wil. You make Charles's memory a mockery."

"I meant my sympathy. He died bravely."

She spat, hitting squarely on the gold embroidery of his sleeve. "I don't know why it couldn't have been you."

"Cheer up, the war isn't over."

"On second thought, dying is too good for you. You're not afraid of death. What's more, they'd probably make you out as some hero. I'd rather see you rot in a Yankee prison."

"I missed you too." The flat of her hand made contact with his face. His beard absorbed the sting, but his head felt like it had suddenly been twisted off. "I'm curious. Why are you here today?"

Her scowl changed to a triumphant grin. "To watch you squirm. Fancy that, Sam marrying Amanda. You wooed her—and lost." Her gaze grew piercing. "She carries his child. Fess up, Wil, you've grown old."

His muscles tensed.

Smiling sweetly, she knew he would control his temper—at least while they were under Amanda's roof. "We also have a little unfinished business of our own."

"I don't have the money with me."

"I suggest you find it—soon."

Her tone sounded like a threat, and he didn't take kindly to them.

Before the stakes went higher, Alice returned, carrying a silver platter. A gracious hostess, she pretended that she hadn't overheard their quarreling.

Pigtails—Wil had visions of Alice wearing pigtails. When had the change come about? Her eyes sparkled the same green shade as Amanda's.

Pouring from a china teapot, Alice served Holly.

Real tea—a rare commodity in the South these days. No doubt remained that he was in a Yankee household.

"Colonel, would you care for some tea?"

Her scent was the sweet smell of lilac. He cleared his throat. "No thank you."

Holly smirked when the groom in full dress uniform and the preacher entered the parlor.

Not that long ago, Wil also had worn Federal blue. South Carolina was his native state, and he had been left with no choice but to resign his commission. He held out his hand. "Prescott, I see you're a major now."

Prescott's hand shook from wedding day jitters, but he shook Wil's hand. "Still not a brigadier?"

Wil laughed and dropped his hand to his side. "Soon. I have been assured it will happen before the coming campaign."

"I trust you're making certain I go through with this."

Wil detected a quaver in Prescott's voice. "Amanda requested that I attend as a family friend."

"Colonel . . . Sam . . ." Alice motioned to the doorway by the stairs.

Amanda's mother and Sam Prescott's toddler daughter from his first marriage joined the guests. Behind them, Amanda followed with a beaming smile. She wore a slightly off-the-shoulder blue dress.

Sighing in resignation, Wil stepped back. She was dressed to appeal to the bridegroom, not him.

Due to the winter season, she carried a dried bouquet. Compared to Amanda's first wedding, this one was a small occasion. But these days a lot of weddings were hurried affairs. One boy in the regiment was married one week, and his young bride became a widow the next. Holly was right. He *was* old—too old for such nonsense. War was a fool's time to fall in love, and men who gave way to the emotion lost sound fighting judgment.

As Amanda joined the groom, Holly's sneer returned.

The joke was on her. He had never let his feelings for Amanda stray beyond friendship. At the same time, he went out of his way to turn a deaf ear when the couple recited their vows.

Alice stood next to him and stole a shy glance in his direction. Not only had she grown up from the freckle-faced adolescent at Amanda's first wedding, she wanted him to take notice. With her upbringing she'd be too proper to admit as much, but he recognized the subtle cues all the same.

If he let his thoughts stray any further, he wouldn't need to fret about Yankee bullets. Amanda would haul out the shotgun herself.

The preacher announced the newly married couple, and Wil let out a frustrated breath. He wished them well, then stepped onto the porch and lit a cigar.

The door opened behind him, and Alice joined him. "Colonel . . . ," she said, greeting him casually.

On the chance that someone might be watching, he bowed slightly.

"I wasn't able to collect much—a few bags of morphine and quinine."

"We can use whatever you got."

With a gracious smile, she glanced in the direction of the barn and breathed deeply. "It's a lovely day for a stroll, don't you think?"

Her meaning was clear. She had hidden the medicine outside the house. "I would be honored to have you accompany me." He stamped out the cigar and held out his arm. She hooked her arm through it, and they went down the steps to the farmyard.

"I hid them in the barn."

"Miss McGuire, your reputation may suffer if anyone should see you accompanying me unchaperoned."

Her smile turned sly. "After what I witnessed between you and Mrs. Prescott, I doubt you have any concern for my reputation. You want the supplies, and you will do anything to get them. You are a dangerous man, Colonel Jackson."

She *had* grown up. "It appears *my* reputation precedes me."

Wil opened the barn door, and Alice led the way inside. "You're well known in town . . ." By an empty stall, she shoved straw aside, withdrawing saddlebags from underneath. Draping the saddlebags over his arm, she continued, ". . . especially with the ladies—Mrs. Prescott rumored as one. Tell me, is it true about the two of you?"

He checked through the saddlebags. Morphine and quinine . . . She had made good on her promise. "Perhaps you should ask her. I'm certain she'd be delighted to fill you in on the details."

Wil retreated to the next stall and threw the saddlebags across the roan's withers.

Alice's smiled widened to a grin. "Shouldn't a self-respecting Confederate officer show more discrimination than dallying with a Yankee?"

Wil pressed a gold coin into her palm. "I have always maintained the belief that one should know the enemy—Miss McGuire."

Her eyelids fluttered and her face flushed. "I should be able to collect more supplies next time. Accompanying Amanda to the hospital has advantages."

Amused by her sudden bashfulness, he studied her. Youthful innocence unspoiled by the ravages of war. The pigtailed child still existed underneath. But there was no turning the clock back. She had witnessed the aftermath of Fredericksburg. He remained uneasy risking a woman's life, but the lack of medicine forced him to take reckless measures. "I must remind you of what will happen if you're caught."

"I will be arrested. Quite possibly imprisoned. I'm aware of the risks, Colonel. I hope your concern is for my well-being and not because of what Amanda might think."

A bad sign—he was feeling protective. "I never fret over what others might think—including Amanda."

"Obviously not, but I thought your regard for Amanda *might* be different."

Almost voicing his thoughts aloud, he caught himself. Amanda was married now. That fact changed the way things were between them. "I should bid my farewells and head back across the river."

"I'm surprised you attended the wedding, Colonel," came a feminine voice.

Fright entered Alice's eyes.

Near the door, Holly held a pearl-handled derringer. "This side of the river tends to be rather dangerous for Rebels." Peering down her nose at Alice with a haughty leer, Holly moved closer. "You wasted no time replacing me."

"I need supplies, and *you* haven't been supplying them—simple as that." Wil stepped between the women. "Any dispute you have is with me."

With a contemptuous laugh, Holly aimed the derringer straight for his heart. "Defensive, Wil? That's unlike you. Because she's Amanda's sister? Or have you been charmed by her?"

If she thought it was in her best interest, Holly would shoot. He was certain of that. No one on this side of the river would mourn the loss of a fallen Confederate officer. Palms up, he held out his hands. "Holly . . ."

Her grin widened. "Now I know you're worried. You've never resorted to the use of my given name before. You can stop fretting. I won't hurt the child. As you may recall, the last time we did business, you paid me in worthless Confederate paper." She opened her left hand. "I require gold."

On one other occasion she had leveled the same pearl-handled derringer at him. Naked at the time, she had held more intrigue. "I thought the sight of blood made you squeamish."

Holly's eyes narrowed. "You're testing me."

Wil shrugged. "Why would I do that? If I'm dead, you don't get paid, nor do you have the pleasure of seeing me rot in some Yankee prison."

Holly's lips curled, revealing glistening white teeth. She shrieked in frustration.

"Here . . ." Alice tossed a gold coin by Holly's foot. "Take it."

Snatching up the coin, Holly lowered the derringer. "This is a start. I want the rest within a fortnight, or I'll inform the Yankees who your new supplier is. With a little luck, they might catch a Reb colonel in the deal."

As Holly scurried from the barn, Wil finished strapping the saddlebags to his saddle.

Alice snapped her fingers. "Just like that."

He tightened the gelding's girth. "Just like what?"

She threw her hands in the air. "How can you pretend nothing has happened?"

"Mrs. Prescott will keep silent as long as she gets paid." Confusion entered her eyes. "Alice, I have men sick and dying. I don't have the luxury of wasting time fretting over little things."

"But she threatened you."

Contrary to his previous thoughts, she had much maturing to do—especially when it came to women like Holly Prescott. "I appreciate your quick thinking, but it wasn't necessary. You're under no obligation to continue smuggling supplies, if that is your choice."

"Mama and I need the money."

If it was his to give, he would do so, but the war had strapped every-one in the South for cash. "Then we shall meet in a fortnight. I'll see that you're paid before then." He glanced around the barn. "Under the circumstances, I think it's unwise to meet here again. Amanda might grow suspicious."

"There's an abandoned servants' shack in the bottomland."

"I know of it. That will do. Remember what you must do if you encounter any Yankees."

Alice kept glancing over her shoulder as if expecting Holly to reap-pear. "I must get rid of the supplies. They're secondary."

Satisfied that she comprehended the risks involved, he untied the roan and backed the gelding out of the stall. She looked nervously to the door once more. Tempted to reassure her, he restrained himself. Amanda might misinterpret any gesture on his part as stepping beyond the bounds of propriety and never forgive him.

Once outside, Alice regarded him with curiosity. "You are concerned for my well-being."

Intrigued by her statement, Wil asked, "What makes you think so?"

"Because you stepped between Mrs. Prescott and me, ready to take the bullet if she fired."

His sword clanked as he mounted the gelding. "A weakness of mine. I have a tendency to rush to the aid of pretty damsels in distress."

She finally relaxed and smiled. "I shall see you soon, Colonel."

"I'll look forward to it." He shoved his hat on his head and reined the blue roan in the direction of the bottomland.

Chapter Two

T HEY'D BOARDED THE WINDOWS over until they could afford new glass and had cleared most of the rubble from the house. Earlier in the week, Wil had sent a courier with the payment for the medical supplies. Finances were stretched to capacity.

Alice had already spent the money on basic necessities—food and cloth for making new dresses. But for furniture—what to do? Odds and ends mended some chairs. The soldiers had kindly contributed a wooden cracker box to serve as a dining room table. With no wood to spare for frames, Mama and she had stuffed burlap bags with straw for beds. Amanda promised the loan of a few items, but even with a pass, the Yankees prohibited them from crossing the river with any goods.

Her stomach twisted in knots, and Alice tossed the scrub brush across the kitchen. Bouncing off the door, the brush thumped to the brick floor near the spot where the dead Yankee had lain. His unblinking eyes . . . Almost every waking moment, she envisioned them staring at her.

Tucking her knees, she curled to a ball and heard the echoes of Yankee laughter—plundering and smashing. Everything was gone. She caught her breath. No, not everything. Their lives had been spared.

"Alice!" Mama called from the parlor.

Alice grumbled to herself. Ever since the servants had run off, hadn't she been toiling hard enough without being at the old woman's beck and call? She should have left Mama with Amanda until the house was presentable. But a single woman—alone; it wouldn't have been proper. Careful not to sound irritated, Alice attempted to keep her voice even. "Yes, Mama?"

"We have a caller."

"I already have enough work . . ." She blinked. "A caller?" Who had time for social calls these days? "Thank you, Mama.'

Alice stood and straightened her rumpled dress. Exhausted, she meandered to the parlor and overheard Mama laugh and a baritone voice—Colonel Jackson.

Uncertain whether to be irritated further or relieved by the break, she pasted on a smile and entered the room. "Colonel Jackson, this is a pleasant surprise."

With a cordial smile, he bowed slightly and took her hand, kissing the back. For some reason his penetrating black eyes made her shiver. "The pleasure is mine."

He certainly knew when to turn on the charm. Definitely not a man to be trusted. "To what do we owe the honor of your visit?"

"I came to see how you are faring. These days it's difficult for two ladies to manage—all alone."

"We've been scraping by. I'd offer some tea, but—"

"Fancy fixings are unnecessary on my account."

"Then please warm yourself by the fire. Some of the soldiers took pity on us and cut some firewood."

"I'm pleased to hear the boys have been helpful. It's a beautiful afternoon. If your mother doesn't mind, I thought you might accompany me on a ride."

So he was going to play the role of a courting beau to speak with her alone. Since he came from a well-respected Carolinian family, Mama wouldn't protest.

"Mrs. McGuire?"

With a nod, Mama waved them on.

Alice resisted the urge of saying she was much too busy for frivolous pastimes. At the same time, she had no wish to admit that she had been on bent knee scrubbing floors like a servant. "I would be honored."

His face brightened, and Mama bid them farewell. On their way out, Wil placed her cloak over her shoulders. As she tied it, their gazes met. Slight wrinkles by his eyes creased into a smile, and he placed his hat on his head.

She hooked her arm through his, and they stepped into the brisk but pleasant winter afternoon. Nuthatches chattered from a nearby sycamore tree. It *was* a lovely day to think of something besides cleaning.

"I wasn't expecting to see you for a few days yet," Alice said, breaking the silence.

Acting every bit the couple out for a stroll, they went down the steps. "I sincerely wanted to see how you were faring," Wil replied.

"And the ride?"

"I thought you might appreciate a diversion."

She broke free of his arm. "As in keeping company with you? You're arrogant, Colonel."

"Alice . . ." Taking her hand, he bowed slightly. "My motives are honorable." He rotated her wrist until her palm faced up.

Her once neatly manicured nails were jagged and her hands had become work-swollen. She clenched it.

"I saw the calluses inside. You needn't pretend—not with me."

"A lady shouldn't be doing the things I have."

He crossed his arms. "There are far worse things you could be doing."

The crude remark should have offended her, but for some reason, his nonchalance made her laugh.

"About the ride?" he asked.

"If you would be so kind and help me saddle the carriage horse."

"Or we can ride mine."

"Don't push your luck, Colonel." She jabbed an index finger his direction, and his eyes sparkled. "It's proper that we ride separately."

"Of course, we must remain in accordance with propriety."

Amusement colored his voice. With no desire to lead him on, she had best ignore such rude remarks. In the barn, Alice rubbed the carriage horse's bay neck. "If I had known you were going to call, I would have brought the supplies I've stockpiled."

"No!" Wil held up a finger. "First order of business, you never bring the supplies across the river. The war was different when Amanda smuggled them. I have scouts and tend to know where the Yanks patrol."

"But the Yankees won't shoot me."

That condescending grin of his returned. "Why Miss McGuire, do I detect concern for my safety?"

"You flatter yourself, Colonel. I don't wish to see anyone hurt."

His sly spark vanished. With a tiredness, suddenly making him look years older, he said, "After what happened to your home, I thought you understood what we are up against. Thousands more will die before this war is over."

Twisting the bay's mane between her fingers, she felt like a wretch for complaining about etiquette. *Thousands more—dead?* How could the South afford to lose their bravest and most daring? Even Wil had nearly died in the foreign land of Mexico. At the benefits, the officers looked so fetching in their finest. She danced and flirted, never lending a thought to battles, and she now understood why Amanda got so distraught when Sam rode away to face the horror. "I'd like to take that ride, and I shall ride with you."

He grasped her hand, and his grip was robust and warm.

By the side of the house, a blue-roan gelding was tied to a tree. She rubbed the gelding's gray nose. "Poker Chip...Amanda told me that he's out of a spotted mare you brought back from the Northwest."

"Indeed—what else did she say?"

"That he has a spot the size of a poker chip on his..." Her cheeks warmed. "...posterior."

He laughed as he untethered the roan and mounted. Extending his hand, he helped her on behind him. She wrapped her arms loosely about his waist, and for a little while, she could even forget the war as the crumbling buildings of Fredericksburg gave way to charred earth.

On the outskirts of town, rows and rows of tents and makeshift cabins covered the countryside. Some had brick chimneys with smoke plumes pouring from them. Others had gaping holes between logs. The army of Northern Virginia was in winter quarters.

At the edge of the Confederate village, an aide led Poker Chip away. Fiddles and banjos strummed around open campfires. Alice gravitated toward laughter—a sound absent since before the battle. Men danced with ladies—some in linen and silk dresses. Not the sorts of women rumored to follow an army, but officers' wives, wearing finery that made her simple cotton frock look frumpy.

"Wil, you should have warned me. I must look a fright."

With a devilish gleam, he replied, "You look delightful."

Joining the group, she danced and sang. A deer roasted over the fire, and she consumed meat for the first time in over a week. Afternoon gave way to evening. Out of breath from dancing and laughing, she spotted Wil near a campfire, smoking a cigar—alone. "Colonel, I must say that I should feel insulted."

He regarded her quizzically.

"You escort me here and have yet to ask me to dance."

His face remained an emotionless mask, but he shook his head. "It wouldn't be proper."

Proper? From the man who scorned propriety. "She stole your heart, didn't she?" she asked.

"Mrs. Prescott? Hardly."

"No. I meant Amanda."

He took a drag on his cigar without a reply.

She hadn't really expected an answer. "Mama will begin to fret if I don't return home soon."

With a nod, he stamped out the cigar, and they retraced their steps through camp. After saddling Poker Chip, he mounted, then held out his hand and helped her aboard. The music from camp faded.

In the crisp winter air, moonlight illuminated Fredericksburg. With tall dreary chimneys and shattered buildings, the town was a mere skeleton of its former self. For a little while, she had forgotten the blue storm—and the bodies.

Outside her house, Wil gently lowered her from Poker Chip's back. He touched his hat. "Good evening, Miss McGuire."

"Please come inside. We may not have tea, but I have some herbs that make a fine drink."

"Thank you kindly, but—"

"Please, Wil. I still see their goddamn faces—their grinning wicked faces as they smashed and stole everything we own. Then I see the bodies on the heights, and I'm glad they died. Lord forgive me, but I'm glad."

In one swift move, Wil leaped from Poker's back and stood beside her. "Alice, you are no lady."

Fearing he would think her godless, Alice sucked in her breath.

"You swear almost as good as some of the boys."

She clapped a hand to her mouth, but couldn't keep from snickering. He hadn't been mocking her the time before, and he was the first man who hadn't.

Inside the house, Mama had left the single lamp left to their name lighted. Candles served the rest of their needs. After lighting a few, she made tea from a blend of chicory and raspberry leaves. Mama must have approved of Wil. She hadn't waited up.

In front of the fire, Alice talked. Not much of a talker, Wil listened, but his company helped her forget the dead Yankee faces.

Growing up on the farm with Amanda, she hadn't ventured far from home—not beyond Maryland. Being a career officer, Wil was well-traveled, and she wanted to hear stories about all of the places she'd likely never see. When pressed, he told her about the New Mexico territory, avoiding any references to the time Sam Prescott served under him.

"I'd be deathly afraid of Indians," she said with a shiver.

"They have more to fear from us than the other way around."

Never having met an Indian, she was intrigued by his sympathy. "Do you believe that because you were married to one?"

His gaze hardened. "Amanda had no right telling you."

Shamed? Embarrassed? No, he was infuriated—by Amanda's betrayal. "She only said that you had a Nez Perce wife when you were stationed in the Northwest."

His eyes remained fixed on her face. "Nothing more?"

"That she died," she answered weakly.

"But not how?"

Alice shook her head.

"She was hanged for stealing supplies."

He said it so easily that she wasn't certain she had heard him correctly. She opened her mouth, but no words came out.

"Forgive me. I don't like people prying, but my abruptness was unkind. I should have guessed you'd react more like Amanda."

"I meant no intrusion."

He clenched his right hand, then released it again. "I still see their faces. I've killed them a number of times—on the battlefield."

Like how she envisioned the Yankees. No wonder he had spared her a lecture for cursing. He knew how she felt. "Wil, thank you for understanding."

His melancholy mood dissolved. "And I thank you for your pleasant company—Miss McGuire."

As a child, she had adored him. Until recently, she thought it had been nothing more than a schoolgirl's passing fancy. But the places he'd been to, and the things he had experienced. Fifteen years separated them. He was much too worldly. Undoubtedly, he'd never see past the adolescent she had been at Amanda's first wedding.

Amanda reined her gray mare to a halt at the picket line, and Alice's carriage horse lumbered to a stop beside her. Since the battle, she had feared the devastation of Fredericksburg might have destroyed Alice's spirit and took some comfort that her sister accompanied her to the hospital to help aid wounded soldiers.

After Amanda had a quick chat with the guard, he motioned that Sam was on picket duty and waved for them to pass. She squeezed her mare forward.

"Amanda, I think we should visit the hospital first," Alice said.

Amanda winked. "What's your hurry, Alice? Is there someone special you wish to call on?"

Alice's nose scrunched in revulsion, but she forced a smile. "Why Amanda, I thought you knew me better than that. I flirt with all of the handsome gentlemen."

Amanda leaned over and gave Alice's hand a comforting squeeze. "Everyone in Fredericksburg is hurting." But she doubted Alice would forgive easily and didn't wish to dwell on it. "Sam tells me the Confederates have remained in winter quarters near you. Have you seen Wil recently?"

Her sister's face paled, revealing the answer to her question.

Uncertain how she felt by that fact, Amanda shoved the thought from her mind. "There's no reason to fret. I was only wondering how he is."

Calming, Alice relaxed in the saddle. "Wil is fine."

The fact that Alice resorted to the use of his given name now gave Amanda a bothersome twinge. On the day of her wedding, she had pretended not to notice the two of them strolling—arm in arm.

Amanda cued the mare to a fast walk. The lazy carriage horse groaned as Alice squeezed him to a trot to keep pace with her mare.

After passing a long line of soldiers, Amanda spotted a big red horse. Bent over in the saddle, the officer was speaking to a soldier in blue. She brought the mare to a halt, and Alice jerked on the reins to keep the horses from colliding.

"Why are you stopping?" Alice asked.

No longer troubled by pesky worries, Amanda smiled as the officer straightened in the saddle and looked in their direction.

Sam's blue eyes reflected a weariness she had witnessed in most soldiers, but upon seeing her, he beamed. He cantered his horse toward them. "Amanda . . ." His voice sounded urgent, and he was no longer smiling. He brought the blood-red chestnut to a halt beside the gray mare. "Sergeant Tucker has taken a turn for the worse. Refuses to see a surgeon."

"Jo?" Amanda asked.

He nodded.

"Where is he?"

"In camp."

Amanda reined the mare around but glanced over her shoulder. "Sam?"

"I can't leave the line."

A musket fired, and several men shouted.

Sam spun the red horse around and shot off at a gallop.

Without bothering to check if Alice was following, Amanda cued the mare to a canter. In her delicate condition, the bumpy ride unsettled her stomach.

"Amanda," Alice shouted after her, "what's the hurry? Who is Sergeant Tucker?"

The sick gnawing in her stomach increased and she slowed the gray to a trot, allowing an out-of-breath Alice to catch up. "A friend who was wounded in the recent battle."

"You can't save every Yankee."

Amanda shot her sister an irritated look.

"I'm worried for you and your baby. If you continue to ride with little concern for your health, you could lose it."

Ignoring Alice's warning, Amanda continued trotting. The mare stumbled in a slushy wagon wheel rut. Nearly slipping from the saddle, she buried her hands in the gray's thick mane and kept her seat. She breathed in relief, only to be swiped by a poplar branch across the cheek. Uncertain how, she stayed on the horse's back, and finally brought the mare to a walk.

At the top of the hill, rows and rows of tents came into view. Amanda halted the gray and slid from her back, and Alice pulled to a stop next to her.

"Soldier!" Amanda shouted to a man huddled near a campfire. "Please see to the horses. It's urgent."

The boy barely had the reins in his hands, and she charged off.

Struggling and wheezing, Alice hurried along behind her. "Amanda!"

Failing to slow her pace, Amanda dodged between the tents. Finally reaching the row's end, the tent flap went up, and Holly Prescott stepped out to greet her. "The poor *boy* is in a lot of pain," she said. "A vile infection has set in."

"Holly," she acknowledged, "if Sergeant Tucker is in a bad way, I don't have time for your games."

A grin spread across Holly's face. Even mourning black didn't keep soldiers from staring. She was a stunningly beautiful woman and obviously well aware of that fact.

Out of breath, Alice reached her side. "Mrs. Prescott—"

"Holly," Holly insisted with a pat to Alice's arm, while giving Amanda a sidelong glance. "After all, with Amanda married to Sam, we are family."

"Holly," Alice agreed.

"Good." Holly nodded in approval.

Worried about Jo, Amanda elbowed past Holly and stooped to enter the pup tent.

Holly's voice came from outside the tent. "Now that we have names settled, I was wondering if you have seen Colonel Jackson since our last meeting?"

Holly inquiring about Wil? An unlikely prospect unless she had returned to supply smuggling, but why was she bothering Alice? Alice had been warned of the danger.

A groan came from the floor, and Amanda bent down to a bob-haired soldier. She opened Sergeant Tucker's shirt to a gaping shoulder wound and caught a whiff of a familiar stench—gangrene. Amanda ripped a section from her petticoat and began dabbing carefully at the wound.

Alice joined her and pointed. "That's not a man."

Amanda covered the girl soldier's tiny but rounded breast with a blanket, leaving only the wound visible. "That's precisely why the sergeant won't see a doctor. Now hush before someone overhears you. Alice, I could use some help."

Alice kneeled beside her. "What are you going to do, Amanda?"

The sergeant's sunken eyes stared up at her. "For now, clean the wound as best as I can."

"But that's gangrene. The surgeon wouldn't bother."

"I'm well aware of what the surgeon would do. I know of an old remedy."

"For gangrene?"

Amanda nodded. The girl soldier's fingers encircled Amanda's arm in sisterhood. "I owe you."

Reciprocating the gesture, Amanda squeezed Jo's hand. "Let's worry about getting you properly mended."

Chapter Three

Alice was late. On his guard in Yankee territory, Wil poised his hand near his gun belt. The sooner he collected the supplies and was across the river, the sooner he could relax.

The night grew colder, and he bundled his overcoat around him. Alice was an inexperienced supply runner. He must give her a chance.

Or she could have been captured. For a moment, he entertained the notion of storming the Yankee camp. Foolish thinking—the cold must have affected his brain. If she failed to show soon, he would notify Amanda. She would *not* be pleased.

Aided by moonlight, he kept the shack in sight from a safe distance in the woods. Despising the cold, he shivered. His fingers could barely grip the reins. His eyelids grew heavy. Damn. He had witnessed men fall into a stupor under similar conditions. He needed to remain alert.

To his relief, he heard the plodding gallop of a carriage horse. Alice pulled up to the shack.

Cautious, he continued waiting behind the trees in case Yanks were on her tail.

Rusty hinges creaked as she went inside. Soon a smoke plume poured from the chimney. Not amused by her lack of discretion, he wondered if she had also invited the neighbors to tea.

Forgive her—she was young and inexperienced. And, a warm fire *did* seem inviting. The luxury of time was long past. Convinced she was alone, he reined Poker to the shack and brought the gelding to a halt next to the carriage horse.

The door flew open. With a pistol in hand, Alice aimed at him. "You're late," she said, lowering the gun.

"I have been here for over two hours. *You* are the one who's late."

"Amanda needed my help with a soldier. I couldn't easily get away."

Nearly frozen, his fingers tingled. With difficulty, Wil dismounted and grabbed the saddlebags from the carriage horse.

"Not even a thank you?" she asked.

"You'll be paid. I hope you have more than this."

"You're certainly in a foul mood."

"Alice, I'm in enemy territory, and I've nearly frozen my . . . " Biting his tongue, he caught himself. " . . . fingers off."

Easily guessing what he had nearly said, Alice giggled. "Come in and warm yourself. I have more supplies."

He tossed the saddlebags over Poker's withers and followed her.

"Besides me," Alice said, "I don't think anyone has been here in years."

As Wil stepped inside, he was greeted with warmth. A single candle lit the one-room former slave shack, and a welcoming pot-bellied stove sat in the corner. Extending his fingers, he gravitated toward the fire. Tingling gave way to burning. He rubbed his hands together, only making the pain worse.

"I didn't mean to keep you waiting."

"No permanent damage done." As normal feeling slowly returned, he wiggled his fingers. "Where are the supplies?"

"On me." Alice lifted her skirt, and a packet dropped to the floor. She hoisted the skirt further, revealing a petticoat bulging at the seams. "Colonel, if you would stop gawking like you've never seen a woman's undergarments before and help me, you would be across the river in short order."

She *had* grown up. The petticoat had pockets sewn inside, each containing a medicine packet. Keeping his head clear, he concentrated on the task at hand. Another packet dropped to the floor and another. A small pile formed. "You collected all of this in one trip?"

"I have more over there." She gestured to a canvas bag beside a cot on the far wall.

A cornhusk doll lay on the floor, and he envisioned her playing with it. But she was no longer a child. With the seams nearly empty of packets, the petticoat framed the spread of her hips and well-rounded buttocks. Amanda would definitely haul out the shotgun if he let his thoughts stray further. He plucked the last packet from her petticoat.

"What was her name?"

He collected the supplies in the canvas bag. "Whose name?"

"Your wife's."

In nearly eleven years, he had uttered Peopeo's name only to Amanda. "I should be leaving . . ."

"And you don't want to talk about her."

"No, I don't care to discuss her."

Spotting a packet on the dirt floor that he had missed, he bent over to retrieve it.

"Or your son?" Alice inquired further.

Amanda had revealed far more than he cared anyone knowing. Wil straightened. "Why the questions?"

"You don't seem the overly sentimental type. I suspect the supply shipments are important because of what happened then."

"Amanda didn't tell you?" She shook her head. "Then I'll forgive your naiveté. Benjamin died when he was three." Her face paled, and he lowered his voice. "Alice, some things are best kept in the past."

"Then I was right."

"Does that fact please you?" He hoisted the canvas bag over his shoulder and hauled it outside. "I shall get word to you when we will meet again." After strapping the bag to the saddle, he withdrew three gold pieces from his pocket.

Looking lost, she clenched the coins.

"*Peopeo Ipsewahk.* It means lone bird. Now I really must be getting back across the river."

Her face brightened, and she smiled slightly. "Of course. I understand."

Wil placed his foot in the stirrup and swung into the saddle, then tipped his hat. "Until next time, Alice." He reined the gelding around.

"Colonel . . . Wil . . ."

He glanced over his shoulder.

"Thank you."

"For what?"

"Taking me in your confidence."

Confidence? He hadn't really. Amanda had relayed bits and pieces—just enough to stir Alice's curiosity. With her youth, she most likely envisioned a dashing romantic notion—not the insanity left behind. He must never drop the mask and let her glimpse behind it.

"Good evening, Miss McGuire." He cued the roan to a trot.

Moonlight illuminated the path. Wil traveled through the forest for a couple of miles until he heard the sound of rushing water. He brought Poker to a halt at the tree line. Two mounted soldiers were near the Rappahannock's ford. Friend or enemy?

The soldiers smoked cigarettes and chatted.

Nasal voices—they were definitely Yankees.

The ford farther up river was miles out of his way, and he couldn't risk crossing downstream in Yankee stronghold. Two against one—the odds could be worse. But there might be another way—without bloodshed. He only hoped there weren't reinforcements lurking in the woods.

Wil drew his pistol and rode into the open.

Two rifles snapped in his direction.

"I'd rather not fight," Wil said.

The first Yank—a sergeant grunted. "No belly, Reb?"

"I'll fight, if that's what you really want. I'll be certain to take one of you with me before I go down. Care to decide which one?"

The rifle on his right lowered slightly.

"I only want to cross the river," he continued. "Seems we should be able to strike a bargain—peaceably."

The rifle sank lower. "What did you have in mind?" the soldier asked.

"These . . ." As Wil reached inside his pocket, the rifle raised. His teeth chattered. The cold was getting to him again. If they decided to fight, his reaction time would be slowed—not a chance in hell of coming out alive. Wil withdrew three cigars. ". . . for allowing me to cross."

The private beamed. "Good Southern tobacco?"

Wil nodded, and the private lowered his rifle.

The sergeant squinted. "What makes those worth more than a Reb officer?"

"All of us live to fight another day."

The sergeant spat on the ground but lowered his rifle. They accepted the cigars, and Wil rode on. He forded the river. The water was icy.

Amanda was right. He gambled too much. One of these days, he'd up the stakes too high and lose. Gamblers often died the coward's way by being shot in the back. He turned slightly in the saddle.

Paying him no mind, the Yanks smoked the cigars.

It didn't matter how one died. Dead was dead. And he had the feeling he wasn't going to survive the war anyway. No use fixating on it.

Poker climbed the bank to the Confederate side of the river. At least with the supplies, there was a chance at life for some.

After two uneventful runs, the few supplies they had managed to smuggle across the river made little difference. A losing battle—the Yanks had greater numbers. Many of the boys were sick, and the medicine was already gone.

So cold . . . Wil wrapped a blanket around himself and edged closer to the fire. Chills, headache—damn, he had it too. The winter river crossings would likely do him in.

"Colonel?"

He hadn't heard anyone enter the hut and glanced around. Alice and Amanda stood in the doorway.

"I knocked," Alice said, "but no one answered."

"My humble winter abode." He motioned for them to come inside the log shelter. "What can I do for you lovely ladies?"

Amanda's hands went straight to her hips. "Supplies are missing from the hospital. Have you enlisted Holly's aid to smuggle them across the river?"

Alice bit her lip.

The gold wedding band on Amanda's finger reminded him that things had changed between them. "I haven't had any contact with Mrs. Prescott since your wedding. Alice can testify on my behalf that she was less than pleased to see me."

Amanda raised a skeptical eyebrow.

"Amanda, if I were smuggling supplies, don't you think I'd be using them for myself?"

"No, I don't, Wil. You had a bullet wound clean through your arm, and you refused laudanum. I also don't like it when you answer my questions with a question."

Alice shifted nervously on her feet, and he held his hands out in a truce. "I haven't enlisted Mrs. Prescott or anyone else to smuggle supplies across the river."

She relaxed her arms, but continued staring at him. "I hope you're telling me the truth. If Sam thinks, even for a minute, that I might be responsible . . ." She finally broke eye contact. "I'm sorry you're sick."

His stomach churned, and he suddenly felt dizzy. "If you stay much longer, you'll be witness to how sick."

"I won't intrude any longer. Come along, Alice."

"I'll stay for a little while," Alice insisted.

"That wouldn't be proper."

Alice's lips curled, and she bunched her fists. "Don't start quoting propriety to me, Amanda. What did propriety get the residents when the damn Yankees burned and looted the town? Wil's division collected money to help the townspeople out. It's time I see to our own, instead of the bastards who did this to us."

Amanda's skirt swirled as she made a hasty retreat.

If he didn't feel like retching his guts out, he would have laughed. No doubt about it, but Alice was a spitfire. "You shouldn't rile her like that."

"She's the one who married a Yankee."

Lightheaded, he needed to sit before he fell. "Prescott's a good man."

Alice gripped his arm and helped him to the cot. "And you weren't disappointed?"

He leaned back. "I wanted to kill him with my bare hands."

She gave him a pat on his shoulder as he closed his eyes. "I may not have quinine, but I'll make some willow bark tea. Meanwhile, you rest."

Wil woke to the smell of herb tea. Seated on the cot's edge, Alice handed him a steaming tin cup. He sat up. "Aren't you concerned about your reputation?"

"You helped Mama and me. My reputation won't suffer for returning a favor."

The warm drink soothed his throat. Not only was she sassy, but confident too.

After he finished the willow bark tea, she took the cup. "Wil, you lied to Amanda."

"But I didn't. I'm the only one who has crossed the river with supplies."

"Which is why you're sick." Her cool hand touched his forehead. "You're feverish. Do you really think Amanda believed a partial truth?"

"Does it matter? She doesn't suspect you."

"That's very thoughtful of you, Colonel, but one of these days, you need to think of yourself for a change. I'm perfectly capable of handling Amanda."

"What about the Yankees?"

A brave front—he saw fear enter her eyes. "The war has forced us to make decisions we'd rather not."

That was definitely the truth. Exhausted, he stretched out on the cot and closed his eyes.

"Now if you get some rest, I shall visit tomorrow," she said in parting.

True to her word, Alice visited each day for the next three days. She brought broth and a feather pillow. Self-reliance had become second nature, and it had been a long time since a woman had tended him. Drifting in and out of a feverish daze, Wil relished the token luxury and looked forward to her visits.

On the fourth morning, he floated in a hazy dream when metal clanged to the floor. Waking with a start, Wil had the kicking and screaming assailant by the arm and flat on his back in a swift move. He blinked—*her* back.

Green eyes—wide as saucers—stared up at him.

"Alice, I should have warned you. *Always* make certain I'm aware of your presence. If I had a weapon—"

"You can let me up now," she said with a quaver.

He lifted his arm that pinned her shoulders, but his leg remained firmly across her thighs. Her hair strayed, making her look vulnerable, and with their bodies pressed so close, she could certainly feel his erection.

She blushed. "Colonel, I said let me up." He let go, and she hustled to her feet. Without looking at him, she straightened her dress. "I'm pleased that your fever seems to have broken."

He picked up the tin cup from the floor. "Please accept my apology. I don't make a habit of flinging lovely ladies to the bed—at least not the first time."

Her face turned a shade pinker. So she had been thinking it too. *Not wise.* He had no patience for proper courting. And she was a lady. Ladies expected a wedding. A part of him that he couldn't give—not again. He had learned that lesson the hard way with Amanda—when she chose Prescott.

Unsteady on his feet, Wil stood.

"Where do you think you're going?" Alice asked.

"It's time to return to duty."

She wagged a finger at him like she was scolding a child. "You'll do nothing of the kind."

His knees were weak, but with stubborn determination he remained standing.

"You need to rest a spell longer. You were mighty sick."

"She died because I rested."

Her brows furrowed. "Your wife?"

And he had said too much. What was the use in fighting it? He sank to the cot in exhaustion.

Bending down beside him, she twisted a dress button between her fingers.

One by one, he wanted to unfasten the buttons of her bodice.

"I'm glad you're taking my advice and getting some rest. There are some matters women are more intuitive about."

Recalling the spread of her hips beneath him, he held his tongue.

"Wil?"

To hell with Amanda seeking a shotgun. "If you'd join me, I'd rest easier."

She swallowed slightly. "Are you propositioning me?"

"Yes."

She poised a hand to strike him, then lowered it again. "Now I know you're feeling better, Colonel Jackson." Her gaze met his and with a swift turn, she left the hut.

Laughing, he rested his head on the feather pillow. She was definitely a spitfire.

Chapter Four

S AM STOOD AS THE LIEUTENANT ESCORTED Holly to his headquarters. He motioned for her to be seated, and she sat on a camp stool, smoothing the folds of her mourning dress.

A mockery... With his brother, Charles, dead only two months, he wondered why she pretended to mourn. Their marriage had been nothing but a mockery. "Holly," he said, seating himself behind the camp desk.

"Sam, get right to the point. I don't believe for a minute that you have summoned me for social reasons."

"How's Jo?" he said, inquiring about the girl soldier.

Holly glanced over her shoulder, but the lieutenant had left them to their privacy. "She had gangrene, but that clever little wife of yours knew an old remedy."

Suddenly feeling ill, he raised a hand. "I know it. Amanda used the same treatment on my leg wound."

With a growing grin, she clapped her hands in delight. "Sam, you never told me. How does it feel having maggots eat you alive?"

"Dead tissue."

"Call it whatever you like. Ugly little worms crawl all over you and eat your flesh. I suppose that's better than rotting on some battlefield."

"Holly..." Sam cleared his throat. "Is Jo going to be all right?"

She threw her hands in the air in annoyance. "How should I know? I'm not a surgeon, and she refuses to see one. She complains she has no feeling in her arm."

His line of questioning was going nowhere, and he drummed his fingers on the desk. "What supplies have you and Amanda used for her care?"

Vexed, she wrinkled a brow. "Some morphine—quinine. Do you wish a detailed report?"

"That won't be necessary. Have you returned to smuggling?"

"I see. We have finally reached the point. Would you believe me if I said no? I haven't seen Colonel Jackson since that farce you call a wedding. And I certainly would have never attended had you warned me that he was going to be there. I wondered why Amanda invited him. Fancy that, an *affaire de coeur* and smuggling supplies on her wedding day right under the bridegroom's nose. Have you ever wondered if the child she carries is even yours?"

Sam gritted his teeth. Holly was only attempting to distract him from the matter at hand with lies. "Try again. Amanda reported the supplies missing."

"What a perfect alibi."

He pounded a fist to the desk and stood. "Holly, I'm warning you."

She withdrew a black handkerchief and dabbed the silk fabric to her eyes. "Sam, I've been so confused since Charles's death. What would it take to prove to you that I wasn't responsible?"

Another front—one he didn't believe. "Cooperation."

Holly leaned forward with a smile. "What is it you want me to do?"

Suddenly, he felt uneasy. If Holly was cooperating, it could only mean that he wasn't going to like what he uncovered.

A regular visitor to Confederate winter quarters, Alice took advantage of the numerous social gatherings. In another month or two, active campaigning would renew, and parties provided a necessary diversion. Before the war, she had donned silk gowns and dashing young men flocked around her, hoping for an opportunity of a dance.

While she had sewn a couple of new dresses, none were silk, nor were they likely to be in the near future. Delighted that plain frocks didn't fail to keep officers from asking, she often danced well into the night. Occasionally, she shared an evening ride, but nothing rekindled the atmosphere of how things had been before the war. Gaiety of the moment covered people's fears of what the coming months would bring.

As Alice crossed the icy path on the arm of a wispy-bearded lieutenant to the columned mansion, she heard a high-pitched yell. Several soldiers formed a line in the falling snow. Across from them, another line took shape. Battle formation. Her heart thumped.

One soldier's eyes blazed, and he scooped up some snow, launching his weapon.

The stricken soldier packed his own snowball and pitched it at the enemy. Soon—snowballs flew every which way. More soldiers, along with several junior officers, joined the battle, and a crowd gathered to watch, cheering the soldiers on.

A lanky private grabbed a bucket and filled it full of snow. He pranced after the soldier who had started the fight. Then all firing stopped as suddenly as it had begun.

To the side of the battlefield, Wil stood with his arms crossed, staring in disapproval at the combatants. The private shoved the bucket behind him and hung his head.

No one moved.

Another high-pitched yell erupted, and the private flung the bucket's contents at Wil. He pointed a finger. "Gotcha, Colonel!"

Unamused, Wil brushed himself off. Carefully, he bent down. He molded a snowball and fired it at his assailant. After packing another snowball, he chased the private, who made a hasty retreat only to slip and fall in the snow.

A mass explosion of snowballs shot the downed soldier's way.

Her escort tugged on her arm. Reluctantly coming along, Alice shook her head and giggled. Fancy that, grown men having a snowball fight.

Inside the mansion, a black servant collected her cloak. After sharing a dance with the lieutenant, a wiry major stepped between them. "Ma'am . . ." He bowed. "Miss McGuire, I'd be honored if you'd accompany me in this dance."

As Alice danced with the major, she spied Wil watching her. Fresh from his snowball fight, he appeared unharmed.

Since recovering from his fever, he had remained distant. He had given her no more rude remarks, and she chalked it up to his feverish state. Yet—he was a man who usually said what was on his mind.

The music stopped playing, and she curtsied a thank you to her partner. Over by the food table, a servant poured her a cup of punch. Not as luxurious of a spread as in years past, the mock oysters looked downright unappetizing. Like everything else in the South, real oysters were in short supply. She sipped the punch. While not unpleasant tasting, it had a bit of a nip. Someone must have spiked it with apple brandy.

She glanced up. Wil continued to watch her. Detecting amusement in his dark eyes, she couldn't fathom why he didn't ask her to dance. She raised her hand to wave at him, but he returned his attention to the lady in his company.

Alice blinked. Holly Prescott—and she no longer wore black. Unlike the day of Amanda's wedding, they seemed engaged in a less heated conversation.

Her escort returned and requested another dance.

Wil laughed, nearly spilling the drink in his hand, and Holly peered her way with a condescending smile.

Alice wanted nothing more than to choke the life out of Holly's long, elegant neck. *Jealousy?* An unbecoming trait. She refused to let Holly's appearance spoil her time.

Pretending Holly didn't exist, Alice raised her chin and held out a hand.

The lieutenant led the way to the dance floor. To the strain of fiddle music, they flowed across the floor together. A spark in his blue eyes uplifted her spirit. She cast a glance in Wil's direction.

He had disappeared—Holly too.

Aware they were lovers, she assumed they had retreated to somewhere more private. She didn't know why that bothered her. It shouldn't. After all, she and Wil weren't courting, and men had physical needs. The music ended all too soon.

With a dreamy smile, the lieutenant bowed. "Miss McGuire, with your permission, I'd like—"

"The lady promised me the next dance," Wil said, cutting in.

Stepping aside, the lieutenant voiced no protest to his superior officer. Wil drew her close as a slow waltz began to play.

"You appear unharmed after your recent battle, Colonel."

"Many of the boys are far from home. They're homesick and bored."

So he wasn't a stuffy career officer. He really cared about his men. "You were rude to my escort."

"I saved him from the humiliation of being turned down. He was about to ask to court you."

If what he said were true, he had done her a favor, but she couldn't let him know that. "How dare you presume. What makes you think I would have turned him down? And wasn't that Mrs. Prescott I saw you chatting with?"

A sly spark entered his eyes as they waltzed across the dance floor. "I believe so."

Uncertain what to make of his behavior, she asked, "Then why are you dancing with me? I thought the two of you—"

"I prefer the company of a lady this evening."

Pressing closer, she felt right with his arms around her, and they remained partners for the rest of the evening. While she laughed and danced, all was right with the world. As a girl, she had worshipped him—a dashing Mexican War hero. His bravery on the battlefield suddenly became a fear within her. All of those bodies—he could have been one of them.

"Wil, I wish to go home. You have frightened off the lieutenant. Would you be kind enough to escort me?"

He held out his arm, and she slipped hers through it.

By the door, Holly waited. "I come on an errand of mercy, and . . . "

Wil shot her a stare to keep quiet.

Holly narrowed her eyes and tugged on the pearl necklace around her throat as they stepped into the foyer.

Outside, where a carriage once would have waited, only a horse stood. After retrieving Poker Chip, Wil helped her mount the carriage horse. He rode beside her to Fredericksburg.

"There won't be any more supply runs," he said, when they reached the steps of her house.

"You've decided to let Holly smuggle them again." She had been fretting herself sick that he would be facing battles in the spring, and she had been nothing more than an adornment for his arm the entire evening. "Wil, take a look around you. This is all Mama and I have. And Mama hasn't been well in weeks. Until this town is back to normal, it's the only compensation we have."

He studied her a moment. "Are you finished ranting?"

Ranting? She hadn't even begun.

Before she could respond, he continued, "I don't trust Mrs. Prescott. After Amanda's suspicions, the timing of her visit is wrong. I told her we were no longer involved in supply running."

"You don't trust Holly?" she asked in confusion.

"Isn't that what I just said?"

"Then you were fretting about . . ." She pressed a hand to her chest.

"Why would you find that so surprising?"

"Colonel, I think you like playing the role of a hero."

"I'm no hero and never have been." With a bow, he lifted her hand to his lips and kissed it. "But I know a lady worth coveting when I see one."

Weary of his rudeness, Alice withdrew her hand from his grasp.

"You needn't fret, Alice. I haven't courted a lady in a long time."

No elaboration was necessary as to the sort of woman he usually kept company with. "What about Amanda?"

He fidgeted with the brim of his hat. "My relationship with your sister never strayed beyond friendship, but even if I were so inclined, the coming campaign won't grind to a halt because I woo a lovely lady."

Progress—at least he hadn't avoided her question about Amanda entirely. Her hands went to her hips, and she ascended another stair, bringing her face-to-face with him. "For the record, Colonel, I'm appalled that you would treat me in such a manner."

He arched an eyebrow in confusion. "Appalled?"

"Yes, I said appalled." For emphasis, she stamped a foot. "You use words that a gentleman would never say around a lady, fling me in bed, then proposition me. What sort of woman do you think I am?"

With a rapid turn, Alice reached the porch. She heard his sword clank, and he was beside her before she got to the door. He grasped her elbow. "As I recall, I wasn't the first to utter the word 'bastard.' And to your other accusation, I was in a feverish state."

"The only thing feverish was your . . ." Daring her to say it, he grinned. " . . . pride."

His eyes held a sly spark. "What would a *lady* know about a man's— *pride?*"

"How dare you mock me."

Before she could turn away, his grip tightened and he gave her a light tug. Her body pressed tightly against him, and with no false pretense for gentleness, his mouth sought hers. Forewarned that such men took without thought, she was tempted to draw away. Other beaus mumbled apologies for stolen kisses. Wil wouldn't. He wasn't the sort. Good sense faded. Unashamed, she parted her lips and reciprocated.

Wil took a swift step back.

"What's the matter, Colonel? Did you think a lady couldn't kiss like that?"

"Alice..." He replaced his hat on his head and turned. He was walking away.

Suddenly cold, she rubbed her arms. She was such a simple fool. A worldly man like Wil wouldn't care for a country girl like her.

At the bottom of the steps, he stopped. "What you want from me died with Peopeo."

"I don't believe that."

With deliberate slowness, he faced her. "Believing what you wish doesn't make it so. Besides, if Amanda gets wind of what happened tonight, and I'm certain we can count on Mrs. Prescott to relay the details, I won't be worrying about Yankee bullets."

She took a hesitant step toward him. "Such a pity..." Feigning innocence, Alice shuffled a foot. "If Amanda's going to haul out a shotgun, shouldn't you make the risk worthwhile?"

He opened his mouth, then closed it again.

She giggled. "I never thought I'd make you speechless, Wil."

He cleared his throat. "Are you propositioning me, Miss McGuire?"

"Not quite. I *do* have a reputation to uphold, but there's no telling where things might lead before I find it necessary to fend you off."

Lowering his hat, he was beside her again. "Alice, you're a fool. If you knew what sort of man I am—"

"I know exactly who you are, Wil Jackson." His eyes grew piercing, and she breathed deeply before he withdrew again. "You're a Confederate colonel, a gambler, sometimes you drink too much, and I don't care to hear about the women in your life since your wife. But the times you've mentioned her, I've seen something in you—lost perhaps, but definitely not dead. Now shall we go inside where it's warm?" Chilled, she tightened her cloak. "Mama stays to her room in the evenings and won't take notice."

He took her hand. "I won't make any promises."

He was lending her the opportunity to change her mind. Even if she could reach the dark depth he had buried so long ago, the war would eventually intrude. All of those bodies . . . After the next battle— he could be one of them. *Draw away—before it's too late.* It was already too late. The warning should have come when she had been a fanciful child at Amanda's first wedding. She squeezed his hand and led the way to the parlor. "You would have surprised me if you had."

Only embers remained in the fireplace. As Alice stoked the flames, she sensed Wil watching her. She turned to him, and in his strong arms, she could easily forget the past few weeks.

He traced a finger over her lips and kissed her.

But she couldn't forget. With a shudder, she drew away. "Before the battle, I never gave any thought to what really happened. A list of names in the newspapers. All of those dead and wounded. The names meant nothing. I fret that yours shall be among them."

In his arms again, she felt a gentle tug behind her head. He un- pinned her hair and ran the locks between his fingers. "Then we shouldn't waste time."

She stepped back. "Don't ever joke about such a thing."

"I beg forgiveness, but I'm well aware of my likely fate."

Did he have a feeling? "Likely?"

Bending slightly, he grasped her hand and kissed it. "I think it's best if I leave. I have enjoyed your company, Alice. You have reminded me what spending a pleasant evening with a lady is like."

As he strode from the room, she followed him. In the foyer, he strapped on his weapons belt. "Will I see you again?"

"I don't think it's wise." He pressed his hat to his heart and bowed. "Good evening, Miss McGuire."

A cold wind swept in the foyer as Wil closed the door behind him. Rubbing her arms, Alice heard the tread of his footsteps on the porch stairs. Just as she thought she understood him, he behaved in an unexpected manner. *Men*—Wil Jackson in particular.

"Alice . . . ," came Mama's voice from the top of the stairs.

Alice quickly pinned her hair.

Mama's dark shape leaned on the rail, gripping it as if she might fall.

"Mama . . ." She raced up the stairs and Mama sagged. Her mother's forehead was feverish. Alice helped Mama to her room.

After serving Mama some willow bark tea, Alice collapsed on the straw mattress in her own bedroom. With Mama sick, how could she have danced the evening away?

For some normalcy. Was that too much to ask? But she had been negligent in her duties to Mama and her chores. With the gold from supply running gone, what was she to do for money? There were plenty of soldiers nearby with uniforms in need of mending. She hugged her feather pillow.

Perhaps, she and Mama should give up the house and catch a train for Richmond.

Chapter Five

A lieutenant bellowed. "ready!"

Wil hated executions.

"Aim!"

A senseless waste—it only made deserters more determined not to get caught.

"Fire!" A round of smoking muskets, and two men fell dead.

At least, he didn't need to tend to the bodies—like he had with Peopeo. He had carried her lifeless form to their log cabin.

"Sir . . ."

Wil blinked at the company captain.

"May I dismiss the men?"

Other companies were already leaving. He nodded, and the captain shouted the order. During moments like this, he wished he were on the battlefield where he could release the urge to kill those responsible for Peopeo's death. But he buried it. Always he buried it, unless he was on the battlefield.

As the men filed to their quarters, Wil lingered. The detail assigned to the bodies flung them in pine boxes with no better treatment than meat carcasses. He had combed and arranged Peopeo's long black hair. His mind was sinking into that awful abyss. Tired of sitting idly, he welcomed the coming campaign. He turned.

A woman ran toward him with her arms waving. Alice was a pretty woman, and he hadn't expected to see her again. After leaving her the other night, he had been in need of a woman. "This is no place for a lady."

"Wil . . ." Alice pressed a hand to her chest to catch her breath. "I need to speak to you—in private."

But the camp follower had left him unsatisfied. "I don't think that's wise."

Her eyelids flickered as if she struggled to hold back tears. "I need your help. Wil—*please*."

The plea drew him from the void, and he led her away from the execution site. Outside his hut, he asked, "What can I do for you, Miss McGuire?"

"I need medicine," she replied in a frantic, high-pitched voice.

Wil withdrew several Confederate bills from his pocket and placed them in her hand. "It's all I have."

Her voice climbed another octave. "I don't mean money. Mama's sick. I've tried home remedies, but the doctor says she needs proper care. He won't give her any medicine. What little there is goes to the soldiers."

Not only was she worried, but frightened as well. "Take her to Amanda. There's plenty of medicine on the Yankee side of the river."

He stepped inside the hut, but Alice followed. "I can't move her. She may die if I try."

As Benjamin had. "Alice, I don't see how I can help. Go to Major Prescott. He'll see that your mother gets the care she needs."

"After a lot of difficult questioning. Mama may not have time for that." With a drawn face, she turned for the door. "My apologies for being a bother. I'll find another way."

When he had been ill, Peopeo had gone alone. *Not again.* Wil grasped her wrist. "Wait. If you go to the Yankee hospital and collect the supplies you need, I'll send a couple of scouts ahead and meet you at the shack. I'll get the medicine across the river. Avoid Mrs. Prescott at all costs. She's not to be trusted. Understood?"

Tears entered her eyes, and her arms went around his neck as she kissed him on the cheek. "Thank you, Wil. I knew I could count on you."

"And I'm a simpleminded fool."

Alice stepped back. "For caring?"

Like a card game, the stakes had risen. The odds—if it had been poker, he would have folded. "For agreeing to this venture." To lower the probability to an acceptable level, his best scouts were required, but he *would* get the medicine across the lines.

The summons was marked urgent. Against his better judgment, Sam met Holly outside the hospital tent. With a smirk, she jabbed a finger for him to take a look inside.

Beside a cot, Alice placed a tin cup to a sick soldier's lips. Alice often accompanied Amanda to the hospital, and he failed to see anything out of the ordinary. Even though only a couple of days had passed since their last visit, he was delighted to see them. He stepped forward. "So what's the urgency?"

Holly thrust an arm in front of him, blocking his passage. "Your dear sister-in-law is the one stealing supplies."

"Alice?"

A grin spread slowly across Holly's face. "Alice."

He searched her face for telltale signs of lying. There were none, but that didn't exactly prove anything as far as Holly was concerned. "Why would Alice steal supplies?"

"Money. As you may recall, the Federals laid waste to her home."

That certainly was a motive. Why hadn't she asked Amanda and him for help? Stubborn Southern pride—not to mention that Amanda's family had a keen dislike for Yankees. "How long have you known?"

Her grin widened. "Since your wedding, but I was well aware you wouldn't believe me without proof. Fancy that, not your wife but her sister stealing right from under your nose."

He couldn't arrest Alice. Not only would Amanda never forgive him, irreparable shame would be brought on the family. "How is she getting the supplies out?"

"I suspect her petticoat has pockets. Quite easy actually. Lean over and slip the medicine in." Holly demonstrated by lifting her skirt. "If anyone sees you, they simply think you're fixing your skirt. No one suspects women. She then meets Colonel Jackson, and he smuggles the supplies across the river."

Jackson—he should have guessed as much. Arresting Jackson wouldn't be much easier than Alice, but he was the lesser of two evils. "Where does she meet Jackson?"

Holly shrugged. "The time I witnessed the exchange was right on the farm, but as you may be aware he is sensitive to Amanda's feelings. Wil may be a scoundrel, but I doubt he would continue to jeopardize her welfare." Her condescending grin returned. "Then again, Wil does love games of chance. Fancy the scandal, if he were caught with the goods in a Yankee household, especially one belonging to a lover."

Sam didn't allow himself to react. Holly was merely attempting to make him jealous, and he'd be playing right into her hand. Anything between Amanda and Jackson was definitely in the past. "You've done your job. Thank you, Holly."

Her eyes narrowed and her hands went to her hips with bracelets clattering. "That's all I get? *Thank you.* Aren't you going to arrest her?"

"Thank you, Holly. Your services are no longer required."

Miffed, she scowled, then hustled off.

The choppy Rappahannock waters were icy cold. Late March, and the air remained nippy. Fortunately, the spring thaw hadn't begun, or the river might have flooded. With a shiver, Wil drew his overcoat around himself. Poker's breathing grew labored as the gelding struggled against the current. He slapped the reins on the horse's shoulder, and the blue roan climbed the bank.

A scout was returning at a gallop and brought his mount to a halt beside him. Out of breath, the red-bearded Sergeant Edmond gave a quick salute. "No Yanks, sir."

Odd—but he had been expecting Yankees. Maybe the game was chess, not poker. He ordered Edmond to survey ahead but remain nearby. With another salute, the scout reined his horse around and cantered off.

Wind moaned through budding dogwood trees, and leafless branches creaked in the gusts. Wil checked his pocket watch. If all had gone according to plan, Alice should be arriving at the shack soon. Eager to return to the other side of the river, he squeezed Poker to a trot.

Near the shack, Poker snorted, and Wil brought the gelding to a halt.

His other scout pulled even with a salute. "Yanks," he reported and leaned over in the saddle, spitting tobacco juice. "...'bout half a dozen, fanned out, on the girl's tail. Don't think she knows they're behind her."

Wil's first inclination was to confront the Yanks and divert them from Alice. Six to three—a move like that was poker. If the Yanks wanted Alice, they would have already arrested her. Undoubtedly, Sam Prescott was behind the chess game, but he couldn't take the risk of Alice getting caught between any cross-fire.

He heard the plodding gallop of Alice's carriage horse. Outside the shack, she reined the horse to a halt and went inside.

Wil scanned the area with field glasses. Definitely chess—no sign of Yanks. As he tucked the field glasses away, Edmond returned, confirming the number of Yanks. "I'll go in and fetch the supplies. No shooting," Wil ordered.

"Sir, if you'll permit, I'll go...," said Edmond.

"I don't think they'll fire as long as Miss McGuire is near. Let them think I'm unaware."

Wil reined Poker into the open. He'd be joining Peopeo and Benjamin soon. No innocents would die this time due to his failure. Dismounting outside the shack, he tied the gelding to the rail.

Alice met him on the step.

His mouth pressed to hers, and his arms locked around her waist.

Struggling against his grip, she pounded his arm with a fist.

Once safely inside, he let go.

"How dare you treat me in such a manner!" Red-faced and with her ruffled hair, she was enticing.

He rubbed his arm. "You brought Yankees with you, my dear. I thought it best to let them think we might be a while."

Her fist flew to her chest. "Yankees? But I made certain—"

"Alice, it doesn't matter how they got there. I promised to get the medicine across the river. I shall."

"What do you want me to do?" she asked.

Relishing the thought of comforting her, he crossed his arms and grinned.

"Wil, how can you think of such a thing at a time like this?"

"Easy. It's more pleasant than the thought of dealing with Yankees."

Her face grew red. "Be serious."

"I am."

She threw her hands up in disgust and turned away.

"Alice—I'm fond of you and your family."

She faced him again. "The situation must be grim if you're making admissions."

Like Amanda, she had seen through him. Given time, she would glimpse behind the mask. He couldn't allow that, but there was no need to fret. He could hear Peopeo's voice. "I want you to ride to Amanda's. Once you're clear, we'll see to the Yanks."

"I'm supposed to ride off and pretend that everything is fine?"

"You can't afford to do otherwise."

"Wil—"

"Alice, my boys can't do their job if they have to fret about a woman getting caught in the middle."

This argument seemed to sway her. She nodded. "What should I tell Amanda?"

"Tell her your mother is ill, and that I think her husband is out there."

"Sam? If it's Sam, then I can explain—"

"I won't use a woman as cover. If anyone talks to Prescott, I will. The supplies." He extended a hand. With a worried frown she raised her skirt, and a packet dropped to the floor from her petticoat. Another—he gathered nearly a dozen packets in the saddlebags. Unlike previous trips, the amount was small, but it would benefit Alice's mother—as well as a couple of sick boys.

Straightening, Alice lowered her skirt. "After I speak with Amanda, I'll return home to tend Mama. That is, as long as Major Prescott doesn't see fit to arrest me. A friend of the family is tending her now. When she's feeling better, I expect you to join us for supper."

"I will."

Tears brimmed in her eyes, and with a quaver, she laughed. "I can only fathom what the rumors shall be after meeting you here, like this."

Wishing he could forget the Yanks, Wil brushed her tears away, then kissed her. "Take care, Alice."

Her arms went around him, and their mouths met.

But Yankees waited. "It's time for you to leave." He escorted her to the front step and helped her mount the carriage horse.

She leaned down to kiss him.

"If you continue in this manner, Miss McGuire, I'll forget there are Yankees."

With a nervous smile, she whispered, "You're incorrigible."

He laughed slightly. "Now I had best get the supplies across the river. Bye Alice."

She mumbled a goodbye and kicked the carriage horse in the side. They lumbered off.

Wil threw the saddlebags over Poker's withers and mounted. It was time for Prescott's move. Reining around, he spotted Edmond ready his shotgun on his hip in the woods.

"Jackson!"

Check—Prescott wasted no time. Motioning to Edmond to hold position, Wil turned slightly in the saddle as Prescott and a junior officer cantered up to meet him. Prescott wouldn't fire—not unless absolutely necessary. Wil left his pistol in its holster and Prescott halted his red horse across from him.

"Jackson, it's unlike you to let your guard down."

"I haven't." Wil pointed to his scout.

Prescott glanced around. His brow furrowed when the scout waved. "I don't want any shooting."

"That suits me just fine. If you move out of my way, then I will leave Yankee territory."

"I can't let you have the supplies."

"Even if they're for your mother-in-law?"

"My . . . Why wouldn't Alice come to me if Mrs. McGuire is ill?"

Wil grinned. "Because she believes all Yankees are thieving bastards. The fact that her sister is married to one doesn't sway her opinion."

Prescott straightened in the saddle. "I could always count on you to be straightforward."

His grin widened. "I'll take that as a compliment."

"You would," Prescott grumbled. He reined the red horse to the side to let him pass. "And since the supplies are for Amanda's mother, I have no choice."

Wil squeezed Poker to a walk and tipped his hat. "Much obliged. I thought you might see things my way."

As he passed, Prescott raised an index finger. "A warning, Jackson—if you're caught in Federal territory again, I will forget the fact that you were once my commander. You *will* be arrested or shot."

"Understood." He rode on, and the veil lifted. Peopeo's voice faded. Too easy—the chess game was a stalemate. He joined Edmond, but the gnawing feeling returned to his gut. They weren't out of danger yet.

Not since the war with the Mexicans had he felt anything similar. Death was near. The threat hadn't been Prescott. Wil ordered Edmond to deliver the medicine and passed the saddlebags to him. He would cross the river upstream.

With a salute, the scout galloped off.

Urging Poker to a trot, Wil followed the meandering stream through the bottomland. A lone rider, wearing blue, appeared on the path ahead. As Wil drew his pistol, a bullet whistled past his ear. He returned fire, missing the target.

Another Yankee on horseback joined the first.

Outnumbered, Wil aimed at the one on his right and fired. The Yank swayed in the saddle, then toppled. At least that evened things a bit. The heat of a bullet clipped the hairs of his beard. Another round of lead, and the remaining Yank galloped away. Wil lowered his pistol.

Clutching his hip and groaning, the wounded Yank squirmed on the ground. Leave the bluebelly be. If he bothered lugging a crippled Yank with him, his journey to the other side of the river would be slow going. Wil gave the writhing Yank a wide berth. Out of the corner of his eye, he spotted movement. The Yank's partner must have circled around to aid his wounded comrade. A warning sounded in his head.

Wil wheeled around and aimed. Before he could fire, the Yank dropped face down in the dirt.

On a ridge his second scout raised an arm in victory with a carbine in his hand.

He had been spared—this time.

Chapter Six

A POUNDING ON THE THE DOOR MADE AMANDA SCURRY. The hammering reached a crescendo before she reached it. Yankees? Confederates? She cracked the door open.

Alice burst through.

"Good heavens, Alice. What's got you so fired up?"

Tumbling from their pins, Alice's locks were in disarray, and she trembled. "Amanda, I need your help."

Amanda hung her sister's cloak on a peg near the door. "Come in by the fire and warm yourself."

In the parlor, Alice held out her hands to the flames and closed her eyes as if collecting her thoughts.

"What's wrong, Alice?"

Wringing her hands, Alice took a deep breath. "Mama's sick, and Wil and Sam are going to kill one another."

Amanda raised a hand for her to slow down. "Start at the beginning. I don't understand what you're saying."

Alice gulped another breath. "Wil didn't want to make any more supply runs. He said there were too many risks, but Mama got sick. Amanda, I was the one responsible for the missing medicine at the hospital."

Her little sister—stealing supplies? How could she—after all of the warnings? Amanda suddenly felt sick to her stomach. She had witnessed all of the telltale signs but refused to believe.

"Wil's caution was justified," Alice continued. "Yankees followed me to the shack in the bottomland. He thought one was Sam."

Amanda gasped. "Alice, how could you? On my land! I warned you that running supplies was dangerous."

"Wil took the worst risks."

"That's supposed to comfort me! For all you know, he could be dead! And if Sam—"

"Amanda, I'm not asking you to believe in what I have done. I'm asking for your help in heading off a fight. Both of them will listen to you."

"They were friends before the war. That should help them see beyond the uniforms." Her stomach gurgled in its queasiness, and she massaged her rounding abdomen. "Alice, you said Mama is sick?"

"Influenza. We needed medicine."

"Why didn't you come to me?"

"Because Holly Prescott knew I was smuggling. I thought by the time I got through the questions, Mama might die."

"So you risked other lives as well? Why I have a good mind to—"

"Spare me the lecture." Alice raised a hand in protest, then lowered it again. "Oh what's the use? Everything makes sense when you do it, even if it's marrying a damn Yankee."

"Alice," Amanda hissed.

"What Amanda? You can blind yourself as much as you like, but it doesn't change the fact that Yankees have invaded our land. None of this would have been necessary if they hadn't."

"You'll not speak that way in my household."

"Fine. Listen to the truth when it comes to slavery, but pretend you don't hear it when the Yankees chant they 'ain't fightin' for no nigger.' "

Alice turned, but Amanda grasped her forearm. "Alice, let's not quarrel. I don't ignore the truth—wherever it comes from, but Sam's not like that. He wouldn't wage war on innocent civilians, and do you seriously think I would have married him if he were the type who would?"

Sheepish, Alice faced her and returned to the warmth of the fire. "So what do we do?"

"Wait. Sam will let us know what's happened, then you can go tend Mama."

"Wait?"

"Waiting is a military wife's duty. Always fretting—whether the knock at the door will be him, or an aide with the news that he's been killed. Then when it is him, you don't let on how much you've been fretting. He knows, but there's nothing he can do to make the wait any easier."

Alice's brows furrowed in distress as she sank to the sofa.

Her sister's pain was obvious, and Amanda surmised she wasn't fretting over Sam's welfare. That bothersome twinge was back. "I see you already know what it's like." She sat next to Alice and grasped her hand.

"Is it that obvious?"

After she had married Sam, it was only natural for Wil to move on with his life. But to her little sister? And why did that thought hurt so much? "You kept pretending you were flirting with sick and wounded soldiers in order to *steal* supplies, and all this time, you loved Wil. Does he..." Wil didn't love easily, and she couldn't bring herself to repeat the word. "...care for you?"

Alice shrugged. "I don't know."

For some reason, Amanda felt relief, but it was typical of Wil—if he did care, he wouldn't let on and would go on to repeat his usual foolhardy pattern. She patted the back of Alice's hand. "Why don't I fetch some tea? It'll make the wait a little easier."

"Thank you, Amanda, and I apologize for calling Sam a damn Yankee." As she left the parlor, Amanda sent a forgiving smile. In the kitchen, she boiled the water on the cookstove, then collected the tea cups and platter.

Ten minutes passed before she returned to the parlor. Drinking and chatting with an occasional forced smile, both pretended they were unbothered by the wait. Another half an hour passed. Amanda heard footsteps on the porch outside. She got up to check. Her freedman, Ezra, carried firewood to the parlor and kitchen.

In need of fresh air, Amanda grabbed her cloak. As she stepped onto the porch, she spotted Sam outside of the picket fence, tying his red horse to the rail. She rushed toward him.

Lowering his hat, he waved that any reunion must wait. "I must speak with Alice—alone."

Duty first. "Then I shall check on Rebecca."

Amanda accompanied him inside and scurried upstairs. Seated on the tapestry sofa, Alice lowered her head. "Have you come to arrest me?" she asked.

He waited for Amanda's footsteps to vanish before responding, "I should."

"What about Colonel Jackson?"

"As far as I know, he's fine. Alice, we need to talk. One of my boys is dead."

The blood drained from her face. "Dead?"

"Alice," he said firmly, "I want to know what happened. Why were you smuggling?"

"After what happened to our house, Mama and I couldn't make ends meet."

"I know. I just wish..." He smacked a fist into his palm. "God damn this war. I ordered my boys not to fire unless absolutely necessary. One's dead, so he's not telling what happened. The other's wounded. He says Jackson fired the first shot."

"What else would you expect him to say?"

Her sympathy had changed to stubborn Southern pride, and Sam shot her a glare.

"My apologies, but it's arrogant to presume that he's telling the truth without hearing Wil's version."

"As a matter of fact, I don't believe him. You forget that Jackson was my first field commander in the New Mexico territory."

"Then arrest me. I'm the one to blame."

"You know I can't do that." Sam sank into the green velvet wing chair and rubbed tired eyes. "I'll think of some way to explain what happened."

"In the future, I shall remember that I can come to you."

"I wish you had remembered this time. Now go tend your mother. Let us know how she makes out." She started for the door, and Sam grew melancholy. With each passing day, the coming campaign got closer. Would he ever see the baby Amanda carried? He needed to shake the mood before he went up to see Amanda.

"Sam," Alice whispered, "I'm pleased that Amanda married you."

"In spite of that tainted Yankee blood," he said dryly.

Alice shrugged. "No one is perfect. Just remember, your child shall be a Virginian."

The tension between them faded. "I'm certain I won't be allowed to forget."

Bending down, she kissed him on the cheek. "Take care of yourself. Amanda needs you."

He rose and bowed slightly, then took her hand and kissed it. "I'm pleased we have finally made our peace. Let us hope the country will follow suit in the near future."

"I think all of us are agreed to that."

As she turned, he thought of the dead boy. There would be a lot more joining him in the coming days.

More than a fortnight passed before Mama was well enough to be up and about. Between the spring thaw and frequent rain, the swollen Rappahannock was impassable. With communication cut off from Amanda, Alice had no way of letting her know Mama would be fine.

For income, she mended uniforms and darned socks—hundreds and hundreds of them, or so it seemed. She hadn't realized there were that many feet in the entire Army of Northern Virginia. With one lamp to see by, she continually strained her eyes, but she pressed on. Without the money, there would be no food for the pantry.

"Alice?" Withered beyond her years, Mama had grown haggard over the past few months.

"Yes, Mama."

"I believe you have a caller. A gentleman just rode up."

Wil? The supplies had been delivered by the time she returned to Fredericksburg, and she hadn't seen him since the day at the shack. She set her darning needles aside. Readjusting pins and smoothing her hair, she faced Mama. "How do I look?"

Wrinkles were prominent around Mama's lips, but she smiled in approval.

Alice's heart flip flopped in that schoolgirl sort of way, and she rushed to the door. *Remain calm*—she mustn't appear too eager. She took a deep breath before opening the door.

About to knock, Wil lowered his right arm. His hat was in his other hand, and he bent at the waist, kissing her hand. "Miss McGuire, I trust you are well."

"Fine, thank you. Come inside, Colonel..." A laurel wreath surrounded the three gold stars on his collar. "I should say, Brigadier. Wil, you're a general." Thrilled with the news, she threw her arms around his neck.

"Much as I'm enjoying myself," he whispered in her ear, "I don't think the timing is appropriate."

Mama was in the parlor. Alice stepped back. Fortunately, Mama hadn't witnessed her unrestrained display of affection.

"I'm paying a call to fulfill my promise."

"Promise?" she asked.

"Supper—I recall that you requested my presence."

Unsure there was enough food for a guest, she said, "There's not much in the pantry."

A devilish spark entered his coal-black eyes. "There's no need to fret if I'm escorting you to dinner."

"What about Mama?"

"I fear Poker can only carry two."

Alone—then his unannounced call was to see her. Her heart started that odd flipping again. "Pay your respects to Mama, and I shall accompany you."

In the parlor, he greeted Mama and inquired about her health. He remained calm and collected. It was no wonder Mama never fretted that she was with him. If she only knew what Wil was really like under the courtly exterior.

After exchanging pleasantries, he escorted her outside. By Poker's side, he faced her. "The Yankees are restless. As soon as the river is passable, they will likely move in force. For your safety, you and your mother should leave Fredericksburg."

Her heart sank. His visit wasn't a social call after all. "What more can the Yankees take from us?"

"Your lives."

"Very well. I'll put Mama on the train to Richmond. We have friends she can stay with, but I'm remaining behind. I'm going to follow Amanda's example and tend wounded in the hospital."

His eyes blazed, and he clutched her arms. "You're a fool."

"Perhaps, but it's what I must do."

With a nod, he released her. "I should have seen this coming."

"Then you're not going to reprimand me on propriety?"

"Would I dare?"

She shuffled her feet in the dirt. "You remind me of a boy I once knew."

"Someone I should be jealous of?"

Jealous? Not Wil Jackson—he was teasing. "Timmy Mullen taught me how to spit and swear—all of the unladylike things that annoy Amanda."

Amusement appeared on his face. "You never told me you can spit."

"I don't anymore. Papa got riled and swatted the backs of my legs. But that was nothing to the licking we got when he caught us smoking behind the barn."

Laughing, Wil mounted Poker and extended a hand, lifting her on behind him. As they rode through town, people chatted with neighbors. Hooves clattered on the dirt streets, and wagon wheels creaked. Just as Fredericksburg was returning to life, the guns would force people from their homes yet again.

At the Fredericksburg Inn, miraculously still standing after the battle, officers with wives and sweethearts dined in a room separate from unaccompanied soldiers. Other ladies wore taffeta and chiffon. Self-conscious of her plain cotton dress, Alice was pleased their table sat in a far corner.

With no sign of his dark moods, Wil soon put her at ease.

Dinner consisted of roast duck, real oysters—not the mock variety so common in the South these days—potatoes, and vintage wine. Having gone months without real food, Alice restrained herself from gorging. Even then, she ate more like a pig, but Wil appeared unaffected by her slight of manners.

Uncharacteristically talkative, he entertained her with tales of Mexico, the West, and Indians. Far from savages, they led a unique way of life that was rich in tradition and folklore. Notably absent from his stories was his wife.

Even so, Alice absorbed each word. Oh dear, Amanda was right. It hadn't been a passing fancy. He had stolen her heart. "I presume we are celebrating your promotion?" she inquired.

With a growing smile, the features of his bearded face were shadowed by the flickering candlelight. "We are celebrating my desire to share the company of a lady."

She had blocked out the true meaning of his evacuation warning. As a brigade commander, he would be facing battle soon. Suddenly cold, she fought to remain brave. "It's been a lovely evening."

His gaze met hers, and his grin turned wicked. "It doesn't need to end yet. If I acquire a room, we can—indulge ourselves."

Part of her wanted to forget the consequences, but Wil wasn't the marrying kind. Though a battle was looming, she mustn't let her heart rule. "I'm not that kind of woman."

So arrogant and sure of himself, he continued to smile. "A pity—it would have been delightful." He reached across the table and grasped her hand. "Alice, I have enjoyed your company."

Under his masculine grip, her hand trembled. Would she regret the decision if he fell in battle? One night was all he asked for. Was the price too high? "Why Wil Jackson, you astonish me. I didn't think you were the sort to give up so easily."

"I'm not, but . . ." He sighed. "The Yankees will likely spoil any future interludes." He left several bills on the table for the meal, then stood.

Outside, they strolled under the hazy glow of moonlight. With so much rain and dampness throughout April, spring barely felt as if it had arrived. Drawing her shawl around her, she shivered.

Dirty, ragged soldiers roamed the streets—laughing and cursing. Inebriated voices sang.

"This is no place for a woman. I'll escort you home."

"Wil . . ." Sound reasoning abandoned her, and she pressed closer.

He leaned down and sought her mouth with his whiskers tickling her nose.

Hooves clattered as artillery wagons and cannon passed. Whips cracked, and more cursing.

Wil broke their embrace. "See that your mother leaves tonight. I wish you would give up this foolish notion of remaining behind and accompany her."

"I can't." Her voice wavered. "Amanda's going to need my help once the baby's born. When it's safe to cross the river, I'll leave. In the meantime, I can be of assistance."

"Very well."

His even, almost gruff response, warned her that he had withdrawn. An emotionless mask fell in place, and the soldier had returned. He was a general of the Confederacy. Duty came first, and she must accept it, but for a little while, he had lowered his guard.

Chapter Seven

"Sir . . ." the lieutenant pointed, and Sam raised his head. Wide-eyed with terror, a deer stumbled and crashed through camp. Muskets were stacked, and several boys made sport of the frightened animal and chased it.

"Make a mighty fine supper," the lieutenant said.

Another crazed deer jumped from the forest.

A gnawing feeling churned in his gut, and Sam stood. The last report said the enemy was heading toward Culpeper.

Another deer leaped into the open, followed by two more, and another. Rabbits—dozens of them, bounded from the woods.

Damn the reports! Sam shouted orders for the boys to form a battle line. Too late. He heard the godawful Rebel yell. He drew his sword and ordered positions.

Under a sharp line of fire, some of the boys ran. Most held their ground. Before they were fully formed, men dropped like flies. The Rebs were nearly on them. Canister sailed into the ranks. More men fell. They wouldn't be able to hold the line for long.

Rebels charged through on their left. Sam ordered for the hole to be plugged. The girl soldier crouched into position. One of his best soldiers—it was good to have her off the wounded list. Like a solid gray mass the Rebels came—lines and lines of them. A courier sprinted toward him with a dispatch from the colonel. The message was a welcome relief. Fall back.

* * *

With whisk broom in hand, Alice swept the farmhouse's wood floor. As cannon roared in the distance, the windows rattled and the floor shook.

A soldier with gaping hole in his trousers stood in the doorway.

Alice threw a hand over her mouth to stifle a gasp.

"Ma'am . . ."

What should she do? *Think.* The blackened face was gunpowder, not burns, and the tear in his trousers wasn't a wound but the rags most of the Confederates wore.

He cradled his arm. "Ma'am, I'm hurtin' somethin' fierce."

"If you're going to swoon at the first sight of blood," the bearded surgeon stepped between them and grumbled, "I'll thank you to leave." He inspected the soldier's arm. "Miss McGuire, either assist me, or leave."

"I'll assist you."

They helped the soldier to the dining room, and the surgeon shook his head at her in disapproval. An assistant surgeon joined them. On a rickety table, the two men examined the soldier.

"Miss McGuire!" The surgeon narrowed his eyes and tapped an impatient foot. "If you are to assist us, you must stop gaping. Perform your duties without being told, or get the hell out."

Alice resisted the urge to run. If she gave in, other women would systematically be dismissed. "Yes, sir." She poured brandy into a tin cup and helped the soldier drink.

While the assistant surgeon cut the soldier's sleeve, the bearded surgeon withdrew a metal probe. Alice grasped the soldier's hand, and the surgeon inserted the probe into the man's wounded arm.

Tears entered the soldier's eyes until he finally relented and screamed. Her words of comfort kept him from thrashing.

The soldier's cries quieted, and the surgeon glanced across at her with interest. "The bullet's not deep," he said, his voice gentler than before. "Miss McGuire, after I've removed the bullet, I'd like you to see to the bandaging."

She agreed, and the day wore on. One wounded soldier soon became ten. Those that were capable walked. Then the ambulances came. Even after tending sick and wounded while accompanying Amanda, Alice had been unprepared for the sights and sounds of a battle. Mangled flesh made her retch and she nearly gave in to the surgeon's protests. Stubborn McGuire determination prevailed.

Whispering words of comfort, bandaging wounds, and washing lice-infested bodies, Alice persevered. She knelt down to a captain, putting a tin cup to his lips. His eyes were fixed in a vacant stare, and he failed to drink. His breathing was shallow and his skin cool to the touch. His trousers were covered in blood. She needed to do something—and quickly—or he'd likely die. Stop the bleeding. But where was it coming from?

Alice reached for the buttons of his trousers, but hesitated. Except for playing doctor with Timmy Mullen, she had never seen a man's private area. *He was dying*. Propriety be damned! She lowered his urine-soaked trousers and drawers to a hip wound.

She gritted her teeth and pressed a cloth to the wound. The bleeding slowed.

"Thank you, Miss McGuire," said the assistant surgeon, bending beside her. "If he survives, it will be because of your assistance."

"Does he have a chance?"

"If the bullet hasn't nicked anything vital. Continue applying pressure until we get him in the other room."

Two men placed the wounded captain on a litter and carried it to the dining room. Outside the open window, she spied flies buzzing around a white mound of lifeless hands, arms, and legs.

Alice tasted bile rising in her throat.

"You can let go now, Miss McGuire," said the assistant surgeon.

Sick to her stomach, she stumbled to the parlor. More and more wounded. She recognized a couple of the pain-filled faces. One of the boys had cut wood for her and Mama. Wil's brigade must be engaged. She mustn't think of individuals. In order to function, they had to remain nameless. She said a silent prayer and returned to her duties.

"Miss McGuire!"

Gathering her bloodstained skirt together, she hustled to the dining room.

The surgeon loomed over a man rolled into a ball. The soldier sobbed on the table.

Alice moved closer. A peach-fuzz face with innocent blue eyes and his cheeks streaked with tears looked up at her. A man? A boy of sixteen at best.

"He won't let us administer the chloroform."

"They're goin' to take my arm!"

Alice hushed him in a soothing way. The boy clutched her as a child would his mama. His arm—she bit her lip. Near his elbow, a jagged bone protruded. She patted his back as he cried on her breast. "I'll stay with you."

Calmer now, he clutched her hand and laid back. The cone went over the boy's face. He muttered obscenities, struggled to rise, then was calm.

The assistant surgeon's hands quickly set into motion retracting skin above the elbow, while the surgeon cut into muscle. He reached for a saw.

Suddenly dizzy, Alice couldn't move. As the saw made contact with bone, darkness engulfed her.

Replenished with ammunition, Wil ordered the brigade to reform. Both former West Point classmates Stonewall Jackson and Powell Hill had been wounded the previous evening. General Stuart ordered them forward.

Wil shouted the command and waved his sword. He entered the dense woods and felt intense heat under his feet. Smoke rose from burning blankets, haversacks, and flesh. Shrieks filled the air. The woods were so dark, he could barely see. He shoved through the dense underbrush. A charred body hugged a tree.

After days of marching and skirmishing, the men took their positions without complaint. Through the smoke and fire, he could not see the Yankees, but knew they were there.

With an unearthly sounding yell, the lines proceeded. Bullets buzzed like angry bees. Bodies littered the ground. Holes appeared. Muzzle flashes discharged in front of them, and he waved the boys forward.

One boy was on fire. He screamed. A couple of the men tried putting the fire out with their bare hands. Blue and gray mingled, helping each other. The blue line wavered and fell back.

Forward—Wil kept waving. He felt a sharp sting in his left thigh. While his scabbard had been dented, he remained unscathed. Forward.

Lead rained in a deadly hailstorm. They reached the breastworks and charged over it. Yankees scattered every which way.

Wil raised his sword, and the earth trembled beneath his feet. Thrust backward, he hit the ground with staggering force. Fiery pain spread from his chest to his back. Gasping for breath, he rose on an elbow. The warmth of blood filled his shirt and covered his jacket. He pitched forward and sank to the ground.

Rough hands rolled him onto his back. A man in blue towered over him.

His vision blurred as he reached for his pistol.

A musket butt crushed down on his hand.

A bone snapped, but oddly, Wil felt no pain. As his breath grew short, he saw Peopeo. Over thirteen years since he had last seen her, and she hadn't aged.

The Yank confiscated his sword and raised it over him in victory.

Wil placed a hand to his chest and saw the blood. *He was dying.* His head grew foggy, and he felt the pressure of a sharp blade against his throat.

Their gazes met.

The sergeant withdrew the sword and vanished in the smoke.

Gunfire surrounded him, and the ground trembled. As his strength ebbed, he closed his eyes. *Not long now.* He drifted toward the darkness and the final abyss.

Hands—no longer rough, were helping him, lifting him. More Yanks? Wil couldn't be certain. Soon—Peopeo, and he would finally join her.

With loss of life and agonized wounds the standard, Alice's mind had grown numb. Bandaging a bloody stump was no different than doling out a bedpan. Shortages abounded—bandages, blankets, medicine. She made do. After learning that her gentle touch possessed a calming effect on panic-stricken soldiers, the surgeon no longer protested her presence.

But when she had swooned, he had left her to lie in the unfortunate boy's blood until she came around. From that point on, she performed her duty with no tears or swooning.

Lines and lines of men waited—some walking, others carried by litter. She avoided their pain-ridden faces. To look into their eyes would acknowledge an individual. There could be no individual, or she would feel. Any grieving had to wait.

The surgeon hailed her.

Another amputation most likely. Careful not to step on any wounded, Alice went to the dining room. A man was on the table, but there were no hysterical screams.

The surgeon tossed a blood-spattered frock coat to the floor. Four embroidered braids were on the sleeve—a general.

Suddenly sick, Alice placed a hand to her belly.

"Miss McGuire, if you're going to swoon . . ."

She shook her head that she wouldn't.

"Then fetch the general some brandy."

General—she hadn't miscounted the braids. Don't look at his face, and he would remain as nameless as the rest.

"Miss McGuire!"

A command—she snapped to attention. Her hands trembled as she poured brandy into a tin cup.

"Alice," gasped a weak voice.

He couldn't know her name. If he did, then she couldn't discount him as another faceless individual. She approached the table. His shirt was open and his chest covered in blood. Unable to look at his face, she didn't need to ask how bad the wound was. Fighting tears, she knew.

Finally her gaze met familiar dark eyes. He watched her as she lifted his head and put the tin cup to his lips. "You did this to get my attention, General."

Finished with the brandy, Wil gasped for breath. "Have I . . . succeeded?"

Always a joke—why couldn't he ever be serious? "It's worked, and now that you have my attention, what do you intend on doing with it?"

He forced a sly smile. Even gravely wounded, he thought about having his way with her.

"Wil Jackson, you are no gentleman, and you had best not go do anything foolish, such as die on me. I shall never forgive you, if you do."

The assistant surgeon placed a cloth cone over Wil's nose and mouth. "Miss McGuire," the surgeon said, "it might be best if you wait outside this time."

Some men went half-crazed when the chloroform was administered. She couldn't leave—not now. "I'll stay with him."

The assistant poured chloroform in the cone, and she reached for Wil's hand. Black and blue, his hand was swollen twice to normal size. Possibly broken, his hand was the least of his worries.

Alice grasped Wil's arm. His eyes darted back and forth and he muttered, while the surgeon sponged away blood. Wil's muscles gradually relaxed, and the surgeon probed in his chest.

She couldn't watch. She rinsed out a cloth in a basin and dabbed it on Wil's forehead. What she wouldn't give for one of his brash remarks. How many days had passed since sharing dinner with him? A week.

For some reason, she thought of Timmy Mullen. A week after they had been caught smoking behind the barn, several boys had taken turns jumping from the hayloft. Too dangerous of a game for her, she had watched from a distance.

Timmy had changed his mind about jumping, but the other boys called him "chicken." Proving them wrong, Timmy grabbed the rope and hurled himself from the hayloft. The rope broke. Timmy fell to the ground with a terrifying thud. He lingered with a fractured skull for days.

And why was she thinking of Timmy now?

The surgeon's nimble hands worked quickly and efficiently—pulling bits of fabric from the wound, tying and sewing until the bleeding was minimal. The assistant lifted the cone from Wil's face. She helped bandage his chest, and a litter carried him to an upstairs bedroom.

Being a general had some privileges. Unlike most of the wounded, Wil had a blanket and a bed. His eyes remained half-closed and his breathing was raspy.

Alice grasped his left hand. She tightened her grip, and Wil squeezed back. Weak—but it had definitely been there. He was coming around.

His eyelids fluttered, and he gasped and coughed.

Beside him, she sat on the edge of the bed and held him as he leaned over the bed and retched.

His muscles quivered, and his body writhed.

Alice mixed water with morphine in a cup. There was so little morphine to spare. To make it last longer, she had been diluting it for days. As she helped Wil drink, she prayed it was strong enough to rid him of pain.

Finally, his trembling halted. A long while passed before he spoke. "How bad?" he asked in a groggy voice.

"Bones are broken in your hand and a couple of ribs."

Deathly pale, he lifted his right arm to view his splinted hand. His breathing was strained, and he fought for each breath.

"You're having difficulty breathing because the bullet hit a lung," she continued. "It went straight through. As long as pneumonia doesn't set in, the doctor says you have a chance."

No reaction—had she been expecting one?

He laid his head to the feather pillow, and she propped it to help him breathe. Around his neck was a leather pouch tied by a deerskin cord. An Indian artifact—she touched it.

"For luck," he whispered.

"You have never struck me as the superstitious sort."

Wil closed his eyes. "Many things . . . that you don't know."

"And you don't know how lucky you were." She traced a finger through his whiskers. "The bullet came within an inch of your heart."

Chapter Eight

Until wil learned his totem, Peopeo's family had refused to allow him to marry her. They feared his guardian spirit might be incompatible with hers. Not knowing what to expect, he had ignored the pain from his Mexican War wound and tromped miles to a clearing in a pine forest. For a day, he sat and waited. Nothing happened. Feeling distinctly silly, he returned to the Nez Perce village.

Peopeo insisted that he try again—and not return until he discovered his guide or admitted defeat. With some reluctance, he went back to the clearing.

Wil watched billowing clouds and heard the cry of a hawk. Was the bird of prey his animal spirit? Peopeo wouldn't be satisfied unless he knew what type. While he grasped the difference between hawks and falcons, the subtleties of the varieties were another matter.

Clouds gathered and pelted him with rain. Wet and shivering, he waited through another day.

The clouds cleared, and on the morning of the third day, a doe entered the clearing to graze. The deer was Peopeo's totem.

Delirious from the elements, he shook his head and laughed. Instead of taking flight, the doe continued to graze. Oblivious to his presence, she wandered so near that if he reached out, he could touch her. For some reason, she must have sensed that he wasn't a threat.

Nimble-footed, she moved with the grace of a dancer. With a flick of her tail, she beckoned him to follow. Her ears remained alert, and her nose sniffed the air as she led him to the edge of the clearing.

Like a house cat playing with a ball of yarn, a mountain lion cuffed and pounced on a twisted root. Aware the great cat wasn't stalking, the doe didn't flee.

Their lives were intertwined. The deer and mountain lion couldn't survive without each other. Peopeo would be pleased. His totem was the mountain lion.

When Wil woke, he expected to find himself in the clearing. Morphine euphoria had unlocked buried memories. More recently, he recalled being wounded, and the agonizing bumpy ambulance ride before being brought to a farmhouse.

The stench of blood permeated the air, and someone moaned from another room. A woman in a blood-stained dress sat in a rocking chair beside the bed.

His throat scratched. He licked his lips and swallowed, but he remained parched. "Alice?" he said in a raspy voice.

Her hair was auburn, and her green eyes filled with worry and fear.

A tin cup went to his lips. Bitter water trickled down his throat and quenched his thirst.

Through clouds of morphine, Wil drifted. A heavy weight was on his chest, and hands pinned him down, keeping him from reaching her. *Peopeo . . .*

Voices shrieked, then thrashing. Violent thrashing.

Her neck was broken.

Sweat poured into his eyes. Wil bolted upright and screamed.

"Wil, you're all right."

Gentle hands pushed him back to the pillow.

Shaking all over, he couldn't make it stop. The pain in his chest grew dull, and he blinked. She was Alice, not Peopeo. "Alice, I'm . . . fond of you."

He had nearly slipped and said love. But he didn't love her, nor did he care to. Peopeo and Amanda had taught him that lesson. Age had crept up on him. Too old for such frivolities, he would be thirty-eight come June. His animal spirit guided the way. Except to mate, the mountain lion lived a solitary existence.

* * *

Day and night, Alice fetched water, washed his feverish skin, and changed bandages and linens. The morphine was gone, and Wil had a restless day. She daubed a cool cloth to his forehead, then his shoulders. A smattering of dark hair poked above his heavily swathed chest.

She wrung the cloth in a water-filled basin and pressed it to his belly. Purposely avoiding his privates, she had discovered quite by accident in the performance of her duties that even men nearly in the grave could be roused by the merest of touches. The first time, she had felt shame in the belief that her gentle cleaning strokes had been too much like amorous touching. Only after it had happened a second and third time did she realize that it was the nature of men's bodies.

But she was fond of Wil, and he would tease her unmercifully if he found out. "Wil..."

Not an eyelash flickered in response.

Cautiously, Alice lowered his drawers. He was far more appealing than a boyish Timmy Mullen. A jagged white scar stretched along his right hip from the wound that had nearly killed him during the Mexican War.

She washed him in long, soothing strokes. He stirred to life, but the man continued to sleep. She thought of Peopeo and wondered if she had comforted him in the same manner. Chastising herself that she was getting carried away, she quickly covered him.

Exhausted, Alice eased into the rocking chair and closed her eyes. Hopefully, he would sleep through the night. Her head lolled.

A groan from the bed woke her with a start. She groped through the dark until she found the lamp. She jerked the chimney away and lit it.

Wil lay on his side and gasped for breath. His eyes were clamped shut, and his muscles trembled. He pressed a hand to his bandaged chest.

Alice squeezed the cloth in the basin and placed it to his forehead.

Though his hand shook, he gripped her wrist. "Alice?"

She sponged his sweaty face. "I'm here."

He let go of her arm. "Thought...you were gone."

"I'm not going anywhere."

Not really seeing her, his dark eyes stared transfixed.

If only she had something to ease the pain. Even brandy would make her feel a little less helpless. Willow bark tea? Not strong enough. Something. Anything. She checked his pulse—flighty.

"Alice . . ." She hushed him to save his strength, but he continued, "I never told Peopeo . . . how I felt." He muttered.

Unable to make out his words, Alice leaned closer. Another language? An Indian language—he was speaking to his wife.

His anguished eyes met hers. "I made the same mistake a second time."

"Mistake?" He had to be hurting something fierce. Wil wouldn't normally talk about his feelings, but did he mean Amanda—or her?

She didn't care. Rules of propriety had already been broken. She clambered under the blanket beside him. She drew him to her, and his body molded against her. Like a lost child, he clung to her.

She fought the tears. "You haven't made the same mistake. I thought you knew. I love you."

He shuddered, and she remained with him until he was still. Outside the window, an owl screeched, and a fox yipped. For now, the guns rested.

Wil's breathing grew easier. To the steady thump of his heart, Alice closed her eyes.

"Good morning."

Wil's voice woke her to sunlight streaming through the window. She stifled a yawn and gazed into his eyes. No longer pain-filled, they were clear. Tending him countless hours must have taken their toll. With her arms around his neck, she had fallen asleep—next to him. Warmth filled her cheeks.

"Waking to your lovely face is most pleasant." His hand rested on her breast.

"I will thank you kindly to remove your hand from my bosom."

Amusement danced in his eyes. "Of course, Miss McGuire."

As his hand slid down the length of her body and under her skirt, Alice chastised herself for not getting up and breaking contact. Nothing of consequence could happen. After all, he had been wounded. Besides, he had his drawers on, and she was fully clothed.

His fingertips ventured inside the opening of her drawers.

No man had ever touched her there. It wasn't supposed to be this way. She shouldn't yearn for a man if not betrothed or properly wed. "Wil, please don't. You're in no condition—"

"Fending me off?" he asked with a wicked grin.

Alice hopped to her feet and straightened her dress. Unable to face him, she swallowed hard. An unwed lady wasn't supposed to tend filthy, lice-infested men, clean their bodily wastes, or view private parts best kept covered. Papa was probably whirling in his grave. But she couldn't forget all that she had experienced—not since glimpsing the bodies on the heights.

"Forgive my weakness."

An apology? She forced a smile. "Why Wil Jackson, there is some hope for you."

"My apology isn't for what just happened. As a matter of fact, when a man wakes to a beautiful woman beside him, it's a perfectly natural reaction. Alice, you're blushing."

Indignant, she waved a fist. "Wipe that smug grin from your face. I have toiled day and night, not knowing whether you'd live or die, and you repay me with insults."

"My intent wasn't to offend."

He did care. "Then why the apology?"

Wil lowered his head. The whiskered face effectively hid his expression, but when vulnerable, she had glimpsed behind the mask. His apology was for showing weakness.

"There's nothing to forgive," she assured him.

"Why haven't I been sent to Richmond?"

Embarrassed for letting his guard down, he obviously didn't wish to discuss it either. "The doctors said you would likely bleed to death before reaching Richmond. They thought it best not to move you, so I agreed to stay behind."

"The army has moved?"

"Most of it. I feared the Yankees would overrun the area, but they seem content staying to their side of the river."

As Wil sat up, his breath grew short. Alice fluffed the pillow behind his back, and he examined his splinted right hand.

"If you wish, I can write a letter for you," Alice said.

"There's no one to write to."

"You have kin in Charleston."

"A brother and sister who would rather not hear from me."

What kind of family didn't long for a letter from relation far away? "But you were wounded. Certainly they will be delighted to know you're alive."

With a devilish spark, he arched a brow. "If I had died a hero's death, then they would care to hear the news."

Crossing her arms, Alice sat on the edge of the bed. "No family can be that cruel."

"Sometimes Alice, you can be very naive. At seventeen, I was shipped off to the Point for transgressions."

Like she had been sent to finishing school to learn proper behavior. "Transgressions? I'd be willing to wager, it wasn't for spitting or swearing."

A slight grin formed on his mouth. "You'd win that wager. If John Graham hadn't taken demerits on my behalf, I would have been dismissed the first year."

She had known that Amanda's first husband and Wil had been friends at West Point. Now she understood how the unusual friendship had formed.

"After that," he continued, "I performed my duty to everyone's satisfaction. The indiscretion my family refuses to overlook is a half-breed son, even though they are one-quarter Cherokee themselves."

Cherokee? Wil was part Indian? His prominent cheekbones and black eyes suddenly made sense.

"Obviously, Amanda hasn't relayed that fact."

"She hadn't. Why are you telling me? You don't usually offer information."

"So you know whom you've been tending."

As they grew closer, he continued to lend ways of retreat. "You can't get rid of me that easily."

He leaned forward to kiss her but gasped in pain. His hand went to his chest, and he slumped to the pillow.

"Serves you right, you fool. If you're not careful, you'll start bleeding again."

"You can't keep an old warhorse like me down for long."

He was trying to placate her. "Wil, I remained with you during surgery. I *know* how bad it was. You're not out of the woods yet. You needn't pretend—not with me."

Grasping her hand, he opened it—palm up. The calluses had grown unsightly, but she was no longer shamed. He kissed the toughened skin. "Old habits die hard."

And some things would never change. He would protect her—fiercely.

Chapter Nine

FOR TWO DAYS IN MID-JUNE Yankees had camped on Amanda's lawn. She woke to wagons creaking on the main road. The Army of the Potomac was on the move. Thankful the squatters had left, she had shooed foragers from the chicken coop the previous morning. A poplar switch had been ammunition enough to send the culprits skedaddling.

Sam had tried to persuade her to seek refuge in Washington, but cut off from her family, she couldn't leave without word of their safety. No news from Alice was an excuse. She had no intention of abandoning the farm.

As Amanda crossed the kitchen's red brick floor, she got a whiff of biscuits laced with honey. Sam kept them stocked in basic provisions, but with the army moving, everyday necessities would likely grow scarce. The warm spring morning suddenly seemed cold.

"Breakfast nearly ready, Miss Amanda." The hunched blind servant pulled a tin of piping-hot biscuits from the oven. "You sit down and rest afore da baby come."

Amanda pressed a hand to her rounded belly. "The baby won't be here for another two months, Frieda."

Frieda pointed a bony finger. "You work too hard. Won't be no time to rest once da baby here."

Amanda sat in a pole-backed chair at the table. "You coddle me."

"If I don't look after you, den who does?" Her sightless eyes widened as if they could see. "Miss Amanda, our comp'ny back."

"Yankees?" Trusting Frieda's instinct, she had best check. Too heavy with child to hustle, Amanda waddled to the parlor. She parted the lace curtain to at least a dozen men in blue outside the picket fence. One man, big as a bull, began ripping the fence apart. As others joined him, she grabbed the rifle over the mantel and went outside.

Fence rails splintered, and Amanda fired over their heads. A chestnut horse reared, nearly unseating its rider. "You will leave the premises," Amanda shouted.

"Ma'am . . . " A bucktooth lieutenant regained control of his mount. "Don't mean to alarm you, but we're requisitioning supplies."

Reloaded, Amanda replaced the ramrod and aimed the rifle. "You have no right to destroy my property. My husband is Major Samuel Prescott—"

"Of the Reb army?" With a sneer, he shook his head. "Sorry, ma'am—"

"Sorry indeed. Major Prescott is Federal infantry."

The lieutenant straightened in the saddle. "Then *Major* Prescott should have posted a guard. I have orders."

Sam had posted a guard, but when the army started moving, the guard went with it. Another board cracked from the picket fence. "I have a small child in the house. Please . . . "

His face held firm. The lieutenant dismounted and confiscated her rifle.

Fearing for Rebecca's safety, Amanda hurried as fast as she was capable to the house and up the stairs. On the trundle bed sprawled Rebecca, her legs and arms tossing in a bad dream. Though she was Sam's daughter from his first marriage, these Yankees didn't care a whit about their own kind.

"Rebecca . . . " Before she stirred awake, Amanda climbed in next to the girl and hugged her.

With a whimper, Rebecca started to cry.

Amanda brushed dark hair from Rebecca's face. "It's all right, Rebecca."

Sniffling, the child tightened her grip. "Mama." Amanda heard the front door open and nasal voices downstairs. Rebecca shrieked as if in pain, "Mama!"

Amanda held Rebecca until she was still. She should have listened to Sam and sought refuge. Only one woman against the entire Yankee army, she wasn't strong enough. Not alone. When Sam found out, he'd have their blue-bottomed hides. But where was Sam? He was most likely moving with the army.

The nasal voices laughed.

What right did they have terrifying innocent women and children? Amanda pressed two fingers to her lips. "You must keep quiet, Rebecca. Mama's going to see that those men leave."

Big blue eyes filled with tears, and Rebecca choked back a sob. Amanda tiptoed from the room and down the stairs.

In the parlor two men in blue stretched on the tapestry sofa. Laughing and joking between them, one smoked Sam's pipe.

Her eyes narrowed, and Amanda made a beeline for the study. She withdrew a pistol from the desk drawer. Trembling, she raised the pistol and returned to the parlor. "Is taking over my house as if you owned it part of your thievery?"

The private with the pipe stood. His wispy moustache turned up slightly at the ends, and he smiled. The smile was a familiar one from the hospital. She had written letters of reassurance to his family in Pennsylvania and washed his feverish forehead. A boyish face in the hospital—it seemed harsher here.

She nearly screamed. Steady—she must keep her wits and hold the pistol steady. "How can you repay my letter writing with treachery? Does your mama know how you treat Southern citizens? She would be ashamed."

With an arrogant grin the private set the pipe down and edged closer. "I'll not have you speaking ill of my mother."

The other Yankee got to his feet and circled the opposite direction. "Stop, or I will shoot."

Daring her, the private kept moving toward her. *Aim to the side of him.* She gritted her teeth and squeezed the trigger. In a puff of smoke, a blast rocked the house. He faltered. Shock appeared on his face, then he clutched his arm. "She shot me! The bitch shot me!"

His partner had her arm, twisting it so hard that the pistol fell from her hand.

"Apparently you boys misunderstood orders," the bucktooth lieutenant said, entering the parlor. "Collect rations."

The private waved a bloody arm. "She shot me!"

"It's a graze, Private. Now see to your duty." The lieutenant scooped the pistol from the floor and tucked it in his belt.

She clenched a hand. "I tended him in the hospital, and this is how he repays me."

"My apology, ma'am."

"How can an apology suffice?"

"Ma'am, quite frankly, I don't give a lick if you accept the apology or not. I have orders."

"And how many more innocent families will you defile?"

The lieutenant glared. "If you cause any more trouble, I'll have you bound and gagged." With an about turn, he followed his men to the kitchen.

The Yankees had won. Except to watch, she was powerless. They would always win. A crash of glass shattering came from the kitchen. More feet stomped around other parts of the house.

Amanda closed her eyes. The Yankees wouldn't be satisfied until all Southerners starved. The kitchen door slammed, and she heard men laughing outside.

A pistol went off. She hurried toward the kitchen. Careful to step over pitcher shards, she went out to the back steps.

Running fingers through Ezra's curly, gray hair, the Yankees pestered him.

She waved a fist at them. "Leave him be!"

"It's all right, Miss Amanda. Dey just funnin'."

"That's right." The private with the wispy moustache sneered and raised his pistol to the sky. "We're just funnin'. Now dance."

Ezra pasted on a compliant grin and jigged. Not a simpleminded Negro, he obeyed to protect them.

Follow his example and don't let the Yankees see humiliation. They would eventually grow weary of no sport. Above all else, they mustn't see her cry. Determined to keep her poise, Amanda raised her head.

A well-fed soldier, unlike so many Southern boys, climbed in the seat of a wagon. Loaded with boards from the picket fence for Yankee campfires, the wagon creaked down the tree-lined lane. Hooting and waving hats, several men galloped after the wagon.

A freckle-faced private in blue led her gray mare from the barn. A hand went to her mouth to keep from crying out. Not her mare—she was the only horse left in the barn. In foal, the gray would be of limited use. Nothing good would come of protesting.

Amanda said a silent prayer, when a warning shot fired from across the farmyard. More Yankees—dear Lord, what would she do now? But a familiar blue-roan gelding trotted into the open with Wil in a simple gray uniform and no insignia. Left-handed, he leveled his pistol to the lieutenant's chest.

Wil wasn't left-handed. What was he up to?

"You boys have overstayed your welcome," Wil said to the Yankees.

The lieutenant's eyes narrowed, and he spat in the dirt. "I only see you Reb."

"I have a boy in the loft and several more in the woods ready to take yours down if the mare isn't returned to the lady. Test me, Billy. You'll be the first to die."

The lieutenant eyed Wil, then glanced to the hayloft. Amanda saw a figure crouch. She swallowed hard. Wil wasn't bluffing.

The lieutenant nodded, and the freckle-faced private draped the mare's lead rope in her hands. The Yankees were getting on their horses and riding away.

As hooves clattered down the lane, the pistol dropped from Wil's hand. With a groan, he toppled from the saddle.

"Wil!" By his side, Amanda kneeled.

"You should...," he gasped, short of breath, "learn poker, Amanda."

"Poker? Wil, you're hurt."

Alice was beside them, bending down and unfastening Wil's jacket. He forced a laugh. "Meet...my boy. Mighty fine looking one. Don't you think?"

Perplexed, she glanced from Wil to Alice. "Alice, what's going on?"

"He insisted on helping you. I'll explain the rest later. Let's get him to the house."

Amanda stepped out of the way as Ezra moved in to help.

After making Wil comfortable in the back bedroom, Alice relayed the events that had transpired over the past couple of months. Though exhausted, her sister beamed when speaking about Wil's heroics. Amanda had already spotted the signs, but she felt uneasy about

Alice's affection toward him. Only after agreeing that she'd check on Wil did her sister relent to getting some rest.

Amanda cracked open the door to the back bedroom. "Wil?" She went inside.

Extremely pale, he was lying on his side. If the bullet had gone through him, it probably helped ease the pain.

She reached for his hand, but thought better of it. "I have some laudanum."

With his splinted right hand, he had difficulty gripping the cup, but he drank the mixture down. Not the sort of man to complain about pain, he was definitely hurting something fierce if he gave no protest.

"I want to thank you for what you did."

He merely nodded.

"Forgive me if I appear insensitive," she continued, "but I'm worried about Alice. It's not proper for her to be caring for you the way she has been."

"Forgive me, Amanda." He handed her the empty cup. "But I'm in no mood to give a damn about proprieties."

"She loves you."

He laid his head against the feather pillow and closed his eyes. "That is her misfortune."

"Then I'd appreciate it if you don't lead her on."

He laughed but quickly sucked in his breath. "Tell me what I should refrain from doing, and I'll gladly stop. But right now, I can barely make it to the chamber pot by myself."

"Wil . . . I have always been able to talk to you in a straightforward manner."

He opened his eyes and met her gaze. "That was then."

She gritted her teeth.

"Amanda, you can stop fretting. I haven't compromised your sister, and I'll leave for Richmond just as soon as I'm capable. Besides, jealousy doesn't become you."

Jealousy? How dare he . . . She crossed her arms above her rounding abdomen. "What makes you think I'm jealous?"

"Because if you weren't, you'd be having this *talk* with Alice, not me."

"A near-death experience hasn't changed you in the least. You're still arrogant and stubborn."

"And you, *Mrs. Prescott*, still have difficulty facing the truth."

"Need I remind you that *you* are the one who burned the letter telling me how you felt?"

His eyes grew harsh. "If I had mailed it, would things have been any different? You certainly didn't waste any time getting knocked up by my former lieutenant when you thought I was dead."

Choking back a sob, Amanda clapped a hand over her mouth. Tempted to bolt, she held her ground, but she mustn't let him see her cry.

"Amanda, I'm sorry," he said in a softer voice.

"For what you just said or for not mailing the letter?" She could no longer fight the tears. He reached out to brush them away, but she stepped back. "There's no sense in discussing this any further. What's done is done."

Without looking back, she left the room.

Smoke puffed from the farmhouse's chimney. Amanda must have already gone to bed. The place was dark. After Sam stabled his horse in the barn, Holly met him on the steps. He pressed two fingers to his lips for her to keep quiet.

Careful not to wake the household, he tiptoed through the front door and dropped his gear in the foyer. He motioned for Holly to wait for him there. His new leather boots creaked, and every step echoed against the wood floor.

By the stairs, he heard a pistol cock behind him. He raised his hands and turned.

The gun lowered. "I could have shot you, Prescott."

"Jackson, what are you doing here?"

Lowering his head as if in pain, Jackson eased into the wing chair. "I received a furlough—courtesy of a Yankee bullet," he said dryly. "Obviously, if you're here, I'm in Federal lines. Arrest me, and be done with it."

Embers in the fireplace glowed, casting shadows throughout the room, but enough light penetrated to see Jackson's drawn face. "Actually, you're in no-man's-land. Most of the army has moved." Jackson glanced up, and Sam pointed. "How bad?"

"Concern? Or comparing battle scars?"

"Captain . . ." His former commander's rank was out before he thought about it.

"Damn Yank nearly killed me."

Betrayed by the edge in Jackson's voice, Sam realized that his former commander wasn't out of danger yet. "I'm relieved you're here."

Jackson eyed him skeptically. "So I can hide from foraging parties?"

"If I had been a deserter, I would have been dead. I wanted Amanda to go to Washington, but she refused to leave."

"That surprises you?"

"I've learned the depth of Southern stubbornness the hard way," Sam admitted.

To this statement, Jackson laughed but his hand went flying to his chest. "Things haven't changed."

Green in New Mexico, Sam had been assigned by Jackson to lead a company, if one could call it a company—a handful of men really. The desert was unforgiving of mistakes. A three-day reconnaissance turned into five. Only severe water rationing had brought his men out alive. It seemed a lifetime ago. "I suppose everything comes easily to you?"

"We're more alike than you might think. Now go see your wife before she accuses me of holding you prisoner." Jackson clamped his eyes shut and leaned his head back.

"That's right, Sam," Holly said, stepping into the parlor, "go see your wife."

Jackson's eyes shot open. "Prescott, you could have warned me."

With a laugh, Sam returned to the stairs. Boots creaking, he reached the top and opened the door to Amanda's room. No fire was lit, and the room was cold. He closed the door behind him and undressed. He joined Amanda in bed. Let her sleep. He snuggled to her prone form, relishing in her warmth.

"Sam?" came a groggy voice.

"Amanda." He touched her rounding belly. The war gave life in peculiar ways, and he sometimes wondered if the baby was the only reason she had married him.

She sat up. "Sam, it is you." With kisses to his face, she threw her arms around his neck.

After the morning, months might pass before seeing her again—if ever. His contrary thoughts gave way to an intense need. In the dark, he lifted her nightdress.

"I'm much too fat."

"You're not fat."

"I have a belly the size of a twenty-pound turkey. You don't call that fat?"

"You're going to have a baby. That doesn't mean you're fat. Amanda, I don't know when I'll get back this way again." He tossed the nightdress to the side and drew her atop him. With him stationed nearby in recent months, they had become complacent, avoiding the day when it would be necessary for him to leave again.

Joined as one, she must have felt it too. Her face was damp, and he tasted salt from her tears. Running his hands down her bare back and around to her belly, he broke the rhythm. Would the baby know him?

"Don't think about it, Sam."

"Can't help it, Amanda. Rebecca doesn't know I'm her father, and now . . ."

Rolling to his side, she fell into the crook of his arm. She placed his hand to her belly.

Beneath his fingertips, the baby kicked. Damn—his moods had a habit of interfering with the precious moments they had.

"Rebecca calls you papa, and you shall see the baby. You must believe that."

"Amanda, I brought supplies and . . . Holly."

Her arms tensed. "Holly? Sam, how could you? You know how I feel about her."

"She tended wounded after the battle. It's not safe for her to return to Washington now. It'll only be for a few days. No matter what else she's done, she is my brother's widow."

"I don't have a room for her."

He snorted a laugh. "Jackson's?"

Amanda whacked a pillow across his ribs. "I'll not have such dalliances in my house. Besides, I don't think they're friendly anymore."

"Friendly? Is that what they were?" The pillow thumped him again. "Put her in the barn. I don't care."

"A big help you are." With a sigh, Amanda added, "I shall move Wil to the empty cabin. I'd rather send *that woman* there, but Frieda would probably pound Holly over the head with a skillet."

He pulled her to him and kissed her on the mouth. With her legs on each side of him and gentle rocking, they coupled. Only after their energy was spent did Sam sleep. At the light of dawn, he woke. Already awake, Amanda watched him. Clinging to what little time was left, they shared each other again.

As the household stirred to life, he heard Alice in the hall with Rebecca. Time to leave. But Amanda was here—in his arms.

The door burst open, and Rebecca charged in, complaining she was hungry. Amanda ducked, yanking the quilt to her neck. He nearly split a gut laughing, while she sent the toddler downstairs with Alice.

All of the precious things he had missed. More of those days were to come. At breakfast, Sam couldn't force himself to eat grits. With the supplies he had brought, there was plenty of food. But for how long?

He played with Rebecca a while, then said goodbye to his former commander. None of them would have needed to fret. Jackson had retreated to the cabin without being asked. Afterward, Sam went to saddle his horse.

The blind servant, Frieda, met him in the barn. "I ain't goin' to be here when you get back, Mr. Sam."

"Where?" His jaw dropped. The old woman hinted that she'd be dead by the time he returned. If it hadn't been for her medicine, he would have lost his leg and possibly his life as well.

"Don't grieve none, Mr. Sam. I live a long life, an' 'cause of Miss Amanda, I be free. Da war goin' to be rough on her. She need you, an' you need to be careful, if you goin' to come out alive."

A warning. The wrinkles on her face were more pronounced than usual. He wondered exactly how old she was. "I'll be careful," he promised. Life around the farm wouldn't be the same without Frieda. He hugged the old woman, and a toothless grin formed on her mouth.

With a goodbye, she waved her cherry walking stick in front of her and shuffled from the barn.

Finished saddling, Sam led the blood-red stallion outside.

Amanda stood where the picket fence used to be, holding Rebecca's hand. Her eyes were puffy from crying, and she crossed the farmyard.

Sam swept her into his arms and kissed her. Rebecca danced up and down for a kiss like Mama's. He laughed at her antics. She did know him—for now. His last sight was the two of them waving. Tears streaked Amanda's cheeks.

He whispered goodbye.

Too late—their pact had been to never say goodbye, unless it was for good.

Wil heard *her* voice—Peopeo's. She had come to him in the night and announced their son was dead. With no emotion, he lingered on her message. *Their son was dead*. When she had needed him most, he had been unable to take her in his arms and comfort her.

Few soldiers cared when measles claimed Indian lives. Day and night, she had tended Benjamin, but with no medicine available, the boy had died. Then when he got sick, she had risked her life to secure medicine and paid the price.

As far as outsiders were concerned, it wasn't a real marriage recognized by the church. She hadn't existed and neither had their son. He vowed no one would ever see that side of him again.

Ready to join Peopeo and Benjamin, he waited for death to claim him, but for some reason, he had been spared yet again.

When Wil woke, a woman in a floral dress sat in a rocking chair beside the bed. His memory was vague, but he had spent most of the night pacing the floorboards. Pain had kept him awake, then when he slept, buried memories returned to the surface.

More recently, he recalled Amanda in trouble and the Yankee foragers. With Alice's help, the Yankees had believed their deception. "Alice?"

"The dear girl needs some time away from you."

Not Alice, but Holly Prescott. Wil blinked, and her beaming face came into focus. "What are you doing here?"

"Paying my respects."

No one would enjoy seeing him suffer more. Short of breath, he waved for her to leave. "You have done so."

A familiar sly look appeared in her eyes. "The least you can do is act happy to see me."

"Why?"

She gave a curt grin. "For old times' sake."

The tattered curtain fluttered as a summer breeze swept through the open window. There was a dull ache in his chest, but he managed to sit. Had he been lying there for hours—or days? Time jumbled in a laudanum haze. "Miss McGuire assured me you were paid."

"Paid?" Fluttering her eyelashes, Holly widened her grin. "Wil, I don't want money. I told you—"

"I heard what you said."

She sent him a look of wide-eyed innocence. "Then I fear I don't understand your foul mood."

She should have been an actress. "Your wish that I rot in some Yankee prison might have something to do with it."

"Oh that . . ." Holly flicked a hand, dismissing it. "I was mourning the loss of my husband. You were an easy target."

As she sidled onto the bed beside him, he caught a whiff of her perfume—definitely up to her old games.

"Sam says the bullet went straight through you. So how do we know you weren't really shot in the back? Tell me, Wil, how fast were you running?"

Baiting him, she was trying to draw anger to the surface. *Ignore it.* His gaze locked with hers. "Obviously not fast enough."

With a laugh, she clapped her hands. "Such wit. But then you always could make me laugh."

Don't react—she'd relish it if he did.

Her finger traced the bandage swathing his chest. "I've been concerned. You were badly wounded."

Sincerity? He doubted it. As the fog lifted, the ache intensified. If she found out, she'd use it as ammunition. "I'm fine."

Her lips curved to a smile. "Faahhn," she drawled. "I love the way you Southrons say that, but to be frank, Colonel, I don't believe you."

"Brigadier," he corrected, "and I shall be returning to the field soon." Gritting his teeth, he laid his head against the pillow and shut his eyes.

"A promotion hasn't taught you how to admit anything, has it? Since we're having such a delightful conversation, maybe you can sidestep another question. Who is *Peopeo*? The name sounds Indian."

His temper grew short, and he glared.

Holly grinned in victory. "You're more talkative when you're under the weather. Wil, you never told me you had a squaw."

He latched onto her arm, and she let out a surprised yelp. Her free hand rubbed his crotch. Though there had never been any tenderness between them, he was tempted to surrender. Anger and danger aroused him. But she wasn't the source of his vexation, and the time had come to bury it. Wil let go of her arm. "What do you want?"

Fluffing pillows to help him breathe, she got cozy. "When you're feeling up to moving to Richmond, I'd like to tend you."

She *did* want money. If it didn't hurt like hell to laugh, he would have snorted his fool head off. "Haven't received your husband's pension yet?"

Fire entered her gleaming eyes. "Your recent experience has only made you more ornery. No, I haven't received Charles's pension, but I shall—unlike those dishonorably discharged for siding with secessionists."

In no mood to continue sparring, Wil gasped for breath. "You win."

Holly opened her mouth, then closed it again. She blinked in disbelief. "You're not the sort to surrender."

Each breath was a struggle, and he closed his eyes. "You sound disappointed."

"I am . . . a little."

Anger had fueled the fire. Without it, the flames were doused. Not dead, sparks simmered—ready to flare. "Then I'll make it up to you—later." Pain hit him like a sledgehammer striking him squarely on the chest. He bit his lip to keep from crying out.

A tin cup went to his lips—water. Nearly choking, he shoved the cup away, and it clanged to the floor.

"Damn you, Wil Jackson," she said with a furrowed brow.

She *was* worried. "Perhaps, we can agree to a temporary truce."

The worry lines faded from her forehead. "A truce? Us?"

"It was only a suggestion."

"Wil, I meant it when I said I'd tend you."

"In exchange for . . ."

Her mouth widened to a grin, and she leaned closer. "Being escorted among Richmond social circles on the arm of a general is repayment enough."

For a change, he knew she was being honest. While far and few, some qualities were in her favor. Publicly—she was well dressed and a proper lady with enticing curves that turned heads. Privately—she thought nothing of strutting around naked except for silk gartered stockings and behaving like a high-priced whore.

Appearances—he had grown weary of them. "I don't think the arrangement would be mutually beneficial."

With a scowl, Holly pursed her lips. "Don't tell me a Yankee bullet has made you sentimental. You're acting more like a lovesick schoolboy. Wil, our type wasn't meant to fall in love."

Lovesick? He settled back in amusement. "You *are* joking? Exactly who is the unfortunate lady?"

She smiled sweetly. "You're still brooding over Amanda."

"I'm not brooding."

"I beg to differ. You've gone out of your way to seek revenge—smuggling supplies under Sam's nose and courting her sister."

"I'm not . . ." Deciding it wasn't worth the bother, he fell silent. She wouldn't believe him anyway.

Her grin turned knowing. "You asked for Amanda the same way as the squaw."

The squaw. Ready to boil, he clenched a hand. "So?"

"I've always wondered what the source of your vexation was. Who would have guessed you were pining for an Indian wench?"

"I strongly suggest that you don't pursue this any further."

Her eyes widened in delight, and she pressed a hand to her breast. "So I am right."

Wil met her gaze in warning as she twisted the deerskin cord of the Nez Perce medicine pouch between her fingers.

"I've heard about military men stationed in the West and their squaw concubines."

He grasped the bedpost to help him stand, and Holly jumped back with a shriek. Pain—he welcomed it. His hands went around her throat. Pressing tighter, he'd watch her suffocate as Peopeo had.

She clawed and struck him to loosen his grip.

More pain—in his healing hand.

Tighter—she couldn't breathe.

"Wil . . ."

Through waves of pain, he couldn't locate the soft and gentle voice.

"Let her go. She wasn't responsible for her death."

He loosened his grip.

Holly coughed and sputtered, darting out of his reach.

He smelled Alice's sweet scent. Thankful she had intervened, he felt her gentle touch, urging him back to bed. "How did you know?"

"You told me that you often killed those responsible on the battlefield. I'm also aware that your association with Mrs. Prescott has been . . . tenuous."

As usual, she was being polite. Green eyes beamed like lanterns, breaking through the abyss of his mind. In some ways, she reminded him of Amanda. He had wooed Amanda—to no avail. No sense in dwelling on that now, since he had known the reason all along why she had chosen Prescott instead. She had glimpsed behind the mask, and now Alice had witnessed it too.

Chapter Ten

VIRGINIA RED CLAY HAD GIVEN WAY to the brown earth of Maryland. The snaking blue column had marched sixty miles in three days through brutal late-June heat. Sam wiped the sweat from his neck. Many boys had been stricken with sunstroke on the march, including the lieutenant colonel. Already ill from dysentery, the colonel had died. Next in line, Sam had received the promotion. Ironic—he was still receiving a captain's pay. Maybe someday the army would catch up.

Unlike in Virginia, the people welcomed the Union with milk and loaves of freshly baked bread as they passed. Sam wished a resident would appear by the road with a dipper of cold water. Rumors floated through the ranks that Bobby Lee was in Pennsylvania. With the breakneck speed of the march, he believed the rumors must indeed be fact.

Feet trod and hooves plodded against the sunbaked surface. Up ahead a flurry of riders and lathered horses caught Sam's attention. A courier brought the word. Halt the regiment and bivouac. Relieved with the break, men began breaking fence rails for cooking fires and pitching tents. Many sank to the ground, falling asleep where they fell. A few boys located a stream and uniforms went flying.

Expecting the rest to be brief, he had an aide see to his horse and quenched his own thirst while the boys frolicked and splashed. He spotted the girl soldier, Jo, standing on the bank staring wistfully at the rushing water. Even her bobbed hair and baggy clothes might not hide her sex if she dove in.

Grateful for the opportunity to jot a few lines to Amanda, Sam returned to the main camp and awkwardly balanced pencil and paper

                    Kim Murphy

on his knee. He barely got settled when shots from the picket line broke his concentration. He tossed his writing equipment to the ground and charged in the direction of the gunfire. Amanda probably wouldn't have received the letter anyway.

By the time he reached the picket, all was quiet.

A private with a pitted face saluted. "Rebel cavalry, sir."

Returning the salute, Sam merely nodded. General Stuart had been hassling their tail throughout the march. One thing didn't make sense—if the Rebel army was in Pennsylvania, what was their cavalry doing in Maryland? He suspected the Rebs were closer than top command let on.

Dizzy from the heat, he trudged over to the stream. As he splashed water on his face, he felt lightheaded. If he keeled over, only junior officers were left to command the regiment.

"Sir," came the girl soldier's wheezy voice, "you're lookin' a might flushed." She grasped his arm and guided him to the shade beneath a river birch, then handed him a tin cup. "Drink."

"Is that an order, Sergeant?"

Jo flashed him a knowing grin, and he obeyed. Although he had come to think of her as one of the boys, he recalled the truth when she doted like a mother hen.

Slightly refreshed, Sam struggled to his feet. Out of the corner of his eye, he caught a glimpse of light reflecting from the stone house on the ridge. There it was again—sunlight glinted off metal from a second-story window. He sent up the alarm. "Sharpshooters!"

Without bothering to don uniforms, the boys scrambled from the stream for their muskets, and Jo shouted for them to get down. Lined up along the bank on their bellies, they waited.

No gunfire, and tense minutes passed.

Weary of the Rebs' recent cat-and-mouse games, Sam motioned to Jo. "Take a few of the boys and flush them out."

She saluted and called out several names to follow her. Snatching up uniforms and dressing in a hurry, the boys crossed the stream. Crouched low in the waving grass, the line made its way to the top of the ridge.

Halfway up, the skirmishers hit the dirt, but no shots were exchanged.

Suddenly uneasy that enemy cavalry and sharpshooters were raising a smoke screen, Sam decided to lead his own group. If Reb infantry lurked beyond the ridge, top command had best be alerted. He motioned for five men to join him and waded across the stream. As they made their way up the hill through the waist-high summer grass, Jo's group began moving again.

Sunlight reflected from the second-story window. Signalling the boys to lie low, he reminded them to hold their fire. Without exchanging a single shot, the first line reached the stone house and disappeared beyond the ridge.

The reflection vanished from the window. Baffled by the Rebs' behavior, he had anticipated the sharpshooters to fire a couple of rounds as they beat a hasty retreat. He ordered the boys to march at the double-quick.

After they scrambled over a snake-rail fence, Sam was finally in range and drew his pistol. A private from the first group reappeared to the side of the house and waved that all was clear. "Colonel, I think you'd best get up here."

Out of breath and ready to succumb to the heat, he holstered his pistol. "Did you nab the sharpshooters?"

"Uh . . . not exactly, sir."

"Not exactly? Then why in the hell did you signal that it was clear?" Before the private could answer, Sam shoved past him.

The girl soldier sprinted down wooden steps of the front porch to greet him. With a snappy salute, she said, "Sir, the house belongs to a Miss Lawson. We couldn't find any evidence of Rebs, but she's visibly shaken and said she'd only speak to command rank about it."

The poor lady was probably frightened out of her wits from the Rebel raids. Accompanied by Jo, Sam climbed the stairs. Inside the parlor, a lean woman with streaked gray hair stood with her hands behind her back. On such a sweltering day, she even wore a cap and shawl.

As he approached, her beady eyes peered over spectacle rims. "General, it's impolite to keep a lady waiting."

He lowered his hat. "Lieutenant Colonel Prescott, ma'am."

She tapped an impatient foot. "You're the one in charge of the men camped along my stream?"

"*Your* stream?"

Indignant, she pointed a bony finger in the direction of the window. "In case you hadn't noticed, my house is only half a mile away."

Beginning to comprehend, he suspected she was about to request protection from the Rebels. "I'll post a guard—"

"Is there something wrong with your hearing, sir? They are in my stream."

Ready to roast alive in the heat, Sam wiped his sweaty brow, wishing he had taken the opportunity to join them. "We've had a long, hot march, Miss Lawson. I'm certain they're staying out of trouble."

Her face turned several shades of red, and he thought she might swoon. He reached out a hand to catch her before she fell, but she swatted his knuckles. "Buck naked, sir. I can see them frolicking through these..."

She pulled her other arm from behind her back. Clenched in her hand was a pair of field glasses.

There had never been any sharpshooters—only a prissy old hag.

Nearly splitting a gut, Jo doubled over in a fit of laughter.

Sam shot her a glare.

She wiped the grin from her face and straightened to attention.

He swallowed hard before addressing Miss Lawson. "I shall tell the boys to be more discriminating. Is there anything else I can do for you, ma'am?"

"That will be all, sir." Tightening the shawl about her shoulders, she gave them a curt dismissal.

Outside, the boys had sought refuge from the scorching sun under the limbs of a spreading oak. Sam gave the order to return to camp. As they regained their feet, they grumbled under their breath and meandered down the ridge toward the stream.

"Why didn't you tell her to put the damn field glasses away?" Jo asked, snorting back a belly laugh.

"Can't afford to make enemies of the civilians, Jo." They reached the snake-rail fence bordering the spinster's house. "Is she up there?"

Glancing over her shoulder, Jo stole a peek. "Yes, sir. And she's still got the dang field glasses."

Who would have thought? Sam shook his head. In the absurdity of the war, he thought that beat all and broke down laughing. His sides ached before he got a grip on himself once more. How many of the boys wouldn't be around after they met the Rebels?

Such little enjoyment these days. When he looked up, a courier on a black horse galloped up the hill with the order to march. God, he was growing tired of this damned war.

Shortly after Sam's departure, Amanda had taken to her bed. Excuses ranged from tiredness to running a fever. Alice believed she was fretting for Sam. With Amanda ill, more chores needed tending. Wil was a large portion of that responsibility. His face was unable to mask frequent pain, and at night she often heard floorboards creak from his constant pacing. At least Holly Prescott had moved on to Washington, making matters less tense.

In the heat of the late-June evening, Alice turned Amanda's mare and Ezra's donkey out to the paddock. As she returned to the barn to fetch Poker Chip, the lantern cast a man's shadow on the far wall.

In the stall beside the gelding, Wil curried the blue-roan's coat. The currycomb went through Poker's guard hairs.

Appaloosa—wasn't that the name Wil had used? A Nez Perce horse. The gelding was a connection to his Indian wife.

Without facing her, he said, "I know you're there, Alice. I'm certain you recall the time when you took me by surprise."

With his West Point background, he was trained to fight, but his experience went beyond formal schooling. He had learned Indian ways. Buried in secrecy, he hadn't let the past go.

"You shouldn't be up," she said, approaching the stall.

After hanging the currycomb on a nail, he threw a blanket and saddle over Poker's back.

"Wil, what are you doing? You're in no condition to be riding."

As he tightened the girth, the gelding bobbed his head. "I'm leaving."

In the humid evening, the sweat beading on her neck suddenly chilled. She folded her arms over her breasts. "Leaving? Where are you going?"

"Richmond. I won't be able to return to the field for a few months, but the War Department will give me a desk job."

Something in the dark depths of his eyes made her hesitate. The familiar mischievous spark was missing. He *was* leaving. "You weren't even going to say goodbye?"

"I thought it best." His voice had remained even and the expression on his face—unemotional. He hid his feelings well. After years of practice, he was an expert—usually.

"Best for me or yourself?"

His jaw tightened. "Alice, by the end of the week, I'll be thirty-eight. While I've done many things I should have been horsewhipped for, I have few regrets, but you saw a part of me that I had hoped you never would."

"Holly was only frightened."

"I wanted to kill her. If you hadn't intervened—"

"Things would have turned out the same."

He slipped a bit into Poker's mouth. "How can you be so sure? I *know* when I'll kill." Finished tacking, he backed the gelding from the stall and snuffed the lantern.

Cloaked in darkness, Alice followed him outside to a chorus of chirping crickets. "Wil, be sensible. This isn't about Holly Prescott, or the fact that you wanted to kill her."

In the moonlight his face—no longer an emotionless mask—twisted in pain as he mounted the gelding. Straightening in the saddle, he groaned. Recovered again, he replied, "Then pray tell, what is it about?"

"Fear."

"Fear of what?"

"That you won't always be able to control the rage because of how *she* died."

"Ride with me."

"An order, General?"

Extending his hand, he softened his voice. "A request."

She grasped his hand, and he nearly doubled over helping her on Poker's back. Stubborn—he wouldn't admit to how much he hurt. Careful not to bump his wound, she encircled his waist with her arms.

Wil reined Poker from the farmyard in the direction of the bottomland.

"I recall after I had been scrubbing floors, you said I needn't hide—not from you. Your words gave me the strength to carry on. Wil, stop being afraid. You would never harm us."

"I wish I could be as certain as you."

Poker started down the hill to the bottomland. As Alice leaned forward, her breasts pressed into his back. His muscles tensed.

The path would take them directly past the shack. At the bottom of the hill, she heard the sound of rushing water from a nearby stream. Wil reined the roan to a halt outside the shack. After helping her from Poker's back, he watched her.

For a moment, she thought he might rein the gelding around and leave her standing alone in the night. The chorus of crickets grew louder, and he dismounted.

He lifted her hand to his lips. "This is where we part, Miss McGuire."

She withdrew her hand from his grip. "Just like that?"

"Alice, you have some romantic notion that by tending me, I will be eternally grateful. My appreciation is all I have to give."

Her heart pounded, and Alice untied the blanket from his saddle. "The night we had dinner, you hinted..." She swallowed hard. "...at more."

Exhaling, he crossed his arms. "I was also aware that you would fend me off."

She laughed nervously. "Then I reacted in the appropriate manner? But what about working on bent knee and scrubbing floors? I've tended wounded. Men I had never met before. I've smoked, and I swear. How can I still be a proper lady?"

"Because a lady demands respect no matter the circumstances."

His answer surprised her. "No matter the circumstances? Then if I carry the blanket inside, and we lie on it together, at what point am I no longer a lady?"

Amused by the suggestion, he smiled a wicked grin. "You will always be a lady."

"Then shall we go inside and 'indulge' ourselves?" Clutching the blanket, she went inside and lit the candle. As a child, she had come to the slave shack often—a place to play hide-and-seek from Timmy Mullen, and she had daydreams about bringing beaus. Until now, she never had the courage to act the fantasy out. Alice spread the blanket over a worn straw mattress.

"Alice." At the sound of Wil's voice, she straightened her shoulders. "If you're under the misguided notion that I will change my mind about leaving, I won't."

Unable to damn him for his honesty, Alice turned and faced him. "I'd be lying if I said it didn't matter, but I know what's in my heart. I want you to . . ."

A grin tugged at the corners of his mouth. Stubborn and arrogant, he was so sure of himself.

She shook her head. It was no use. He wasn't going to change, and she couldn't bring herself to say it.

"Alice—"

"What, Wil? Another lecture from the man who says he doesn't care about what others think?"

"Actually, I was going to say that I'd be delighted to accommodate your desire."

Laughter helped relieve her nerves. "Damn you. I serve my heart on a silver platter, and you make it sound lackadaisical."

"That was not my intent." He traced a finger over her lips, then kissed her, gently at first. "But I must ask, what about your reputation?"

"You tarnished that ages ago. Wil, I—"

He pressed two fingers to her lips, then unfastened her bodice buttons. "Don't say it."

He was right. While tending him, she held a romantic notion of being the woman to get him to recite wedding vows. Foolish thoughts, but he did care. After nearly losing him, nothing else mattered. Or was she fooling herself in her own naiveté? After all, she was nothing more than a sheltered country girl.

She was bare to the waist. He cupped her breast and kissed it, playfully teasing the tip with his tongue. His name formed on her lips, and she closed her eyes. No man had ever touched her in this way.

But his touches vanished. She reopened her eyes. He stared in a curious way. Withdrawing again, he *was* afraid—afraid to care for her. With a giggle Alice tugged on his hand, and both of them tumbled to the blanket. Soon—they were naked as jaybirds.

Delightfully unashamed, she kissed him, kissed his chest, luxuriating in his scent and coarseness of male skin. While tending him, she hadn't allowed herself to think.

If any doubt lingered, it vanished when he pressed his face with loving eagerness between her thighs. Tingly and warm, she felt his tongue. No wonder young women were warned that anything more than stolen kisses were improper. Inappropriate touches felt good and led to other things. Did that make her a strumpet? As he rose above her, she forced her eyes shut.

"Alice?"

She reopened her eyes. "Amanda told me that . . . that it hurts the first time."

He smiled at her in a whimsical way. "I shall endeavor . . ." He brushed the hair away from her neck and kissed her there. " . . . to distract you. Let me know if you wish for me to stop."

"Stop?" Just as she had got to feeling so good, his touches vanished. He had that teasing smile again.

After Amanda's warning about her first time, Alice had been expecting an ordeal, not a carefree milestone. "Damn you, Wil Jackson. You know very well that wasn't a command."

The swear only heightened his arousal. With his breath hot on her neck, his heart beat rapidly against her breast. His private member was warm against her skin. She winced. He was inside her and touching her again with his mouth and hands. The pain lessened.

Alice floated among the layers of new sensations. Through the smells of straw and sweat, her body was joined with his in perfect unison. No longer so gentle, he was lending her more than a passing moment in time. He possessed her—heart and soul. He always had.

His chest hurt like hell. With a groan, Wil put a hand to the slow-healing wound.

As Alice rose on an elbow, her bare breast brushed against his arm. "And you thought you were fit enough to make a journey to Richmond." She giggled. "It seems our little rendezvous has demonstrated to the contrary."

Bewitched by her spell, he had been snared before making his escape. "If Amanda finds out about 'our little rendezvous,' I don't need to fret about any damned Yanks," he grumbled, reaching a hand to her cheek.

"She won't find out," she said, with her voice nearly a whisper. "Wil, I'm not ashamed."

It had been a long time since he had been with such a woman—too long. "I haven't declared undying love."

"You wouldn't. It's not your way."

Only Peopeo had known him this well. No, not even Peopeo. Such familiarity made him downright nervous. Time to bid their farewells and be done with it. He rolled to the side, but intense pain caused him to drop back to the blanket.

"Sometimes you can be very stubborn. What were you trying to do?"

"I was attempting to get dressed, escort you to the farm, then leave for Richmond—as planned."

"Leave . . ." The shine faded from her eyes. "I thought—"

"Alice, I warned you about romantic notions."

Without looking at him, she nodded. "I know," she said weakly, "but you're in no condition to travel."

An excuse—to keep him from leaving. He did enjoy her company, and he had another thought. "You could accompany me to Richmond."

"As your wife or mistress?"

Obviously, he hadn't thought the notion through. As a farm girl most of her life, she could make new discoveries in the city—and partake in more nights like this one. "I would treat you royally."

"As a kept woman? Thank you, no. I have more dignity than that."

Many women of her social standing tended to restrain themselves—but not Alice. "Then I fear I don't understand."

"You will," she said softly, "if you ever learn to be honest with yourself."

He had said it himself—she was very much a lady. Unless she got with child, one night with him didn't change that fact. He was foolish to have risked it.

As she reached for her chemise, Wil nodded that he understood.

The candle had burned down hours ago, but morning sun cast enough light to see by. Her girlish shyness had vanished, and she pulled the chemise over her head, breasts jiggling. Delighted with the view, he continued watching as she tugged her drawers past the spread of her hips.

"Wil Jackson, are you going to loll in bed all day?"

Grasping her arm, he drew her to him and kissed her on the mouth. "I can't think of a better way to spend the day, can you?"

She wiggled free of his grip. "I know you fancy yourself a dashing knight, but unlike some people, I have chores that need tending."

Her message was clear. She wasn't about to lend him a free hand. When he departed, she'd probably wave her handkerchief goodbye, pretending nothing had happened. She finished dressing, and as he struggled to do the same, she waited outside the shack.

Poker swished his tail and nickered a greeting. Alice was perched astride the gelding with her hair fluttering in the morning breeze, reminding him of Peopeo. When taking a Nez Perce bride, he had been presented with two spotted mares. Out of one mare, Poker was the result, and it was all that he had left of Peopeo and Benjamin.

"Alice, I truly meant no insult by asking you to accompany me."

She leaned over in the saddle and kissed him on the forehead. "I know."

Ignoring the pain in his chest and back, he gathered Poker's reins and mounted behind her. As he reined the roan around, he retraced their steps of the previous evening. At the top of the hill, Amanda's whitewashed farmhouse came into view. He kicked the gelding on, and they arrived in the farmyard.

Early yet, no one rummaged about. Outside where the picket fence once stood, he helped Alice from the saddle. "I shall see to Poker," he said.

"You look a little pale. Will you come in and have breakfast before leaving?"

He nodded. As she turned, long auburn hair flowed behind her. For a brief moment, he saw pigtails. With fifteen years separating them, only in the past year had he thought of her as a woman. Clenching his teeth, Wil slid from the gelding's back and led him to the barn.

He barely had Poker in a stall, when an angry voice shouted, "Wil!"

As Amanda approached, he faced her. Her arms were crossed above her rounded belly, and her green eyes smoldered. Not just angry—she was seething, and he had a fair notion as to why.

"Fancy my surprise when I started downstairs to fix breakfast, and Alice was sneaking to her room. Her bed hadn't been slept in. I tried not to let my mind jump to conclusions, but you were missing as well.

Do you care to tell me where she spent the night?"

Friends for years, they knew each other's moods. An admission was not what she was looking for. "I suggest that you ask Alice."

"So she can lie for you? Why, if Papa were still alive he'd take a shotgun to you, Wil Jackson. I thought we were friends."

"We are. Amanda, it's not the way you're thinking."

Her hands went to her hips. "Tell me in all honesty that you didn't bed her."

He lowered his head.

"How dare you treat my little sister as one of your strumpets. I shall thank you to leave my land and never set foot on it again."

"It's not like that—"

"Then you've set a wedding date? You were aware that she isn't as well-versed as you in the ways of life. Now get out!" Red-faced, Amanda pointed to the door. "Get out before I fetch the shotgun myself!"

Don't respond—it would only make matters worse. Untying Poker Chip, he backed the gelding out of the stall.

"Wil . . ." Her voice wavered. "Was this some sort of revenge?"

Confused, he looked up. "Revenge?"

"Because I chose Sam."

Something had remained unsaid between them. He had loved her. She had been the first woman to penetrate the dark abyss of his mind, but he had been unable to commit. Caught in an endless cycle, he had repeated the mistake with Alice. "No Amanda, it has nothing to do with you and Prescott."

Outside the barn, he mounted up. A wave of pain coursed through him, but he managed to straighten in the saddle—barely.

Alice stepped in front of Poker and grabbed the reins. "Wil, what did Amanda say that you would leave without saying goodbye?" She glanced in Amanda's direction. "Amanda, what did you say? I can't believe you would take your jealousy this far."

He heard Amanda's footsteps on the bricks, rushing to the house. Not only had he wronged Alice, he had set off feuding between sisters. "Alice, you wanted the truth, then you shall have it. Peopeo's death was a convenience. The week prior, I received orders for a transfer. It spared me from leaving her behind."

"Leave her behind?" Tears formed in her eyes, and she shook her head. "I don't believe you."

"Believe what you wish. Now if you will kindly step away from my horse."

Her hand curled to a fist. "You're much crueler than I could have ever fathomed. If you will excuse me, I won't weary you with my presence."

Gathering her skirts together, Alice hustled away.

Other men had fallen victim to the allures of a woman. When they had, their sense of duty vanished—some to the point of desertion. Governed by military protocol, Wil didn't look back. So why was he fighting the urge to rein Poker around? Nothing short of a wedding would keep Amanda from hauling out the shotgun. Resistant to committing to one woman exclusively, he had thought himself unaffected by sentimentality. He was an even bigger fool than he thought.

For a brief moment in time, he had cared for Alice, a woman barely out of her childhood. He kicked Poker in the side. His responsibilities as a Confederate officer came first.

Rebel shells sailed harmlessly over their heads. Bored by the wait, a couple of boys stood. Sam reminded them the next one could be lower. They hunkered behind the stone wall. At least in this fight, they possessed the wall.

Another shell struck a caisson. Wood splintered and horses screamed as smoke billowed to the sky. With its tongue flailing and legs kicking, a blood-spattered horse writhed on the ground. When had he come to think of such scenes as commonplace?

In a deafening roar, the Federal cannon responded. Back and forth, the bowels of hell opened and swallowed the Pennsylvania field. Two days of hard fighting, and some of their most precious blood had been spilled.

Orders were to sit tight and wait. Wait until the Rebs came. Thank goodness for the wall. In Fredericksburg, bodies had given Sam shelter, while the Rebs crouched behind the stone wall.

One boy prayed, and another sat reading a book, laughing. A strange place to laugh, but certainly not the first time he had witnessed it. Sam started counting exploding shells—one, two, three ... By the time he reached a dozen, he gave up.

Federal guns fell silent as Rebel shells continued to whistle across the line. Still overshooting. Casualties would remain low until the Rebs came.

In the previous day's fighting, one of the line officers killed had a wife waiting at home who would soon birth their first child. She wouldn't know of her husband's death yet, and the child would never meet his brave father.

Sam thought of Amanda. She would be birthing soon. Maybe she already had, and the news hadn't reached him. Son or daughter? He didn't care as long as Amanda was all right. Unlike Kate—she had bled to death birthing Rebecca.

Silence descended over the battlefield. His stomach knotted. It wouldn't be long before the Rebs came.

Sam looked through his field glasses, but couldn't see through the smoke. After it drifted, he spotted *them* across the field. A long gray line—waves and waves of them in one solid mass. Sun glistened off their bayonets, and the gray line moved forward with rustling feet. Dust rose with their steps. They marched closer as if part of a dress parade. Awed by the performance, he momentarily forgot they were being sent to kill him.

Federal cannon quaked, sending him a reminder. Holes appeared, breaking the gray line. Filling the gaps, they came—closer and closer. Rebel shells flew over the ranks. Smoke grew thick again, and the acrid scent of gunpowder was everywhere. Out of the smoke, the Rebels came. Firing broke out along the line. The Rebs weren't in range yet.

"Hold your fire, boys," Sam shouted, crouching low.

The red-bearded soldier nearest him began chanting, "Fredericksburg ..." Several others joined him. "Come on, Johnny. Fredericksburg!"

Rebel cannon stopped firing. The gray line was nearing the stone wall. Federal canister whistled through the thinning gray ranks. Bodies, screams, and moans came from everywhere. Like a flag, they waved but kept coming. Rebs charged, and Sam expected to hear the accursed yell.

Finally in range. Sam drew his sword. "Ready! Aim! Fire!"

A sheet of flame ravaged the gray line. Rebel officers bellowed the same command. Muzzle flashes nearly blinded him. Men in blue fell.

"Fire!"

More Rebels went down.

The remaining graybacks reached the stone wall and sent up a Rebel yell. Sam emptied his pistol in rapid succession. As the swarm reached them, an officer raised his sword—not fighting, but offering it in surrender.

Chapter Eleven

A SUMMER SHOWER HAD COOLED the July night. The rainstorm brought out frogs, croaking and chirping in their quest for mates, and the haunting cry of the screech owl filled the air. Even though the lace curtain fluttered in the open window, the less humid evening hadn't helped Amanda sleep. Throughout the day twinges in her abdomen made her aware that her birthing time was near.

No guns. During each thunderstorm, Amanda would give her little sister a knowing glance of relief. The war had moved north to Pennsylvania. After a great battle near a small town by the name of Gettysburg, she had received no word from Sam. With the Yankees gone from the Fredericksburg area, Federal casualty reports were difficult to come by. In the meantime, she waited and prayed.

"Alice . . ." She heard Rebecca tossing on the trundle bed from Alice's room, but not a stir came from Alice.

The pangs grew stronger, and Amanda moaned. She sat up and clutched her belly. "Alice, I think it's time."

Minutes passed, and she called Alice again.

In a rumpled nightdress, Alice appeared in the doorway and gulped for air. "I'll fetch Frieda."

"Leave Frieda be—unless there are difficulties. She's old and needs her rest."

Alice approached the bed. "But I don't know what to do, Amanda. I've never had a baby."

Amanda rubbed her belly. "Neither have I, but I've helped Frieda deliver a couple. Alice?"

"Yes, Amanda?"

Sam's first wife had died in childbirth. Amanda's mood turned somber. She should have made plans—just in case. "If I should die, will you look after Rebecca and the baby?"

Alice sat beside her. "You know I will, but I don't want to hear any nonsense about dying. Soon, you shall have a bouncing baby...boy. I should like a nephew, since I already have a niece. So hush up about dying and tend to your business of birthing."

Her sister had grown up in the past year. Was that why she continued to feel pangs of jealousy? Neither of them had spoken about that morning a fortnight ago, and she couldn't rest with it on her conscience. Amanda touched the side of Alice's face. "I'm sorry for interfering."

Alice squeezed her hand. "You did what you thought was best."

"But I had no right. I told Wil to never set foot on my property again. I know how much you love him."

"I was foolish to let my heart rule. You did the right thing, Amanda. I'm no longer infatuated by Wil."

The edge in Alice's voice betrayed her true feelings, but a birthing pain distracted Amanda. She groaned between clenched teeth, "I wish Sam were here."

Alice tightened the grip on her hand. "He's with you in spirit."

"Alice, help me up." Alice tugged on her arm, and she got to her feet. By the window, Amanda lifted the lace curtain. Streaks of yellow tinged the sky. Morning would soon arrive. The curtain fell from her hand. "I almost expect him to come riding up."

"I know."

"I keep telling myself this war can't last forever, but it goes on and on with no end in sight. I've never told anyone, and I'm certain you've heard the whispers, but this baby was begotten in love."

"I never doubted that."

"Alice..." Amanda felt another pain and clutched her belly. Alice supported her elbow until the pain passed. "Have I spoiled it for you? Foolish family pride got in the way. I saw you making the same mistake I have, and with Wil no less. You were right, I was jealous."

"Jealous? Because I courted Wil? But you're married to a loving husband."

"I love Sam with all my heart," Amanda agreed, "but Wil and I have been friends for a long time. After John died, he looked after me and gave me a shoulder to cry on. I always suspected there was another side to him that he didn't let others see, then when he told me about his wife and son..." Was she still feeling regret? "Well, I know how easy it is to feel like someone special in his arms."

"Why are you telling me this?"

Amanda rubbed her belly and started pacing. "I'm aware of the whispers about my baby. Few are going to miss the timing between the wedding and his birth. But the other one the rumormongers like throwing viciously about is that Wil is his papa...Alice, it was never like that between us."

Alice let out a noticeable breath. "I've heard the rumors, but I didn't believe the one about you courting a Yankee either."

In a time of sorrow, Amanda had turned to Sam when she had thought Wil was dead. But she couldn't tell that to her little sister. Near the dresser, she glanced in the mirror at her bulging shape. "I fear that one is true."

Another birthing pain gripped her, and Amanda pressed a hand to her belly. Alice grasped her arm and helped her to bed. Sunbeams danced with the spreading morning light, and tears trickled down Amanda's cheeks.

"Another pain?" Alice asked.

"Oh, Sam," she moaned. "Why can't he be here? What if he never sees the baby?"

"You mustn't think that way, Amanda. He'll return and be very proud of both of you. You must believe that."

As morning gave way to afternoon, Amanda's pains got longer in duration and more frequent. The blind Frieda had joined them, lending her guidance. Amanda felt cool water on her sweaty forehead as Alice sponged it.

"It's time to push," Amanda groaned.

Alice covered her legs with a clean linen.

Panting, Amanda shoved it to the floor. "I want to see my baby born."

Alice fluffed the feather pillows behind Amanda's back.

"Alice...?"

"I'm here, Amanda. I'm not leaving." Alice gave her a reassuring squeeze.

Amanda's grip tightened, and she bent her legs in the birthing position. Her nightdress was soaked crimson.

"Frieda?"

Amanda overheard a quaver in Alice's voice.

"It all right, Miss Alice. Things as dey should be."

Trusting the old servant's instinct, Amanda breathed out in relief. The red circle grew larger, spreading from her nightdress to the linens. Bleeding was normal, she reminded herself. She wrinkled her face in pain and closed her eyes. Suddenly, she felt like she was on fire and let out a cry.

"That's it, Amanda," Alice shouted in encouragement. "I see a head. Your baby is almost here."

"I can't go on."

"Yes, you can. Keep pushing."

Amanda strained again, and she saw the baby's head. Another push, and a blood-covered form dropped to Alice's waiting arms.

"It's a boy," Alice said.

His skin was blue, and Alice's pale face revealed her fear. "Alice, what's wrong?"

Alice quickly passed the baby to Frieda. "Frieda?"

The old Negro woman clutched the baby in one arm and touched his face. "I need a cloth, Miss Alice."

Alice handed Frieda a linen. "What's wrong?" Amanda repeated, nearly hysterical. "What's wrong with my baby?"

"Ain't nothin' wrong." Wrinkled hands worked expertly as if Frieda could see, cleaning the baby's nostrils. She rubbed the tiny blue body, and a squall pealed through the room. "He needed some warmin', Miss Amanda."

As the baby changed to a healthy-looking pink, tears streamed down Amanda's cheeks. She reached for him.

"Let me clean him a little." Alice took the baby from Frieda and wiped the blood from the tiny body before placing him in Amanda's outstretched arms. She unbuttoned her nightdress and snuggled the baby to her breast. He began to suckle.

Alice stroked the damp brown hair. "He's beautiful, Amanda. His eyes are as blue as his papa's."

A tired smile crept to Amanda's face. "All babies have blue eyes."

"Not like Sam's. Amanda, he will be so proud. What are you going to name him?"

Name him? "Benjamin."

A worried look crossed her sister's face. "But Amanda—"

"Alice, do you think Sam won't like it? We should have discussed names, but never got around to it. There was so little time together."

Worry changed to delight. "No, Benjamin is a fine name. Sam will think so too."

With pride Amanda watched her baby nurse. "Benjamin, it is."

Oh Lord, what had she done? Alice obviously knew that Benjamin had been the name of Wil's son. No one else ever need know. She had banished Wil from her land. For Alice's sake—or hers? She caressed the baby's smooth cheek, and tears—mixed with joy and sadness—crept to the surface.

Crunching through the snow-covered valley, Wil encountered the remains of a deer encrusted in a drift. Nearby a black wolf whimpered with its left foreleg caught in the jaws of a leghold trap. The deer carcass had lured the starving predator.

An icy wind moaned through the pine forest. Detesting cold weather, he bent down to release the wolf. But his hands had no strength, and the trap held fast.

At the bottom of the hill, oblivious to the cold and captive wolf, an otter slid on its belly along a snow bank. The otter splashed into the freezing lake water, and bubbles rose from the spot where it had submerged.

Sweat beaded on his forehead when Wil woke. It was summer—not winter. The heat never used to bother him, but the trip to Richmond had caused his wound to reopen.

Drifting in and out of a fever for days in a hospital bed, he kept having dreams of deer in various stages of decomposition, the black wolf, and the ever playful otter. What could they symbolize?

The deer represented Peopeo. Of that, he had no doubt. But the wolf and otter?

The mountain lion wasn't near. Until the noble cat entered the scene, the significance would continue to elude him.

After the glorious Union victory at Gettysburg, the opposing armies had been playing games of cat-and-mouse. A couple of times, the regiment had camped within several miles of Amanda's farm. Sam's requests for leave had been denied. Finally with a pass in hand, he cued the chestnut stallion to a gallop. After traveling a mile, he brought the horse to a trot.

Another mile went by, and he got an odd feeling in his gut. The forest had grown mighty quiet—not even a bird sang. He was being watched. Unwilling to take chances, he drew his pistol.

A deer bounded across the road.

Easing Red to a walk, he spotted a rider ahead—in blue. Breathing easier, he shoved the pistol in his holster.

Astride a lathered horse and out of breath, the girl soldier pulled even. "I know you're anxious to see if the young 'un has arrived, but the colonel says you got to wait, sir."

"Damn," he said under his breath. With the curse, he heard Amanda's voice chastising him. "What is it this time?"

"Movin' out."

"Moving out . . . ," he grumbled. "Moving in circles is more like it."

Not today, Amanda. He waved his hat in front of his face, but the air flow did little to cool him. He uncapped his canteen and took a swig. In less than a week it would be September, and the broiling days should soon end.

"Let me water my horse." Sam dismounted and led Red from the road down the bank to the stream. As the stallion drank, that peculiar feeling returned. "Jo, did you bring anyone with you?"

"No, sir."

"Then I suggest we head back to camp—nice and easy." As Sam swung into the saddle a shotgun blast echoed from the woods on the opposite side of the stream.

Blood spurted from Red's neck. *Not Red!* The horse wobbled but remained standing. Another shot of gunfire, and Jo's horse pitched over on its back with the girl soldier barely scrambling clear of flailing hooves.

He reached for Jo's hand to haul her on behind him. Another shot landed in a nearby tree, splintering wood. Red reared, and Sam hit the ground.

Dazed, he looked up and found himself staring at the end of a double-barreled shotgun. The bearer wore a ragged butternut jacket and trousers—a Rebel scout. "Make one wrong move, Yank, and you're history. Mighty fine boots. I could use a new pair."

Realizing the remark hadn't been a request, Sam sat up and tugged the boots off. He counted five men, plus two guarding Jo.

"Thank you kindly."

Rough hands jerked him to his feet and searched his pockets. Two silver quarters, a greenback dollar, and his pocket watch dropped to the ground. Grimy hands snatched up his belongings.

The scout with the shotgun opened the watch to Amanda's picture inside and smiled. "Mighty purty lady."

Jo screamed and the scouts near her hooted. "A girl!" One scout groped her, while the other dropped his trousers.

Sam moved toward her, but a shotgun butt struck him on the side of the head, hurling him backward. A booted foot kicked him in the groin, and the shotgun went straight to his temple. "I won't warn you again, Yank."

"Don't fight 'em, sir. It ain't worth gettin' killed over." Resigned, Jo closed her eyes and undressed as the scouts fondled and pinched her cruelly.

If he could provide a distraction, Jo might have the opportunity to make a run for it. Menacing brown eyes stared at him, almost in a dare, from the other end of the shotgun, and a finger was poised and ready to let both barrels loose.

A horse nickered from the road, and a Rebel officer astride a splendid black mare looked on. The scout atop Jo tugged on his trousers faster than he had lowered them, and Jo covered her nakedness with her uniform.

Smartly dressed in a gray jacket with a yellow cavalry sash, the captain had a moustache and a neatly trimmed goatee—a gentleman officer. He dismounted and approached the group. "My apologies, sir, and, uh, ma'am," he said in a thick Virginian accent. "Are you all right, ma'am?"

Jo nodded, and a couple of the scouts, who had been lingering to the side, went to her aid.

"Return the watch and help him up, Shifflet."

The scout shoved the watch into Sam's palm and dragged him to his feet. Still numb from the blows, Sam didn't know which hurt worse—his head or genitals.

"You should remove the picture if you wish to retain it."

"Thank you, sir." Sam extracted Amanda's picture and held out the watch.

The officer shook his head. "I will not steal from a prisoner, but others down the line are likely to. Captain Reid Woodward, Seventh Virginia Cavalry."

An honorable gentleman officer—that might work to his advantage. "Lieutenant Colonel Samuel Prescott." He stuffed the watch into his pocket and surrendered his sword to the captain. "Sir, I request that my sergeant be released on the grounds that she is of the fairer sex."

"Sam . . ."

He shot Jo a look not to say anything further.

The scouts hooted, and the captain held up a hand. "Request denied, Colonel. If the sergeant assumes the role of a man, then she should be punished as such."

The captain motioned for his boys to bring them along. The pain in Sam's groin had finally eased enough that he could stand straight. "Sir, I beg you to reconsider. You saw with your own eyes. Your boys weren't going to punish her as a man. If you hadn't happened along, they would have raped her. What do you think will happen as soon as your back is turned?"

The officer's eyes narrowed in disgust.

"My wife lives near Fredericksburg—"

"A Virginian?"

"Yes, she's a Virginian. I was on my way to see her. She should have recently given birth to our first child. If you would allow my sergeant to deliver the message of the events that have transpired—"

"You trust her that much?"

"I do, sir. I owe her my life."

The captain's dark eyes softened. "Let the girl go."

"Much obliged, Captain."

Weariness entered the captain's eyes. "I only wish I was at liberty to do more."

"You have done as much as your duty will allow."

The captain nodded. Under a different set of circumstances, they could have been friends.

Finished nursing the baby, Amanda tucked Benjamin in the cradle beside her bed. More than six weeks had passed since the battle in Pennsylvania, and still there was no word from Sam. Often his presence seemed to be watching over them, but in the last day or so, she felt nothing. Fearing he was dead, she fancied she was her own worst enemy.

"Miss Amanda!" Startled by Ezra's shout, she rushed to the top of the stairs. At the bottom of the stairwell, tears streaked the old man's face. "Miss Amanda, I cain't wake Frieda."

Frieda—not Sam. "Where is she?"

"In da shack. She lay down to take a nap afore fixin' supper. I shake her, but she don't move."

His description of Frieda sounded like what had happened to Papa before he died. "Alice," she shouted over her shoulder, "keep watch of the children."

She hurried down the stairs and outside to the walnut grove at the side of the house. Inside the shack, Frieda lay on the bed—motionless. With a sickly pallor and a smile on her wrinkled face, the old woman looked at peace.

"Frieda?" Amanda checked her pulse and breathing. "She's alive."

Relief spread across Ezra's grizzled face. "Thank da Lawd. I thought she be dead."

Amanda poured water in a tin basin and wrung out a cloth. The old woman was dreadfully hot—just like Papa had been, and Papa had lingered for months. She began washing Frieda's feverish body. No change—if only she possessed Frieda's medicinal knowledge, but in her heart she knew Frieda was beyond herbal cures. "I'll sit with her, Ezra."

Several hours later, Alice brought the baby in to nurse. After Amanda fed the baby, Alice said, "Amanda, you need to keep up your strength. Let me stay with Frieda for a while."

"I can't leave her, Alice." With some reluctance, Alice carried the baby to the house. Not yet fully recovered from the birth, Amanda sat beside the bed in a rocking chair with a threadbare cushion. Nursing Benjamin had sapped the rest of her energy. She closed her eyes. So little food had been planted this season, what would they do come winter? And Sam—where was he?

In the morning, gurgling woke her. Frieda . . . The old woman's right arm hung limply at her side, and she showed no recognition of their voices. Amanda gave Frieda another sponge bath and struggled trying to dress her in one of her handed-down cotton nightdresses. The size was much too large for the old woman's slight frame. How much alike Benjamin and Frieda were.

When a knock came to the door, she let Ezra answer. "Miss Amanda, Miss Alice is outside."

Her breasts were engorged with milk, and she suspected Alice must be bringing Benjamin to nurse. She shoved back loose strands of hair. "Tell her to bring the baby in."

"Amanda, I think you had best come outside." She turned to Alice standing in the doorway. "There's someone here to see you."

Alice's tone warned her that it wasn't Sam—unless the two had schemed a surprise. That was it—he wanted to surprise her. "Sam," she squealed.

"It's not Sam."

"Not Sam? Alice, if this is some sort of prank, it's gone far enough. My heart nearly stopped just now."

"It's no trick," Alice replied softly. "Come outside."

Amanda stepped into the brisk morning air. With fall nearly here, the days were cooling. By the porch stood a small-framed soldier dressed in blue—much too tiny for Sam. A lump caught in her throat.

The bob-haired soldier spat, then tipped his hat—*her* hat. She hadn't immediately recognized the girl soldier's charcoal-blackened face.

"Mrs. Prescott—"

"Jo, since when have you been so formal?" Her voice quavered. As long as she didn't let Jo speak, Sam was alive. "Let's go inside where we'll be more comfortable."

"Best come straight to the point—"

"Not here. Alice, would you fetch Benjamin?"

"Of course, Amanda." Alice ran inside the house.

Amanda led the girl soldier to the parlor and motioned for her to have a seat in the wing chair. "I'll make some tea."

"Don't go botherin' none on my account."

"It's no bother." Amanda rushed to the kitchen and collected a copper kettle from the cookstove. With tea being a luxury good, no real tea had been in the household since Sam had left. Frieda had made a blend of blackberry leaves and chicory root that tasted quite nice. She strained the herbs and poured hot water into tin cups.

Since the foraging Yankees had broken her china, she placed the cups on a silver serving tray. The arrangement looked ridiculous, but people made do with what they had these days.

By the time she returned to the parlor, Alice had Benjamin in her arms. "Mighty fine young 'un," Jo said, standing.

"He looks like his papa." Setting the serving tray on a table, she handed Jo a tin cup.

"Much obliged."

Jo had avoided eye contact. The news definitely must not be good. Amanda held up a tin cup. "Alice?"

"No thank you, Amanda. Sit down."

An order. "If you'll stay with me."

"I shall."

Alice sat on the sofa. More than ever, she needed Alice's strength. Amanda sat beside her and grasped her hand. "He's dead."

"He ain't. Least as far as I know."

Sam wasn't dead. Had she heard right? Amanda looked up with new hope. "Then he's been wounded?"

"Nope. To be honest, Amanda, you got a plumb fool for a husband."

"What do you mean?"

Jo slurped from the tin cup. "He went and forgot I ain't one of the boys. Rebs nabbed us, and he talked them into lettin' me go." Her arms waved as she got more excited, and she spilled tea onto the floor. "... 'cause of my sex."

Sam wasn't dead or wounded—but captured. A blessing or a curse? With some Confederate prisons' reputations, he could be as good as dead. She tightened her grip on Alice's hand. "Do you know where he is?"

The girl soldier shook her head. "It happened the day before yesterday. Ain't enough time for the Rebs to let us know."

Amanda wrung her hands. There was nothing left to do but wait.

With the baby snuggled in her arms, Alice stood. "Wil can help," she said.

"Wil?" Fighting tears, Amanda glanced up at Alice. "After what I said to him, why would he be willing to help?"

Alice placed a hand on her shoulder and gently squeezed it. A sympathetic gesture that tugged at every woman who had ever sent a loved one off to war. "Because he and Sam were friends."

"Beggin' your pardon," Jo said, "but who's Wil?"

"Brigadier William Jackson—Sam's commander before the war."

Jo whistled. "A Reb general. Can't get much better help than that."

Amanda shook her head. "I can't ask Wil."

Alice slipped the baby into her arms. "Amanda, you have Benjamin to think of. Stop letting your stubborn, foolish pride get in the way. Sam's life is at stake. If you won't ask Wil, I shall."

As Amanda stood, she met Alice's gaze. "You're the one who hasn't thought things through. General or not, Wil can't just wave a hand and have Sam released."

"He might be able to speed up an exchange."

Although slowing over the past few months, prison exchanges took place all the time. Amanda still didn't like the idea. "I can't ask Wil to risk his life for Sam's. Sam wouldn't want it that way."

"If Wil merely makes an inquiry, he won't be risking his life."

Amanda tightened her grip around Benjamin and closed her eyes. "I said no!"

Defeated, Alice fell silent.

Jo broke through the tension and said, "Amanda, it ain't much, but I returned his horse."

"Red?"

Jo fidgeted with her hat. "The Rebs didn't take him 'cause he was wounded. A little mendin', and he'll be as good as new."

"Where?"

"Left him outside the barn."

Amanda rushed over to the window. Near the barn, a blood-red chestnut stood, flicking his tail at a fly. She groaned. "Oh Sam..." Suddenly nauseated, she hurried from the parlor and up the stairs to her room. After placing Benjamin in the cradle, she made a fist. "Damn you, Sam! Yes, you heard me right. I said damn you!"

She flung a pillow against the bedpost. Here was where she had conceived Benjamin, and now she was left alone to raise him. She hurled the pillow again, and feathers went flying. She fell to the bed and wept.

Alice's gentle but firm arms went around her. "I'm here, Amanda."

Amanda sobbed on her shoulder until she had no tears left. "Sam will die in prison. I've heard stories of men coming out looking like skeletons."

"Let me write to Wil," Alice suggested once more. "He went to Richmond. He can confirm where Sam is and how he's faring."

Amanda wiped away her tears. "You've been in contact with Wil?"

"No, stubborn pride kept getting in the way—for both of us." Tears formed in Alice's eyes. "Sometimes, we forget what's important in life. I don't know whether Wil can ever let go of the past. Unless he can, I doubt he'll ever return my love, but I can't change my feelings, any more than you can change yours about Sam. I'll write for Sam's sake. One never knows. The time away may have given him a chance to think things through."

Or find another woman to frolic with. Amanda kept that thought to herself. "For your sake, I hope so, but I won't lay blame if he refuses to help Sam."

"Amanda, how long have you been friends? Wil Jackson can be a rascal, but when it comes to people he cares about, honor is stronger. He won't say no."

Alice *did* know Wil. Maybe he had finally met his match in her fiery little sister. "Alice, can you ever forgive me for interfering?"

"You're my sister, Amanda. You were trying to protect me, but I don't need protecting anymore."

With the war often on their doorstep, no one could stay blind. Not only had Alice grown up in the last year, but she had matured.

Amanda hugged her sister, and Alice whispered in her ear, "Let's see what we can do to help Sam."

Chapter Twelve

The mountain lion had nearly died. Otter's medicinal power had been strong, and she had breathed life into him. Mischievous and playful, the otter represented Alice. After receiving her letter, Wil had checked the prison rosters. The black wolf was Prescott—trapped in Libby prison. But a new animal spirit had entered the scene. The master of trickery, a raven flew overhead.

When the guard opened the heavy-wood door to the pitch-black underground cell, the hinges creaked. The stench—men forced to live in their own wastes. Wil nearly gagged.

The guard raised a lantern. "See the one you're looking for? We send 'em down here when they get too rambunctious for their own good."

Three officers huddled against the wall with wrists and ankles shackled. Wil recognized Prescott on the right. "Get the chains off."

"I don't take orders from you, sir."

"And I don't take kindly to repeating commands. Get the chains off, or your name will feature prominently in my report to General Winder." The guard spat but followed orders. Chains clanked to the dirt floor, and Wil bent down to the nearest officer. "Prescott..."

Sunken eyes looked up at him as Prescott rubbed his wrists. "Fancy meeting you here, Jackson. Been stealing any Federal supplies lately? A few of us around here sure could use them."

"I'm sorry to report that I've given up that pastime, but I'll see if there's a way to hasten the exchange process."

Prescott nodded that he appreciated the effort. "They've confiscated the letters I've written to Amanda. How is she?"

"As far as I know, she's fine. I wasn't informed of his name, but you have a son."

Prescott lowered his head to his hands and wept.

Wil squeezed his arm and straightened. "What were these men's infractions?"

The guard squared his shoulders defiantly. "You heard him. He writes letters, sayin' things he shouldn't. He don't learn neither. Keeps breakin' rules. Three days bread and water in isolation is lenient, sir."

His voice edged on insubordination. Ignore it, or the guard might take his anger out on the prisoners after he left. For now there was nothing more that he could do. Wil turned to leave.

"Captain . . ." Prescott always referred to him by his rank before the war—out of respect. "Thank you."

Without facing him, Wil responded, "I haven't done anything."

"You'll do whatever you can."

Whatever he can. The dream had warned him. He lacked any real authority, and his hands were tied—unless he determined the meaning of the raven.

Nightfall had arrived by the time Wil reined Poker up the tree-lined lane. A cold wind hinted at winter. Uncertain what sort of reception he would receive, he brought the blue roan to a halt in front of the farmhouse.

A rail had been constructed where the picket fence once stood. He dismounted and tied the gelding to it.

Alice stepped onto the front porch. "Wil?"

With her voice barely above a whisper, his thoughts returned to that hot June night. The day no longer seemed chilly.

Clasping her hands together, she approached him. "I wasn't certain you had received my letter."

He lowered his hat. "After receiving the transfer, my intent was to resign my commission. Peopeo died before I had the opportunity."

Her face brightened with his confession.

A curtain fluttered in the front window, warning him that his actions were being monitored. "I have news of Prescott. If Amanda prefers that I remain outside, I can relay it here."

"Don't be silly. Come inside. Is Sam all right?"

Even with his iron stomach, he couldn't rid himself of the stench from the old warehouse. They reached the porch, and Wil answered, "He's alive."

She let out a relieved breath. "Thank goodness."

"Alice . . ." The words wouldn't come. She faced him, and he traced the brim of his hat.

"Say what's on your mind, Wil. You don't usually hedge."

"If I said what was on my mind, I'd likely be threatened with a shotgun again."

She pressed a hand to her breast and giggled. "I missed you."

Good reason abandoned him. He leaned down and kissed her.

The door opened behind them, and Alice stepped back, clasping her hands behind her back.

"I didn't mean to intrude," Amanda said. "Alice, where are your manners? Invite Wil in, so he can warm himself by the fire."

Only emptiness registered in Amanda's green eyes. The war had robbed her of much, and she wasn't going to like what he had to tell her. As he stepped into the foyer, Alice took his hat and overcoat and hung them on pegs by the door, then led the way to the parlor. Delighted to be out of the cold, he held his hands near the warmth of the fire.

"I shall make something warm to drink," Alice said, excusing herself.

Unaccustomed to awkward feelings, Wil watched her rush from the room in silence. He withdrew a wood carving in the shape of a horse from his pocket.

Amanda's eyes brimmed with tears as she grasped it. "Where did you get this?"

"In Richmond. Yankee prisoners make them to buy food."

Tears streaked her cheeks, and she clutched the figure in her hands. "Then he's—he's—"

"Alive in Libby prison."

With her lower lip quivering, she swallowed noticeably. "Libby—you've seen him?"

"I have. Since visiting, I've had him monitored. He's holding his own."

"Take me to him."

"I refuse to take a woman."

Her eyes smoldered.

"Amanda, conditions are deplorable. Libby is overcrowded and rat infested. He wouldn't want you to see him there."

Her gaze softened. "So what do I do? Wait for it to get the best of him?"

"Our boys in the field face similar conditions."

"That's supposed to comfort me? Wil, what about an exchange?"

The frustration in her voice was evident, but posturing on both sides had broken down exchanges. He lowered his head. "One isn't likely in the near future." Though her dignity remained strong, she was too proud to come straight out and ask for his help. "Amanda, there is another way."

She hugged the wood carving to her breast. "And that is?"

"With the overcrowding, the guards can't be everywhere at once."

Amanda's eyes widened in horror. "I won't hear of it. I can't ask you to risk your life."

"You didn't ask."

Skeptical, she raised an eyebrow. "Why are you suddenly helping me?"

His indiscretion with Alice had forced a wedge between them. "We're friends."

Her brow crept higher. "And?"

"I'd like to see Alice. I had hoped you might have changed your mind in that regard."

"She's of age. It's not my place to interfere."

"I had hoped for your approval."

Her voice got louder. "My approval is not up for bargaining, and if you think you can gain it by helping Sam, then you're sadly mistaken."

He let out a weary breath. "Regardless of your position, I will help your husband. If you wish, I'll leave."

"Do you love her?"

Unable to openly confess something that he hadn't come to terms with himself, Wil replied, "She's kind and caring—very much like her sister."

With a groan, Amanda closed her eyes.

"Amanda, I meant that as a compliment, but if we're being totally honest, Alice is far better at swearing."

A twinkle appeared in her eyes. "I should have known you'd like that trait, Wil Jackson. Papa spoiled her. He pretended not to hear when he should have been using the soap." The tension between them faded, and Amanda turned serious again. "Wil, your suggestion to help Sam. Are you scheming something foolish?"

She had sidestepped giving her approval as neatly as he had her question. Before he could respond to Amanda's latest query, Alice returned to the parlor, carrying a silver tray. His mind wandered to June. And that was precisely the reason why Amanda wouldn't grant her approval. He had crossed the line.

As Alice handed him a steaming tin cup, it nearly slipped from his hand. A scalding drink would have quickly solved the problem of his arousal. That thought helped him refocus his attention to Amanda's question. "I'm not scheming anything, but I'll think of some way to get Prescott released."

Alice chewed on her lip but said nothing.

He sipped the hot liquid—an intriguing blend of herbs. Some people went to great lengths to replace unavailable goods. "Alice informed me that you have a new addition in the family."

A delighted smile replaced Amanda's frown. "Would you like to meet him?"

"Of course."

"Then I shall fetch him."

Amanda disappeared from the parlor, and the tread of her footsteps retreated up the stairs. Alice's brow wrinkled. "Are you serious about getting Sam out of Libby, or were you humoring Amanda, so she won't lose hope?"

He resisted the urge to touch her. "I'm serious. I'll find a way to get him out."

She lowered her head.

Wil set the tin cup on the mantel, and his hand went under her chin, tilting her head to meet his gaze. "I don't expect you to understand, but he was once part of my command."

She pressed close and put her arms around his waist. "Even as a girl, I knew you were brave. Fancy that, one of the things I fell in love with terrifies me now."

Unprepared for the admission, he stepped back, breaking the embrace. Careful—he was getting too entangled again. "Would you have me do otherwise?"

Alice shook her head. "No, you wouldn't be the man I love if you did. I daresay I knew as much when I wrote to you."

Footsteps sounded behind them, and Alice drew away. "Brigadier Jackson," Amanda said, "I'd like you to meet Benjamin Prescott."

Benjamin . . . She had known that was his son's name, but beaming with pride, Amanda slipped the baby in his arms. He hadn't held a baby, since—his own son. Wil forced a smile. "He's a handsome boy."

"I hope his papa approves of the name."

He cleared his throat. "He will. It's a fine name." How many birthdays had passed in silence? Ben would have been thirteen come spring. If he had possessed the courage and told Amanda his feelings, this child could have been *their* son. Was that why she had chosen the name?

The baby opened his eyes with a smile that only babies can give.

"He's such a good baby," Amanda said. "Hardly ever cries."

"Must take after your side of the family. Prescott often voiced his dissatisfaction."

"No, I see Sam." Tears trickled down her cheeks. Sniffling, she brushed them away. "Forgive me . . ."

Like when Peopeo had announced that Benjamin had died, he was unable to react. He returned the baby to Amanda's arms. "If you will excuse me."

Alice stepped toward him, but he motioned for her to stay put. Once outside, he lit a cigar. *But he had reacted*. When there was a medicine shortage, he had smuggled supplies so others' sons would live. The one thing he could give Amanda was to make certain Prescott didn't become a casualty of Libby.

He stamped out the cigar and went down the steps. By Poker's side, he tightened the girth. The farmhouse door flew open, and he untied the gelding from the rail.

"Wil . . ." Alice charged down the brick walk toward him. "I can't fathom how someone can be unafraid in the line of battle, but runs at the sight of a baby, or when he finds himself caring for a woman. You ran from Amanda, and now—I had hoped . . . How old was Benjamin when he died?"

"He was a month shy of his third birthday."

In the fading daylight her green eyes filled with sympathy. She leaned forward and touched him on the arm. "I can't say that I know how you feel, but I reckon there's no greater loss than that of a child."

With her gentle touch, his thoughts shifted to June. Her long auburn hair draped across him. Her cries... "I need to be leaving." He turned to mount Poker.

"Back to Richmond? Tonight? Wil, I don't believe you made the trip only to deliver a message to Amanda. You haven't even bothered telling me how you're recovering."

Wil pulled off his hat and faced her once more. "The wound still bothers me—some days more than others. Alice, my intent was honorable. I had hoped for Amanda's approval to court you."

"Did you receive it?"

Restless to be on his way, he shifted uneasily on his feet. Damn—he hadn't felt this awkward since Peopeo. "No."

Her tone turned light and sassy. "What is your intent now? You're not one to let an honorable notion get in the way of something you want."

"Meaning?"

Alice tilted her head shyly. "Really Wil, from the moment you rode up, you wanted more than to court me. Did you seriously expect Amanda's approval for anything more?"

Amused he was that transparent, he laughed. "I had hoped to start somewhere."

"But Amanda knows you better than that—as do I."

Her voice was suggestive, and Wil met her gaze. "What would you advise as my next course of action?"

"Join us for supper. It wouldn't be proper to send you on such a long journey without being fed. If you're in a hurry to return to Richmond..." Up close, he could smell the sweet scent of her perfume. Her smile turned sly and giddy. "...morning will be soon enough. If you leave Poker here, Ezra will tend to him."

Persuaded to stay, Wil tethered Poker. A courier would have sufficed if he had no intent besides delivering a message. With the mountain lion guiding him, he could no longer resist the power of the otter.

* * *

Casual and carefree, Alice should have felt guilt for laughing, but Wil's presence made her twitter like a schoolgirl. Throughout the chicken and dumpling supper, Amanda forced a cheerful face, but her sister's pretense was obvious. By the scores, soldiers died in prison. With Sam in Libby, Alice should have restrained her smiles. But Wil's promise gave Amanda hope.

Following supper, they retired to the parlor for polite conversation. Alice's giggles were gone, and she sat a respectable distance from Wil on the tapestry sofa. After four months' separation, she smoothed folds in her dress to keep from staring. Not Wil—there were no taut lines near his eyes nor fidgeting in his seat. She wished she possessed his calm. With the exception of an occasional glance, he showed no tension at all, but facing enemy gunfire would have perfected his collected demeanor.

Almost an hour passed before Amanda rose from the wing chair. Wil stood to bid her goodnight.

"If you'll excuse me," Amanda said, "the baby needs to be fed. Alice, do you mind lending a hand?"

As she left the parlor, Alice cast a glance over her shoulder at Wil. His dark eyes turned pensive. She sprinted up the stairs. Expecting a lecture from Amanda, she tapped a foot. "You wanted to speak to me?"

In the rocking chair, Amanda nursed the baby. "I don't expect you to change your mind on account of anything I say. I'm all too aware of how easy it is to lose your heart. I also know what it's like after not seeing him for months."

"Then why?"

"I wanted you to take a good look at your nephew."

The baby suckled, and Alice bent down to stroke a chubby cheek. "He's beautiful, Amanda, and I love him with all of my heart."

"I know, but I never thought I'd be alone with a baby to raise."

Her message was clear. Alice straightened and squeezed her sister's hand. "It's a dangerous time to love, but Sam will survive because he has you and this wonderful little baby to come back to."

Amanda forced a smile. "You had best not keep Wil waiting. Men get . . . irritable if it's been a while since their needs have been met."

Her jaw dropped. Amanda had always been so proper, and Alice would have never expected such a remark. "Amanda . . . "

Amanda's eyes sparkled slyly. "You're a woman now. I thought you should know." Her smile faded, and she whispered, "Be careful, Alice. Be very, very careful. Don't let him break your heart."

Amanda lowered her head and wept. Many tears had been shed since Sam's capture. Wil's verification that he was in Libby probably added to Amanda's worries.

Torn between comforting her sister and returning to the parlor, Alice turned away. So weak—she was turning her back on Amanda for a man who had never promised his love. Love was truly blind.

Downstairs, Wil no longer waited in the parlor. She heard a sword rattle and headed to the foyer. "You agreed to stay."

Readying to leave, he strapped on his weapons belt. "My presence has distressed Amanda."

"It's not you. She's fretting over Sam."

"Prescott's not all she's fretting about—for good reason." Wil yanked his hat from the peg.

He *was* irritable. Alice clamped a hand over her mouth and chuckled.

"I don't believe I said anything humorous."

She bit her lip to keep from laughing. It was no good. She only snickered harder.

Not amused, he fixed his gaze on her.

Alice struggled to regain a semblance of poise. "Amanda warned me that men get irritable when their—uh—needs haven't been met."

His eyes narrowed. "Sometimes your naiveté can be irritating." He grabbed his overcoat and stepped onto the porch.

Following him into the brisk evening air, Alice wished she had brought her shawl. With a shiver, she crossed her arms. "You could have sent a courier with news about Sam. Why did you make the trip?"

In the lamplight shining through the parlor window, his gaze softened, and he threw his overcoat over her shoulders. Leaning against the porch rail, he glanced out at the growing darkness. "If I had wanted nothing more than to satisfy my needs, I would have found a whore in Richmond."

Direct, honest, but evading the question—so typical of Wil. "Did you come to see Amanda?"

He faced her. "When I set out, I wasn't certain why, but no, I didn't come to see Amanda." Relieved, she breathed out, and he laughed slightly. "I've already told you that our relationship was based on friendship."

"I believe you." But both of them had wanted more. She heard it in their voices when each spoke about the other. Something had happened that neither was willing to talk about, and it wasn't her place to pry.

The screech owl wailed a haunting cry. Alone, yet unafraid, it reminded her of wounded men crying for the homes they might never see again.

As if reading her thoughts, Wil broke the silence. "I had hoped you would remain untouched by all of this. I should have kept my word and never allowed you to run supplies."

"It wouldn't have sheltered me from the war. Nothing could have, and now I understand what's at stake."

"Do you? Alice, come spring, unless by some miracle the war ends before then, I'll be returning to the field."

Amanda's warning had come too late. He had already broken her heart. Never giving her a second glance, he had broken it the first time when she was a girl. Once she was grown, he broke it by loving her in the only way he could. Until the war was over, he would continue breaking it. Faced with no other choice, he was a general of the Confederacy first. "As much as I'd like to pretend otherwise, I'm aware of that."

"Alice . . . " He wasn't sure what he had been about to say, and it didn't matter anyway. "It's time that I leave."

"Leave? But I thought . . . "

"I know what you thought, but . . . " Wil heard a horse nicker and voices near the barn area.

"What's the matter?"

He made a motion for her to lower her voice. There it was again—at least two voices. Alice nodded that she had heard them.

Wil unbuckled his weapons belt. Before handing it to her, he withdrew his pistol. "Go inside, and lock the door."

As he turned, he felt her hand on his arm. "Wil, be careful."

Without responding, he continued on. A clear night—at least there was enough light to see by. Whether the unannounced visitors were Yankee or Confederate mattered very little. If they were lurking around the barn area, they certainly weren't paying a social call. He edged his way across the farmyard.

Two distinct nasal voices came from inside the barn—one sobbing. Yankees—scouts most likely. Wil moved toward them. A pair of light-framed horses built for speed with McClellan saddles and U.S. brands stood just inside the door—definitely Yankee scouts. One man leaned against the other, and a stubble-faced man looked up as he approached. "We don't mean no harm. My brother's been hurt."

Wil lowered his pistol. "Let's get him to the house." He tucked the gun in his waistband and lent a hand, drawing the injured Yank's arm over his shoulder. With each step, the wounded man moaned.

As they went up the stairs, the Yank stumbled. Amanda met them on the porch with John's hunting rifle. She lowered it, and a hand flew to her mouth. "Dear Lord."

Once inside, they helped the Yank to the sofa. Amanda bent down to examine the wound. Gutshot—even if a surgeon were available, there was nothing he could do. Peach fuzz covered a freckled face. Nothing more than a boy, he cried for a home he'd never see again.

Tears filled his brother's eyes, and he latched onto the boy's hand, while his body quivered in a trembling fit.

All too familiar with death throes, Wil realized it was only a matter of time. His own wound throbbed, and he sank into the wing chair.

Alice dropped his sword to the floor with a clang and a gentle hand touched his shoulder. "Wil . . ."

He looked up into lovely green eyes and grasped her hand. Wartime was a hell of a time to care, but he would have been fool enough to take on a dozen bluecoats if he thought *her* life had been at stake.

The boy's twitching intensified, and he howled in agony. Hours might pass before he breathed his last. Someone should relieve him from his misery. He had best leave the boy be. The brother would think hate guided him. Death was near enough.

"Reb . . ." The stubble-faced Yank narrowed his eyes in contempt and pointed a finger. "You're responsible."

Wil held out open hands. "If you feel better blaming me, then so be it."

Tears streaked the Yank's cheeks. "He's my only brother. Ma told me to look out for him."

Nothing made sense these days. Misled by war's glory, boys signed up, hoping to become men. Straight from the Point as a raw cadet, he had believed the same. Eager to see battle, he quickly discovered that war led not to glory but early graves. Damn—he felt old.

While the women spoke words of comfort, the boy clutched his belly and wailed. The Yank returned to his brother's side, and Wil blocked out the cries. Like on the battlefield, one learned to disregard the screams, or the mind went.

"Wil . . ." Alice stood before him. "He's dead."

Bent over the dead boy, the Yank sobbed.

"I'll help bury him," Wil said, standing.

Wiping tears away with his sleeve, the Yank lifted his head and clenched a hand to a fist. "In Virginia—Reb country? I'm sendin' him home."

The Yank's eyes glazed over. Wild and predatory, they no longer seemed human. He reached for his sidearm.

Almost too late, Wil reacted. He shoved Alice aside and fired his pistol. Hit in the head, the Yank tumbled backward across his dead brother with his gun clattering to the floor.

Though his left eye was gone and the back of his head spread across the sofa, the Yank still breathed. At least he wouldn't linger as long as his brother had.

Wil disliked the notion of watching another man die—especially one he claimed responsibility for. "Let me know when he's dead. I'll bury both at the same time."

Alice huddled in Amanda's arms. He headed for the study. Without bothering to light a lamp, he slumped into the leather chair behind the desk and searched through the drawers where Amanda's first husband had stashed the whiskey.

In the lower right-hand drawer, he found an untouched bottle just as John had left it. After the firing on Fort Sumter, they had toasted for a short war. Both veterans of the Mexican War, they were well aware that more than one battle would be fought. True to their prediction, the war had continued year after bloody year, and like so many others, John lay in his grave.

After uncorking the bottle, Wil set it on the desk top. His first duty was to the Yankee family. Although he had written many such letters, it was the first time writing one where he also carried the blame. The family would hate him as much as their son had.

"Wil..." Amanda stood in the doorway.

All too aware of the rage he buried, Alice probably feared him. "Is the Yank dead?"

"He's passed on."

"Passed on..." Leaning back in the chair, he snorted a laugh. She couldn't even say the word. "He's dead, Amanda. D–E–A–D. That spells dead."

Amanda approached the desk and lit the lamp. She gestured to the whiskey bottle. "How much of that have you had?"

"Not a drop. But if you come back in an hour, I'll have a different answer then."

"Wil..."

Holding up a hand, he let out a tired breath. "Spare me the lecture of how we've been friends for years, so I'll listen to whatever you say. Tell me, Amanda, how many men have you killed?" He seized the whiskey bottle and took a swig. Fiery liquid washed down his throat.

"None. I have never killed anyone, and I hope to God I never have to find out what it's like. But this isn't about the war."

He took another gulp. "Then perhaps you can enlighten me."

"Why must you be so simple at times? You saw us in danger—*her* in danger, and you were ready to give your life."

"Rather noble, don't you think?" With a smirk Wil raised the whiskey bottle. "Care to join me in a toast? To rescuing damsels in distress."

He placed the bottle to his lips, and Amanda stamped a foot in disgust. "You fool. Don't make the same mistake that you did with us."

Us... He had written the letter, expressing his feelings, but burned it before mailing it to Amanda. "Is that why you named your son Benjamin, *Mrs. Prescott?*"

As she hustled from the room, Wil thought he saw tears fill her eyes. He returned the bottle to the desk. As usual, he was alone. He searched through the drawer for some paper. Duty came first. He had another sort of letter to write.

Chapter Thirteen

Blood trailed across the wood floor where Ezra had dragged the bodies away. Alice dabbed the sofa with a wet cloth. It was no use. The two brothers' blood remained soaked in the tapestry pattern. In large circles, she scrubbed and bumped against something soft—part of a man's brain. No tears, no sympathy—why couldn't she feel?

"Alice . . ."

Ignoring Amanda, she continued scrubbing.

"Alice, you need to talk to Wil. He won't listen to me."

Alice glanced over her shoulder, and Amanda approached her. Pressing the cloth down, she scoured harder. "Amanda, can't you see that I have work to do?"

"Alice, please talk to Wil."

Wil? The stubborn red stains endured. "Brothers. They're both dead."

Amanda patted the back of her hand. "One of those brothers was ready to kill us."

Alice recalled Wil shoving her. Had she screamed? She couldn't remember—only his hand tossing her aside like a rag doll, and then gunfire. Afterward, she had scrambled across the floor to Amanda's arms. She shivered. "How can there be so much hatred?"

"It seems it's all too easy these days, but Wil risked his life for ours. He reacted out of love, not hate. He loves you, Alice. Talk to him."

"Loves me?" She placed a hand to her throat. "Why can't he say the words?"

"Some men see it as weakness. John was that way. Wil is more stubborn than John. Weakness is the last thing he wants to show. He'll admit it when he realizes he's stronger because of it."

Sometimes Amanda was the wisest soul she knew. Fancy that, only three years separated them. Finishing school hadn't prepared Alice for real life, but Amanda's front didn't fool her. Beneath the bold exterior, her sister hid her worry, and she must follow Amanda's courageous example. Alice raised her head high. "Where is he?"

"In the study. He's found a bottle of whiskey. I think it's best if Ezra and I attend to the Yankees."

Alice straightened her dress. Amanda nodded that she looked fine, but she had no way of hiding the blood stains. Taking a deep breath, she crossed the parlor to the study and peered around the half-open door.

Behind the desk, Wil gripped a pen and stared at the paper with a vacant expression. Either his attention lay elsewhere, or he had drunk too much whiskey. The bottle was half-empty.

Alice entered the study, and he looked up. She neared the desk. Her throat constricted. The letter was addressed to the Yankees' family.

Wil tossed the pen aside and crumpled the paper to a ball. "It never gets any easier."

With his rank, he had probably written many such letters. Swayed by the dash of his uniform, Alice had never really understood the meaning behind it—not just bravery, but honor as well. She edged her way around the desk. "I don't suppose it does. Perhaps we should write the letter together."

His gaze softened, and he drew her into his arms. Alice ran her fingers through his thick black hair. After a long while, his taut muscles relaxed. "Things will get worse before they get better," he said.

Worse? The Yankee blockade had nearly choked off all supplies to the South. Thousands—both blue and gray—rested in their graves. How could things get worse? "You're just saying that because of what happened."

His eyes remained pensive. "Should the war continue another season, it'll get bloodier and harsher. Tonight was only a sample. Outnumbered as we are, the South doesn't have a prayer of winning."

She blinked back her surprise. "The South lose? I never dreamt of that possibility."

"Not only will the South lose, it will be punished for firing the first shot. Alice, even if I survive the war, there will be nothing left—no land, no career, no money. The Yanks will possess everything we hold dear."

So matter-of-fact, so straightforward—was he trying to frighten her away? She still trembled from the shooting and curled her hand around his.

He stood. "I said that I'd bury the Yankees."

More than anything she wanted to hold him in this place. "I'll wait for you," she said softly.

With a nod, Wil left the room. Several minutes passed before Alice gathered the courage to return to the parlor.

On her hands and knees, Amanda scrubbed the blood stains on the wood floor. "Thank you, Alice."

"For what?"

Amanda continued scrubbing. "Speaking to him."

Alice shook her head. "I didn't . . ." But she had. "Amanda, let me finish here. You need to keep your strength for nursing Benjamin."

With some reluctance, Amanda agreed. She hugged her sister, and Amanda went up to her room. Alice took over the tedious job of scouring.

Nearly three hours passed. Most of the stains were gone, and Alice pulled a braided rug over a stubborn red blotch.

"I'd like you to accompany me to Richmond when I return."

So engrossed in her work, she hadn't heard Wil enter. Had it been a command or request? She turned to him. He held his hat in his hands, but his expression was unreadable. "We've already been over this. Besides with Frieda ill, Amanda needs my help with the children."

"As my wife."

Wife? Her heart performed an odd thumping. "You're not serious?"

"I don't tend to make a habit of proposing. If you prefer, I can do so in time-honored fashion."

He gripped her hand and got on bent knee, placing his hat over his heart.

Alice stifled a laugh. "That won't be necessary."

Wil regained his feet with a groan and a joint popping. "I fear the war is making an old man of me, and I understand if you say no."

"Wil, stop teasing. You should know that my answer is yes. Is it because of what happened that you're asking now?"

"No, it's because I like a woman who can swear."

Though he kept a straight face, love reflected in his coal-black eyes as his hand went around hers. Amanda had been right. It would take him a little longer to lower the mask completely. "Then I shall do my best to not disappoint you."

He grasped her elbow and led her along the hall. No lamp or fire lit the back bedroom where she had nursed him to health. In the darkness, all pretense of calm vanished. Her dress, crinoline, and petticoat tumbled to the floor.

His hands fumbled with the laces and stays of her corset. "I don't know why women wear these damn things."

"To make things more entertaining."

He mumbled another curse, and she realized that his jokes were a sham. He needed her as much as she needed him. With his breath hot on her neck, his fingers worked frantically to loosen the laces.

She gave a slight laugh. "You *are* irritable."

"I'm pleased you find it amusing."

The last of the laces came free, and her breasts were released from their binding. Unrestricted at last, she could breathe. The room's chill nipped at her nakedness. Dashing beneath the covers, she heard his gun thump to the floor. *What if Wil hadn't been here? They could be dead now—all of them.*

His warmth moved in next to her, and she clutched him like a frightened child. "He wanted us dead. He didn't care which of us or how many . . ."

Wil hushed her, but she could no longer hold back and burst into tears. His quiet strength was what she needed. As his mouth met hers, her worry faded, but she couldn't forget. He had warned her that things would get worse, and until the war was over, each moment together could be their last.

Cherish it.

They touched and fondled until his familiar weight was atop her. With his face next to hers, his whiskers scratched—so coarse, yet pleasurable. He put his fingers through hers, and the bed creaked to their rhythm.

Only her—she wanted him to think of nothing else. Gripping him tighter, she held on as if she'd never let go. More rhythmic rocking, and the chill in the room suddenly felt gloriously warm until they fell to the bed, exhausted.

Nestled in the crook of his arm, Alice listened to the faint echoes of his heartbeat. "Wil, you haven't said anything about children."

His arm tensed. "What about them?"

Because of the death of his son, she worried how he might react. "Do you want them?"

He laughed slightly. "If we continue in our present manner, I doubt that I'll be consulted."

"And you have a knack for evading questions."

"Alice, I shall cherish you as well as any child that may result because of it."

Progress—but he still hadn't said the word, love. Have patience—give him time. Whispering her love, she hugged him close.

Mama had made a special trip from Richmond to attend the wedding. As Alice dressed, Amanda realized how difficult it must have been for Wil to watch her recite her vows with Sam. Part of her wondered if Wil would actually go through with the ceremony. She'd have his hide if he reneged on his promise to her little sister. Still another side of her wanted him to do just that. *Why couldn't she rid herself of such shameful thoughts?*

"Amanda . . . I could use a little help."

Alice stood in front of the dresser in the blue silk dress, waiting for the back to be buttoned. Amanda's stomach knotted. It was the same dress she had worn to marry Sam.

Amanda buttoned the dress. "I wish we could have sewn a proper wedding gown rather than having you wear my hand-me-down."

Alice smiled dreamily. "The dress doesn't matter. Wil only has a ten-day pass. I wasn't going to wait for any silly dress." She held up a shaking hand. "Now if I could only keep my hand steady."

"Relax, Alice. Mama and the preacher's wife are the only guests. And Mama's quite pleased, unlike when I married . . ." *Sam . . .*

"He'll be back."

"This is your day. Don't let my worries spoil it. Wil's a good man. I always suspected he'd settle down if he found the right woman. Little did I know she was my own sister."

"When I met him at your wedding to John, he was so handsome. Even then, I had fantasies of this day. Amanda..." Alice beamed when she glanced over her shoulder. "What's it like?"

Popping out of her gloomy mood, Amanda got a sly grin. "I fancied you had already found out, and if you know what's good for you, you'll pretend innocence when Mama rushes up here to give you the wedding night lecture."

"Amanda..." Alice's face reddened. "...that's not what I meant."

Like when they were girls, Amanda covered her mouth and giggled. Alice joined her, then took a critical look in the mirror. Her sister's auburn hair was coiled in ringlets.

Amanda added fresh sprigs of chicory. This late in the autumn season, it was the only flower that readily bloomed. By a stroke of luck, the pale blue blossoms matched the dress.

The awaited knock came, and Mama poked her head in. "Alice." Fidgeting with her bead necklace, Mama stepped into the bedroom. "It's a mother's responsibility to advise her daughter about the wedding night."

Alice exchanged a sly glance with Amanda. "Yes, Mama, what is it you want to tell me?"

Mama twisted the beads between her fingers. "A good man will be gentle the first time..."

Alice flickered her eyelashes. "First time for what, Mama?"

Amanda elbowed Alice in the ribs as Mama cleared her throat. "Once married, a man has...uh...certain rights..."

"Certain rights? That sounds serious."

Amanda jabbed her sister again. "I've already warned her, Mama."

The pronounced wrinkles in Mama's forehead faded, and she stopped tugging on her beads. "Then I'll wait downstairs."

"Alice," Amanda chastised as Mama shuffled to the stairs. "You can be wicked at times."

"You said to pretend innocence."

"Innocence," Amanda repeated, "not ignorance."

With another laugh, Alice hugged her. How many times had they quarreled over silly things like dress color? Or which of them had the most handsome beau? When her sister's girlhood friend, Timmy Mullen, had died, Amanda had held Alice until she had nothing left to cry, and they'd taken turns consoling the other after Papa's death.

Stepping back, Alice grasped the chicory bouquet from the dresser. "I'm ready."

As Amanda led the way from the bedroom, her stomach churned. *This wasn't the way things were supposed to be.* Dreams had been ruined, not by war, but foolish pride. *Lord, what was wrong with her?* She should only be thinking about Sam's well-being and safe return.

At the bottom of the stairs, Amanda gave Alice a reassuring squeeze and took her place beside Mama.

Without even giving Amanda's entrance a glance, Wil stood beside the preacher. Cleanshaven except for his moustache, he looked particularly handsome in his gray jacket with shiny brass buttons and fine gold embroidery on the sleeves. And so typical of Wil, he failed to show any trace of nerves. His eyes sparkled when Alice approached.

The preacher began to speak.

Instead of being relieved that she wouldn't have to haul out the rifle, Amanda's whole body ached. *He was going through with the ceremony.*

In a daze, she listened to the couple recite their vows. Wil slipped a gold band on Alice's finger.

All this time, she had blamed Wil for lacking the courage to mail the letter expressing his feelings. But why should she be held guiltless? Equally stubborn, she had failed to tell him how she felt. Now it was too late. Her little sister *was* Mrs. Brigadier William Jackson.

Over the next fortnight, the dream—or vision—became clearer. The raven, a master of trickery, was the key to the plan. Once the black wolf altered color, Wil was capable of opening the leghold trap. While staying at an inn on the return trip to Richmond, he had dispatched a request for the raven to meet him.

With a contented smile, Alice slept in his arms. As an unexpected side effect of marrying Alice, he no longer felt the rage simmering beneath the surface. The family would be relieved that he had finally taken a bride—a white one. In all likelihood they would never recognize Peopeo as his first wife, but that union might be overlooked for Alice's sake.

A knock came to the door, and Alice's eyelids fluttered. "Brigadier Jackson, you have a caller."

"I'll be right there." He lowered his voice for Alice. "Duty calls."

Wil got up to dress, and Alice sat up and rubbed her eyes. She exposed a plump, round breast. Tempted to return to bed, he finished dressing. Duty came first—unfortunately.

In the hall, the boardinghouse mistress sent him a piercing look of disapproval. "In the parlor, sir."

Wagering that the raven had arrived, he went downstairs. An unescorted woman waited in the parlor—Holly Prescott. "Outside."

Collecting his overcoat on the way out, he stepped into the clear but cold night.

"Aren't you going to wish an *old* friend hello?" she asked drolly.

"You weren't supposed to come here."

Joining him under the gas lamppost, she gave a triumphant smirk. "You're lucky I came at all." She placed a hand to her throat. "Need I remind you about our last meeting?"

As if he could forget. He had wanted to choke the life out of her. "You have my apologies."

Her gaze hardened, and she narrowed her eyes. "You tried to kill me, and I'm supposed to dismiss it with a simple apology?"

Wil shoved his hands behind his back. "Holly, if I had wanted you dead, you would be. Now I presume you have answered my summons because you need the money, or you've suddenly developed a soft spot for your brother-in-law."

"And I have recently learned Sam is your brother-in-law as well." Baiting him, she licked her lips. "Is the little woman keeping you entertained? My recollection is that you could be annoyingly difficult to satiate."

Wil held his tongue and silently counted to ten. "It seems we will always bring out the worst in each other. Shall we accept it and move on for Prescott's sake?"

She held a dubious expression but nodded. "Pray tell, what do you have in mind?"

"I'd like you to become friends with a respected Richmond citizen. You do remember how to be friendly?"

Holly waved a fist. "How dare you, Wil Jackson. You always were a smooth talker. I'm *not* some strumpet for hire."

As she turned, Wil caught her arm. "I meant what I said—friends. Rumors abound that Miss Van Lew is a Yankee spy. With her help, we can get Prescott out of Libby." He let go of her arm. "I think even you are capable of understanding why I can't go to her myself."

She bunched her hands. "Insult me again, and I'll return to Washington now. Tell me honestly, are you doing this for Sam...or Amanda?"

He shrugged. "Does it matter?"

"*Mrs.* Jackson might think so if she thought you were still pining for her sister."

He fought the building rage. No more—he needn't resort to anger. "Holly," he replied evenly. "I'm not pining for Amanda."

Suddenly amused, she placed her hand to her heart. "*Au contraire*, I think you want to believe that. Even so, how will you explain that *I'm* in Richmond?"

"If things go according to plan, Alice needn't know."

"And if they don't?"

Delight had lingered in her voice, and he surrendered to her sarcasm. "If plans go awry, I trust the gallows can be arranged so we hang side by side. A fitting end, don't you think?" All traces of her smile faded and fear crossed her face. He had gone too far. Respond, or she might give in to her fear. "If you're caught, tell them I coerced you."

"You did!"

"You had best think of some reason besides my making it worth your while in gold." Her eyes darted back and forth as if she were ready to flee. "Holly, I need your help if I'm going to get Prescott out of Libby."

"You've become chivalrous of late, Brigadier Jackson," she said with a waver. "A bad habit that is becoming most annoying."

"You complained that I never defended your honor."

She stepped closer—near enough to smell her perfume, and her hands went to her hips. "Are you going to stand there and pretend nothing ever happened between us?"

The sweet fragrance revived memories. She sought to control him through her wily seduction. "I don't deny our liaisons."

"Liaisons," she muttered as if mortally wounded. "I'm shattered that it meant nothing more."

"I'm certain you are," he said dryly.

"Wil, sometimes you underestimate me. I wouldn't have come to Richmond if I had no intention of helping my dear brother-in-law."

Progress. Once and for all, the cycle must be broken. "After this meeting, we won't be seen together. Is that clear?" With some reluctance, she nodded. "In the next few days, you'll be paid half. By that time, you will have made your acquaintance with Miss Van Lew. The remaining amount shall be paid when Prescott is out of Libby."

She regarded him quizzically. "You're a fool to think you can pull this off."

"Maybe..." True, he hadn't sorted out the details, but there had been other prison escapes. With most able-bodied men at the front, prisons were understaffed. That fact could be used to their advantage. Poker or chess? Definitely poker. "I'll be in contact with you."

"Wil..." He turned but didn't look back. "If you should hang, I assure you I'll lead the round of applause."

Deadlock—he shook his head and laughed. Holly would make good her threat. Nothing gained, nothing lost. Returning to the boarding-house, he made his way up the stairs to the second story and down the hall. Inside the cramped room that he shared with Alice, he sat on the edge of the bed and tugged off his boots.

Alice covered her mouth and stifled a yawn. "Anything serious?"

He finished undressing and climbed in beside her. "No."

"Then what took you so long?"

On the chance that his plan failed, he wouldn't risk dragging her down with him. "Nothing you need to fret about."

"Wil—"

He pressed two fingers to her lips. "Alice, I have an early morning."

Without further questioning, she snuggled in his arms. So young—in many ways she remained quite innocent. If she discovered how much he sheltered her, she'd be furious. He didn't care. Determined not to repeat the mistakes that he had made with Peopeo, the only thing that mattered was her safety.

* * *

A brisk north wind and a layer of snow welcomed 1864. Uncertain who needed more care, the baby or Frieda, Amanda finished washing the old woman. Frieda's sightless eyes rarely blinked, and her right hand resembled a misshapen claw.

Ezra sat on the opposite side of the bed and lovingly held the old woman's hand. His own eyes were sunken and his skin, withered. Facing everyday life must be worse when a body got older. At least she had the children to keep her days occupied and the hope that Sam would return.

Amanda finished dressing Frieda and sat in the rocking chair to rest her feet a spell. There had been no word from Alice or Wil concerning Sam. Knowing Alice, she was donning ball gowns. With Wil's influence, she had likely become a Richmond socialite. Not that she begrudged Alice enjoying the moment—there was so little of that anymore, but Sam ... Did he even have enough to eat?

"I be goin' now, Miss Amanda."

"Frieda?" Amanda opened her eyes and glanced in the old woman's direction. Her mind must be playing tricks. She could have sworn she had heard Frieda's voice.

Tears streaked Ezra's brown cheeks. He gathered Frieda's slight frame in his arms and wailed.

Always more of a doting Mama than a servant, Frieda was gone. Why couldn't she cry? Too much grief these days. A fact of life—birth and death. Fewer chores for her aching body—no more cleaning Frieda's helpless body or spoon-feeding her feeble face.

Amanda buried her face in her hands and slumped in the chair. *Oh, Sam—please don't die.*

Chapter Fourteen

COLD—SO COLD. SAM PACED the floor of the old warehouse in a use-less effort to remain warm. There was no glass in the windows, and the bitter winds swept straight off the canal from the James River. During warmer days, he had whittled to keep monotony at bay, then he turned to visiting with other prisoners. After days turned into weeks of repeating the same stories, they simply ran out of things to talk about.

He heard excited muttering near the door and Major Bowen thumped him on the arm. Several Confederate officers touring the prison had caused the commotion. At least two of the officers were generals. Just what the prisoners needed—more dignitaries promising they would personally see to the improvement of conditions.

Sam resumed pacing. As the generals made the rounds, he watched them.

While conversing with the prisoners, they seemed polite enough. Finally they reached his sector. The one on the left was General Morgan. The other bearded general reached out a gloved hand. "General Hill," he said, introducing himself.

Though his fingers were numb, Sam shook his hand. "As in General A. P. Hill, sir?"

"I am."

"I've met your boys a number of times. Brave soldiers, sir."

"Much obliged that you would admit as much."

"As a matter of fact, I believe my former commander serves under you."

Intrigued, the general raised an eyebrow.

"Brigadier William Jackson," Sam said.

General Hill laughed, and as they talked, Sam discovered he'd been a friend of Jackson's at West Point. They had several escapades of sneaking off to Benny Havens for a drink during midwinter.

Sam finally understood what Jackson had meant by being more alike than he thought. Small world—and when General Hill left, he made no empty promises. Definitely a man he could respect, and a few minutes had passed without boredom.

Life in Richmond was near idyllic. While Wil worked at the War Department during the day, Alice spent time calling on neighbors and newly made friends. With the blockade having little effect on parties of the elite, evenings treated her to numerous social gatherings. On one occasion she met President Davis and his charming wife, Varina. At another reception, General J.E.B. Stuart and Wil's West Point friend General Powell Hill attended. She overheard them conversing about the upcoming spring campaign.

Being far from the guns, she had blocked the war from her mind. With snow and ice on the ground, spring was a long way off, but she had secretly hoped Wil would retain his position in Richmond. As a Confederate field officer, he was honor bound to return to the front. As his wife, she must dutifully keep any concern to herself. But if it was truly a lost cause as Wil believed, then what glory was there in fighting for it?

How quickly she had turned a blind eye to Fredericksburg's devastation—the loss of her home and all of those bodies on the heights. Dancing and parties shrouded the truth. While Richmond streets swelled with refugees, Chimborazo housed Confederate wounded, and Libby imprisoned Yankee officers. Could Amanda forgive her negligence?

Caught up in playing the role of a brigadier's wife, Alice had left the details to Wil, and he had made no mention of Sam's release since leaving Amanda's. Out of guilt, she had hired a carriage, and the driver halted a block from the canal near the James River. He extended a hand and helped her down. "Would you like me to wait, ma'am?"

Wait? Exactly what had she been expecting? March up to the door, knock, and ask for Lieutenant Colonel Samuel Prescott? "Yes, please wait, if you don't mind."

He assured her that he would. "It ain't safe for a woman alone."

"Thank you, sir." She pressed a bill into his palm, and he tipped his hat.

Recent thawing and refreezing of the roads had left them rutted. Carefully negotiating over wagon wheel grooves, she nearly tripped. A cold wind whipped off the canal, and she bundled her cloak around her. Finally, she spotted the sign on a three-story, brick warehouse—L. Libby & Son, Ship Chandlers.

Bars covered the windows. Many were without glass. Not a single face peered out. Perhaps the overcrowded conditions were nothing more than a rumor. She knew better. Wil had been inside, and he wasn't prone to exaggeration.

Alice stepped forward but quickly halted. A plain-looking, dark-haired woman in her mid-forties stood outside the main door. She carried a basket on her arm, and her blue eyes darted back and forth in a frenzied fashion.

"Are you going in?" Alice asked.

"No time . . ."

What could she mean? "I'm Mrs. William Jackson. My husband . . ."

Her eyes danced, and she patted Alice's hand. "In there. So sorry, child."

"No, you misunderstand. My husband is a Confederate . . ." Alice bit her tongue. She had already revealed too much to this eccentric stranger. ". . . soldier."

The woman threw her hands in the air, nearly toppling her basket. "No time for this. The boys depend on me."

"My brother-in-law, Lieutenant Colonel Samuel Prescott, is a prisoner."

Her blue eyes continued looking from side to side. "Prescott?"

The odd woman must be simple-minded or mad. "Do you know him? Is he all right? My sister is very worried."

"Prescott?"

The woman was definitely simple. She was getting nowhere. The trip had been a foolish venture. With no notion of what she had hoped to gain, Alice turned.

"On the third floor."

Alice glanced over her shoulder, and the strange woman muttered to herself. Could Sam really be on the third floor, or was it a crazy woman's gibberish? She looked to the warehouse. "Take me to him."

The woman gave Alice a crooked smile and shoved the basket over her arm. "I've been feeling poorly. You can assist me today."

The weight of the basket caught Alice off guard. She sagged before getting a firm grip on the handle. "Thank you. I don't even know your name."

The lopsided smile widened to a grin. "Bet. They call me Bet."

Edging to the prison doors, Alice overheard a guard refer to Bet in a less polite manner by calling her "Crazy Bet." Bet seemed to be a familiar sight. Other guards simply ignored her.

Alice praised her good fortune in crossing paths with the simple-minded woman. Inside the warehouse, she stifled a gasp. The stench of human waste assaulted her nostrils. Nauseated, she pressed a hand to her stomach, and Bet lent her a steadying hand. Nodding that she would be fine, she wished for Bet's poise. In spite of the cold, she was sweating.

Up a flight of stairs, Bet strolled to the nearest room.

Alice pointed to the third floor. "You said he was . . ."

Two fingers went to Bet's lips. "Be patient, child. Assist me." Sallow, bearded faces peered at her with interest, and Bet's weird smile returned as she gestured to the basket. "My niece," Bet said.

When Alice lifted the linen from the basket, some of the men started chatting. With sunken eyes and withered hands, they all looked elderly, rather than men in their prime.

Alice passed out freshly baked bread and dried vegetables from the basket. All around her, men coughed, and high-pitched squeaking surrounded them. Rats scuttled along the floor. On the other side of the room someone played a harmonica, and the faint melody of another man singing drifted to her ears.

In the next room, more coughing—all of the prisoners had it. Under the poor lighting of gas lamps and candles, nothing seemed quite real. Looking more like ghostly apparitions than real flesh and blood, some men were hardly more than skeletons.

She shuddered. Wil had said he'd rather die than be captured. Now she understood why.

Too weak to stand, one gaunt form held up a bony hand.

Alice placed a loaf of bread in his hand. Another prisoner snatched the loaf and gorged, while others stood around like buzzards ready to catch the crumbs.

Bet tugged on her cloak to keep moving, and they reached the landing of the third floor.

More lean faces watched from the corridors. Eager for any scrap of news, the healthier prisoners spoke as they passed. Alice followed Bet through the rows of men.

With little space between them, some had no blankets and huddled on the bare wood floor. That sickening smell reached her nostrils again. It wasn't human waste alone—but the smell of death. All of them were dying, and Sam was here—somewhere.

She resisted the urge to call his name.

Among the cluster of arms and legs, none had enough space to stretch out. Many were curled for warmth on the filthy floor. In the corner one man sobbed—probably from hunger. An emaciated form stared at her.

Low on food, Alice placed a Confederate bill in the man's palm. She'd fret about how to pay the cab fare later. Another man slipped her a letter. She stuck it in her cloak and nodded that she would mail it.

"Colonel," Bet whispered.

No one responded.

"*Pssst*, Colonel . . ."

A scruffy, bearded officer cracked open his eyes.

Bet reached in the basket and handed Alice the last portion of bread.

Why would Bet give her the bread now? She needed to find Sam.

A thin face with familiar blue eyes looked in her direction. Not the strong, rugged man she had known, he slept on the bare floor with his feet wrapped in dirty cloths. *He couldn't be Sam.*

Fighting tears, Alice handed him the bread.

He grasped the bread with shaking hands and coughed—the same hacking cough as the others.

"Sam?"

"Alice," he answered in a low voice. "How is Amanda?"

"She's fine."

"And the baby? I don't know his name."

Before she could respond, Bet tugged on her arm to be moving. But she couldn't leave Sam behind—not in such filth. She'd visit with Bet again, and bring him food, a blanket, and some warm clothing.

After returning to the boardinghouse, Alice went up to their room and sank in the wing chair by the window and watched the sun go down. She wondered how cold the warehouse got at night. With their stomachs empty—and no blankets—how did the prisoners survive?

The sun sank further until the only flicker of light was from the gas lampposts on the streets.

"Alice? Why are you sitting in the dark?" Wil lit a lamp.

She hadn't heard Wil come in. "I wasn't feeling well."

"No wonder. The fire's nearly out." He bent down to stoke the ashes.

"Wil, I saw him."

Wil tossed a log on the fire and straightened. "Saw whom?"

"Sam."

His dark eyes grew fixed, but his voice was even when he spoke. "Perhaps you should tell me what you did today."

"I hired a carriage and went to Libby. A simple, but kind woman took me to him. Her name is Bet. She feeds—"

"Bet..." His jaw tensed and his hands curled to fists. "Of all the goddamned fool things—"

"Sam doesn't even have a blanket."

He raised a hand. "Not now. I'll deal with you later."

Turning swiftly, Wil slammed the door behind him, and the thud of his angry footsteps retreated down the hall.

Confused by his outburst, she stared at the door. With Libby located in a squalid section of the city, she had expected concern for her well-being. Even anger for disobeying his orders she would have understood, but not full-fledged fury.

At supper time, Alice kept normal appearances and went to the dining room. When the topic of Wil's absence entered the conversation, she made believe that he was working late. After supper, unable to make idle chitchat, she retreated to their room instead of socializing with the other boarders. By midnight, she began to fret. She nervously readied for bed and climbed between cold sheets.

On other chilly nights, she had grown accustomed to snuggling up to Wil. Without his warmth, she shivered. She had no right to complain. In the drafty, filthy warehouse, Sam would be colder.

No matter how much Wil protested, on Bet's next visit, she would return to Libby and make certain Sam got a blanket, along with some decent food and warm clothing. But what about the other prisoners? Under the circumstances, Bet was doing the best she could.

Around two, Alice heard Wil's footsteps outside the door. Relieved that he was safe, she breathed easier.

The door banged, and she closed her eyes. Several hours away hadn't simmered his temper. All these nights while she had been attending parties, Sam was shivering sick and hungry in a foul warehouse. Why couldn't Wil understand her concern? She turned to her side and pretended to be asleep.

The mattress shifted as he got in beside her. His breathing was raspy. The wound, especially at night, often bothered him.

"Wil—"

"I don't care to discuss it."

She touched the taut muscles in his shoulder. "After so much time, I had to see how he was faring. After all, he is Amanda's husband."

"I'm aware of that," he snapped. "Are you satisfied I relayed the truth about the conditions?"

"I never doubted . . ."

He faced her. The gas lampposts outside shed enough light to see his drawn face. "Then why did you make contact with a Yankee spy?"

"Yankee?"

"Miss Elizabeth Van Lew is a Yankee spy."

Elizabeth? Bet? He stated it so matter-of-factly. "But she seems so simple."

"She has fooled you too. Did you doubt I would get him out of there?"

"I thought you had forgotten," she said, suddenly unsure of herself. "Sam's ill, and there's not enough food. He doesn't even have a blanket."

Wil sucked in his breath and sat up.

"And you're hurting. Let me get something . . ."

He caught her wrist. "I am sick of you telling me what conditions are like. I *know*. I've checked into prisoner exchanges. It could take months before they resume."

"Sam may not survive months."

"I'm aware of that fact. I've monitored his condition—discreetly. I didn't want you involved."

"Involved in what?"

A hand went to his chest, and his breath grew ragged. "For the past month, Mrs. Prescott has been following Miss Van Lew's social circle to gain her confidence."

No longer caring how much he hurst, she clenched her hands. "Mrs. Prescott? As in *Holly* Prescott? Is *she* the reason you were out half the night?"

He grasped her hand and lightly kissed the back. "I assure you, I've done nothing to warrant suspicion."

"Then why is Holly in Richmond?"

"To gain Miss Van Lew's confidence."

Sidestepping again—he never gave a straight answer. "Wil, please—"

"Despite her disagreeable nature, Holly is capable of talking her way out of precarious situations. After she gained Miss Van Lew's trust, the plan was for her to deliver a Confederate uniform to Prescott in Libby. Because of his weakened condition, I would then bring him out."

By visiting Libby, she had interfered, and he had been protecting her. "It seems I've botched up. Let me take the uniform to Sam."

"Alice, if you're caught, it won't be like smuggling supplies. Because you're a woman, they *might* give you a prison sentence."

Or hang her—like Peopeo. But what of Wil? He would certainly be handed a death sentence. Why had she been so blind? Damn him for being so secretive. "I'll take food and supplies to keep him alive until this asinine war is over. He's my brother-in-law. No one will question my actions."

"Too late." His hand touched the side of her face and stroked her cheek. "Against my better judgment, we shall alter the plan to include you."

Careful not to hit his wound, she put her arms around him. "I can do it. Bet said I was her niece. No one need know otherwise." Alice drew away from him. "Wil, I told her who I was."

"Miss Van Lew?"

She nodded.

"I'll see if Holly can discover what she knows. We'll take it from there."

How could she have been so foolish? Not only had she implicated Wil, but she had endangered all of their lives further.

The carriage halted outside the columned mansion surrounded by the white iron fence. Hopping to the brick walk, the driver helped Holly down and opened the creaking gate with a bow.

Not only was Wil paying too little for her taking such life-threatening risks, he had grown downright tiresome of late. Fancy that, Wil Jackson smitten and expecting her to remain satisfied with nothing more than befriending a middle-aged spinster. She just might have to rustle up an engaging romp with some Rebel cavalry.

A massive split staircase loomed before her. After climbing the right section, she tapped a brass knocker on the door. A black free servant escorted her to Bet's sitting room. Iron pilasters capped with crouched lions edged the fireplace.

A simpleton's smile formed on Bet's lips, and she motioned for Holly to have a seat. "I've been expecting you, Mrs. Prescott."

As Holly eased in an overstuffed chair, Bet continued to smile. "I trust you have."

Anyone who smiled as much as Bet had to be daft. Holly caught herself. Don't fall for that one. Looniness was part of Bet's role. "Shall we get straight to the point?" Holly asked.

Bet's smile never faded, but she nodded.

"I presume you have guessed why I'm here?"

"Really, Mrs. Prescott, you didn't need to go to the trouble of pretending to be my friend."

Couched in riddles, Bet rarely spoke plain English. Damn Alice for interfering, and damn Wil for involving her. Holly had a notion to flee from Richmond without Sam.

But that wouldn't be sporting. After all, he was her dear, dead husband's brother. If she were caught, she'd just make certain to drag Wil and the little strumpet down with her. "You don't fool me, Miss Van Lew. You have already put two and two together. Lieutenant Colonel Prescott is my brother-in-law, and I aim to get him out of Libby."

Bet stood. "Some tea?"

The black servant poured from a silver teapot into finely gold-etched china cups.

Holly fished a note from Alice out of her crocheted bag. "Will you see that Colonel Prescott receives it at the appropriate time?"

Bet unfolded the note, and her smile finally faded. "She's married to a Confederate brigadier."

As Holly had suspected, Bet's demented routine was a sham. "He served with my brother-in-law before the war."

Bet's head tilted, and her daft looking smile returned. "Does the colonel like Shakespeare, Mrs. Prescott?"

At a loss, Holly had no idea how to respond.

Bet carefully folded the note. "I have a room where weary soldiers can rest."

Relieved, Holly accepted the china cup from Bet's servant and leaned back in the overstuffed chair. She'd inform Wil that Bet would help. Meanwhile, she'd sit back and wait. Sam didn't have a chance in hell of coming out of Libby alive, and poor Amanda would wear black yet again.

A cough racked through Sam's lungs. The previous night was so cold that icicles hung from the windows. *Write to Amanda.* He struggled to wrap numb fingers around the pencil. The Rebs would confiscate any letter that mentioned seeing Alice. Hell—they appropriated anything beyond the weather. He tried once more, but his hand shook. His letter would remain unwritten for another day.

Huddling on the bare floor, he curled into a ball and closed his eyes. Nearly four in the afternoon, and no rations had been served yet. The day before, they had received half a loaf of gritty cornbread. Barely noticing hunger pangs anymore, many officers had become proficient at snaring vermin. Rats weren't any worse tasting than the meat the Rebs served—on the few occasions the prisoners got any.

All he cared about now was sleeping—where he could dream about Amanda. The way she tilted her head, or the satisfied glint in her emerald eyes after making love. And their son. *What was his name?*

Sam coughed, bringing up phlegm. Amanda's world was fading from his grasp.

"Colonel . . ."

With all of the colonels in Libby, the woman's voice could have been addressing any number of them. He had no desire to answer and stayed where he was.

"Lieutenant Colonel Prescott," the voice came again.

Go away. He wasn't leaving the one place he could be with Amanda.

"Colonel!"

He squinted an eye open to Crazy Bet, smiling in that inane way of hers. He glanced around for Alice. No sign of her—she hadn't accompanied the eccentric spinster this time.

Bet shoved a book in his hand.

"You woke me for a goddamned book?"

In his mind, he heard Amanda chastise him for swearing, but Bet wasn't swayed. "Enjoy the book, Colonel. My niece will call *tomorrow* to pick it up."

Bet ambled on, passing out bread from her basket.

Hungry as hell, and he got a book. While some of the men snatched up the few books and newspapers that made it past the guards, he was indifferent. Any hopeful attitude had changed when he got sick, but the only way to see Amanda again was to hold on.

Sam flipped through the pages. The wretched tallow candle lighting made reading difficult. He stretched his arm to toss the book, and a small scrap of paper fell from between the pages. He unfolded it.

A new uniform is ready. Will you need help trying it on?

A

A? Alice. Uniform? His mind worked slowly these days. Why would she bring him a uniform? The guards wouldn't withhold a uniform, unless . . . He looked over at Bet.

With a nod, she smiled. "What's the matter, Colonel? My niece was certain you'd like Shakespeare."

Her niece? Was she speaking about Alice? "I've read it before. Thank your niece kindly."

"She'll bring something more to your liking—*tomorrow*."

Tomorrow? That was the second time Bet had stressed the word. Alice must be bringing a uniform—tomorrow. He crumpled the note.

"Do you have a special request?"

Answer Alice's question. "Tell her that I'm not well. If the book is heavy, I'll need help holding it."

Still smiling, Bet nodded that she understood.

Damn—the guards were watching. They sprinted over, and Bet smirked as they searched her basket.

Sam passed the note to Major Bowen, lying next to him. Rough hands jerked him to his feet, and the guards searched him.

"My apologies, Colonel," Bet said, "I didn't know they'd have such a conniption fit over Shakespeare."

"Where is it?" the first guard asked.

Sam shrugged. "Where's what?"

The guard loomed over him. "The note."

Bowen had likely passed it on, and it was probably halfway across the prison by now. Sam pointed to the letter he had tried writing to Amanda earlier.

The second guard bent down to check the letter. "That ain't it."

"It's the only note I have."

The first guard gave him a long, searching look and jabbed a finger to his chest. "If I find it, you know what happens."

Sam's skin crawled—the pitch-black, underground cells. Rebellious in the beginning, he'd rather face death than the cavernous cells again. As prison authorities had hoped, the punishment made him more compliant. He couldn't risk being sent there now—not if Alice was coming tomorrow. "There's no other note."

Doubtful, the guard continued staring. He motioned to the other guard. "Let's send him below ground."

Strong hands seized his arms, when Major Bowen stood. If the guards got possession of Alice's note, he'd never see the light of day again.

The major held out a plug of tobacco. Accepting the bribe, the guards let go of Sam's arms and wandered off.

Sam nodded his thanks to Bowen and slumped to the floor. Tomorrow—God, what was Alice planning? Temporarily forgetting his hunger, he rested his head on the filthy floor and thought of Amanda. She might be closer than he had fathomed possible.

A fortnight earlier, Wil had been summoned to the field, inspecting troops and conditions. A message from him by courier the day before alerted Alice that the time had come.

Outside Libby, she waited for Bet. Spying the spinster, she climbed from the carriage.

"He didn't like Shakespeare, child. I hope you brought something more to his liking."

Good—Sam had received her message. As Bet muttered nonsense, Alice grasped the basket from her arm. At the first sign of guards, she shuddered. *Keep your wits. Let Bet do the talking.*

Bet mumbled hellos, and the little girl in Alice wanted to run screaming to the safety of Papa's arms. The way he had held her as she bawled her eyes out after Timmy Mullen had died.

Inside the prison, she gasped for air from the stench of overflowing sinks. Were the prisons where they sent women like this? *Get a hold of yourself*. She thought of Wil and momentarily yearned for him. He was probably outside, waiting. Most likely, he had even watched her enter the prison.

Alice formed her most gracious smile and helped Bet distribute bread and dried vegetables. By the time they reached the third floor, she spotted Sam.

Sitting up and chatting with the major next to him, he glanced in her direction.

As they got closer, a rat brushed against her legs. She startled a cry, nearly dropping the basket.

A toothless lieutenant laughed at her.

She mustn't let anything distract her from her mission. Closer—finally near Sam, she whispered, "Lift my skirt."

The major's hand went under her skirt and fondled her leg.

She swatted his hand with a loaf of bread. Even here, in this vile warehouse, men thought of having their way with women.

Sam hesitated.

"Go ahead. Lift it," she repeated. Alice prattled on with the major and felt a tug under her skirt. Good—Sam had found the gray jacket pinned to her hoops.

He wadded the jacket and slipped it under the major's blanket.

So the major was aware of the plan. "The boots too."

His hand went under her skirt again for the cavalry boots she had tied there.

"Be ready in two hours. Wil shall fetch you."

Tears formed in Sam's eyes. "Alice..."

She placed a finger to her lips and continued on until the basket was empty. By helping Sam, she was doing her share, but what of all the others? Such living conditions were an atrocity, and it didn't matter if they were the enemy.

Chapter Fifteen

TWO WEEKS IN THE FIELD PROVIDED time to grow some semblance of a beard. After watching Alice enter Libby, Wil returned to the hospitals a block from the prison and paid his respects to the sick and wounded. Attired in cavalry gold with captain's bars, he gave reassuring words of their bravery. He checked his pocket watch—only half an hour had passed. It had been a long time since he'd played a good game of poker. Wedded life must have mellowed him.

Another hour passed. Wil stepped outside and waited. As afternoon shadows on the streets lengthened, the buggy rounded the corner. With Poker in the field, he mounted a dark bay horse. He reined the bay around but brought the horse up short before colliding with the buggy.

Wil tipped his hat. "Beg your pardon, ma'am. My thoughts must have been elsewhere. I didn't see you."

Startled, Alice put a hand to her collar.

After a fortnight away, he'd prefer to return to the boardinghouse and spend the evening in bed with her, rather than playing poker.

She met his gaze, but quickly glanced at the road ahead. "Apology accepted, sir. Now if you don't mind, I must be on my way. I have an appointment with my husband, and he gets testy if I'm late."

Damned right. Wil said a silent goodbye, and she clicked her tongue. The carriage horse trotted on. *Clear your head*. Caring so much weakened men into making foolish mistakes. She was out of danger now, and he focused on the task at hand.

He squeezed the bay to a trot until arriving on Canal Street. Two blocks from Libby, he tied the horse to a rail and checked his papers—Captain John Cole, First South Carolina. As long as the guards didn't examine the paperwork too closely, they would never know the name was as fictitious as the papers.

Waiting until nightfall, Wil lowered his hat over his eyes and strode to the prison. In the rat-ridden, squalid section of the city, he hoped the bay would still be tied to the rail when he returned with Prescott.

If not, matters would be complicated, but they'd be able to walk to refuge. Unless of course, they were shot while making the escape. *Don't think that way.* Alice was too young to wear black.

Outside the main door, a guard saluted and gave a cursory glance at his paperwork. Wil entered the old warehouse and breathed in the stench of unwashed clothes and bodies. A familiar scent on the battlefield—only here death was slower.

At the bottom of the stairs, another guard—the same one who had taken him to the underground cell—snapped to attention with a salute. "Captain, what can I do for you?"

Wil breathed in relief that the guard hadn't recognized him. "My assistant surgeon was to meet me here."

Confusion crossed the guard's face. "Sir?"

Grumbling at his ignorance, Wil replied, "General Winder expressed a need for surgeons. Colonel Black—First South Carolina—sent our assistant by earlier in the day to look over the prisoners. You do know where he is?"

"Yes, sir. He's in with the uh . . . prisoners. Shall I fetch him?"

"No," Wil said in disgust. "I'll fetch him myself."

"Yes, sir."

Wil stepped forward.

"Uh, sir, you'll need to leave your weapons here."

"Of course." Wil unbuckled his weapons belt and draped it over the guard's outstretched arm.

With a salute, the guard stood aside.

Too old for high-stakes poker, Wil let out the breath he was holding in. On the second floor, he repeated his story to another guard, stopping long enough for appearance's sake of searching for the surgeon.

Under long shadows of flickering candlelight, sickly bearded faces stared at him—most with lost expressions. Others narrowed their eyes in contempt. *Yankees,* he reminded himself, but even he couldn't wish such a lingering death on his worst enemy.

Continuing on, he reached the third floor. Upon Wil's arrival, most prisoners stopped talking, and the grimy whitewashed room filled with persistent coughing. Rows and rows of men huddled on the floor.

Wil made his way through, and a rat scurried past his feet. Behind him, the rodent squealed.

A soldier smacked his lips. "Hey Reb, care to join us for supper? Fry it in a pan, and you can't tell the difference from that tasty Southron specialty—possum."

Stripped of all dignity in this place where rats were a delicacy, the Yanks joined in a round of laughter.

Ahead of Wil, a scruffy, bearded officer groaned and got to his feet. In the faint light a moment passed before he realized the officer's uniform was gray. The jacket bagged on Prescott's lean frame, but he looked like a ragged Confederate from the field. The black wolf had changed to gray and could be released from the leghold trap.

"Prescott..." The name was out of his mouth before he gave it a thought.

"Jackson?"

"Cole. Captain Cole."

Prescott coughed with the same raking sound from his lungs that most other prisoners had. "Captain Cole..." He wheezed and caught his breath. "...you're just going to walk me out of here?"

"Something like that."

Prescott grinned in amusement. "We'll both be shot."

"Would you rather stay here? Now shut up. With that head full, you sound more like a Yank than usual." Wil grasped Precott's arm to lend support. "You must walk on your own when we meet guards. Can you do that much?"

"I think so." Prescott took a shaky step and sagged.

"He ain't going to make it, Captain Cole," a major hissed.

"He will if he wants to see his son."

His statement had the desired effect. More determined, Prescott's steps grew stronger.

A prisoner claimed the dead rat for himself in an overly loud voice and tugged on its tail.

A defiant voice responded.

A diversion—the prisoners were helping Prescott escape. As the two men squabbled, other soldiers gathered around, goading them further. The guards charged over to the angry-sounding mob.

At the top of the stairs, Prescott leaned on him and wobbled. He gasped and stopped to catch his breath.

"You need to keep moving, Prescott."

Prescott managed a weak laugh. "Is that an order, Captain?"

Ironic—the rank he had held when they had served together in New Mexico. "Consider it an order."

They reached the second floor. Prescott's gait faltered.

Wil gave him a shove and nearly sent him plummeting down the last flight of stairs. He latched onto Prescott's arm.

The guard who had met him on the way in appeared at the bottom. "Is there a problem, Captain?"

Wil's forehead broke out in a sweat, and he straightened. He *was* getting old. "My assistant surgeon has no stomach for this place. The smell sent him reeling."

The guard laughed. "Don't blame him none. These bluebellies are hogs."

Wil felt Prescott's muscles tense, but he drew away and stood under his own power. Prescott covered his mouth and coughed as if he might retch.

"Tell me your name, Private," Wil said, "and you'll appear prominently in my report to General Winder."

The guard snapped to attention with a salute. "Elisha Taylor, sir."

Wil returned the salute, and the guard resumed his station near the door. While he collected his weapons belt, the guard watched him closely. After two flights of stairs, they still had to get outside the prison and down the street to his waiting horse. With Prescott trudging along like a doddering old man, it could take them all night to walk two blocks, leaving the bloodhounds a very short trail to follow. They reached the door.

"Sir, haven't we met before?"

Without turning, Wil halted by the door. "I don't believe so."

Taylor stepped closer and regarded them curiously. "I'm certain of it."

Wil handed the guard his papers, but Taylor studied Prescott with a suspicious frown. Even under the dismal gas lighting, the guard would eventually recognize him as a prisoner.

"As you can see," Wil said, "everything is in order. Now if you don't mind, we need to be returning to camp."

Taylor examined the paperwork and returned it to Wil. "Sir . . ." He extended a hand for Prescott's paperwork.

Prescott lunged with both hands.

Reacting instinctively, Wil brought his pistol butt down on the guard's skull. Taylor toppled. But Prescott failed to release his stranglehold grip on the unconscious guard's throat.

Wil seized Prescott's arm and jerked him to his feet. "There's no time for this."

The fire hadn't faded from Prescott's eyes. "He's not dead."

"Move on, Lieutenant."

Prescott shook his head in defiance but obeyed the command. They were at the door again. It creaked on its hinges, and the guard stationed outside saluted. "Captain."

Feeling more like his old self, Wil grinned slightly. Safely out of the guard's sight, he grasped Prescott's elbow, supporting him down the street.

"Jackson—Wil, I want to thank you for stopping me before I killed him."

Wil nodded that he understood.

"But I still haven't figured out why you're doing this."

"Old times, Amanda's sake—take your pick."

Prescott's hand went to his chest. He halted to catch his breath. "The fact that we're brothers? I saw the ring on Alice's finger. You're the last one I expected to tie the knot."

Amused, Wil arched a brow. "Times change." He hustled Prescott to resume moving.

A pocked-faced soldier lingered by his horse—home guard. The private raised a pistol.

"Soldier, stand aside," Wil ordered.

The gun lowered slightly. "Sir, is this your horse?"

His suspicion was already aroused—not good. "My assistant surgeon had a little too much to drink and started wandering the streets. You can rest assure he'll be appropriately disciplined."

The boy glanced from him to Prescott, then back again.

"Private, I don't have time to waste. I believe I gave an order. Now stand aside."

The boy hesitated, but lowered the pistol and stepped away from the horse. Wil untied the bay and mounted. He extended a hand and helped Prescott on behind him. Prescott clutched his overcoat and sagged. A block away, Wil heard him laugh.

"If this don't beat all. I always knew you were loony, Jackson, but this is your best yet."

Exhilarated, Wil could feel it now as if he were holding a royal flush. They were almost home. "It's been a long time since I've played high-stakes poker," he admitted.

"This isn't about poker, Captain, and I want to thank you. Amanda—how is she?"

"As far as I know, she's fine."

"And my son?"

"His name is . . . Benjamin."

Arriving at Grace Street, Wil reined the bay toward the outbuildings behind the columned mansion. He helped Prescott from the horse's back, then slid from the saddle.

The back door opened, and Holly scampered down the steps. "I feared the two of you had been shot. Come in and warm yourselves by the fire."

Tempted by the invitation, Wil declined. She would expect more than a simple warming by the fireside. He reached into his pocket and withdrew a pass. "They'll hide you here until you're well enough to travel. This will get you through the city's defenses."

Prescott unfolded the pass. "I'll never be able to repay you, Captain."

"You can, by not calling me Captain."

"I meant . . ."

Wil held up a hand. "I know what you meant. We're not in New Mexico anymore, Sam."

Sam held out a hand. "True, in New Mexico the boys nicknamed you—Attila the Hun."

Wil grasped it and shook it. "I hadn't realized I left such a lasting impression. Do you recall the widow, Lucy?"

Sam shuffled his feet in the dirt.

"She was a mighty fine woman, don't you think?"

As Wil remounted the bay, Holly placed her arm through Sam's. Her lips formed a sly grin. "I'd like to hear some tales about New Mexico."

"Jackson . . . ," Sam grumbled.

"No need to be embarrassed. You were between wives. Now tell me that Attila the Hun would have seen to his men in such a manner."

Delighted, Holly clapped her hands.

Ignoring her, Sam straightened and saluted his thanks. "Godspeed, Wil."

Wil gathered the leather reins and returned the salute. A feeling stopped him cold. The game wasn't poker, but chess. One day they would meet—on the battlefield. But for now, honor was satisfied. He reined the bay around and kicked the horse into the Richmond streets.

After dropping off Sam's uniform, Alice had journeyed to the Confederate winter quarters south of the Rapidan River. The following day, she remained in seclusion under the pretense that she had spent the day with Wil. By nightfall, she was fretting. A simple plan—he'd take the train to Gordonsville, dispose of the Captain Cole disguise, and ride the remaining distance of eight miles. So where was he?

Already General Hill's aide had visited with a summons for Wil to meet with the corps commander in the morning. Fortunately, the aide had no qualms about her delivering the message.

Floorboards creaked beneath her feet as she got up from bed and paced. Thankfully, Wil had acquired a room in a farmhouse owned by two spinster sisters, not the makeshift huts that the soldiers constructed for winter. She would have scoured a rut in the dirt floor if he had done otherwise.

Beside the bed, she sat in the rocking chair and nibbled her fingernails to the quick. By the time her fingers were raw and bleeding, she got up and resumed pacing. He could have been caught while helping Sam escape. Or lying on some Richmond street—dead.

With sunrise a few hours away yet, the next person to request Wil's presence could be the general himself. Wil would want her to feign innocence about her involvement. Unable to lie to protect herself, she entertained the thought that perhaps Holly would have been a better choice after all.

She returned to bed and reached to the opposite side. The sheets were cold beneath her fingertips, and she drifted.

When Alice woke, her heart pounded. How long had she slept? Dawn hadn't arrived, and the farmhouse was quiet. So what had startled her?

She rose and peered out the door to the hall. *Wil* . . .

Clad only in a flannel nightdress, Alice scrambled down the stairs. No one. Chilled, she rubbed her arms. No hoof beats outside . . .

The last time she had felt this uneasy, Wil had been lying on the surgeon's table—more dead than alive. "Damn you, Wil Jackson, you had best have a good excuse. You're scaring the hell out of me."

With a silent prayer, Alice sat next to the window and waited. Five minutes became ten. What was she expecting to see in the darkness?

Wil was out there.

Half an hour passed.

She thought she saw something move—a dead leaf blowing in the wind.

Another hour—and the moon shed a little light.

A figure.

She blinked.

The shadowy form remained. It hobbled toward the house.

"Wil . . ." With no thought for the cold, she shot out the door to greet him. "Wil, I didn't think you would make it."

He groaned when she threw her arms around his neck. "Nearly didn't. My horse snapped a leg in a gopher hole. Had to walk most of the way from Gordonsville."

Thrown from a horse and traveling on foot in the dark, he down-played the incident. She touched his face to make certain he was real. His whiskers tickled beneath her fingers. "As long as you're here. What about Sam?"

"He should be out of Richmond in a few days."

Relieved, Alice seized his hand and nearly dragged him up the porch steps. A victim of her blind enthusiasm, he stumbled. Once inside the bedroom, she could finally see his rugged bearded face. His jacket was smudged with dirt and the right sleeve, torn, but he was very much alive.

After kissing deeply, they hustled beneath the bed covers. He tossed his clothes to the floor and shoved her nightdress above her thighs.

Merely a child in the ways of life, she was startled by his lack of ceremony. He barely had her cotton drawers open and was inside her. Somewhere between ecstasy and pain, she shrieked until her body ached and she lay dazed. Dear Lord, she had entered his world.

Her lips curved to an involuntary smile, then she remembered the farmhouse owners slept two doors away. "What if someone heard me?"

Rolling to her side, Wil chortled. "They'll think you have a considerate husband."

"But they're spinsters."

"Then they'll be envious."

As he gave her a good-night kiss, she gritted her teeth. "Wil . . ."

His breathing was even, and he was already fast asleep. She ran her fingertips through his whiskers. "Your actions are most unbecoming for an officer. I know, it's partly my fault. I should have realized long before now that you'll never be a gentleman." Satisfied with life, she kissed him on the cheek and nestled into his arm.

An hour later, Wil woke. The lamp flickered shadows on the wall. Asleep in his arms, Alice slumbered with a contented smile. Holly had been right. He wasn't meant to love. All too often, he had witnessed men pining for wives and sweethearts and scorned their weakness.

But on this night, nothing short of a Yankee brigade would have kept him from reaching her side. So why couldn't he say the words she longed to hear? "Alice, I no longer feel the need to kill the bastards."

She stretched her arms and sat up. "Did I hear right?"

"You did."

"Then you've finally accepted her death?"

He untied the deerskin cord from around his neck and dropped the Nez Perce medicine pouch into her hand. "It's not a matter of accepting her death, but how she died. Blood has surrounded much of my life, and I felt I should have found a way to save her. I reckon I always will."

Tears formed in her eyes, and she clutched the medicine pouch. "You said it was for luck."

"At Sharpsburg, it took a direct hit."

"You also survived this . . . " Alice touched the reddened scar on his chest, then tied the deerskin cord around her neck. "Maybe it'll bring me luck as well."

An odd feeling—knowing her for as long as he had. She had been nothing more than a girl when they had first met, and he could have never fathomed that as a woman she would raise his mind out of the murky abyss. All this time—she was the simple answer to what he had been missing. He drew her to him and tasted her mouth.

"As I recall you have an early-morning meeting with General Hill. If you don't get some sleep, how will you explain your exhaustion?"

"I'll say my wife kept me pleasantly occupied most of the night."

"You wouldn't."

Grinning wickedly, he lifted her nightdress over her head and tossed it to the side.

"I should have known better. You would. Then I had best make certain you speak the truth."

As she placed her warm legs on each side of him, Wil recalled his vow to never love another as he had Peopeo. But here he was caught in the otter's spell. With the gentle rocking of her hips, the medicine pouch swayed between her breasts, distracting him.

A soldier can't function like this. If he let emotion rule, others could die. He felt himself falling through a chasm. The darkness of his mind lingered, but the medicine pouch was a lifeline lifting him to the surface. "I love you, Alice."

Tears streaked her cheeks, and she fell gently to his chest, exhausted. "You don't know how long I have waited to hear you say that. Wil, did you mean it?"

He watched her as she moved to his side. "I'm not in the habit of saying things I don't mean."

An affectionate smile formed on Alice's lips, and she combed her fingers through his beard. "There's no reason to be afraid, Brigadier Jackson. I was well aware of what you were when I married you. You're a Confederate field officer first. I wish to God you weren't, but there's nothing I can do to change that fact. You won't react any differently on the battlefield."

He heard a soft choking sound at the back of her throat. In a moment of passion, he had lapsed. Breaking his vow, he had made the admission she longed to hear. With the spring campaign several months away, the soldier needed to regain control before then.

Chapter Sixteen

Too tired to hold the baby, Amanda rested on the bed. She unfastened her dress and let him suckle. His cries quieted, and she drifted.

"Amanda . . ."

Not Mama again. Running Amanda ragged with foolish demands, the old woman was sometimes as helpless as the baby. She hoped she never lived to be as old and ornery.

Footsteps scuffed outside her room. "Amanda!"

Wide awake, she shouted, "What is it, Mama? I'm trying to rest."

Mama stepped inside the bedroom. "There's a soldier outside."

"Blue or gray?" Covering her breast, Amanda hurriedly buttoned her dress.

"Gray."

Her hope evaporated. The soldier couldn't be Sam. "Mind the baby. I'll see what he wants."

He was probably begging for food, most likely, but she'd fetch the rifle in case he had come to rob them. Amanda sprinted down the stairs and peeked out the front window.

Sure enough—a man in gray tied a skinny nag to the poplar tree. An officer—the uniform bagged on his thin frame. Although he was stooped, there was something about his walk.

Sam? She shook her head. He couldn't be Sam—not wearing gray.

He trudged along the brick walk, and she caught a glimpse of familiar blue eyes. She squealed. "Sam!"

Amanda bolted out the door and nearly toppled him flat.

"Amanda, I wasn't certain I'd ever see you again."

Giddy, she danced up and down. "Sam, it really is you. But gray?"

"Long story. I'll tell you later. Let's get inside before someone suspects I'm a spy."

She seized his hand and brought him to the warmth of the parlor. "Mama, could you please fetch the children?"

Worn and haggard, Mama scowled. She shuffled off, grumbling something about damn Yankees.

Amanda hooked her arm through Sam's on the tapestry sofa. After a throaty cough, he said, "Wil tells me the baby's name is Benjamin."

She should have known Wil would make good his promise of getting Sam out of Libby. The gray uniform suddenly made sense. "I hope you approve of the name. I had forgotten until after I had named him that it was the same as Wil's son."

His brow furrowed, and he held up a hand. "Slow down, Amanda. I haven't any idea what you're talking about."

"Never mind, there's plenty of time for explanations."

As she wrapped her arms around him, she stifled a gasp. He wasn't just thin, but bony. His eyes reflected—*hell*.

"I'm luckier than most. I couldn't have survived without you to come back to."

Amanda grasped his hand. "I never gave up hope."

He began to kiss her, tenderly at first. His hand touched and fondled the way she liked, and she felt a longing that had been suppressed with his capture.

Mama cleared her throat. "I think you had best meet Ben before giving him a brother or sister."

Heat rose in her cheeks, and Amanda drew away. She took the baby from Mama and placed him in Sam's waiting arms. "I'd like you to meet the other man in my life—Benjamin Prescott."

A smile swelling with pride formed on Sam's lips, then he looked up. Rebecca sucked her thumb and clung to Mama's skirt.

"Say hello to your papa, Rebecca," Amanda said.

The toddler dug deeper into the folds of Mama's skirt.

"Rebecca . . ."

"It's all right, Amanda. It's been the better part of a year. How could you expect her to remember me?"

A brave front—she heard the ache in his voice. "You're here now. That's what's important."

His attention reverted to the baby, and his smile returned.

"He's got his papa's eyes."

He met her gaze. "Not a day went by without thinking of you. I'm sorry, Amanda."

Mama snatched the baby from his arms. "If the two of you are going to start that mush, I'll take the children to a proper environment." She padded to the kitchen with Rebecca in tow.

"Her bark is worse than her bite," Amanda said. "She loves her grandchildren very much."

"That may be, but I get the distinct impression she hasn't changed her mind about Yankees."

"True, but you didn't marry her. She's a cranky old woman no matter the circumstances." Amanda got to her feet and tugged on his hand. "The first thing we're going to do is put some meat on your bones."

With a laugh, he stood. "Amanda, not so fast."

His blue eyes flickered in a familiar, loving way, and she wrapped her arms around his neck with a kiss. Winter cold melted, and the day suddenly felt delightfully warm.

The April morning dawned with trilling robins and puffy white clouds. So much for spring showers. The least it could have done was spit rain, then the day would have matched her mood. Alice bent over the chamber pot and retched.

"If you're ill," Wil said, "you should postpone your trip."

They'd had many heated quarrels over whether she would remain in Richmond upon his return to the front, and she detected irritation in his voice. Unaccustomed to anyone disobeying his orders, he continually reminded her of that fact.

She rinsed her mouth and stuffed a dress into the trunk. "I'm going to Amanda's."

"Suit yourself." He held out a pistol. "But take this with you."

"So this is what it has come to?"

"The fighting is likely to come close. I'd feel better if you have it. Use it if necessary."

His voice remained lifeless and dull. He might as well have been speaking to a fence post, rather than fretting about her safety. The change had been gradual but dramatic.

After helping Sam out of Libby, he had been unusually talkative, telling her tales of his travels and Indian legends. In recent weeks as the general reemerged, so had the somber moods. For so long she had attributed his melancholy to the death of his first wife, but she had been wrong. They were caused by the war.

Alice curled her fingers around the gun and held it next to her. "I wonder if anyone ever fancied we would pay so dearly. Three years . . . Even you thought it would be over by now." She packed the pistol away. "Wil . . . "

His dark eyes remained distinctively cold.

No longer able to see behind his emotionless mask, she debated what to say. "I shall give Amanda your regards."

He watched her a moment. "Do that."

Finished packing, Alice closed the trunk. No goodbyes . . . No kisses of longing . . . Pressing a hand to her stomach, she thought she might be sick again. "Wil—"

"What is it?" he asked with impatience.

"Never mind."

The nausea faded, and she collected her cloak and went down the steps to the waiting carriage around back. Poker Chip stood tethered to the rail.

She rubbed the gelding's nose. "Take care of each other," she whispered.

The blue roan nickered, and the humid spring day suddenly seemed more like summer. Clouds were building. Maybe she'd get her wish after all. Not just spitting rain, but a thunderstorm. The crashing and booming reminded her of the guns. Guns that would soon be firing across the land, spilling their most precious lifeblood.

Her throat constricted. "Wil, I love you."

Barely breaking stride, he loaded her trunk on the carriage.

"The least you can do is acknowledge that you heard me."

"I heard you. We've already been over this."

"Have we? Sometimes you can be so damnable stubborn." She saw a brief flicker of amusement tug at the corners of his mouth.

"Alice—"

"No Wil, for a change you're going to listen to me. If you hadn't been so busy playing soldier, you would have noticed I've been sick all week—retching my guts out. It's not because I'm acting like some teary-eyed female. I'm . . . I'm going to have a baby."

His mouth opened as if to say something, but he closed it again.

Alice covered her mouth and snickered. "I think it's only the second time I've caught you at a loss for words."

His eyes narrowed in annoyance. "How long have you known?"

Impatience again—she wiped the smug grin from her face. "A few days."

"And you only saw fit to inform me now?"

"I should have told you sooner, but I thought the news might make your moods worse."

His rigid features softened. "I have been a bit of a bastard."

With a sheepish smile, she replied, "You won't get any quarrel from me."

Wil tugged on the chain of his pocket watch and checked the time. He replaced it and held out his hand. "We have a few minutes before you leave."

Fighting tears, she grasped his hand. "Then you're not upset?"

"I said I would cherish any child. I meant it."

As the upcoming campaign got nearer, the bravery she had fallen in love with was definitely her greatest fear. And like Amanda, she would birth alone.

After pacing the floorboards most of the warm May night with a feverish baby, Amanda tucked Ben in his crib. Having been ill earlier in the week, Alice remained confined to her bed. Between sitting with Alice and Ben, she could barely keep her eyes open. Without taking the time to change into her nightclothes, she slumped to the bed and dozed off.

A cannon rumbled in the distance and rattled the window.

Startled awake in the murky dawn, Amanda ran over to the window and clutched the curtain. *Sam . . .* She said a silent prayer as another blast shook the house.

From across the river, the guns of war had returned to Virginia.

"Amanda . . . " Frightfully pale, Alice, clad in a cotton nightdress, poked her head in from behind the door. "So you heard it too." Alice joined her at the window and asked in a low whisper, "Have you ever thought that they might meet?"

Amanda gripped the lace curtain tighter. *Sam and Wil meet on the battlefield?* No matter how much she wanted to pretend otherwise, it could happen. Sam and John had confronted each other during the opening battle at Manassas. "It's not good to think about such things."

"But it's possible."

Amanda bit her lip. Wil would kill Sam, or die trying. "I pray that it doesn't happen."

"Amanda—"

"Alice, you shouldn't be out of bed. You've been sick, and in your condition—"

"I'm not that far along. Besides, carrying Ben didn't stop you from nursing wounded soldiers." Alice rubbed her belly and padded over to the crib. "And he's beautiful." She leaned over and stroked Ben's cheek. "Amanda, he's awfully warm."

"He was running a fever last night."

Alice gaped as she lifted the baby's gown. "He's doing more than running a fever."

Amanda went over to the crib and sucked in her breath. Bright pink spots covered Ben's chest and neck. *Scarlet fever. No—keep calm.* Many illnesses caused rashes. She lowered the gown and scooped Ben into her arms.

He squalled.

"Alice, is there a doctor in Fredericksburg?"

"Confederate cavalry was there. They'd have a doctor."

But it had been two weeks since Alice had traveled through town. Chances were good that the cavalry had moved on. Another boom rattled the windows.

Amanda looked toward the sound. Near the guns there would be doctors. "Alice, if you can fetch his basket, I'm going to find a doctor."

"Amanda..." Alice grasped her arm. "You can't go out there."

"I don't have a choice. If it's anything more than a food rash, I need medicine." She exchanged a glance with Alice. How often had they smuggled medicine for others? Now her son was sick, and no medicine was to be had.

"Then I'll go with you."

"I need you to stay with Rebecca."

"Mama can look after her. You need someone to help you. I'll have Ezra saddle the horses while I change." Alice rushed from the bedroom.

Amanda rocked Ben in her arms, but his wails grew louder. She sat in the rocking chair and unbuttoned her dress, offering him a milk-laden nipple. He quieted down and suckled. Back and forth she rocked. Here, she had been jumping to all sorts of conclusions when he was simply hungry.

By the time, Alice returned with the baby's basket, Amanda finished nursing. She placed Ben over her shoulder and rubbed his back. "He's not sick, Alice. He just needed something in his tummy."

Alice pressed a hand to Ben's forehead. "He's running a fever."

"A baby usually feels warmer after eating."

"He's burning up, Amanda." Alice gathered him in her arms and gently placed him in the basket.

With a whimper he scrunched his legs to his belly and retched.

Terrified, Amanda covered her mouth. "Alice..."

Alice mopped up the mess with a handkerchief. "We'll find help." She clutched the basket and stood. Her face paled, and she placed a hand to her stomach.

Amanda seized the basket. "I won't have you risking your baby."

"Morning sickness. I'll be fine."

In need of Alice's support, she nodded. Outside, Ezra had the horses waiting at the end of the brick walk. Amanda tied the baby's basket to the gray mare's saddle and mounted. On the main road beyond the tree-lined lane, not a wagon rumbled or a person strolled. The guns grew steadily louder.

At Bank's Ford on the Rappahannock River, a handful of Yankee cavalry waited. A sergeant with a wispy moustache held up a hand. "No citizens are allowed to cross."

Amanda brought the mare to a halt. "My baby's ill. He needs a doctor."

He shook his head. "The reason doesn't matter. There's fierce fighting on the other side."

Guns rattled several miles away—near the Chancellor Inn, where the two armies fought the preceding year. "We won't go near the fighting. Please—"

"I wish I could help, but—"

"His papa's a Yankee," Alice chimed in.

The sergeant spat. "I don't give a damn if his father is General Grant himself. I have orders . . . "

Undeterred, Amanda said, "Lieutenant Colonel Samuel Prescott. Could you send him a message?"

He motioned to one of his men to check the basket. A private lifted the blanket and peered at Ben. "It's a baby. He looks sick."

The sergeant's stern expression softened, and he lowered his hat. "Sorry ma'am, but if Colonel Prescott is already engaged, only command messages have a chance of getting through. As I recall, there's a hospital on this side of the river. Near the fork of the two rivers—a blue house."

"The Monroes," Amanda replied with all hope fading. "That's nearly five miles away."

Sympathy crossed the cavalryman's face. "It's the best I can do."

A risk, but she must try. Amanda reined the mare around. "Thank you, kind sir."

"I wish I could do more, Mrs. Prescott. I have a son of my own."

"I appreciate your help, Sergeant. I hope this war ends soon, so you will be reunited with your family."

Squeezing the mare to a trot, Amanda passed the soldiers and followed the road's twists and turns. By the time they reached the hospital, it would likely be overflowing with wounded. Would a doctor have time to look at Ben? *Stop fretting.* Children outlived their parents, didn't they? She kicked the mare in the side for more speed.

Finally, a blue frame house came into view with a red flag hanging out front. Groans reached her ears before she saw the wounded on the ground.

Already dismounted, Alice tied the horses and was helping with Ben's basket. What would she have done without her sister's help? Carefully, they stepped over bloody bodies and went up the steps. From beside her, Amanda heard a scream.

Inside, more wounded sprawled across the floor. A soldier tugged on her skirt. "Water . . . ," he pleaded through powder-blackened lips.

"I have none."

Alice grasped her arm to keep moving. In the kitchen, a red river flowed from the table to the floor. The surgeon bent over a soldier's leg with a saw against flesh. She had no right asking for help.

Amanda turned away, and a strong hand gripped her elbow. "Ma'am, what are you doing here?"

She faced a bearded man in a blood-covered apron. "My baby is sick. I didn't know where else to go. His papa's a Yankee. I thought the doctor—"

"I'm the assistant surgeon. I'll take a look at him."

Amanda lowered the basket to the floor.

The surgeon kneeled and lifted Ben's gown. The scarlet spots had spread to his belly. "You said his father is with the Union?"

"Lieutenant Colonel Samuel Prescott."

The doctor palpated Ben's abdomen. The baby tucked his chubby knees to his body and cried. He examined Ben's throat, then lowered the gown. He stood. "Mrs. Prescott, you should notify the colonel at once. There's nothing I can do. Take the baby home and make him comfortable."

Nearly toppling, Amanda felt faint. "Make him comfortable . . . For a food rash?"

The doctor's face remained grim. "Scarlet fever, ma'am. I'm sorry."

Children died of scarlet fever. "That's not possible. I have another child at home."

The doctor searched through his medicine chest and withdrew a bottle of quinine. He handed it to Alice. "I really shouldn't be doing this, but since his father's a Union man . . . It will make the children comfortable."

There was that word again. When the wounded were feverish, she had spread cool cloths across their foreheads. Had that made them comfortable? And later, she had peered into their dying faces, whispering that everything would be all right. Had they died in comfort? With Frieda's help, Sam had survived. But Frieda was gone. Amanda felt life slipping through her fingers.

Chapter Seventeen

DURING THE PREVIOUS YEAR, the armies had fought in the same
woods—the Wilderness. Winter rains had washed skeletons in rotted blue to the surface, bringing the ominous sign of grinning skulls with them.

The brigade commander galloped down the line from Sam's right, waving his sword. With a yell, the regiment charged across a field. Survivors from the column in front of them had broken through the Rebel line. Opportunity was on their side, and they could crack the hole wide open.

Sam carried his pistol in one hand and motioned with his sword in the other for the boys to keep moving. As the regiment joined their comrades, the grassland gave way to woods. Lead filled the air.

Among brambles and dense undergrowth came groans and shrieks. Thick with smoke, the woods blazed. Muskets roared, and Rebels bolted. Sam shouted for the boys to pursue the retreating Confederates. The billowing cloud stung his eyes until he could barely see. He continued forward.

In a small clearing, the hazy veil lifted.

No Rebs.

Sam turned to re-form his line. No line either—only a handful of men. Equally confused, Sergeant Tucker joined him. Although there was nothing in front to fight, they couldn't withdraw. Retreat was the way of cowards.

He ordered the boys to form a battle line, and they marched forward—quietly and swiftly. Near the meadow's edge, they encountered a small group of Rebs crouched behind earthworks—with backs facing them and waiting for Union soldiers.

In the confusion of the woods, Sam's group of men had circled them. Again, they held the advantage. Sam lowered his sword, and the boys advanced with a bellow as if they numbered a thousand.

Caught unaware, some Rebs threw their muskets down and thrust hands into the air. Others fled through the woods. A lanky Reb raised a musket at the girl soldier. Jo hurtled forward and plunged her bayonet in the Reb's chest, pinning him to the ground.

Another filthy Reb readied his musket. Sam shoved his empty pistol in its holster and leveled his sword. As he leaped forward, the Reb turned, and the sword sliced through the back of his jacket. Without looking back, the Reb skedaddled.

A gray line formed.

Outnumbered by the enemy, Sam gave the order to collect their wounded and withdraw at the double quick. Determined not to return to Libby, he whispered an apology to Amanda. He'd choose death over returning to hell.

Reinforcements should have arrived by midnight. At 2 A.M., a courier brought a dispatch. Support would definitely relieve the brigade by morning. For now, the orders were to let the boys rest. Finished reviewing the battle-weary line, Wil regarded the message with concern. After a full day of heavy fighting, his line was spread thin and vastly outnumbered. If reinforcements were late again, the line would crumble.

He dismounted Poker and leaned against a tree, pulling his hat over his face. With Yankee lines only a few feet away, he overheard nasal murmurs. Pine smoke drifted his way, along with the stench of burning flesh. As in the previous year, the woods had caught on fire. But he was capable of sleeping anywhere, and the shrieks and groans of the wounded faded.

Someone shook his arm. In one swift move, Wil was on his feet and had the assailant pinned to the tree by the collar. He blinked—a staff officer. "My apologies, Captain Hanes. Someone should have warned you of my tendency to wake fighting." He let go of the trembling officer. "Is the First Corps up?"

Swallowing hard, Hanes straightened his jacket. "No, sir."

"What time is it?"

"Almost five, sir."

Nearly dawn—and with its arrival the Yankees would attack. He should have known better than to trust the repeatedly tardy General Longstreet to have his troops in position on time.

Wil called for the regimental commanders and mounted Poker, but the Yanks were already open firing along the battle front.

At a disadvantage, the boys faced the rising sun, and the glare camouflaged the blue shadows hidden in the murky forest. As seasoned soldiers, the men needed little rallying and returned fire. Bullets sliced branches. Blood splattered trees, and pieces of uniforms draped limbs. Inch by hard-fought inch, the line fell back.

Wil raised his sword and raced into the fray. Hit in the shoulder, Poker reared. Barely keeping his seat, Wil shouted for the men to hold their ground. No use—hardened veterans were turning tail and running. Blood streaked Poker's foreleg as Wil spurred the roan on, attempting to get behind the men and regain order.

On the main road, General Lee sat astride his gray horse. His eyes blazed. "My God, General," he shouted to Wil. "Is this splendid brigade of yours running like a flock of geese?"

Rarely bothered by reprimands, Wil was stung. His boys had given everything they had, and then some. "General, these men aren't whipped! They only want a place to form, and they'll fight as well as they ever did!"

Wil galloped on to restore some discipline to the confusion. Behind him, the Wilderness blazed. Another group of soldiers marched past. General Longstreet's First Corps had arrived.

The pine box rested on the grassy knoll beneath the expansive limbs of the old oak. With a final prayer, the preacher closed his bible, and Ezra lowered the tiny box to the red earth.

Alice dabbed her eyes. Oddly enough, Amanda didn't cry. Like Wil—she was burying her grief. No, in that regard, she suspected Amanda was stronger. Give her time. Burying her firstborn—she was in shock. She grasped her sister's elbow and led her down the hill to the farmhouse.

On the porch Amanda sat in the rocking chair and stared at the yard without blinking. She began to rock.

"Amanda, I'll check on Rebecca."

Alice patted Amanda's shoulder and heard a rumble. She looked to the sky. Thunderclouds were building, but she heard the guns. Although more distant than in recent days, cannon fire broke the solitude.

"Alice?" Amanda clutched her so tightly that fingernails dug into her forearm.

"I'm here, Amanda."

Green eyes searched—and finally found her face. Still Amanda shed no tears. "What shall I tell Sam?"

"You don't fret. I'll get word to him."

"Thank you, Alice." Amanda let go of her arm, and the blank expression on her sister's face returned. "Alice?"

"Yes, Amanda."

Back and forth, Amanda rocked. "Tell Wil I never meant to revive hurtful memories."

A lump formed at the back of Alice's throat. "He understands."

Amanda smiled in a peculiar sort of way. "Now you're going to have a baby. I used to have a baby. His name was Benjamin."

Was this how Wil had felt? Afraid to express her own mourning, Alice wanted to offer something—anything. Amanda needed her strength. With no words of comfort forthcoming, she wrung her hands. With the loss of his son, Wil had buried the pain and channeled it to something productive. She vowed other sons wouldn't die due to lack of medicine.

Captain Hanes had relayed the message to Wil that Alice was tending wounded. Bent over a yellow-haired boy, she whispered words of comfort. She wore black. *Prescott? Amanda?*

Careful not to step on prone forms, Wil negotiated his way over to her. "Mrs. Jackson."

Startled, she jerked her head up. "Wil, you gave me a fright."

"Alice, what are you doing here? It's not safe."

Straightening, she faced him with bloodshot eyes—like she had been crying. "Tell me where it is safe. How many mothers' sons need help?"

"Alice . . ." He grasped her clenched hands and led her from the farmhouse.

Outside—wounded stretched across the grounds, overflowing to the outbuildings. Agonized groans surrounded them as guns rattled in the distance. Another skirmish—*when would it all end?*

Past the line of wounded, he stopped by the sycamore tree where he had left Poker tethered. With his own wound causing discomfort, he waited a minute to catch his breath. "Alice, what has happened?"

"Poker?" She fingered lightly near the raw, but healing wound on the gelding's shoulder.

"He's a war horse. It's not his first wound, and it's unlikely to be his last." He hadn't meant to be sharp. Wil lowered his voice. "The horse is fine. He was only grazed."

Her arms went around his neck. "Oh, Wil."

As she pressed against him, he thought of the winter nights in Richmond—holding her and touching. *Not here.* Someone had died, and she was crying. *Don't pull away—as you did with Peopeo.* "Prescott?"

Brushing tears from her eyes, she stepped back.

He tugged a soiled handkerchief from his pocket and handed it to her.

She seemed unaware of the mud and dabbed her eyes. "I tried to get in touch with Sam. After all, I promised Amanda."

He gripped her arm. "Alice, what has happened?"

"Ben came down with scarlet fever . . ." There was a soft choking sound at the back of her throat. "He's dead, Wil. Amanda apologized for reopening old wounds."

He released her arm. *Benjamin.* Peopeo had held the lifeless body in her arms. *Their son was dead.* When he spoke, he struggled to keep his voice even. "How is Amanda holding up?"

"Not good."

"Then you should be with her."

"It's not that easy, Wil. Besides—Mama is with her. I've decided . . ." She shook her head. "No, I went to the Yankees, hoping I could find Sam. He's over there somewhere." She gestured in the direction of the booming guns. "He could be as stone-cold dead as his son."

"Alice," he snapped.

"The truth never used to bother you. Why now?" Alice straightened the folds of her mourning dress. "As a matter of fact, until a few moments ago, I didn't know whether you were alive or not. When I couldn't locate Sam, I tended their wounded. A kindly Yankee doctor gave Amanda some quinine. I had to repay him someway, then I got to thinking about our own boys . . ." She tugged a small bag from her sleeve and poured a trickle of white powder into his hand—morphine.

"Where did you get this?"

"When I tend their wounded, they don't question my reason for being there." Almost in a frenzy, her eyes widened and she whispered, "I slipped it in my petticoat—just like before."

Just like before. Like him—she *had* reacted. "The war has changed. We can never return to our old ways."

Her lips curved to a smile. "Never?"

"Alice, if you're caught, they could hang you."

"Like Peopeo."

He clenched his hands to keep from screaming. "They left her for me to cut down!"

She lowered her head. "Forgive me—that was unkind. But I can do some good, if I continue to help others."

The insanity from the loss of his family wasn't gone. Buried deep, it was still very much a part of him. He struggled to keep his mind from sinking into that horrible abyss and dropped his voice to barely a whisper. "Alice, if anything should happen to you, I have no reason to survive this goddamned war."

Her knowing smile returned. "Sometimes, you have a peculiar way of saying that you love me, but I accept it." Her arms went around him, and her forefinger slid through a hole in his right sleeve. She lowered her arms. "That's a bullet hole."

"Bullets do have a tendency to fly on a battlefield."

"Dammit, and you take it so lackadaisically."

"I wasn't hit. The boy beside me died."

"When will it end?"

The war was going badly. Hadn't he sworn an oath to the Union? But he had sided with his state instead. Since he rarely returned to South Carolina, he often wondered why. From the beginning, he had known it was a lost cause. "Alice, promise me that you won't run any more supplies."

She glanced beyond him at the wounded. "I wanted to help."

"Then be with Amanda. She needs you now more than ever."

"What about Sam? Someone should tell him about Ben."

"I'll send a courier under a flag of truce."

"A courier seems impersonal."

Wil shrugged that it was the best he could do. After a farewell kiss, he watched Alice as she turned to leave. Never knowing if each time might be their last parting, he nearly called after her. There was nothing he could do to change that fact—not until this foolish war was over. But he could seek permission to deliver the message to Sam personally. Powell Hill had also lost a child and would be sympathetic.

He mounted Poker and rode to the general's headquarters.

With a sick pallor from recent illness, Powell remained seated behind a camp desk. "What can I do for you, Wil?"

Benjamin—both boys were dead. "My wife has informed me that her sister's infant son has died."

What little color remained in Powell's face drained.

"The boy's father doesn't know. I'd like to request permission to meet him under a flag of truce and notify him."

"Isn't your wife's sister married to Lieutenant Colonel Prescott?"

Wil had a gnawing in his gut about Powell's line of questioning. "Yes, sir."

"Didn't Prescott also serve under you as a second lieutenant in New Mexico?"

The feeling intensified. "Yes, sir."

"General . . ." Despite being weak, Powell stood, and an edge of impatience crept into his voice. "I met your former lieutenant in January when I toured Libby."

Although they had been friends for years, Powell would be unable to overlook a transgression of this magnitude. His errand of mercy had gone awry, and he'd most likely be facing a court-martial and a firing squad.

"Wil, I'm not going to ask the next obvious question. If Old Jack were here, I'd be required to."

Stonewall—dead and buried for over a year now—had carried out his duty to the letter.

"But I can't risk losing a brigade commander. Not now, and certainly not like this."

"Then may I ask your intent, sir?"

Powell's eyes blazed, and he slammed a fist to the desk. "If we both survive, I shall ask at the war's end and take appropriate action then."

Both had risked their careers by resigning their commissions, and honor wouldn't have let Wil choose any other course of action. Sam would have died in Libby. A loyal Virginian, Powell was not ready to hear that sort of truth.

"Return to your duty."

As Wil saluted, he had an odd sense that the court-martial would never take place. Outnumbered and outgunned by the Yankees, Richmond and the Confederacy would likely fall in a matter of months.

Chapter Eighteen

AFTER WIL HAD LEFT the general's headquarters, Powell had sent a message granting him permission to meet with Sam. Stripped of honor due to an unasked question, he retained his rank. He would rather have lost it. With a little sweat, a man could work his way through the ranks. But there was only one way to regain honor—die in a glorious battle charge. But what of Alice and the unborn child? His shame would spread onto them.

Benjamin ... Wasn't he also supposed to be shamed for begetting a half-breed son? No shame—only sadness. After all these years, he grieved.

Although his courier carried a white flag, the nervous pickets had nearly shot him. With a salute, Captain Hanes brought his horse to a halt beside Wil. "Sir." Out of breath, Hanes handed him a dispatch. "The Yankee colonel's reply."

"Thank you, Captain." Unfolding the note, Wil recognized Sam's handwriting, agreeing to a meeting under a flag of truce. He tugged on the chain of his watch and checked the time.

Army maneuvers were no longer like chess—or poker, but something between screaming children. The Yanks threatened Richmond, and *tag— you're it.* The Confederates would make a countermove.

He handed the note to Hanes and let out a weary breath. "See to the details."

"I already have, sir. The colonel informed me of his reply. He waits for you at the bottom of the ridge. I will accompany you." Hanes raised a white cloth.

Wil swore the young and brash captain had begun to read his mind. He wondered if the aide's enthusiasm would be dampened by the fact that his recommendations for promotion carried little influence.

"Very well." Wil returned his watch to his pocket and eased Poker to a trot.

At the bottom of the ridge, Sam and an aide waited by a flag of truce. Once on open ground, any wrong move could be misconstrued and result in either side opening fire. He cued Poker to a walk and passed the Confederate picket. Some of the boys watched the enemy while others engaged in idle chatter. Concealed behind earthworks, a blue line waited on the other side.

Urging the gelding on, Wil moved between lines into the open. For some reason, he thought of Peopeo. He heard her voice. *Why now?* The last time he had this feeling, he had nearly died.

Wil halted Poker beside Sam's red stallion. "You appear to have regained some weight since our last meeting,"

Sam acknowledged him with a nod of his head. "I have you to thank, Captain."

Captain again. In New Mexico, they had been so much younger, with no concept of the choices honor would force them to make. His palms were sweating. Faced with the same decisions, he wouldn't change anything. Honor would have prevented him from siding with the Union—or standing idle and not helping Sam escape Libby.

Poker detected his nervousness and pawed the ground. "Sam, I have bad news. Your son is dead."

"My . . . " Sam's face paled, and he swayed in the saddle as if he had been struck by a Minié bullet. "How?"

Wil lent a hand to keep him from falling. "Scarlet fever."

His brows furrowed in pain. "Amanda? How is Amanda?"

And honor would prevent Sam from going to Amanda when she needed him most. "Alice is with her. Sam, I understand how you feel. I've buried one myself."

Tears formed in the other man's eyes, which was more of a reaction than he had been able to give when Benjamin had died. Yet, he knew Sam was holding back.

Sam glanced to the Confederate lines, and a wild gleam entered his eyes. He clenched the red stallion's reins.

"Don't even think about it. The pickets are on edge, and you wouldn't be the only one to die."

"I didn't think you were afraid of death, Jackson."

"I'm not, but what about our aides? Should they be dragged into your personal hell? Amanda has already lost her son. There's no reason for making her a widow too."

Sam relaxed the grip on his reins, and Wil heard Peopeo again. She was no longer resorting to her halting English, but her native Nez Perce tongue. Many years had passed since he had last spoken the language, and the meaning of her words were lost.

A Yankee soldier moved from behind the earthworks with a message.

The hand of death—Wil felt it near. "I expect you to take proper care of Amanda. She and her sister are much alike. They are women to be cherished. If you do not, I shall meet you in hell to settle the score." He waved to his aide and reined the gelding around.

"Jackson!"

A shove from behind sent him reeling from the saddle, and he heard gunfire. He thudded to the ground to shouts for the pickets to hold their fire.

Numb from the fall, Wil felt a strong pair of hands go under his arms. Sam helped him sit up, and a dead Yank sprawled near his feet. The messenger had been nothing more than a damned coward trying to shoot him in the back under a flag of truce.

Wil got to his feet, and Poker swayed. With a groan, the old war horse sank to his knees and toppled to his side. Legs flailing, the blue roan struggled to get up. After all of the battles they had survived—*not like this.*

"Sir—orders?"

Wil blinked, and Captain Hanes's face came into focus.

Blood bubbled from Poker's nostrils, and he gasped for breath. "A war horse deserves some dignity," he said to Sam.

Sam nodded. As Wil drew his pistol, he heard Peopeo. The gelding was all that remained—from a spotted mare known as Appaloosa.

He took aim.

Along with Peopeo's voice came a toddler's laughter—Benjamin.

He fired.

Poker snorted, then lay still.

He dropped the pistol to the ground, and the voices faded.

Wil looked up. Dashing unseen by the pickets, a doe flagged her tail at a trailing fawn to follow. With the grace of a dancer, she leaped a tree felled by battle and vanished into the woods.

Barely had Alice returned to the farm when she found Rebecca had taken ill. In her grief, Amanda had grown mechanical in caring for the child, and Alice scrambled a fast return to the Yankee hospital. Pleas for medicine fell on deaf ears. Defeated, she left the hospital tent and passed the medicine wagon.

One last time. Under the circumstances, Wil would forgive her for disobeying his orders, and she retraced her steps.

As she passed wounded and sick soldiers, Alice offered a kind word, ladled out water, and changed dressings.

Beside a strawberry-blond boy, she pressed a hand to his forehead. Sick with fever, the poor boy was burning up. Taking advantage of the opportunity, she sought a doctor for some quinine. After lacing the bitter liquid with molasses, she bent down and helped the boy drink.

"Isn't it peculiar that a Confederate brigadier's wife would help Union wounded?" asked Holly Prescott.

Straightening, Alice stood and faced her. As always, Holly's black hair was pinned in a neat chignon at the nape of her neck.

Holly's eyes danced, and she folded her arms across her chest. "Are the doctors aware of your husband's occupation?"

"I thought I could help."

"In other words, no. Did Wil send you?"

Should she tell her the truth? Holly wasn't gullible enough to believe a lie. "Wil doesn't know that I'm here. I require medicine for Rebecca. Neither army believes civilians need medicine as long as there are suffering soldiers, but Ben has already died."

Holly's brows furrowed. "Sam told me."

Sympathy? From Holly Prescott? Had she misjudged the woman? With her breath quickening, Alice shuddered. "Are you going to have me arrested?"

Holly's hands went to her hips, and a smirk appeared on her lips. "I have nothing to gain by turning you in. Unless, of course, you think

Wil would come dashing to your rescue." She shook her head. "Even Wil's not dimwitted enough to play war hero against thousands of Yankees for the sake of a bed partner."

"How dare..." Alice raised a fist in protest, blinked, and lowered her hand. Though her tongue was biting, Holly *wasn't* going to have her arrested. "What my husband ever saw in you, I shall never know."

Holly's grin widened, and she opened her mouth to answer.

Alice held up a hand. "I also prefer to remain ignorant in that regard. Holly, Rebecca may die. I don't know how Sam is faring, but Amanda will likely up and die herself if she loses another child."

"I'll help. Follow me."

They passed through rows of wounded soldiers. Few had cots, but unlike in the Confederate hospitals, most men had blankets or a bed of straw to lie on. In the day's heat, flies buzzed around festering wounds.

Alice's stomach churned, and she thought she might retch. Outside, several yards from the medicine wagon, she felt lightheaded.

Holly lent a supporting hand. "You're looking rather pale. Wait here."

With the rough travel of recent days, she could be endangering her own baby. She rubbed her belly—only a matter of time before she could no longer conceal her condition. What sort of rude retort would Holly utter if she knew?

Holly strutted to the wagon, and sidled up to the assistant surgeon. She shimmied into the man's arms.

A crooked grin appeared on his face.

Holly shoved a tin, then a bottle into her dress pocket without the doctor noticing. She pressed her hips against the unsuspecting man in a shameless manner.

In broad daylight, no less. Alice's hand flew to her collar. Dear Lord, she *knew* what Wil had seen in Holly. No mortal man possessed the resolve to resist such temptation.

More medicine vanished, and Holly stepped away from the man's embrace. He grasped her arms and drew her back. Holly popped the side of his face with an open hand.

The surgeon bellowed a string of curses as Holly strolled away. She approached Alice. "Where is your horse?"

"Over here." Alice pointed. "Holly, you took a dangerous risk."

"Will the little girl ever grow up? Men are very simpleminded. Give them the impression that they'll get a good roll in the hay, and they can't do enough for you." Holly winked. "But then, I bet you've already absorbed that little trick."

Alice felt her cheeks warm. "I have no need to resort to such practices."

"My, my," Holly clucked with a mocking laugh, "it appears wedded bliss has changed Wil. Only time will tell if one woman can keep him suitably entertained."

It was best to ignore such rude remarks. What's more, if it suited her fancy, Holly was the sort to change her mind about helping Rebecca.

Once beside Amanda's gray mare, Alice grasped the saddlebags.

Holly checked over her shoulder to see if they were being watched, then tucked the medicine into its pockets.

"I shall find a way to repay you, Holly."

Holly squeezed her hand. "It's for my niece. Be careful. General Sheridan's cavalry is roaming the countryside. I've heard frightening stories of them terrorizing Southern citizens."

Common ground—Alice never thought she'd find it with such a self-centered woman. The war had a way of changing most people's hearts. She tied the saddlebags behind the saddle. "I appreciate the warning."

"Alice . . ." Holly's brows knitted together, and she gripped Alice's arm. "A Yankee soldier nearly killed him when he met Sam under a flag of truce."

Alice's heart thumped. "Wil?"

"Don't fret. He's fine. Sam repaid the debt of helping him escape Libby. The coward hit Wil's horse instead."

Alice choked back a sob. Poker Chip . . .

"Oh dear, don't tell me you're going to get blubbery over a horse. I thought you'd be relieved it wasn't your husband."

"Is Poker . . . ?"

"Dead? Afraid so. Wil put the poor beast out of his misery."

Poker—gone. Among all of the dead and wounded, she felt silly crying over a horse and brushed back the tears. With no time to grieve over Poker, she mounted Amanda's mare and kicked the gray in the side. The only important thing now was delivering medicine to Rebecca.

* * *

Two days had passed without rations. Nothing to eat, but Sam had earned his silver eagles. He focused the field glasses. Someone in the army with a sick sense of humor must have thought he could dine on the promotion.

Sunlight glinted off something shiny in the woods. The reflection wasn't one object, but two bronze cannon.

"Anything of interest?"

At the sound of Holly's voice, he held his tongue that she had no business being at the front. "Wait a minute, Holly. You'll see something interesting."

Both guns boomed, and shells whined over their heads.

Holly's eyes widened in sheer terror, and she bolted. "I think I'll return to the hospital."

Sam slapped his hands to his sides and nearly choked laughing. Tears entered his eyes. *God, he was gone. His son was dead.* Surrendering to his grief, he dropped to his knees and wept.

A gentle hand went to his shoulder. "Sam . . ."

Holly again. Forcing the image of a soldier to the forefront, he wiped the tears and stood. "Forgive me. That was cruel, but you have no business being here. It's too dangerous." Why was he suddenly being sympathetic to Holly?

"Rebecca is ill."

"Rebecca?" *Not his daughter too.* "She can't be sick."

"Alice was here. The doctors wouldn't give her any medicine, so I helped her appropriate some."

For the first time, he truly understood what Amanda had been trying to tell him all along. With medicine scarce, men wearing gray died who shouldn't have. The shortage was worse among the civilians, and Ben had died as a result. "Thank you, Holly."

"I warned her about the cavalry."

The cavalry? For some reason, he was slow to think. General Sheridan's men looted and burned Southern citizens' worldly goods. "I'll send a scout to help her get through."

Rebel shot whistled overhead, and Holly instinctively ducked.

"By the time you hear it, it's too late. Now if you've said all you've come to say, skedaddle to the rear where it's safe."

Holly gathered her skirts together.

"Holly...Can you check where our rations are? I've got some mighty hungry boys who are likely to start slaughtering mules soon."

With a nod, she hustled off.

Sam crouched behind the breastworks as another stray shot sailed past. Among the boys, he heard grumbles for food and water. He gave the order for a private to collect canteens and fetch water. Still no rations arrived. How long before they'd be trapping vermin—as he had in Libby?

"Sergeant..."

The girl soldier straightened, but didn't look up from her musket sight. She fired.

A Reb hit the ground, and she lowered the musket. Cold and efficient, she was one of the most lethal soldiers he had.

"Jo, I need your help."

"Yes, sir."

"My daughter's ill. Take my horse..." He went on to explain the situation.

Gunfire shattered the night. Alice brought the nervous mare to a halt. Holly hadn't lied. The woods crawled with Yankees, and she had limited her travel to the cover of darkness. Residents were kind enough to loan her a room or a barn to sleep in. The gray's ears twitched. Squeezing the mare forward, she spotted a flicker of light on the road ahead. *Morning*... She had best seek shelter.

In the warm breeze, she smelled smoke along with the acrid odor of burning wood. The light expanded, and she heard a loud whoosh.

Panicked screams shouted above crackling flames. It wasn't morning light. Yankees were burning a Southern family out of their home.

Alice jerked the mare around, urging her to a gallop. Hoofbeats charged after her.

The mare stumbled as a bullet whistled past her ear. A narrow miss. Clutching the gray's mane in one hand, she slung the saddlebags over her shoulder with the other. She slowed the mare and slid from her back. Without missing a beat, Alice slapped the mare on the rump and ran for the cover of the woods.

The troopers raced past, and she let out an uneasy breath. Alice pulled the pistol Wil had given her from the saddlebags and headed deeper into the forest. Brambles caught her skirt.

From the road, a trooper yelled. They must have caught up with the mare.

Stumbling through the woods, she stopped to listen. Something slithered near her feet. A copperhead or black snake most likely—she struggled to keep from screaming. Her heart pounded wildly, and she could only hear her own ragged breathing in the darkness.

With a silent prayer, she aimed the pistol toward the road.

Horses clattered past. The troopers must not consider her worth their effort. If the mare had indeed been captured, daylight would be soon enough for them to flush her out.

Her abdomen ached. Exhausted, Alice sank to the ground with the pistol tucked beneath her arms.

Wil had told her about nights of sleeping on guns. Was he doing that now? Waiting for morning light, so some Yankee had yet another opportunity to make her a widow? What would *these* Yankees do to her if they found her? If she discarded the medicine, they'd likely be content with stealing the mare and leaving her be. But Rebecca might die.

Recalling the snake, Alice sat up. Rebecca's life was at stake. No matter the cost, she must keep moving. She flung the saddlebags over her shoulder and got to her feet—a little unsteadily at first.

Trudging along, she followed the road and wished she had brought a shawl to break the morning chill. As she traveled, the sky lightened. Like sparkling fingers, the sun's rays poked through the leaves, and a thrush in a nearby tree announced the new day with a song.

Morning gave way to afternoon, and the day grew hotter. Her throat was parched. Why hadn't she thought to grab the canteen before bailing out? With each step, the saddlebags grew heavier.

Muddled and alone with her thoughts, she kept moving. Her mind wandered. Until the battle of Fredericksburg, she had believed in war's glory. The loss of her home forced her to realize otherwise.

The clip-clop of hooves made her look up. A lone red horse came into view, and she sought the cover of a gnarled oak tree, taking careful aim with the pistol.

The rider wore gray—or faded blue. Unable to tell which, Alice called out, "Confederate or Federal?"

"Depends on who's askin'?" came a high-pitched, wheezy voice.

The blood-red chestnut looked like Sam's horse, and the voice . . . Alice lowered the gun. "Jo?"

"Mrs. Jackson . . ." With a broad grin the girl soldier tipped her hat. "Been lookin' for you for nearly a day. Sam sent me."

Breathing out in relief, Alice tucked the pistol in the saddlebags and stepped into the open. "Sam?" Holly must have been an informant again—only this time for her benefit. Over by Red, she patted the stallion's velvety nose. The horse nickered softly. "How is he?"

Her gaze hardened, and Jo uncapped a canteen, handing it to her. "Fine. Been doin' his share of dodgin' Rebs' bullets lately."

The insinuation wasn't lost as Alice quenched her thirst. "I meant how is he taking the loss of his son?"

Jo tossed the saddlebags across Red's withers.

"Careful—that's valuable medicine."

"I kinda figured that." Jo replaced the canteen on the saddle and extended a hand, pulling Alice on the stallion's back behind her. She placed her arms around the girl soldier's waist. "The colonel don't bitch none, but he's grievin'. I hope his mind don't wander at the wrong moment and get him killed."

Unable to miss Jo's dedication to Sam, Alice couldn't damn the girl soldier for her loyalty. "You're helping me because of him?"

Jo cued the horse forward. "Mostly—but you helped me when I was down. Kept my secret. I owe you for that, but it ain't worth Sam riskin' his career tryin' to keep you outta Sheridan's path."

The girl soldier's tone had turned biting. Sam must not have told her why she had risked smuggling supplies again. "Sometimes there is more to life than a career."

"Durin' war, men don't think of much else, 'cept bein' with women— the more the merrier."

Before she could respond, Alice felt a sharp stab in her abdomen. "Jo, I need rest."

Jo reined the stallion from the road down an overgrown lane to an abandoned shack. "We'll rest 'til evenin'. I'll see you to your sister's. After that, you're on your own." She brought Red to a halt and jumped from his back, then helped Alice.

As Alice's feet touched the ground, her knees buckled.

Jo lent an arm for support. "You're sick."

Alice met the girl soldier's gaze. "I'm . . . in a family way."

The girl soldier gave a low whistle. "You don't say."

Recovered slightly, Alice jerked her arm free of Jo's grip. "I don't need your coddling." Alice seized the saddlebags and went up the shack's rickety steps. Once she was past the door hanging off its hinges, the pain returned.

"Sit down."

Feeling as if she might swoon, Alice obeyed and sat on the dirt floor.

"Are you bleedin'?"

"I don't think so." Jo lifted her skirt, and Alice snapped the hem from the girl soldier's hands and hugged it against her knees. "What on *earth* do you think you're doing?"

"Checkin'."

Alice's jaw dropped.

"This ain't no time to be playin' no role of a prissy lady. If you're bleedin', you'll likely lose the young 'un. 'Sides—you had to have done more than lift your skirt to get in this fix."

Alice narrowed her eyes, but let go of the hem. "Where did you learn so much about having babies?"

Jo raised the skirt. "Ma had eight—only three of us lived. You gotta spread your legs some so I can see."

Alice hesitated, but she spread her legs.

Jo lowered her skirt. "Ain't no bleedin', but you gotta be careful."

Still embarrassed, Alice tugged on her collar. "I appreciate your concern, especially with your feelings toward—*Rebs*."

"Ain't nothing personal, but I don't like gettin' shot at."

"I seriously doubt anyone forced you to join the army."

Rolling a cigarette, Jo squatted in the corner where she could monitor both doors. "Ma needs the money. Wasn't born privileged, like you."

"And thanks to Yankees invading our land, we've lost nearly every-thing we own."

Jo struck a match to the cigarette and inhaled deeply. "Still got a man to support you."

"One that you'd just as soon see dead. As you may recall, you were personally responsible for my sister's first husband's death."

Smoke plumed from Jo's nostrils. "Killed lots of men. Bet your Reb husband has too."

Even though his action had saved her life, Wil had shot the Yankee through the head. The dead boy's face would haunt her to the end of her days. "Your situation must have been desperate to lead such a life."

Jo cracked a smile. "See, we ain't so different. Wouldn't you have done the same if it'd saved your nephew?"

Pretend to be a man? "Growing up, I was a bit of a tomboy, but I wouldn't know how to act like a man." Alice placed a hand against her belly. "Even if I knew where to begin, I don't think I could hide it for long."

Jo snorted. "I was discovered the first week in camp. Kinda hard to hide when sleepin' three men to a tent. The boys agreed to keep my secret in exchange for favors."

"Favors?"

The girl soldier took a drag on the cigarette. "Don't go flittin' those lashes in your innocent belle routine." Jo tossed the cigarette butt into the crumbling fireplace and straightened her faded jacket. "The first time I didn't even know what they were doing—only that it hurt."

Alice thought she saw tears. "I'm sorry you had to endure that."

Jo laughed again. "Joke's on them. I outlived 'em all."

Afraid to ask the obvious question, Alice had to know the truth. "Why has Sam kept your secret?"

"I ain't never laid with him if that's what you're askin'. He found himself a high class *lady*. And I can always gauge his mood as to how long it's been since he last saw your sister."

"I pity you, Jo. Your experience has been trying, but I happen to know that Sam and Amanda are very much in love."

"I reckon so, and you're right smart to have latched onto a brigadier. He ain't bad lookin' neither. 'Sides . . ." Jo shrugged. "Once they get their trousers off, they all look the same."

Alice sputtered, and both women doubled over in hysterics. Breathing deeply, she waited until she was calm again to speak. "Each day, I fret. I worry I shall receive word that he's dead."

Sympathy crossed Jo's face. "He'd fret about you too, if he knowed you was smugglin' again."

The girl soldier was right. Women often noticed things that men missed. While Wil wasn't the sort to say so in words, she saw it in his eyes—when he had found out where she had got the morphine.

"I was smuggling supplies because my niece is sick. I can't let my sister and Sam face the death of another child." Alice stood and put her arms around Jo.

Uncomfortable with the gesture, the girl soldier kept a stiff, soldierly stance, but her muscles gradually relaxed. Finally, Jo reciprocated the gesture. "I reckon I've played the part of a man so long, I forgot what it was like to have a woman friend."

Alice stepped back. Suddenly sensing a foreboding, she went to the doorway and looked outside. "We need to be leaving."

"Be safer if we wait 'til dark."

"Rebecca may not have that long." All appeared quiet as the red stallion grazed on green shoots of spring, but someone or something watched them. Then she spotted it—a sleek tawny shape padded through the woods. Not a threat, but an omen. Alice pointed for Jo to look.

Jo drew her pistol but shook her head. "Don't see nothin'."

"It was a . . . " Alice clasped the Indian medicine pouch around her neck. Wil had said it was for luck. Before now, she had only half-believed the Indian legends. " . . . a mountain lion."

"In these woods?" With a sharp whistle, Jo lowered the pistol. "Now I know you've gone plumb loony. Ain't no mountain lions 'round here for years."

"He's watching over us and leading the way."

The girl soldier's brows knitted together in confusion. "Who?"

"The animal spirit." Alice returned to the shack and snatched the saddlebags from the dirt floor. "Jo, I don't expect you to understand, but we must leave—*now*."

"No need to get your drawers knotted."

Once beside the red stallion, Alice untied him from the post. Jo joined her as she placed the precious cargo over the horse's withers.

She mounted up, and Jo climbed on behind her. Reining Red around, she cued him to a trot down the overgrown lane. Alice clicked her tongue to the horse for more speed.

"You could still lose that young 'un if you ain't careful," Jo reminded her.

"Rebecca's life is at stake."

After traveling two miles, a downed oak barricaded the road. The tree's end was neatly cut and hooves of many horses were stamped in the dirt—Yankee cavalry. She must choose her path wisely.

Alice reined Red from the road and skirted the tree. She heard hoofbeats. Jo drew her gun. With a silent prayer that Red wouldn't cry out, Alice brought the red stallion to a halt in the dense foliage.

A Yankee column traveled by. A trooper in blue spurred a gray mare in the side.

"That's Amanda's mare," Alice whispered.

"Not anymore. She belongs to Union cavalry."

"They take and burn . . . They won't be satisfied until all of us are dead."

Jo squeezed her arm. "Not all Yankees are like that. Let's get the medicine to your niece."

With resignation, Alice waited for the cavalry to pass. She guided Red past the fallen tree before returning to the road. As they got closer to Amanda's farm, Red's ears pricked. Familiar with the route, the stallion pranced. By the time shadows grew long, they entered the tree-lined lane.

In the farmyard, Ezra sprinted to greet them, waving and wearing a broad grin. Jo jumped from the red stallion's back, and Alice lowered the saddlebags to her. Ezra grasped her waist and helped her dismount. Blinding pain. With a shriek, Alice clutched her abdomen.

Chapter Nineteen

Near Petersburg, Virginia
June 1864

FOR THREE DAYS, THE SOUND of Federal guns pounded Petersburg. General Grant had shifted his focus from the vicinity of Richmond to the major supply lines south of the capital. Red dust and the baking sun took their toll as the Confederate column marched along the Petersburg pike.

At one time, Wil would have taken pride in heading up the brigade. *Only a matter of time before the South crumbled.* It wasn't good to think about such things. Duty came first. As best he could, Powell Hill kept an eye on him. Trust and friendship were broken, but he'd make certain the general would have no cause to complain.

Buzzards floated overhead. A bad sign—men were dying on their feet. Wil uncapped his canteen and swallowed dust. Choking, he spat the grit out of his mouth.

A freckle-faced private, looking more like a haggard scarecrow, offered his canteen.

Grateful, Wil accepted. With water scarce, he gulped only a swallow and returned the canteen, thanking the boy for his thoughtfulness.

Poker's replacement, a chestnut mare courtesy of a Yankee prisoner, plodded on. Wil's hand went to his chest. The march had begun at three in the morning, and the old wound was acting up something fierce. He sagged in the saddle.

"General . . ."

Wil straightened, saluting General Hill.

Powell had protruding cheekbones and held a gaunt weariness about him. He looked in worse shape than himself. Two aides flanked him. "If you're ill, you can ride in an ambulance."

"No, sir, I'm fine."

"Wil..." Powell halted his gray stallion even with the mare, so the aides wouldn't overhear. "I know why you're pushing yourself."

"Because there's a job to be done, sir."

For the first time since the unasked question, anger faded from his old friend's eyes. "Then carry on, General." With a salute, Powell reined the stallion around and the two aides trailed after him.

Guns grew louder, and the column would reach Petersburg soon. By mid-afternoon, they entered the streets. Women, children, and Negro servants came running to greet them with a cheer.

Wil waited for orders to position the brigade and dismounted. He leaned against the mare for support.

A kindly woman with a servant carrying a wood bucket offered him a metal dipper. Cool water at last—he quenched his thirst. Revived slightly, Wil thanked her, and she gave a cordial smile. Her auburn hair reminded him of Alice as she passed the dipper to the next man. He wondered if a spitfire lurked beneath the gracious hostess image.

Damn, he was simple. Fighting a war couldn't change the way things were meant to be. Only once had he said the words that she needed to hear, and he had dismissed them as weakness. It wasn't weakness—but a gift of strength. His was a slow world. Unafraid of the consequences, he could finally admit it to himself. He was in love.

Confined to bed for nearly a month, by some miracle Alice hadn't lost the baby. Over the past fortnight, she had regained her strength and was feeling like she might go out of her head.

Recovered from her bout of scarlet fever, Rebecca charged into the room with a delighted squeal.

Dressed in black from head-to-toe, Amanda poked her head in the room and spoke in a monotone voice, "I'm sorry she disturbed you."

"She didn't disturb me, Amanda. I enjoy her company."

Through lackluster eyes, Amanda frowned. Nothing helped her sister's mood, and with her own condition becoming noticeable, Alice feared Amanda wept secretly in her bedroom. The child she had so desperately wanted was buried on the hill.

Amanda held out an insistent hand to Rebecca. "It's no call to forget her manners. Come along, Rebecca."

"Amanda..." She squeezed Amanda's arm, but her sister's gaze remained empty. Alice let go. "I'll be out in a minute."

By the time she finished dressing, she found Amanda on the porch, rocking in the morning sun, totally oblivious to three soldiers in butternut leading a string of horses in the farmyard.

"Ma'am." Ragged and lean, a corporal sporting a scraggly beard lowered his hat and with a bowlegged stride moved toward her. "We tried gettin' the other lady's notice, but she didn't pay us no mind."

"She's been ill," said Alice. Judging from the number of horses in their possession, they had stolen from a fair number of citizens. Why hadn't she carried the pistol with her as Wil had warned?

"Is this the Prescott farm?"

The situation was worse than she thought. Confederates had sought out a Yankee household.

"We don't mean to frighten you, ma'am, but the general said to deliver this here letter to the Prescott farm." He withdrew a crumpled envelope from his pocket.

"General?" She recognized Wil's scrawl, and her heart fluttered. "I'm his wife."

He handed her the envelope and turned back the way he had come. With no intent of robbing them, he had only stopped by to deliver the letter.

"Wait—there's not much to be had, but you're more than welcome to stay for breakfast."

"Thanks ma'am. Much obliged."

Fighting tears, she hugged the letter to her breast.

"Ain't you goin' to read it?"

"Was he all right when he gave it to you?"

"Yes'm."

Alice broke the wax seal and unfolded the paper. The letter was dated two weeks before. Wil confirmed the newspaper reports. The fighting had shifted to Petersburg. As soon as he could secure accommodations, he wanted her to join him. Then what she read next—her cheeks warmed. She shoved the letter into her pocket.

"Bad news?"

"No, sometimes my husband has a wicked sense of humor. If you'll come around to the side of the house, I'll get breakfast started."

"Alice, you should be resting." Life had temporarily returned to Amanda, and her sister motioned to her pocket. "Did you say the letter was from Wil? How is he?"

Amanda often shared Sam's letters. How could Wil write about such a private matter? What if someone else had read it? Yankees confiscated citizens' letters and published them in Northern newspapers. "Lonely."

"Wil admitted that?"

"Not phrased quite so delicately."

As Alice's cheeks grew warmer, a hint of a smile appeared on Amanda's face. The first time she had smiled since Ben died. Amanda clapped a hand to her mouth and snickered. "I see."

Relieved to see Amanda smiling, Alice forgave Wil. "It's good to see you smile again."

Amanda stopped laughing, and her eyes dimmed. "I know I haven't made things easy for you."

She put an arm over Amanda's shoulders and hugged her. "Don't fret. It's understandable after what you've been through. We have guests to attend to. I'd be grateful for your help."

Once in the kitchen Alice fried eggs in the skillet, while Amanda set the table and popped golden brown biscuits from the oven. Adding smidgens of ham to the griddle, she fretted there wouldn't be enough to feed three hungry men. Embarrassed by the meager portions, she set a platter on the table. Without complaint, the scouts dug in hungrily.

Glad to take the weight off her feet, Alice eased in a pole-backed chair and joined them at the table. "You didn't say where you met my husband, Corporal . . . "

"Hatcher. Frank Hatcher—Third Virginia, General Fitz Lee's division." He stuffed the remains of a biscuit in his mouth before continuing, "Many of the boys are ridin' mules or transferrin' to infantry. Afore we set out, Colonel Owen introduced us, and I agreed to deliver the letter."

The letter remained hidden in her pocket. Warmth returned to her cheeks. Thank goodness, the scouts hadn't read it, or they'd be hooting and hollering.

Alice cleared her throat. "That was very kind of you."

"My pleasure, ma'am." Corporal Hatcher split another biscuit and wiped the last morsel from his plate. "Much obliged for the meal."

"I only wish it had been more."

The other scouts added their thanks, and Alice and Amanda accompanied them outside to their waiting horses. Dust trailed behind them as they trotted down the lane.

Amanda turned to her with a sly grin. "So what did Wil say?"

"I fathomed you had guessed." Alice pressed a hand to her rounding belly. "And Lord knows, when I see him again, I shall be much too fat for such . . . intimacies." Amanda's face twisted. Wrong words—she had reminded her of Ben and wished she could take them back. "Amanda, I didn't mean—"

"I know." Tears filled Amanda's eyes. With her voice barely a whisper, she said, "Don't let my mood spoil your happiness. Besides, when he sees you, he's not going to care if you're as big as a stuffed turkey."

Voice of experience? Amanda blushed and Alice giggled. Little by little, her sister was rejoining the world of the living. Should she break the news now? She clasped Amanda's hand. "Wil wants me to join him in Petersburg."

Amanda withdrew her hand from Alice's grip.

"I can tell him that you're not well enough—"

"Don't be foolish. Your place is with your husband, and with a little luck, he won't be absent when the baby's born." Dissolving into tears, Amanda went up the porch steps and disappeared inside the farmhouse.

No use fretting. Only time would help Amanda. Already behind her schedule, the day had grown miserably hot. Alice set out to finish morning chores.

By late afternoon her ankles puffed, and she kicked off her shoes, propping her feet on the sofa. Upstairs, she heard Amanda rummage about in her bedroom. Her sister had probably spent the morning sobbing in her pillow. Rubbing her swollen ankles, she'd check on her after she rested her feet a bit.

Rebecca pointed out the window with a squeal. "Look Mama, blue coats."

Footsteps thumped from upstairs, and Amanda hurried down to the parlor. "Sam..."

Edging to the window in bare feet, Alice parted the lace curtain. Not Sam, but three scouts—Yankee this time. A rope trailed behind a black horse. Tied to the other end... She closed her eyes—Corporal Hatcher.

As Alice fetched the hunting rifle from over the mantel, Amanda yanked Rebecca away from the window. Alice stepped outside. Taking a deep breath to steady her nerves, she mustn't let them see the gun shake. "What can I do for you—gentleman?"

A lieutenant with ears that looked like they belonged on a jackass lowered his hat. "We'll be staying the night, ma'am."

She aimed the rifle. "When hell freezes over."

He gave a curt smile. "Apparently, you didn't understand. That wasn't a request." He ordered a private to secure the prisoner. "We are staying the night, or you shall be removed from the premises."

Her eyes narrowed, and her finger hovered over the trigger. Yankee bastard—if she pulled the trigger...

"Alice," came Amanda's voice from behind her, "do as the lieutenant says."

Blinking back the vision of a bullet sailing smack dab between the lieutenant's flapping ears, Alice lowered the rifle.

"Lieutenant," Amanda said, joining them, "I'm Mrs. Samuel Prescott. My husband is a Yankee colonel and will deal with you if you don't listen. There are only women, a small child, and one free servant here. You are welcome to camp in the yard, but there shall be respect to all family members. Furthermore, no human will be treated like an animal on my property. Even when the family owned slaves, that was never allowed. Is that clear?"

The lieutenant's gaze met Amanda's in a challenge. Finally he glanced away and ordered the private to untie Corporal Hatcher.

The corporal nodded his gratitude. With her head held high, Amanda retained her poise. She turned and headed to the house.

"I'll bring you some supper," Alice said to the corporal. "I doubt these Yankees—"

"Alice—"

"Coming, Amanda." Alice hustled after her to catch up.

Once inside Amanda closed her eyes with her back to the door and sagged. *All an act.* Her sister was as terrified as she.

"Amanda, we've got to help Corporal—"

"No." Still trembling, Amanda reopened her eyes. "These men are dangerous. They're Sheridan's scouts."

The same troopers who burned and looted citizens from their homes. "Then what shall we do?"

Amanda swallowed. "No more Rebel talk, Alice. We'll be thrown out if you do, and I doubt Sam can help us. General Sheridan is free to do as he pleases. Mama will sleep in my room tonight, and Rebecca shall stay with you. Hopefully, they'll be gone in the morning."

"With Corporal Hatcher as their prisoner."

"There's nothing we can do about that!"

"You're right, of course, but what if Wil had said there was nothing he could do to help Sam?"

After retrieving her shoes, Alice retreated to the kitchen. Sweat trickled down the back of her neck. It was too hot to cook, but with Yankees camped on the lawn, she wouldn't chance preparing a meal in the summer kitchen.

Barely had she got a fire in the stove burning and bacon grease in the skillet, when a knock came to the door.

The lieutenant stepped inside. "Good evening." He lowered his hat and revealed his oversized ears. "My apologies for my earlier abruptness. It's been a while since I've shared the company of lovely ladies."

Although he had changed his attitude, Alice didn't trust him. Remain polite—nothing more. She forced a smile.

"That smells mighty good."

"Hog slop—a common dish in the South these days."

"Alice . . . " Amanda crossed the red brick floor.

"Forgive my manners, we're not used to such . . . " Alice caught her tongue and took a whisk broom to the dirt he had tracked through the kitchen. " . . . untidy guests."

Laughing, the lieutenant withdrew a chair from the table and eased in it. "We've been in the saddle for more than a week. Lieutenant Michael Wade. Mrs. Prescott, would you care to introduce your charming friend?"

Alice clenched her teeth as his eyes raked her in an ungentlemanly manner.

"My sister," Amanda said evenly.

"Mrs. . . ." Alice snapped the broom to the spot beneath his feet, " . . . as in married, William Jackson."

"And your husband, I presume he doesn't serve the Union?"

She couldn't come right out and admit that Wil was a Confederate brigadier. "A most astute observation. As you can fathom, it makes for some mighty heated conversations in this household."

He clutched his sides and laughed harder. Good—she had tempered him, but he showed no signs of leaving and obviously expected a meal. She'd fry up some salt pork and save better fare for after he and his men left, presuming they didn't steal their supplies. He wouldn't chance it—not in a Yankee household.

Careful not to antagonize him, she fixed the meal and like a dutiful servant waited on him hand and foot. She sent Ezra with a plate for Corporal Hatcher, and to their relief, as Amanda helped her wash dishes, the lieutenant thanked them and left.

Maintaining a semblance of normal routine, the family gathered in the parlor after supper. While the evening was too warm for a fire, they engaged in chitchat.

A gunshot went off in the front yard, and the Yankees hooted. Nasal voices raised in an off-key song.

Alice exchanged a nervous glance with Amanda.

"Mama . . ." With a whimper Rebecca covered her ears and curled in Amanda's lap.

"Time for bed, Miss Rebecca." Amanda clasped the toddler's hand and vanished up the stairs.

Another gun fired, making Alice jump. Mama clutched her beads and cursed, "Damn Yankees."

"Mama, why don't you retire? I shall see to the lights and be straight up."

Mama agreed and followed Amanda. As she went from room to room, Alice left a few lamps burning low. For added safety, she'd tuck the pistol under her pillow once in bed.

A gun popped, and like a wild animal, someone howled.

Alice peered out the window, but saw nothing in the darkness. The wailing stopped, and she turned for the stairs.

A fist pounded on the front door.

Her heart felt like it had drifted to her throat. "What is it?" More banging. From behind the door, she asked again, "What's wrong?"

With the rifle gripped in her hands, Amanda joined her.

"Dang Reb," a voice called out. "Tried to escape and got shot. He's bleedin' mighty bad."

Amanda nodded for her to open the door, and Alice cracked it to a wide-eyed private. "Bring him to the house."

"Don't think it's serious, but he's hurtin'. He's in the barn, ma'am."

Was it a ploy to get her outside? "I'll be right there."

"Alice . . ." Amanda's face was lined with worry.

"I'll be careful." She stuffed some linen in a bag for bandages, and Amanda slipped the pistol Wil had given her in.

Alice nodded and went out to the warm evening. Crossing the farmyard to the barn, she heard a whimper and quickened her pace.

Inside a stall, Corporal Hatcher clutched his right arm.

"Someone fetch a bucket of water," she said.

Alice grasped a clean linen as the private brought in a wooden bucket. She dipped the cloth in water and dabbed the corporal's arm. As she wiped blood away, he sucked in his breath. His skin was broken, but no bullet had lodged in his arm. Although painful, the wound wasn't serious.

"Much obliged, ma'am," he said.

Outside the stall, Amanda watched. Apparently satisfied the Yankees spoke the truth, she turned away.

Alice wrapped the corporal's arm and finished tying the cloth. Slinging the bag over her arm, she straightened.

"Mighty fine work, Mrs. Jackson." Lieutenant Wade blocked the stall.

She swallowed hard. "Thank you."

He stepped aside to let her pass. "I admire a woman who knows her own mind. Strong and independent—like you Southron gals."

Out here with one flickering lantern to see by, his face seemed less clownish.

"Tell me Mrs. Jackson, in what capacity does your husband serve the Rebs?"

Alice glanced around. The private guarded Corporal Hatcher, but the other Yankee scout was nowhere to be seen. "A captain—Third Virginia."

He moved closer, and she smelled the grime and dirt of an unwashed body. She stepped back, and a jagged stall rail jabbed her in the spine.

"A captain? Our Reb friend over yonder says he delivered a letter from Brigadier Jackson."

Her heart pounded as she rummaged through the bag for the pistol. "There must be some mistake. My husband is a captain."

His face twisted in a cruel smile. Moving closer still, he seized the bag and looked inside. "What have we here?" He withdrew the pistol from the bag. Tossing the bag and pistol to the straw floor, he leaned in to her with the brunt of his weight. "You're gonna be sorry you tried that, Mrs. Reb brigadier."

Pinned against wooden rails, Alice felt his erection against her. A scream caught in her throat as his mouth met hers with his tongue probing.

She beat her hands against him and broke his grip. His fist connected with her cheek, and she staggered to get away. He shoved her down. Straw scratched her face, and she smelled his sweat along with horse manure. He unbuttoned his trousers, exposing his male organ as if it were some sort of prize.

"Let my sister go!"

Dazed, Alice saw Amanda with the rifle clasped between her hands.

"She came on to me, ma'am. A swishing and swaying. It's only natural for a man—"

"I said let her go!"

He fastened his trousers.

None too steady, Alice regained her feet.

"I will be reporting this disgraceful act to my husband. Alice, are you all right?"

"I'm not certain." Her eye throbbed and her vision blurred, but she thought she saw a shadow move behind Amanda. The other Yankee scout. "Amanda!"

Amanda turned, and the rifle flew from her hands.

Alice scrambled for the pistol in the straw and snatched it up. She fired. The lieutenant reeled back before dropping to the straw. Her sides heaved, and she aimed at the other Yankee. He shoved his hands skyward.

"Get out! And leave Corporal Hatcher behind." The scout gestured to the lieutenant. Bent beside Lieutenant Wade, Amanda shook her head. Alice motioned with the pistol to fetch him. "Take his filthy hide with you."

As the Yankee trooper helped the lieutenant to his feet, he clutched his belly with a groan. Gut shot. He'd linger for hours, maybe days. And she had killed him. Shouldn't she feel guilt—or shame? Her knees were weak from shaking, but she felt no remorse. She was elated.

Corporal Hatcher had helped her on the long roundabout journey around Richmond to reach Petersburg. Exhausted, Alice inspected the smoke-blackened, windowless kitchen. In the main section of the two-room cottage, walls were unplastered and earth was plainly visible between the floorboards. Not much different from her home in Fredericksburg after the battle, a table with two chairs and bedding with no frame were the only furniture. "I suppose with all of the refugees in the city, it'll have to make do," she said.

"I'll secure better quarters when some become available," Wil assured her. "For now, we have a table and a bed. What more do we need?" He flashed a wicked smile, and without ceremony, he unbuttoned her dress and lowered it to the floor.

She kept silent about her frightful experience and didn't resist. Layers of clothing gone, only her chemise and drawers remained. After four months apart every part of him was anxious, and his hands touched her everywhere. As he sought her mouth, she thought of the Yankee lieutenant violating her.

Gooseflesh prickled her arms, and she shoved away from him.

"Alice, what's wrong?"

"I suffered a chill." She rubbed her arms.

His dark eyes danced in amusement. "Then I shall warm you." He reached for her, but she stepped back.

Wil's grin faded.

She couldn't explain—not yet, and she mustn't let him think. Over on the mattress Alice curled her legs underneath her and slid the pins from her hair as he looked on. She shook her head, and hair tumbled past her shoulders.

Naked to the waist, Wil tugged off his boots and joined her.

She shouldn't have fretted. Her body molded to him, and she breathed in the sweet aroma of cigars. In his strong arms, she felt safe. She traced a finger across the rippled red scar on his chest. A graphic reminder of the bullet that had nearly claimed his life. Like a tormented child, she clung. She laid her head on his shoulder and sobbed.

"Alice?" He held her head between his hands, and his gaze met hers. "Tell me what's wrong."

He brushed away her tears with his thumb, and she swallowed. "The pistol you gave me—the one you told me to protect myself with. I used it . . ." Her voice cracked, and she gulped back a breath. " . . . to kill a man."

His muscles strained as his right hand curled to a fist. "I had hoped you would be spared."

"You don't understand, Wil. I wanted him dead."

"You wanted him . . ." Ready to boil, his black eyes simmered. The dark place he usually kept suppressed had been rekindled. "*Why* did you want him dead?"

"He . . ." Alice wrung her hands. "He tried to rape me."

No longer simmering, Wil's eyes blazed. Like a madman, he shot from the bed and slammed a fist into the wall. Cursing in pain, he cradled his bleeding hand.

"Wil—oh Lord, the same hand you hurt before. I hope you haven't broken it again." She tore a section from her petticoat and began wrapping his hand.

"I should have been there for you."

"You're here now."

He only got angrier. "Did he hurt you?"

She tied off the bandage. "He gave me a black eye, but, otherwise, I was unharmed."

"Then it's good that you shot the bastard."

The oath reminded her of when they were courting. With his rage mostly under control, he buried his fingers in her hair. She bowed her head to his chest and listened to the rhythm of his heart, when she felt a sensation of rushing water in her abdomen. It wasn't dyspepsia, but the baby. She pressed his hand to her belly. The stoic mask dropped as he murmured the words she longed to hear.

Chapter Twenty

Near Petersburg, Virginia
October 1864

DAY AND NIGHT, SHELLS WHINED. Sam wondered how the civilians survived under such intense pounding. While the soldiers were protected behind earthworks, shells frequently lobbed into the city. He had a personal stake now. Amanda's recent letter disclosed that Alice lived behind Confederate lines with Wil.

Under twilight with field glasses in hand, he crawled beyond the picket line on his belly. Encroaching darkness made separating inanimate objects from live ones difficult. Counting eight cannon, he feared one of these days he'd see the colors of Wil's brigade across the way.

A ping of a bullet near his arm warned him that sharpshooters had spotted him. He scrambled back to the trenches.

As he dropped down behind the earthworks, another bullet whirred over his head. His hat flew off. "Damn Rebs," he said, leaning over to fetch it, "that hat cost me seven dollars." He poked his index finger through a hole.

"Could've been your head, sir."

The girl soldier had a point, and she grinned in smug victory. Annoyed, he hated it when she was right and shoved the hat on his head. "Rebel pickets look fully defended," he said.

Like half-crazed Indians, Rebel yells came from all directions. Jo drew her pistol, and began firing. More screams and shooting broke out up and down the picket line.

Before Sam could shout a command, he struck the ground. A sharp pain traveled the length of his torso—he thought he was hit, then he felt the deadweight of a Rebel sprawled across him.

Sam clambered from underneath and checked for wounds. Except for the dead Reb, there was no blood. He must have been swiped by the edge of a musket butt. Jo had dispatched the Reb and moved on. No time to thank her.

With bayonet extended, another ragged Reb charged. The blade sliced through Sam's forearm and pinned him to the side of the trench, stretching his arm like he had been nailed to a cross. He beat a fist at the earthen wall. The bayonet wouldn't budge, and he felt the warmth of fresh blood flow along his arm and fill his sleeve.

In wide-eyed amazement, the Reb stared with his jaw agape at the bayonet lodged in Sam's arm.

A dull ache was growing, and Sam grew dizzy. *Think.* His left hand worked just fine. Their gazes met in a final challenge. As Sam reached for his pistol, the Reb went into motion and wrenched the blade free.

Sam screamed and fired.

The Reb's head twisted and his arms flailed as he tumbled back with shock on his face. Sam's pistol clattered to the ground. He clutched his arm and fell to his knees as the remaining Rebs scurried from the trenches and vanished in the growing darkness.

Silence. Firing along the line halted as quickly as it had begun.

Lightheaded, Sam wrapped a handkerchief around his arm. "Anyone hit?"

The boys muttered and mumbled that they were all right. A private offered a supporting hand, and he waved him on.

Grateful no one else was wounded, he stood. With at least three dead, the Rebs hadn't been as fortunate. Pain pulsed through his arm, and he gritted his teeth.

A private grasped his elbow. "Sir, we need to get you to a doctor."

"Later." Time to thank Jo for saving his hide yet again, Sam glanced around for her. "Sergeant—"

"Sir . . ." The private pointed to a prone form.

The motionless body had smaller hands than most men. "Tucker!" How many times had he watched men die? But one bob-haired girl soldier who had no business being in the war . . . No, it couldn't be

Jo. She had moved to the other end of the line. "Tucker!" he bellowed again.

Shaking his head, the private faced him. "He ain't breathin', sir."

He . . . Was he the only one left alive who knew her secret? Bending down, he struck a match to see.

In Jo's temple was a neat bullet hole with very little bleeding. The dead face smiled in a curious way. With her wicked sense of humor, it was probably her way of telling him, "I told you so." From the beginning she had said he'd come to think of her as one of the boys. Most of the time that was true, but he never had completely.

So senseless—women had no place in the army. Yet Jo had more grit and determination than most of the boys, and she had died with her face to the enemy.

His fingertips burned, and Sam dropped the match. He straightened. Honor bound to keep Jo's secret, he'd have her buried alongside the men. No one else needed to know the truth of her sex. Following standard protocol, he'd write to her mother and inform her how her daughter had died bravely in the line of duty for her country. A hero's death—with full military honors.

On the grassy knoll behind the house, Amanda stared at the tiny grave. Still numb from Ben's death, she had a gaping hole in her heart. *Did the pain ever go away?* Frieda had always been a source of comfort, and she wished the old woman were here to talk to, but she, too, was at rest in her grave.

Grasping her black mourning skirt, she turned. Her breath caught in her throat. At the bottom of the hill stood a man in blue. To the best of her knowledge there hadn't been any Yankees in the area since before Alice had departed for Petersburg. She had never thought to lug the rifle along.

With his right arm in a sling, the soldier had probably stopped by looking for a handout. He wandered toward her. She blinked. An officer, and his bold, long-legged stride seemed familiar.

Tears streaked hot on her cheeks as she dashed down the hill and nearly bowled him over, knocking his hat from his hand. "Sam, it is you." She kissed his face. "Your arm. You've been hurt."

"It's not serious, but it gives me a chance to spend some time with you." His blue eyes were etched with grief. "Amanda, I'm sorry I wasn't here."

She glanced over her shoulder at the cemetery. "Would you care to see where he's resting?"

Sam nodded. As he retrieved his hat from the yellowing grass, she spotted a bullet hole. *Stay silent.*

Amanda grasped his hand and led him up the hill. At the sight of the cross at the head of the tiny grave, tears filled his eyes. He placed his hat over his heart and bowed his head.

Their son. His presence had been on the earth for such a short time. *How could there be any meaning?* As Sam's good arm went around her, she prayed for strength. Sam was here now. Together, they'd grieve.

The warm days of autumn faded to numbing winter winds. Although wood was growing scarce, on this night Alice had the urge to make a toasty fire. A shell whistled overhead and landed somewhere in the city. She rarely paid the shells any notice.

Day and night, they screamed. At least Wil had procured better living arrangements. In a private cottage near his headquarters, she tossed in bed.

Something pinged against the tin roof. She thought a shell had hit the cottage, but Wil's face remained squashed against the feather pillow. A light sleeper, he would have woken if it had been a shell.

Heavy with child, she was unable to get comfortable. Fluffing pillows behind her back, Alice sat up and rubbed her tense belly muscles. Other officers' wives had alerted her that her time for birthing was near.

"Alice?" Wil touched her belly, and the baby kicked.

"He's been very active this evening, not to mention that I feel like a trussed turkey." But she heard even breathing beside her.

Her back ached. Alice got up and paced the floor. She sank in the rocking chair and the distress in her belly eased. What sort of country would the baby enter?

Wil assured her the war would be over by spring, but he also predicted a Union victory. If that happened, what would become of them?

The fire had been dampened down for the night, and she got a chill. She returned to bed, snuggling next to Wil's warmth. "Wil, I'm afraid."

His arms went around her shoulders. "Of what?"

"Women die birthing."

"You're not going to die."

She felt shamed. All around her, men died of disease and horrendous wounds. "Forgive me, I shouldn't have brought my foolish fears up."

"There's no shame in being afraid."

She placed her head to his heart and stroked across the expanse of his broad chest, twisting curly hair between her fingertips. "What would you know about being afraid? You never show fear."

"That doesn't mean I've never felt it."

Astonished by his admission, she sat up. "When have you felt fear?"

He laughed softly. "To know the answer will set your mind at ease?"

"Yes."

Wil stopped laughing, and she felt his cozy naked warmth beside her. "My first battle. I was afraid I might not stand my ground, and when Peopeo died..."

There had been a time when he wouldn't have shared such things with her, but he stated them easily now. Progress—Alice smiled to herself and clutched the Indian medicine pouch around her neck for luck when a muscle spasm caught her off guard. *The baby would soon be here.*

A rap came at the door. "Sir, sorry to wake you, but I have an important dispatch from General Wilcox."

With a grumble, Wil lit a lamp and rolled from the bed. After tugging on his trousers, he threw on a shirt and strode to the door.

Alice drew the quilt to her chin as an arctic blast filled the cottage.

A staff officer saluted. "Beg your pardon for the intrusion."

Returning the salute, Wil unfolded the dispatch and read it. "Summon my staff. I'll be right there." Another salute, and the staff officer about-faced, closing the door behind him. Wil returned to the side of the bed and finished dressing. "Yankees have threatened the supply line. We're to assist the cavalry and intercept them."

Not now. "Wil..."

His sword rattled as he strapped on his weapons belt and looked up.

She couldn't let on that she'd be birthing soon. "I thought the campaign was over for the season."

"Apparently General Grant has decided otherwise." His eyes flickered in concern. "Alice, will you be all right?"

Her abdomen constricted once more, and she glanced away. "If you would call a servant to sit with me, I'll be fine."

With a kiss to her lips, he turned to leave.

"Wil, I love you."

He fidgeted with the brim of his hat but made no response. At the general's reemergence, Wil, her husband, was gone. A sharp wind blew in as he closed the door behind him.

She laid her head against the feather pillow. With another contraction, she moaned. The pains were getting closer together—and stronger. Closing her eyes, she wished Amanda were here. Her life would be entrusted to a stranger, and Wil wouldn't even be present to pace in time-honored tradition.

Ten minutes later, a knock came to the door. A Negro servant who belonged to an officer's wife stepped in. "Lily, fetch the doctor. I'm having birthing pains."

"Straight away, Miss Alice."

Rain pinged against the tin roof. Oh Lord, on such a cold night, if a Yankee bullet didn't find Wil, pneumonia certainly would. Warmth of rushing water flowed between her legs. "Lily, please hurry."

Nearly half an hour passed before the servant returned. "Da doctor say he be here, Miss Alice. I's make a nice, warm fire."

"Thank you, Lily." As Lily stoked the embers in the fireplace, Alice's abdomen tightened. She gripped the quilt in her fists to keep from crying out. The contraction ended, and she breathed out. "Why did he have to be called away tonight?"

The fire began blazing, and Lily grasped her hand. "Don't know da answer to dat, but you got to rest between pains, Miss Alice. Da birthin' go easier dat way."

Easier? But women died in childbirth. Alice clutched the medicine pouch. For luck. She imagined the mountain lion padding along a rocky cliff surveying a tree-studded valley below. Wil had said such visions were symbolic. The rocky cliff represented—what? The war? No matter—the mountain lion shared Wil's strength and courage. He was with her in spirit. When the next contraction came, she breathed evenly and the pain lessened.

Lily mopped Alice's sweaty brow. Her muscles tensed, warning her of another pain. Breathe—in, now out. Her muscles finally relaxed. Exhausted, she attempted to rest, but the break was short.

A knock at the door irritated her, breaking her concentration. Hearing a man's voice, she let out a strangled cry. "Wil?"

"No, ma'am. It da doctor. Mr. Wil be back," Lily said, patting her hand, "but afore he is, you's goin' to have da baby." She fluffed pillows behind her back.

"I need to push."

"Not yet," the doctor's voice cautioned.

"What would you know? You've never had a baby!" Alice began to weep. "Where's Wil?"

"He be here just as soon as he can, Miss Alice."

She felt cool water spread across her forehead as the ground trembled from a shell burst. Tail twitching, the mountain lion scanned the crumbling buildings and charred remains. Buried beneath the rubble, an otter quivered in pain. The vision forecasted her own death. "No!"

"It's time, Mrs. Jackson."

Time? Time for what?

The doctor bent her legs to help her birth. Her brow furrowed as the pain became blinding. A damp head with black hair appeared between her legs, then shoulders. The baby dropped to the doctor's waiting hands. A girl—she had a daughter. A wail filled the cottage. "She's beautiful," Alice said.

The doctor placed the wriggling baby in her eager arms.

Exhausted, Alice held the baby to her breast and traced a finger through the damp hair. Overcome by emotion, she sobbed. She looked so much like Wil. Their daughter was going to be a spitfire.

Snow had changed to sleet. After a miserably cold night spent in the open with scant rations and wrapped in blankets and gum cloth, the Third Corps resumed its march at daybreak. The sound of guns several miles ahead warned Wil they would be engaging the enemy soon. If the Yanks didn't break the supply line this time, they would another. It was only a matter of time. Like a simpleton, he'd lay down his arms and stop fighting when he was ordered to. *Why?* The South would lose whether he fought or not. His duty was not to question.

As darkness settled, the guns fell silent. Around midnight, the dispatch came. There would be no engagement at dawn. The Yankees had withdrawn. Wil called the regimental commanders and relayed the order to return to camp.

After another biting night in the field, Wil woke to find himself covered by ice. Barely able to move, he struggled to his feet and the column trudged back to camp. With a shiver, he opened the door of the cottage to an inviting fire.

The Negro servant, Lily, put two fingers to her lips for him to keep quiet. "Miss Alice sleepin'."

After two days with little sleep, Wil relished the thought of huddling next to Alice. Before he could dismiss the servant, a squall filled the cottage—a baby's cry.

Lily ran over to the cradle beside the bed and picked up a bundle. She carried the fussing bundle to the bed.

Alice cradled the baby in her arms and beamed. "Wil, aren't you going to come over here and meet your daughter?"

"It's a girl?"

Her smile faded. "You're disappointed."

He hadn't meant to sound miffed. "I'm not disappointed."

As she put the baby to her breast, he strode over to the bed. Careful not to jostle her, he sat on the edge. The baby's skin was brown and her hair, black—like Benjamin's. *All of his birthdays passed in silence.*

"You know I'm not very good about such things," he said.

"Lily..." Alice dismissed the servant. "I know you're thinking about him. I don't expect you to ever forget, but she's here. She needs her papa."

She knew him well—better than anyone. Wil touched the tiny hand while she suckled. A perfect hand—four chubby fingers and a thumb. Overcome by the moment, he swallowed hard.

"If you don't mind, I'd like to call her Emma Kate."

He nodded that he approved of the name. "Alice..." His voice broke.

Her knowing grin returned. "It seems I've made you speechless again. Wil..." She moved to the opposite side of the bed and patted the mattress for him to join her.

He removed his weapons belt and boots, then climbed in next to her, placing his arms protectively around them. Unlike with Peopeo and Benjamin, he would see to it that they remained safe.

Another Christmas clouded by war drew near. Mama had stayed behind on the farm with Rebecca, and most of the visiting wives remained at City Point. Though she was far from the delicious smells of fruit-filled cakes baking and gaudy decorations, Amanda insisted on being with Sam—in the trenches. Soon after her arrival, the shells pounding Petersburg screamed to a halt in observance of an unofficial truce.

Around the Christmas Eve dinner table overflowing with smoked ham, potatoes, and pumpkin pie, officers toasted, chanting the end was near. Having wished for peace for so long and so fervently, she should have been happy.

"Amanda..."

Forcing a smile, she looked over at Sam.

"Three years ago, you said we can't give up hope."

All too clearly, she remembered uttering the words. With so many friends and loved ones called to their graves, she had lost sight of her own preaching. "I was thinking of Alice. With the supply lines to the city nearly gone, I wonder if she has enough to eat."

He leaned back in the chair with a smile. "Why don't you call on her and find out?"

His teasing could be wicked at times. "And how do you propose I do that?"

"I have a hunch the pickets will allow you to cross—tomorrow. Should I send a message for her to expect you?"

Amanda's arms went around his neck, and through the night with Sam's blessing, she prepared her articles for smuggling. After breakfast,

Sam escorted her a couple of miles to the south by wagon. The opposing picket lines were separated by a few hundred yards, but as Sam had predicted, both sides let her freely pass.

Once past the Confederate picket, Wil waited beside another wagon. Upon seeing her, he lowered his hat, and they exchanged Christmas greetings. His uniform bagged slightly, and he looked *thin.* "It's been over a year," she said. "You're looking well."

Amusement danced in his eyes. "And as always you look ravishing, Amanda."

Warmth rose in her cheeks. And he could still make her blush. "I thought Alice might be here to greet me," she said, attempting to keep her voice even.

"She's recovering."

Recovering? "Has she been ill?" Before the words were out of her mouth, it dawned on her. "The baby... She's had the baby. What? When? Is Alice all right?"

He held up a hand for her to slow down. "Alice is fine. The baby is a girl, and she was born two weeks ago."

His reluctance to say anything more than necessary was as aggravating as ever. Amanda grew impatient. "Well, does she have a name?"

"Emma. Now we can stand here jabbering all day, or you can go meet her." He helped her in the wagon and groaned, "Amanda, I believe you have put on a few pounds."

"Sometimes I still wonder what my little sister saw in you."

With no sign of the dark moods, he only laughed and climbed into the wagon from the opposite side.

As he settled on the seat beside her and grasped the reins, she touched his hand. "I never had the chance to thank you for helping Sam, then again for letting him know when Ben..."

His gaze met hers. "Friends lend a hand in moments of crises. Isn't that true?"

Her hand still rested on his. She suddenly felt awkward and drew it away. "I never thought I'd have the opportunity to say this, but marriage becomes you, Wil."

"It does have *certain* advantages." He sent her a sly grin. "Although I must admit—not recently."

His insinuation was all too clear, and she felt herself blushing again. To ease her discomfort, she chatted about her trip to Petersburg. The wagon traveled through rows of log huts, and soldiers clad in tattered butternut coughed—deep, hacking coughs. Not much more than skin and bones, the men were so thin. Conditions were far worse than when she had run supplies at the war's beginning. She suddenly fell silent.

After a mile, Wil brought the wagon to a halt outside a cottage. The door flew open and Alice rushed out with arms spread wide to greet her. "Amanda . . ."

Without waiting for Wil's help, she clambered from the wagon and hugged Alice. Wil led the horse and wagon away, and she stepped back. Unlike the soldiers, her sister retained her plumpness. "I'm anxious to meet Emma."

Alice led the way inside. The welcoming warmth of a fire blazed in the hearth, and near the bed of the two-room cottage was a cradle. With a delighted smile, Alice lifted a swaddled bundle from the cradle. "Amanda, I'd like you to meet Miss Emma Jackson."

Carefully taking the bundle in her arms, Amanda hadn't held a baby since Ben. Her throat constricted. The baby's dark hair resembled Wil's, but her eyes were going to be green like Alice's. "She's beautiful, Alice. How's Wil taking his new role?"

Wiggling a finger in front of Emma's face, Alice cooed. "He's smitten. I never thought I'd have competition from a lady so young."

His gruff exterior *was* a sham. Amanda giggled. "I always suspected he was soft at heart."

Alice's brows furrowed, and her smile faded.

"What's wrong?"

"I fret what shall become of us. I'm sure you're aware the end is near. Wil won't talk about it, but I hear rumors from others about desertions and know they're not just some idle gossip. I see the men and how they live. Can anyone blame them when they're nearly naked and half-starving for giving up on a lost cause?" Alice waggled her finger at Emma once more. "I can't say this to the other wives. They say I must believe the Confederacy isn't lost, but the military is all Wil knows. Come spring, what he has worked a lifetime to build will be gone."

Maybe Christmas three years ago wasn't so different from the present. With a long, difficult war ahead, Sam had given up hope.

Now they dreamed of the war's end. "It's Christmas. Spring is a long time away."

"To disregard what's happening doesn't make it go away."

"I know, but you have a beautiful new baby and a loving husband. Together—you'll work it out when the time comes."

Alice forced a smile. "You're forgetting the man I married. He doesn't tend to openly discuss such things."

"I'm not forgetting, but you mustn't give up hope." Reminding her of one of the reasons she had come, Amanda returned the baby to Alice's waiting arms and hoisted her skirt. "I brought you a little Christmas present."

Ecstatic by a surprise, Alice beamed. "A Christmas present?"

Amanda untied a tiny smoked ham and a small bag of flour from her hoops. A fierce wind blew through the room as Wil entered the cottage. She unpinned strings of dried apples, peaches, and carrots from her petticoat. As she shed her extra pounds, he laughed. The tricks she learned while smuggling supplies had come full circle.

Chapter Twenty-One

With the ranks growing thin, Wil trotted the chestnut mare along the picket line. Barefoot soldiers spaced yards apart behind breastworks stood in icy water to their ankles. No reserves remained in wait to plug the holes. No shoes, and so little food.

And Yankee shells continually bombarded the city. He had ordered Alice to seek refuge at Amanda's. Stubborn woman—he should have known better than to order her to do anything. It only made her more determined to behave in the opposite manner, and for all the good it did her, she remained at his side in Petersburg.

The line stretched for miles, and the better part of his day was spent inspecting it. Shouts came from behind him, and Wil wheeled the mare around. A soldier with tattered trousers clambered the breastworks, waving his arms in surrender.

Duty bound to shoot deserters, Wil drew his pistol, but lowered it as the man carefully made his way through the point-sharpened abatis. No sense in killing him. Desperate men took equally desperate measures. *The Cause was lost—it was only a matter of time before the Yankees came.*

Less forgiving, Captain Hanes fired. The soldier stumbled, then clutched his arm. Shouts from the Yankee side encouraged the soldier to persevere. Up and running, he continued on.

With a quizzical look, Hanes ran a hand through his beard. "Sir?"

"He's out of range." Feeling no need to explain his rationale, Wil reined the chestnut around.

The captain brought his mount beside Wil. "Sir, if you let one man get away, others will follow suit."

Although less common in his brigade, desertion happened nonetheless. "Others will follow, regardless of what action I take."

Hanes opened his mouth to say something, but apparently changed his mind and closed it. Smart man—while Wil refrained from killing a man for desertion, he held no reservation in issuing insubordination charges. It was a peculiar sense of priority, but no stranger than taking an oath to honor the flag—the Yankee flag—then fighting under another.

As he reached the end of the brigade's line, cannon rumbled further ahead. A battle? A skirmish—there wasn't enough firepower for a battle. Battle, skirmish—what difference did it make? His line would likely be stretched thinner.

Weary, he turned in the direction of his headquarters and the cottage, where Alice would be waiting.

In early March, daffodils bloomed. As a child, Alice had loved spring. The season of rebirth brought endless hours of rolling in fields and Mama scolding her for rough-and-tumble behavior. These days, spring brought death.

Wil's brigade had been shifted to the west. Most nights, Emma had her final feeding of the day and was soundly asleep before he returned to the cottage. Other nights he spent on the line and failed to return at all.

Each morning brought new worries. While she exchanged visits with other wives, only wide-eyed looks confided their greatest fear. Every knock brought the expectation of a courier bearing the news that one of their husbands was dead.

With the room still dark when Alice woke, she heard Wil rummaging about. His sword clanked as he strapped on his weapons belt. Someday soon—there would be no need to fret about him leaving in the morning.

"Let me make breakfast," she murmured, half-asleep. She felt his weight on the mattress beside her.

"You rest. I'm late."

Sitting up, Alice lifted the chimney beside the bed and lit the lamp.

His heavily bearded face had a broad grin. "You look lovely first thing in the morning. Although you're even more enchanting with nothing on."

"Wil, don't pretend."

He arched a brow. "Pretend? I meant every word."

His mouth met hers, and his hand went under her nightdress. He squeezed her posterior. Alice drew away. "The pantry's low, and you leave what there is for me. Don't pretend I don't see."

His eyes sobered. "You're feeding two. It's essential that you keep your strength, but..." He pinched her backside once more. "I truly meant what I said."

"And you're incorrigible."

He got to his feet. "You were fully aware of that when you married me."

She wanted to be mad, but couldn't. Cherish their time together—each moment might be their last. "Wil..."

"Yes, Alice."

She untied the medicine pouch from around her neck and held it out to him. "Please take it—for luck. You'll need it more than me in the days to come."

His gaze met hers. Grasping the medicine pouch, he nodded. "Now I must be leaving, or face a court martial."

After a goodbye kiss, Wil cast a glance at Emma in the cradle with a smile before turning to leave. Alice whispered her love, and he closed the door behind him. A sick feeling rose in her stomach. Slapping a hand across her mouth, she scrambled for the chamber pot and retched. A ritual—every time he left.

Her stomach settled slowly, and she remained hunched on the floor with her knees drawn to her chest until she was certain she wouldn't repeat the ceremony. She rinsed her mouth and grew conscious of the whistling shells.

Day and night, they buzzed. On warm evenings, one could stand in the yard and watch a firework display. Glowing like singing angels, they fluttered across the sky. With so many shells sailing through the air, she had learned to disregard them. Another boom sounded—much closer than the rest. Confederate guns were signaling a warning.

The door flew open. Dripping wet from running through rain, Lily screamed, "Miss Alice!"

"I heard." Alice bolted for the cradle and seized Emma.

Outside, she fled through the drenching downpour. A mortar shell whined and the ground trembled with a terrifying explosion. She fell to her knees, but clutched the squalling baby to her bosom. Dear God, if they lived through this...

Lily grasped her elbow, helping Alice regain her feet. Finally they reached the safety of the bombproof. Underground in a foot of water, she heard a rat squeak. She grasped the back of Lily's dress. "We need some light."

"Da matches wet, Miss Alice. Dere, I found a dry one." Lily lit a candle.

Alice sat on an earthen shelf and put Emma to her breast. Cold and wet, she half-expected Wil to reappear. He had most likely ridden a mile or two when the shells had hit. He knew she would seek shelter. She prayed that he had done the same.

"Miss Alice." Lily draped a blanket over her shoulders. Underneath the relative warmth of damp wool, the women huddled together.

As shells exploded above ground, the earth shook. "My sister's husband is one of those on the other side firing at us."

Lily cast her gaze downward.

"You have everything to gain when the Yankees win, don't you?"

The servant's dark eyes looked up. "You say when. Da other ladies—"

"Say the Confederacy shall succeed." Alice shook her head. "It won't happen."

"Miss Alice..."

She squeezed Lily's hand. Alice guessed by the servant's smooth, caramel complexion that she was probably close to her own age. "If I could, I'd buy you and set you free."

Lily's gaze met hers. "I believe you."

"Do you have any family?"

"Da man I jump da broom with go fight for da Yankees. Nathan come back for me, and we get married proper, when dey win."

So matter-of-fact—there was no doubt in Alice's mind that she believed it. She hoped Lily would see her dreams. As shells whined and the ground trembled, she wished she had supplied more provisions in the bombproof. With the cottage located southwest of the city, this section wasn't normally shelled, and she had little reason to think of it. Besides—there weren't many supplies to spare. Barely had she finished nursing Emma, when Alice's stomach rumbled. Her fingers and toes had gone numb, and she shivered.

By mid-afternoon, the shells stopped screaming. Alice exchanged a nervous glance with Lily. Both afraid to say the bombing had halted, they waited another hour to make certain. "I'm going to fetch something to eat, Lily."

"I go. You got da baby to think of."

"Then we both shall go."

Resigned, Lily nodded. Sloshing through frigid water, they went above ground. The rain had stopped, and it was easier to see. A shell had smashed an outbuilding to tinder, but the cottage, thankfully, remained standing. Inside—to Alice's relief—a shattered lamp was the only damage. She changed out of her saturated nightdress and ate a meal. At long last, her trembling began to subside.

A rap came at the door. Unable to breathe, she felt a lump in her throat.

"Mrs. Jackson . . ."

She recognized the voice of Wil's aide, Captain Hanes. More rapping, and she clutched her collar. As long as she didn't answer, Wil was fine.

"Mrs. Jackson, are you all right?"

Lily strode for the door. "Don't answer it, Lily."

"But Miss Alice . . ."

The captain was pounding. The door burst open, and she covered her ears. "Don't say it! Wil's dead."

He lowered his hat. "The general's fine, ma'am."

"Fine?" Blinking back the words, Alice dropped her hands and let out a ragged breath. "Then why are you here?"

"He wanted me to make certain that you're all right."

Bless Wil's heart—he was always thinking of her. Her fear gave way to a smile. "We're fine, thank you. A lamp is the only casualty."

"Very good. Do you have a message for the general that you'd like me to relay?"

Alice joined him at the door. "Tell my husband—"

A shell whistled, and the Confederate warning gun sounded. Too late to seek the shelter of the bombproof, the captain shoved her to the floor. An explosion rocked the cottage. She heard Lily scream, and pain—more than she had ever experienced—traveled the length of her right arm.

Lily grasped her hand and helped her sit up. "I think he killt, Miss Alice."

Blood covered the back of the captain's head. Still alive, he moaned. But her arm. Red pools splattered across the floor and on her dress. She had difficulty distinguishing between her own blood and the captain's.

Something jagged poked through her dress sleeve. She reached for it, then realizing it was a bone, she grew faint. "Help him, Lily." Darkness enveloped her, and she slumped.

When Alice woke, coal-black eyes peered at her in worry. She had never seen Wil fret before. She struggled to get up, but pain shot through her arm. He helped her lay back. "Save your strength. Remain still."

The strong scent of blood mixed with gangrene and human wastes penetrated her nostrils. A hospital—after all the long hours she had spent toiling in them, she'd recognize the smell anywhere. "Wil, your aide—Captain Hanes..."

He hushed her. "He had a knock on the head, but he'll be fine. The surgeon will be here to check your arm."

A surgeon? "How...how bad?"

"You've lost a lot of blood."

The pain made it difficult to think. "Emma?"

"She's fine. She's with Lily."

"Wil, it hurts," she whimpered.

A red-bearded face joined Wil's. She should know him, but couldn't place the face. As she drifted, the two men spoke. She couldn't make out their words. The man with the red whiskers shook his head.

Wil grasped her good hand. "Alice, your arm is peppered with shrapnel."

She had witnessed enough such injuries to know what he meant. He was trying to tell her... "Are they going to take my arm? Tell me the truth. How shall I care for Emma? You won't want to look at me anymore."

Wil hushed her once more. "The surgeon is going to try and save your arm, but there is a chance . . ." He squeezed her hand. "If it comes to pass, it won't stop me from looking. I thought you knew by now. I love you."

As she had done for him, he was lending his strength. She reached her hand to his face and stroked her fingers through his whiskers. "Stay with me."

He tightened his grip on her hand. "I shall."

Closing her eyes to shut out the tears, she absorbed the mountain lion's courage. The cone went over her face. When she woke . . . So tired. Unable to finish the thought, she was engulfed by blackness.

When Wil had discovered Alice with a broken arm, not knowing the extent of her injuries, he had nearly gone on a rampage. His duty—kill Yankees. *For a dying cause?* He struggled not to let insanity win.

Unlike Peopeo, he could help Alice. Lily sat with her when duty required his presence. As the line stretched thinner and longer, he rode more miles each day inspecting it. The precious few remaining hours, he stayed by Alice's side and got very little sleep.

For nearly a week, she fought a fever. Self-sufficient for most of his life, he felt impotent. At the back of his mind lingered the thought that she might die. If she did, he'd be unable to control his urge to kill those responsible. But as the days passed, life returned to her green eyes.

Wil wrung a cloth in a basin and helped her wash her long graceful neck, her shoulders, and full, firm breasts. His body reacted. *Not now.* She wasn't ready. She'd let him know when the time came.

In wide arcing circles, he massaged the irregular pale marks stretched across her belly. He lowered her nightdress. "The Yankees will be moving soon." Idle conversation? No, the truth. Soon—duty would make no allowances. He'd be unable to return to the cottage. "I'd like you to go to Amanda's before that happens."

"An order?"

"A request. If Lily accompanies you, she'll be free."

"I'm not feeling up to a journey." Her lips formed a sad pout.

Damn, she was beautiful. Unable to resist, he kissed her on the mouth.

"Wil . . ." She twisted from his arms. "I'm loathsome."

"I beg to differ." Though it wasn't the stump she had feared, she lifted her right arm from under the blanket. Pitted with oozing sores and raw, healing wounds where the surgeon had removed bits of lead, her arm was useless all the same. She tried to remain brave, but he caught a glimpse of tears in her eyes. "The doctor says it may take time for any feeling to return."

"Or never."

"A possibility," he agreed.

"Damn you—for being so honest."

She wouldn't have respected anything else. In time, she'd realize that fact. "None of this changes who you are." But she didn't move. Tired of her self-pity routine, he resisted the urge to shake some sense into her and got to his feet. Wil shoved his hat on his head and strode for the door. "Suit yourself. I need to return to the line."

"Wil, I'm sorry. I'm afraid. I want to be more like you and not show fear, but I can't. What use am I this way? I don't want you to feel obligated to stand by me out of duty."

He lowered his hat and reseated himself on the edge of the bed. "Alice, I don't find you loathsome. You're as charming as when we first met."

She clapped her good hand over her mouth and giggled. "I was barely past being an ungainly, small-bosomed girl when we met, and you didn't even notice me."

"Amanda wouldn't have been the only one to fetch a shotgun if I *had* noticed."

She only laughed harder. Turning serious once more, she grasped his hand. "I'm truly afraid you'll be humiliated to present me as your wife and take another woman."

Wil squeezed her hand. "There is no other—in my mind or heart."

"Not even . . ."

Amanda. He let out a weary breath.

"Even if you won't admit it to yourself, you cared for her."

Women possessed a peculiar sentimentality that he doubted he'd ever comprehend. "I cared for Poker too, but never had the desire to make him my bedfellow."

"Wil, don't make fun of me. You know it's not the same." Tears returned to her eyes, and he handed her a handkerchief. Although awkward, she dabbed her eyes with her left hand. "You loved her."

The letter that never got mailed. "Did Amanda say something...?"

More dabbing. "She didn't have to. Even after all this time, I see it in your eyes—and hers."

How did he feel? He thought he had come to terms with the way things had turned out. But at Christmas, seeing Amanda again and thinking of Prescott violating her body... Wil took out his pocket watch and checked the time. "What is it you want me to say?"

"Nothing, but sometimes I fret that you wish I were her."

"Nonsense." He tucked his watch in his waistcoat. "You should know by now that I prefer a woman who can swear."

She giggled again. "And the bawdier it is, all the better." Her good arm went around his neck, and she kissed him on the mouth. "Thank you, Wil, and I wish I didn't have to leave—not at a time like this. But I will take your suggestion and go to Amanda's."

"I'll see to the arrangements." Wily and mischievous, otter's powers were tempting to reel him in. But the mountain lion was solitary. Until the war was over, he would wander along the ever darkening chasm.

Ambling hooves and creaking axles traveled the length of the tree-lined lane. With rifle in hand, Amanda met the wagon in the farmyard. Not a military wagon—but two women. A lovely Negress and Alice. She lowered the rifle.

Alice handed her a basket containing Emma. The baby smiled at her. As she thought of Ben, her heart tugged.

"Amanda..."

She looked up as the mulatto woman helped Alice from the wagon.

Her sister clutched her right arm next to her body. "This is Lily." They exchanged greetings. "Wil sent me. He thinks once the Yankees move, Petersburg will fall, and Richmond won't be far behind."

The war would be over soon? After four years, she prayed it was true. "Alice, I'm relieved you're safe."

"I wanted to stay in Petersburg."

"An' Miss Alice would've. She'd follow dat man to da ends of dis earth."

"That's what it will be for us," Alice said. "I wanted to be with him when the moment came. I know neither of you understand. Amanda, you're married to a Yankee, and Lily, you have everything to gain. You're in Yankee territory. You're free now."

A broad grin appeared on Lily's face. "An' you didn't have to buy me to get it neither."

Alice grasped Lily's hand—in sisterhood. "Is Lily the reason you changed your mind?" Amanda asked.

"Lily and Emma. I'd never forgive myself if anything happened to either of them—the way it did to me." Alice raised her right dress sleeve.

Amanda stifled a gasp at the pitted, limp arm. "The Yankees did that to you?"

"One of the missiles hit near the cottage. The surgeon struggled to save it. I'm beginning to get a little feeling back, but there's no way of knowing if it will ever be the same."

Amanda hadn't thought civilians were targets. No, Sam had warned her, but she had shoved the thought from her mind—for this very reason. "Come inside. I'll fix some tea."

"Tea? I don't know when I last had any tea. It sounds delightful."

As they went up to the house, Amanda gave Alice a quick hug. A thunderclap rumbled in the distance, hinting at rain. The storm brewing was far from over.

Barely able to sit in the saddle, the gaunt frame halted the gray stallion abreast with Wil's mare. He saluted General Hill.

Fresh from sick leave, the haggard general appeared as if he should have remained in Richmond, but rumors abounded that General Grant was ready for an all-out assault on the Petersburg line. To the end, both of them would fight.

"General . . . ," Powell said, his voice sluggish as if he were having difficulty concentrating. "Wil, we have some unfinished business."

The unasked question. "I thought I had a reprieve until the end, sir."

Weariness and pain reflected on his old friend's face. From the days of playing pranks on Old Jack at West Point to the trenches of Petersburg, the war had turned them into old men. Illness had plagued Powell for so long that his hazel eyes warned Wil that he wasn't going to get better. *Was this their final meeting?* He hated for their friendship to end in this manner.

Wil reached for his sword and presented it to the corps commander.

Powell stared at it in a lingering sort of way, then looked up. A younger, more robust Powell would have snapped the sword over his knee. He placed a gloved hand on the sword as if ready to accept it. "If I said I wouldn't ask until after the war, then I won't, but Wil," he said with a shake of his head, "I no longer recollect what the question was."

"Powell?"

Powell raised a hand. "I know you will perform your duty in the days ahead. If a question would keep that from happening at such a dire time, then it's best I don't remember. Don't you agree?"

Managing a weak nod, Wil sheathed his sword. Not only was his honor restored, his hands were washed free of shame. Had Powell really forgotten the question? Or was he using his illness as a pretense? Wil saluted. "It has been an honor serving under you, sir."

With a frail smile, the corps commander returned the salute and cued the gray stallion on. The Yankees were coming, and Wil had the feeling he would never see Powell Hill again.

Chapter Twenty-Two

Petersburg Front
April 2, 1865

IN THE ROLLING MIST the dappled horse was barely visible. The courier halted with a salute, and Wil read the dispatch. His gut feeling had been right. Lieutenant General Powell Hill was dead. No details—only an announcement of the change in command and his orders to hold the line for as long as possible. *So many dead—friends and enemies alike.*

With no time to mourn, he supposed it was a fitting paradox that the war would end the same way it had begun—with the loss of a dear friend. This day would mark his last battle as well.

But hold the line? For what purpose? So the rest of the army could escape Petersburg. The revolution that never happened was drawing to a close. The ragtag army of Northern Virginia must be retreating. "Tell the general we'll hold two, maybe three hours."

The courier saluted and reined the gray around. Vanishing into the mist, they galloped off. So little time. Preparing for the blue storm, Wil ordered the men to throw up breastworks.

Muskets rattled to their left.

As the morning passed, the mist burned off. While Wil inspected the line, men continued digging. A mound of dirt wouldn't hold the Yankees at bay for long. Through field glasses, he spotted a gleam of sun shining off bayonets in the woods to the south. The Yanks were on the march toward them.

Wil checked his pocket watch. Almost noon—he should have written to Alice. And said what? The Yankees were coming, and when the day's fighting was finished, she'd most likely be a widow. That wasn't the sort of thing a man wrote to his wife. What a fool—he hadn't learned as much as he thought. *Write the things a woman needs to hear.*

It was too late for writing letters. A blue mass rushed forward, yelling and shouting. Behind the earthworks, his boys waited with muskets ready to greet them.

Steady.

The howling mob came closer. Firing broke out to their right. Wil raised his sword.

Closer.

He lowered the sword, and with deadly accuracy, his boys fired. The enemy line vanished in a cloud of smoke.

Holes gaped where men once stood. Still, they came. His boys fired steadily and heavily. Like a flag in the breeze, the blue mass waved. A hole in his line opened on the right. No reserves waited to plug it.

Wil spurred his mare that direction. He jumped from her back and raised his pistol, joining the fight.

"Sir . . . Please get back."

As the firing lessened and smoke drifted away, Wil turned to Captain Hanes. The Yankees were retreating—for now. "They're re-forming. Prepare the line for the next attack."

The captain saluted and trotted off.

The wound in his chest was acting up. After taking a moment to catch his breath, Wil remounted the mare and inspected the damage along the line.

A few men had fallen, but their losses were minimal—this time. Some of the boys strengthened the earthworks. They could probably withstand one more onslaught before the line crumbled. Unless the Yanks flanked them. Damn—there were no men to spare to safeguard against such a maneuver.

Cannon roared to the left. Hell was opening up and swallowing the Confederacy. Wil heard them before seeing them. A yelling mass charged straight at them. He reminded the boys to hold their fire. Closer. Old Glory waved—the same flag he had taken an oath to defend. He mustn't think about that now. "Fire!"

Smoke filled the air, and bullets whined. He felt a sharp stab in his lower right leg. He was hit. *Don't look and keep going.* A Yankee clambered over the earthworks.

Wil aimed and fired his pistol. The Yank screamed before going down. Another Yankee scrambled over their defenses, followed by another. His boys dropped both of them. Holes opened in the Yankee ranks. The enemy line wavered, but continued forward.

Through the smoke he could barely see. The pain in his chest and leg was spreading, making him dizzy. Finally, the smoke cleared.

The line had held. The only Yankees within it were dead or dying, and a carpet of blue lay on the other side.

From the relative safety of the woods, Sam glanced at the breastworks through field glasses. After two failed assaults resulting in the same number of wounded brigadiers, the division commander had sent a skirmish line to the Reb's right flank as a distraction while their brigade formed on the left.

Choking back his worst fear, Sam snapped his eyes shut. The colors of Wil's brigade were positioned on the opposite ridge. *Not again.* He rubbed tired eyes.

Waiting was always the worst, and this time more so than usual. While some of the boys chatted, he distracted himself by rereading Amanda's latest letter. She proudly announced she was in a family way. Should he shout for joy or weep?

Barely had he met his only son before his tiny life had been snuffed out. With so many friends and loved ones gone, there had to be a reason. Would Amanda be able to carry on if he joined them? The war had begun with the death of her husband. What if it ended the same way?

After carefully folding the letter, he tucked it in the pocket nearest to his heart. A silly superstition—a letter couldn't keep him out of harm's way. He peered to the breastworks.

"Colonel . . ."

Sam saluted the general's staff officer.

"You're to take the enemy's works no matter the cost. We shall be in Petersburg by nightfall. On to Richmond!" With a triumphant grin, the officer raised his sword heavenward. "God go with you."

His orders were clear. Sam called his company commanders to relay the orders and focused on the job of taking the enemy's works. It wasn't just anyone he was facing. *Wil Jackson is on that hill*. Sam raised his sword.

Cannon fired at the entrenchments as a signal for their advance. "Forward!"

Out of the ravine and woods, the brigade charged. Rebel canister responded, shaking the ground and tearing through the ranks.

Dress the line. Sam waved his sword. *Forward*.

A musket volley fired into the tattered gray ranks. Smoke burned his nostrils. The field cleared.

Already battered by previous assaults, the Rebs threw their muskets down and bolted. Another volley, and more Rebs skedaddled. Others surrendered. Yet, a tenacious handful remained planted on the enemy line.

Aware the Rebs couldn't hold their ground for long, Sam admired their perseverance and grit. Among the men crouched behind breastworks, a hatless Rebel officer limped, waving his sword and rallying them further.

Wil . . . *No matter the cost.*

Alice would never forgive him. Could Amanda? Sam couldn't think straight and said a silent prayer. Give the command or *his* men would die. Closing his eyes, he shouted, "Fire!"

The ground rumbled, and the ragtag defenders vanished in a cloud of smoke. As the veil lifted, the remaining Rebel hands shot skyward, but the officer was gone. Rallying his men, Wil had been a conspicuous target. Most likely, he was among the dead or dying.

Sam ordered his boys to round up the prisoners and checked the prone gray-clad bodies for his former captain. A red-haired boy moaned in death throes. Beside him, another boy gripped his arm. He continued checking faces and uniforms. None of them were Wil.

A dark-haired officer sprawled face down in the dirt. Dropping to his knees, Sam turned the limp body over. A colonel, not a brigadier.

"Sir, why are you frettin' over dead Rebs?"

For a moment, Sam thought he heard Jo's wheezy voice. Like so many others, the girl soldier was dead. He focused on the private's peach-fuzz face. "You wouldn't understand."

The private plunked his musket butt to the ground. "I reckon you're right. If'n you want my opinion, all the Southron traitors should pay for the sufferin' they've caused."

Sam straightened and looked the private in the eye. "My wife is Virginian, Private. Now return to your duties."

Red-faced, the boy saluted.

Could he blame the private? Everyone felt the strain of the war's four long years. With it rapidly coming to a close, they mustn't lose sight of who they were or why they were here. To let one's guard down— even now—could be lethal. He continued searching for Wil among the fallen.

Overhearing shouts, Sam jerked his head up.

Four defiant Rebs were turning a cannon, aiming it for one last deadly assault. If the gun was ready, it would tear a hole through his regiment.

As Sam raised his pistol, several of the boys readied their muskets. He aimed and froze. *Shoot.* His finger hovered over the trigger, refusing to obey his will.

Bullets whined, and one Reb went down. One grayback was an officer. God help him, he couldn't pull the trigger and now knew why. "Hold your fire!" he shouted to the boys. "Jackson!" He sprang forward.

The Yankee officer charged straight for Wil, screaming.

Determined to take as many of the bluebellies with him as possible, Wil reached for the lanyard. Before he could fire the cannon, the full brunt of the Yankee's weight struck him square in the chest, slamming him to the ground. He ignored the pain. This was his last fight, and his hands sought the officer's throat.

The Yank gasped. Struggling to break Wil's grip, he countered with a blow to the face.

Dazed, Wil tasted blood and loosened his hold. The Yank yelled, but the horde of faces laughed at the squaw perched on the spotted horse with a rope around her neck. *His last fight* ... Once and for all, he would avenge Peopeo's death. He landed a crunching blow to the bastard's jaw.

The Yank successfully deflected several swings. After an exchange of bruising impacts, a doubled fist met with Wil's chest. Pain swept through him like wildfire. Finding it difficult to breathe, he pounded his last remaining strength to the bluebelly's midsection.

Wil fell back and tried to catch his breath. "You've won."

The Yank staggered to his feet. "For an old man, you pack a hell of a wallop."

The officer's blue eyes held no hatred, but recognition. "Sam?" His hands trembled, and Wil spat the blood from his mouth. "Just who are you calling old?"

Breathing heavily, Sam rubbed his jaw, then offered a hand in truce. "Come back, Captain."

Captain . . . Though they fought on opposite sides, they had shared life and death once more in an ironic twist of fate.

Wil glanced to the side. The Yankees had rounded up a number of his boys as prisoners. A few were dead or wounded. The rest had run. With his command gone, the Cause was dead. There was no honor in keeping a lost cause alive or glory in dying in battle. Or—in seeking revenge for Peopeo's death.

A color-bearer carried Old Glory.

"I could have killed you, Prescott."

"But you hesitated. I thought that was *my* failing, Captain." Sam thrust out his hand once more, and Wil reached to accept it. "Welcome back, Wil."

As he got to his feet, Wil pressed a hand to his chest. Blood seeped between his fingers. Under the stress of the fight, the old wound had reopened. "I fear it will be a short reunion."

His left arm was being drawn over Sam's shoulder. "I'll get you to a surgeon."

"To die in a Yankee hospital." Wil managed a ragged laugh. "Do you detect the irony?"

Wil swayed on his feet, and Sam tightened his grip to help steady him. "You're not going to die . . . "

Captain . . . Even though Sam hadn't said the word, Wil heard it all the same. "I accept my fate. I don't need consolation."

"And I wasn't giving it. You're too much of a hard-headed son of a bitch to die."

He gasped for breath, and his legs buckled. Sam caught him. With a groan, Wil clutched Sam's jacket. "Tell Alice—tell her—"

"You'll tell her yourself." Two Yankees grasped his arms, and Sam let go. "See that the general receives proper treatment. Captain . . . " Sam saluted.

Though weak, Wil returned the salute. Between them, blue and gray had always stood still. "Thank you . . . Lieutenant." New Mexico seemed a lifetime ago. Four years of war made everything feel that way.

"Ma'am . . ."

Holly withdrew the tin cup from the wounded private's lips and glanced up.

A Confederate captain leaned on a crutch. "Ma'am, we've been here for over a day and haven't had anything to eat. I was wondering if you could . . ."

She nodded that she would fetch some rations and overheard a Federal patient taunt the captain. "You had best scoot back to your ward before someone thinks you're trying to escape," she said.

The captain hobbled in the direction of the Confederate ward. Holly made a quick trip to the kitchen with the inquiry, and the cook assured her the Rebels would be fed. She collected some fresh-baked bread and returned to the ward, making the rounds of the patients capable of eating solid food. With a gentle smile, the captain was most appreciative of her efforts.

"I thought the sight of blood made you ill, Mrs. Prescott."

The sound of Wil Jackson's voice chilled her. She straightened, then cautiously turned. Heavily bearded, he lay on the cot with his chest swathed in bandages. Another bloody dressing wrapped his right leg.

"Wil," she said, "you appear to be in one piece."

Though he forced a laugh, his dark eyes couldn't mask pain. "You should get your wish," he replied.

"My wish?"

He struggled to sit up. "That I rot in some Yankee prison."

"I told you . . ."

He waved a hand. "That you were grieving over the loss of your husband. I'd wager you were mourning the loss of his income."

Before she could respond, the captain hobbled between them. "Sir, are you acquainted with this charming lady?"

Wil laughed, but he doubled over in agony.

It served him right. Holly pasted on her most alluring smile. "Yes, Wil, why don't you introduce us?"

Wil struggled to catch his breath. "Captain Hanes—Mrs. Prescott, my former . . ." She shot him a glare, and a wicked grin tugged at the corners of his mouth. ". . . informant."

The captain kissed her hand. "A pleasure, ma'am. Your generosity won't be forgotten."

Ready to gloat, she flashed Wil a haughty smirk, but he had clamped his eyes shut and gasped for breath. "Wil Jackson," she chastised, bending down and readjusting the feather pillow to help him breathe, "when are you going to learn you can fool others, but not me?"

Breathing easy again, he studied her, and the captain discreetly returned to his cot. No simpleton, the subordinate officer had likely guessed she had been more than an informant. "I underestimated you, Holly."

The admission stunned her to silence. She regained her poise. "No, you didn't. I think it's likely we know each other far better than either of us care to admit. If we hadn't parted ways, one of us would have wound up dead." A tired smile crept to his face, and she jabbed a finger in his direction. "And if you get any fool notion in your head about gaining the upper hand with me again, I still carry my derringer."

His smile widened to a grin. "You have my word. I'll try not to rile you. Is it possible to get a message to—"

"Alice." She shook her head. "They won't let any messages from senior Rebel officers through—not now. General Lee is on the run, and everyone is a little tense. Even if I wrote one for you, it would likely get confiscated."

His breathing suddenly grew ragged. He leaned back and closed his eyes.

She fluffed the pillow behind his head, but he didn't move. "Wil?"

No response. His pulse was flighty and his skin—cool to the touch. *Oh God . . .* She had witnessed it often enough. Wounded men who were fine one minute, then the next . . . "Wil, don't do this. You're too much of a prick . . ."

Still no response, and goddamn him for making her fret over whether he lived or died.

* * *

Wagons, broken wheels, and knapsacks littered the road. General Lee's army was on the run. As the regiment formed near the white clapboard house, Sam lowered the field glasses. An aide led Red to the rear. In three lines, the brigade marched down a hill toward the waiting Rebels.

By the creek, the Rebs opened fire. The once clear-running water already trickled crimson.

Sam waved his sword for the men to continue forward. Under a barrage of flying bullets, he jumped waist-deep into the water and, once on the other side, re-formed the line. Up a rise toward a copse of woods, they marched, and the Rebels began to flee. The regiment reached the trees.

A Reb officer sprang forward and yelled, "Fire!"

Gray-clad figures rose from camouflaged hiding spots behind felled trees. Burning lead skimmed Sam's cheek. Boys dropped faster than buzzing flies, but he shouted the order to return fire as the Rebels charged.

Bayonets sliced through flesh, and screams filled the air. Blocking their avenue of retreat, the Rebs got between his boys and the creek.

Before the enemy had a chance to re-form, Sam called for a counter-charge. More screams, and more boys fell. Metal struck metal in hand-to-hand combat. The Rebel line gave way, and the regiment slogged its way in retreat across the red-running stream.

The division commander galloped a lathered bay and slid to a halt beside him. "Colonel . . ."

Sam saluted the general.

"As senior officer present, take command and recross the stream. Swarm the Rebel line, but I want those people driven from that hill." Another salute, and Sam rubbed war-weary eyes. He retrieved Red from behind the clapboard house.

He mounted the red stallion and motioned his line forward.

Bullets whined anew, and the regiment crossed the scarlet water. Up the hill, Red snorted and pitched. He was falling.

Before Sam could jump clear, he heard a sickening snap as the half-ton horse slammed onto his right leg. Unable to move, he pounded a fist to the bloody ground and screamed.

* * *

More than six weeks had passed since General Lee's surrender at Appomattox Court House. With no word from Wil or Sam, Alice slept little. Tossing and turning from the next bedroom during the night warned her that Amanda fared much the same. Both kept from speaking their greatest fear.

Occasionally, soldiers clad in gray would tramp through in search of a bite to eat or to bed down in the barn. Mostly northern Virginians on their journey home, none had heard of Wil. She hadn't expected them to recognize his name. Still, she never gave up hope and repeated her inquiry to the next straggler.

Each passing day brought more feeling to her arm. In a melancholy state, Alice tucked some Confederate bills and stamps into an envelope, then sealed it with wax. She'd save them for Emma. One day her daughter would ask about the troubled times of her birth. Had it really been two years since the destruction of her home in Fredericksburg? All of those bodies... Already it felt like a lifetime ago.

Wagon wheels creaked along the lane. Wil... She jerked her head up. In a mad dash to reach the door, she nearly slipped across the wood floor.

Once on the porch, a rickety wagon entered the farmyard, leading a flea-bitten red horse. She barely recognized the chestnut stallion. "Amanda, come quick!"

The wagon halted out front, and a soldier in blue shoved a crutch under his arm and struggled to rise from the bed of straw.

"Sam?"

His blue eyes gleamed. "Alice, you're looking lovely."

Finally securely balanced on the crutch, the blue-clad officer was definitely Sam. Once again, she called for Amanda. "You've been wounded."

"Not wounded. Leg's broken, but..." Hobbling closer, he motioned to Red. "...he got the worst end of the deal. Took a bullet in the neck and fell on me. Fool horse nearly died."

Behind her, Amanda squealed and sailed past her with outstretched arms, nearly knocking Sam from the crutch. Feeling distinctly out of place, Alice lowered her head and turned away.

Sam called after her. "Alice, haven't you heard from Wil?"

She faced him. "No."

With a properly restrained smile, Amanda draped her arm about his waist to help support him. "I don't think he was hurt bad," he said.

"You've seen him?"

"A few days before this happened."

"Sam, tell me what you know."

Even Mama delighted in welcoming Sam home as they helped him inside. Once he was comfortable in the green velvet wing chair, Amanda propped his broken leg. Occasionally exchanging glimpses and admiring smiles with Amanda, Sam relayed how he had met Wil on the battlefield during the fall of Petersburg.

Chilled, Alice rubbed her arms. So where was Wil now? Dead? Alive, but detained in some Yankee prison camp? On his way back to her? "If you'll excuse me . . ."

"Alice . . ." Amanda grasped her arm. "He'll be back. You'll see."

She nodded and glanced over her shoulder. "I'm glad you're home, Sam." Gathering her skirts together, Alice hustled outside to the porch and down the steps.

In the farmyard Ezra curried the stallion's lackluster red coat. She stared down the empty lane. Sam had spoken to Wil a little more than a month ago. That thought gave her hope.

A bobwhite called from the pasture. As she moved toward the sound, she wandered through the shoulder-high grass. Arriving at the knoll, she sat and watched clouds. In a gentle breeze a red-tailed hawk sailed overhead, then dove.

Unable to see through thick blades of long grass, she heard a high-pitched squeal. The bird flew to a bare oak branch with a limp field mouse grasped in its talons. After gulping down the mouse, the hawk preened. Fluffing feathers, its dark eye watched her. Finally, with a cry, the hawk gracefully took to the air.

Wasn't the hawk a warrior? It must be a sign from the animal spirits. Wil was on his way back to her.

With renewed hope, Alice rushed back to the house to feed Emma. By the time she returned, it was nearly dark and her breasts were swollen.

Mama passed her a squalling baby.

Alice hurried to her room and hummed while Emma nursed. She traced a finger across a chubby cheek. "Your papa will be home any day now, Miss Emma."

With Emma's black hair and brown skin, she reminded Alice so much of Wil. Only her daughter's eyes were more like her own. Sinking into despair, she fretted over meaningless words. Emma might not know her papa's love. But the hawk . . . Certainly it was an encouraging sign.

Rhythmic creaking came from Amanda's room. She conjured up a delightfully wicked vision of Sam flat on his back with his broken leg and Amanda, growing heavy with child, poised above him. The bawdy distraction only made her yearn for Wil.

After tucking Emma in her cradle, Alice went outside to check the tree-lined lane. Empty—she turned away.

Each day, she made it her business to pass the lane several times. More stragglers lumbered by with the same shake of their heads upon mentioning Wil's name.

Two days later, she spied the hawk hunting the same field and discovered it had a nest high in a sycamore tree. At the end of the week, a familiar figure limped up the lane. Wil . . . She ran toward him, but pulled up short when he entered the farmyard. The stooped frame wasn't Wil, but Captain Hanes.

He lowered his hat. "Mrs. Jackson . . . "

Squeezing her brows together, Alice swallowed hard. "I presume you have news of my husband."

"The Yanks were detaining senior officers, ma'am."

Her heart lurched in relief. Then Sam could help Wil. With an overjoyed whoop she called for him.

"Ma'am . . . " The captain shook his bearded face. "While it's true the Yanks were holdin' officers, I'm sorry to say, the general has passed on."

"Passed . . . on? As in . . . " Frozen in place, she couldn't utter the word.

He bowed his head slightly. "You have my condolences."

"Details, Captain." With the crutch under his right arm, Sam hobbled between them.

"The old wound was botherin' the general something fierce. He started bleedin' and . . . passed on. I saw the Yanks carry, beggin' your pardon, ma'am, the body out."

The body. Wil wasn't some frozen corpse—like those on the Fredericksburg heights. A tear streaked her cheek. "That's not possible. That wound was completely healed."

Speaking gently, Sam faced her. "Alice, you tended wounded in the hospital. Sometimes these wounds never heal. You know from my account that he . . . well, I'm sorry."

Sorry? Refusing to believe, she clenched her hand to a fist. Wil was a warrior. He wouldn't just up and die. "But I saw the hawk."

"The hawk?"

"The hawk is a sign that Wil shall be returning soon."

Sam shook his head that he didn't understand. "Alice . . ."

To shut out his words, she clamped her hands over her ears. "Sam, you don't know Wil as much as you think you do. He wouldn't . . ." Wouldn't what? Die?

The word sank in. Not Wil—he couldn't be dead. Suddenly lightheaded, she sank. Strong hands caught her before she hit the ground. Half-expecting to find herself on the Fredericksburg streets and gazing into familiar black eyes, she smiled a thank you. But his eyes were blue, and Wil really was dead.

When Amanda had lost her son, Alice remained steadfast, offering comforting words, but, most importantly, sharing a sister's love when she needed it most. She searched the knoll where Alice spent the best part of her days, sitting and staring at the sky. What kept her so preoccupied with the spot Amanda couldn't fathom. Had Alice met Wil on the grassy hillside in the past? If circumstances had turned out differently, *she* could have been the one on the hill waiting for him and struggling to face the notion that he was really gone.

Dead, Amanda. Unable to say the word, Amanda heard Wil's voice at the back of her mind spell it out. She crossed her arms above her rounding belly, and a red-tailed hawk floated across the sky, finally coming to rest on a branch in the bottomland.

Of course, why hadn't she thought of it sooner? Alice had retreated to the shack where she had met Wil while smuggling supplies. She suspected more had gone on at the secluded shanty than supply running, but none of that mattered now.

Raising her black skirt, Amanda scurried down the hill to the rushing stream. She followed the path along the bank until arriving at the shack.

With the door opened wide, Alice stretched on a straw mattress.

"Alice..." No answer. "Alice, Sam received a response to his inquiry."

Alice's cheeks were streaked as if she had been crying.

When her sister sat up, Amanda cleared her throat. "Hospital officials can find where Wil's buried. If you'd like to bring him home..."

Without looking up, Alice blinked. "But I don't know what place he regarded as home."

Fighting tears, Amanda struggled to keep her poise. Stay strong—for Alice's sake. "He'd want to be near you and Emma."

Alice traced a hand along the straw mattress with a reminiscent smile, confirming Amanda's suspicions. "Amanda, you warned me. You said 'Don't let him break your heart.'"

All too clearly, she recalled the words. With arms spread, Amanda sat beside her sister and hugged her to her breast.

"He has. Damn him, he has."

Her own tears were near the surface, and Amanda forced a smile, wiping Alice's smudged face with a handkerchief. "If he were here, he'd tease you about the swear."

Alice's lashes flickered. Amanda thought she might cry again. Instead, she giggled. "Not a very endearing trait, is it?"

"Maybe not, but he loved you all the same."

"Because he's no gentleman." Present tense. Realizing the mistake, Alice bowed her head and dissolved into sobs.

So much waste. There had to be a reason for all of the suffering countless families had endured. None that she could see. John and Wil were in their graves for no reason at all.

Chapter Twenty-Three

For so long, clouded moods and melancholy had been a part of him, but Wil was at peace. Whether it was a permanent state or not, he couldn't be certain, but he accepted it. Holly had confiscated a Confederate uniform from a dead private and brought him to a one-room house falling to disrepair and long abandoned by war.

With the wound in his lower leg nearly mended, he decided it was time to make the journey home. He scrubbed his face with the cool spring water from the bucket. *Home.* At one time, home was determined by his location. Now Alice was the defining factor.

"Wil, you're a fool."

He patted his face dry with a soiled linen. "Been called worse."

"That's more than fifty miles—on foot without a pass."

Had that been worry in her voice? He straightened. "And I have finally lived to see the day that you fret over my well-being." Holly cursed, and a smile crept to his face. "I see things have returned to normal."

"Don't be mean." Her lip curled to a pout.

"Holly . . . I thank you."

"Thank you," she repeated dryly. "I risk my life by sneaking you to a safe haven, then tending you, and I get a mere thank you?"

"You knew from the outset that's all I had to give."

Hesitant, she met his gaze. She had never been the sort to be unsure of herself.

He finally understood that greed and lust *hadn't* been her primary motivating factors. "I don't know what to say."

Suddenly miffed, Holly pointed her chin and tightened her shawl about her shoulders. "Don't say anything, you fool. You'd only embarrass both of us, and we'd fall into our usual bickering routine."

So true. Wil lifted her hand to his lips and kissed it. "I never thought I'd say this, but you have my respect."

Poised to slap him with her free hand, she jerked free of his grasp. "I told you not to say anything." Before he could turn away, she pressed several greenbacks into his palm. "It's not much, but I know what the war has done to Southerners. You can repay me when you're able."

Left speechless by Holly's uncharacteristic generosity, he fidgeted with the bills.

"Tell me that you'll accept it." He nodded, and her familiar biting tone returned. "Besides, do you seriously think I'd be seen with the likes of you now that you've lost your rank and are a pauper?"

Comforted to know she would never truly change, he laughed and tucked the bills into his pocket.

Outside the shack, the road stretched through the morning mist. During the war, he would have been able to march the route in several days. Weakened from the wound he had taken in the Wilderness and the still-mending one from Petersburg, he'd be unable to set such a blistering pace.

Wil stepped from the creaky porch and began the journey home.

As the late-spring sun burned the mist away, Wil passed once-stately manors and barns reduced to blackened timbers. Fencing destroyed, fields trampled and scorched, and the rest left to weeds, the countryside had been laid almost completely to waste. Odd—what four years of war did to the land and mind alike. Now that it was over, what next?

Short of breath, he sat by the roadside and rested. Holly *was* right. He was a fool. At his current rate, it would take him more than a week to reach Fredericksburg. As long as he got there, little else mattered. He regained his feet and pressed onward.

Morning gave way to afternoon. Hatless, Wil sought relief from the sun along the bank of a stream. Barely had he got comfortable beneath the shade of a poplar tree, when he heard the hammer of a rifle cock.

Instinctively he reached for a sidearm that was no longer there. Raising his hands, he got to his feet and turned slowly.

A pint-sized woman in a pronounced family way haphazardly clutched a double-barreled shotgun.

"If you're going to shoot, I suggest that you brace the gun against your shoulder, or I guarantee the recoil will be most unpleasant. In your—*delicate* condition, it could be downright dangerous."

Her eyes blazed, and she lowered the shotgun slightly—just enough that if she fired, it would hit him squarely in the groin.

He arched an eyebrow.

"You are no gentleman," she muttered. Though her dress was threadbare and sorely in need of mending, her accent betrayed a former elite status.

"Even the missus has accused me of that from time to time, but I must confess, I have never been threatened in such a manner."

Her gaze followed the gun barrel. Flushing, she lowered the shotgun. "My apologies."

"Much obliged, ma'am. Now if you don't mind, I'll bid you farewell. After making it through four years of war in one piece, I'd prefer to keep it that way."

As Wil turned, she hailed after him, "Mr. . . . ."

Mister—after more than twenty years in the military, it would take time to get accustomed to a civilian title. "Jackson," he said, turning back.

"Mr. Jackson, I don't have much to spare, but if you'd care to join me for supper, I'd appreciate the company."

Torn between staying and continuing on, he realized that most of the day had passed without eating when his stomach rumbled a reminder. Meal opportunities were rare. "I'll accept as long as the shotgun isn't invited."

She smiled in a gracious hostess-like manner, reminding him of Alice on Amanda's wedding day. "Agreed. I'm Mrs. Robert Boyer."

As she lifted her skirt to climb the bank, he grasped the shotgun to keep her from blasting something or someone unintentionally, then gripped her elbow to aid her up the incline.

At the top of the bank, they reached the road. Several hundred yards farther, overgrown boxwood hid the entrance to a lane lined by dogwoods. She chatted about her husband, serving as a captain in Fitz Lee's cavalry and how there had been no word since the surrender.

While her expression remained stern, the quaver in her voice betrayed her distress from waiting. "Forgive me. I'm prattling on about my troubles and haven't given you the opportunity to speak."

"Understandable in your condition."

At the mention of her pregnancy, her face reddened. "Tell me, Mr. Jackson, as I recall you said there was a missus." He nodded. "So she knows what it's like."

"I reckon so," he agreed.

She stopped walking. "You don't talk much, do you?"

Without facing her, he halted. "Not usually—but I can listen."

To this response, she smiled and continued on. At the end of the lane stood a brick-columned house with sagging shutters. Where immense shade trees once framed the building, jagged stumps left a wartime reminder. "I'm alone," she said. "The Yankees allowed me to stay because I signed their oath."

His own dilemma—senior officers were required to sign the Yankee oath in order to secure a pardon, or uphold a cause that had been lost from the very beginning. Even if amnesty were granted, any future military career would be out of the question.

"He'll be shamed to call me his wife, but I wasn't in any position to travel . . ." She pressed a hand to her rounded belly.

"He'll think you made a difficult decision to the best of your ability."

Suddenly suspicious, she examined him from head to toe. "Do you know what's in the oath?"

"I do, ma'am—all too well."

"You've signed it?"

"Not yet, but I reckon I will."

"You're not a private."

It had been a statement, not a question. Wil gestured to the frayed butternut jacket. "The Yankees pay less notice to a private slipping out of their camps than an officer."

As she ascended the stairs, she asked, "Colonel?"

"Brigadier."

Inside, a few makeshift chairs were the only furniture in the parlor, reminding him of Alice's house in Fredricksburg after the battle. She set about to preparing supper—a simple meal of greasy broth with a few turnips and carrots along with a roll of hard cornbread. Famished, he devoured the soup as if it were gourmet fare. While he ate, she spoke of her life being threatened the past few months by Yankees. As she talked about her husband, she grew solemn.

"Begging your pardon, but what do you aim to do when your time comes?" he asked.

She avoided eye contact, but her face no longer flushed from embarrassment. "A neighbor calls on me daily. She'll be here to assist."

That answered only part of his question. Wil got to his feet and tucked a dollar into her hand. With a wife and child of his own waiting for his return, there was little else he could do. Yet, he *should* do more—cut wood, mend fences.

If he started in on chores, the delay could cost him weeks, and he was barely fit enough to carry them out. Only enough stamina—and determination—to make the journey home. "You're a most generous woman. I appreciate your hospitality."

She clutched the greenback to her chest. "Brigadier Jackson, can you afford such extraordinary expenditures?"

No. "There are some advantages to having been a general."

He hadn't answered her question any more than she had his. She looked up and met his gaze. *She knew better.*

"If you need a place to bed down for the night, you're welcome to stay in one of the cabins. The servants are long gone."

He pressed another dollar to her hand. "Your offer is a welcome relief."

"Let me fetch a blanket." She vanished from the room, momentarily reappearing with a wool bundle in her arms. "This is foolish. Even on these warm nights, the cabins are plenty drafty. Goodness knows, I have rooms to spare."

"That's most kind of you, but the cabin will do."

She shoved the blanket to her face and sobbed into it. His first instinct was to do as he had always done—withdraw. Always—he pulled away. He forced himself to stay and comfort her. Wil put his arms around her, stiffly at first, and held her. He couldn't think. Wouldn't think. Not the sort to reach out to others' grief, he buried it.

With a tear-streaked face, she looked up. Her face flushed, then she stepped back and wiped the tears from her cheeks. "Forgive me."

He shrugged. "There's nothing to forgive."

Clutching the blanket tighter, she gave an appreciative smile. "What's your given name Brigadier Jackson?"

"William, but most folks call me Wil."

"I'm Anna."

Given a choice, he would have preferred for her to remain nameless. Forever her name would be burned in his memory, a vulnerable woman called Anna—alone, when things shouldn't have been that way.

But nothing would keep him from achieving his goal—to reach Fredericksburg or die trying. After bidding her good evening, he took the blanket, still damp from her tears, and went outside. As he strode to the cabin, Wil heard the haunting cry of the screech owl. He knew then as Anna already must. Captain Boyer wouldn't be returning to his grief-stricken wife, and she would birth alone as she now lived.

The following day, Wil meandered through Richmond streets. Battle scarred and with many buildings reduced to burned rubble, they no longer seemed familiar. Women in black drifted through the charred ruins. Old Glory flew from Libby—the prison Sam had nearly died in. In a park, officers—former Confederate and Yankee alike—strolled with women.

He should feel something. Four years of trying to keep the Yankees out, and there was nothing inside. Only one thing was on his mind now. He spent the last of his money for a decent meal and set out on the road again—to Fredericksburg.

By early evening, the clouds unleashed gathering thunderstorms. Wil sought shelter in a leaky, abandoned shack. With no blanket, it wasn't much different from many nights spent in the field, but he was fitter then. A cough racked through his lungs. He spent the night huddled in the driest corner, shivering.

Though the sun returned in the morning, mud slowed his pace. Later in the day, the road dried, but not soon enough to keep his boots from being caked with red Virginia clay.

A column of Yankees—most likely heading for Washington—marched past him. A few glared, one spat, and finally the taunts came. Ignore them. If he responded in kind, they might keep him from arriving at his destination.

A mounted lieutenant reined away from the column and brought his horse to a halt in front of Wil. *Be cautious—very, very cautious.* If he were suspected of being a former Confederate officer, he'd likely be detained.

The lieutenant leaned against the pommel of his saddle and extended a hand. "Your pass."

Careful not to make eye contact, Wil rummaged through the frayed pockets of his jacket. "I must have lost it."

"Lost it...," the lieutenant grumbled.

Wil opened the tattered jacket. "I'm unarmed, sir."

A couple of soldiers, all too eager to disprove him, shoved him against a tree and searched him. Hands probed every pocket and fold of clothing until the men were satisfied he carried no weapons. "What should we do with him, sir?"

"Bring him along."

Wil remained silent to the order. To protest would only make his circumstance more complicated—plus, they were marching in the right direction. Joining the column, he remained under the watchful eye of two privates. The pace was faster than he had established on his own, and by the time the Yanks bivouacked for the night, he was footsore and barely able to breathe. At least the guards freely shared their rations of hard bread and salt pork.

As pots of coffee boiled over blazing campfires, he heard a voice sing of home. The war was over, giving soldiers both blue and gray—hope.

Determined not to let the Yanks keep him from his destination, Wil stood.

Armed with a musket, one guard got to his feet. "Where do you think you're goin', Reb?"

The urge to reach Fredericksburg had grown so strong, he had stopped thinking things through. The Yanks weren't going to just let him walk out of camp. So as not to alarm the guard further, Wil kept his hands in plain view and reseated himself.

The guard relaxed with a snicker. "You know, I don't blame you for fightin' to keep your niggers."

"I never fought for the right to own slaves."

"Couldn't afford none, huh?"

Even in the name of war, he couldn't completely wipe the blood from his hands, and ignorance of the truth could never forgive him for owning other humans as livestock. "I had a couple of servants—long ago."

The guard only chortled harder. "I would've liked one of them mulatto gals for myself. If'n you didn't fight for the niggers, then what did you fight for?"

Annoyed with such asinine stupidity, Wil met the guard's gaze. "To keep Yankee bastards like you from soiling the South."

The musket butt struck him in the face and sent him reeling backward. Flat on his back, Wil heard shouts from other men as they gathered round. Groggy from the blow, he opened his eyes slowly and found himself staring at the end of a musket barrel.

"Come on, Reb. I need little cause to blow your head off."

An officer shoved the musket to the side and stepped between them. "The war is over, Private."

Rough hands jerked Wil to his feet. Soldiers on each side held his arms fast. Glaring at the private, he strained against the stranglehold grip.

"What is the meaning of this disruption?" the officer inquired.

The guard stood at attention. "He insulted me, sir."

"It must have been *some* insult." The captain sent an irate glance in Wil's direction. "Well?"

As his anger faded, Wil felt a painful throb in his cheek. "I reacted to some rather ignorant misconceptions without thinking. My humble apology, sir."

With a slow, appraising glance, the captain stepped closer. "You speak more like a gentleman officer. Colonel Jackson? Release him," he ordered the soldiers, and thrust out a friendly hand. "Captain Shaw..."

The captain's eyes flickered in familiarity, but Wil had no recollection as to where they had met. Confused, he accepted the officer's hand and shook it. "Do I know you, sir?"

"I believe so. You are Lieutenant Colonel William Jackson, are you not?"

No sense in lying—the man obviously knew who he was. Wil nodded.

"At the beginning of the war, you came to the aid of a Union scout. An overenthusiastic boy wanted to join the fighting and was prepared to execute the scout in the name of the Cause. You saved my life, sir."

It dawned on him. Under the pretense that the scout was his escaped prisoner, he had paid the boy in silver and sent him on his way. He released the scout with the warning that if they ever met in battle, circumstances would be different. "This isn't exactly a battle situation . . ."

Captain Shaw smiled. "Which delights me to no end. Why have my men detained you?"

"I don't have a pass."

"Where are you headed, Colonel? I'll see what I can do to get you one."

"My destination is near Frederickburg, but I was a brigadier at the war's end."

Indifferent to the revelation, the captain widened his smile to a grin. "Then when we reach Fredericksburg, you shall have a pass, Brigadier Jackson."

Pain spread throughout his cheek. Wil rubbed it and choked back a cough. "I'm much obliged, but I can't keep a marching pace these days."

"If you will allow me the honor of repaying my debt, I'll take care of that as well." He held out his hand once more—as a friend, not an enemy.

Relieved, Wil accepted the captain's aid.

For two days, Wil listened to the groaning axles of wagon wheels. While traveling in a tumbledown army wagon made the journey more bearable, he noticed more than a few soldiers sending him scowls.

True to his word, Captain Shaw secured a pass upon their arrival in Fredericksburg.

Wil ventured the battle-scarred streets until he stood outside the boarded-up red-brick house. More than two years had come and gone since courting Alice. Facing the prospect of battle, he had been noncommittal then. No, the reason wasn't due to the war, but ghosts from the past. Maybe he'd return with his family here—or head west.

With only a few miles to Amanda's farm, he was wasting time. The war was over. Rejoice in that fact and make plans later. Wil set out on the final leg of the journey.

On the outskirts of town, devastated streets gave way to charred fields and ruined fencing. A red-tailed hawk floated overhead in search of prey, and he wondered if the entire South had been equally plundered.

An elderly farmer struggled with a plow and a bone-thin mule. Life recovered slowly to fields once littered by bodies and filled with death. Thunder rumbled like cannonfire from the distant woods ahead. The same woods where he had fought and been wounded, then a year later led an attack against near impossible odds. Even now, he recalled the intense heat from the fires and heard the screams of men burning alive.

Another thunderclap, and Wil blinked. The dead were long buried, and he quickened his pace. If the storm expanded beyond the Wilderness, the Rappahannock River could easily become impassible. A mile from the crossing, the wind kicked up gusts and rain pelted the ground. He was soaking wet by the time he reached the ford, and the sound of rushing water alerted him to what he already feared. The waters had churned to rapids and were still rising.

Half a mile back, he had passed a farm. He'd seek shelter and wait out the storm. Discouraged that his goal was so near yet out of reach, he turned.

A woman shouted.

Wil shielded his eyes from the lashing downpour.

In the middle of the ford, a mulatto woman slapped a whip across the thighs of a mud-drenched horse. The horse strained in its harness, but the cart behind it failed to budge. Frantic, she struck the poor animal again. Eyes bulging, the horse only grew more nervous.

Damn—she'd likely drown if he didn't go to her aid. He gritted his teeth and plunged into the chilly water. The water wasn't just cold, but downright bone-chilling.

Already in waist deep, he slogged toward the cart. The woman whipped the horse again. With the rising water and increasing current, Wil struggled to keep from being swept away. He reached the cart and pushed from behind as the horse pulled. The cart rocked forward, then back again, but remained mired in the mud.

No use. His feet went out from under him. Sucked under the water, he grabbed the edge of the cart and righted himself. He extended a hand to help the woman from the cart.

Her eyes were wide with fear, and Lily screamed. "It cain't be. You're dead." She struggled against him and screamed louder. "Miss Amanda say dat you dead."

He had her in his arms. "I assure you I'm not, but if we don't get to the bank . . ." His hands were nearly frozen, and he barely managed to release the horse before it broke free of its own accord.

"I cain't swim, Mr. Wil."

As panic set in, she flailed her arms harder. With one arm locked around her waist, he suffered the blows and gripped the horse's mane. The horse pulled them toward the bank. Lily stopped hitting him and contained her fear long enough to clutch the mane with both hands.

Relieved she no longer fought him, Wil boosted her on the horse's back. She leaned low against the horse's neck and trembled. The bank got closer.

A swell hit him and towed him under. Before he could hold his breath, he swallowed a mouthful of water. A hand gripped his forearm and helped him shove his head above the surface. Sputtering and coughing, he fought to breathe. *Damn, the water was cold.*

His muscles ached and his mind was growing numb. *Don't think about it.* He had faced worse.

Near the bank, the water seemed less deep. An illusion—an undercurrent tugged at his feet. Even the horse strained against the flow. His grip on the mane was the only thing that kept him from going under. They reached the slope to the bank, and the horse skidded in the mud, dropping to its knees.

Though a blur, Wil saw Lily's face contort as she sailed overhead. Then nothing. Only cold water surrounded him, and there was a roaring in his ears. Unable to breathe, he struggled to get his head above water as the current swept him downstream.

* * *

Even senseless pounding couldn't make Alice look up. On the wet afternoon, she stared at the flames in the fireplace while Amanda answered the door.

Shrieks and sobs came from the foyer, then a drenched Lily rushed into the parlor. "I saw him, Miss Alice. He save my life."

"Saw whom?"

"Mr. Wil."

Wil . . . Nearly bursting into tears, Alice stood. "You're playing a cruel joke, Lily."

Upset further, Lily flapped her arms like a bird. "I don't lie, an' I ain't jokin'. Mr. Wil save my life."

Her knees went weak, and Alice reseated herself before she fell. She exchanged a glance with Amanda.

"Could Captain Hanes have been mistaken?" Amanda asked.

Alice shook her head. "He was on Wil's staff for more than a year."

Lily's fingers traced over her heart. "I swear, Miss Alice. I wouldn't kid 'bout such a thing."

"Lily," Amanda said gently, "tell us what happened."

As Lily recounted her experience at the river, Alice clutched her collar.

"Alice . . ." Amanda called her again before she looked over. "I'll have Sam and Ezra check the river."

Unable to allow herself the hope that Wil might have been alive an hour ago only to have him taken from her grasp yet again, she wanted to scream. "Suit yourself."

"You know we must—for Wil's sake."

For Wil's sake . . . Don't dare hope. The ache would only begin anew. Alice watched as Amanda hurried from the parlor. *Get up and go with her.* Frozen in place, she tried to move. A foot, then the other . . . There— she was standing.

Lily seized her sleeve. "Miss Alice, leave it to da men. You bin through enough."

Dazed but focused on her duty, Alice replied, "No Lily, I must know."

"Den I come too."

"You had best get out of those wet clothes."

"Yes'm."

As Lily scooted from the parlor, Alice collected her cloak and stepped outside. Amanda spoke to Sam under the barn's overhang, explaining Lily's ordeal crossing the Rappahannock, and here she stood dressed in black—widow's black.

Slightly dizzy, Alice clutched the porch rail for support. Over the past month, all hope for any future had been dashed. Tears moistened her pillow every morning, and each afternoon while Emma napped, she sat on the knoll and watched the hawk. Long ago, the noble bird had sent her a message.

Wil *had* returned to her, but he couldn't complete the journey without her help. Her heart pounded, and Alice sprang down the steps through sheets of rain. She clasped her hands together and held them up, pleading, "Sam . . ."

"As I've been explaining to Amanda, don't get your hopes up. He could have been carried miles downriver."

Miles? If that were the case, she might never find him. "But I have to know. Certainly you can understand that?"

"Of course. We can't search the other side of the river until the rain eases some, and we won't be able to dredge it."

Alice swallowed but kept her poise. "I'm aware of that."

"Then I'll help Ezra with the team."

No longer requiring the crutch, Sam limped inside the barn, and Amanda opened her arms with a hug. "I'll say a prayer."

"Thank you, Amanda. He needs all the prayers we can give him. You'll keep an eye on Emma for me, won't you?"

"Just scoot back here before her next feeding. The last thing I need is a fussy baby on my hands."

What would she have done without Amanda? Alice clutched her sister tighter. Freshly changed in a dry dress, Lily rejoined them. The clip-clop of hooves rounded from beside the barn. Ezra brought the wagon to a halt, and Sam helped the two women beneath the safety of a gum cloth in the back.

As the wagon bumped along, axles creaked. A rut jarred her teeth and lurched her backward. At least under the gum cloth, they remained dry. *Would they find Wil? What condition would he be in?* Oh dear, she had allowed herself the hope they might find him alive and prayed harder. At the sound of rushing water, her heart felt like it had drifted to her throat.

The wagon grated to a halt. Sam lifted the gum cloth and helped her from the wagon bed. While the rain had eased to misting, the Rappahannock waters remained too high and choppy for crossing. "We'll cover more ground by splitting up," Sam said, taking charge. He placed the haversack on his shoulders. "Ezra, you and Lily drive the wagon downriver to the next ford, and we'll meet somewhere in the middle."

"Yessir."

The wagon creaked on. Sam immediately set out along the river's bank, while Alice stood on the ford's slope. Not more than two hours before, Wil had been here—alive. She thought of his strong arms around her and ran after Sam. Her feet slipped in the mud and skidded out from under her. Nearly twisting an ankle, she slid. A bush slapped her in the face, and she came to a halt near the river's edge.

"Alice, you don't need to put yourself through this. I'll let you know if I find him." Sam gripped her arm, and she regained her feet.

So kind and gentle—in spite of being a Yankee. She was all too aware of why Amanda loved him. "By now you should know the McGuire sisters can't sit idly on their posteriors. Amanda would have accompanied us too if she wasn't getting so heavy with child that she's begun waddling."

They continued on. Overgrown with vegetation and brambles, the trail along the river was barely more than a deer path. She kept glancing to the river, then back again.

Bubbles—she blinked. Yes, bubbles were definitely rising to the surface. She pointed. "Sam . . ."

"If he's been in the water this long, he won't be breathing."

Uncertain whether she should be relieved or not, she suspected he knew more about such matters than she did. Like Wil, he was a military man, and his experience surpassed her own country upbringing.

The path sloped away from the river. To keep her from slipping and falling again, Sam grasped her hand. She glanced over the edge. Poplar and river birch leaves made seeing the river's edge difficult.

After they trudged over rocks and slogged through mud, the trail aligned with the river once more. When they rendezvoused with Ezra and Lily, the old Negro shrugged and shook his head—no sign of Wil. Her hope was rapidly diminishing, and the next section of water revealed more of the same.

The parties split up and combed another mile. The sun poked through the clouds, but mist steamed over the water. At the top of a ridge, footsore and weary, she heard the cry of a red-tailed hawk. The noble bird soared overhead.

Alice halted.

"What is it?" Sam asked.

"The hawk." She understood now. A surveyor of the skies—the hawk saw things ordinary people could not. "Sam, he's here."

He raised a skeptical brow. "Because of a hawk?"

Sam peered over the edge, and she called out. "Wil . . ." No answer. He might be dazed or hurt. She called again. Still no response.

"Alice, he's not here."

"He is."

Sam secured a rope from the haversack to a poplar trunk.

"What are you doing?"

"If you're that certain, I'll check."

As he wrapped the other end of the rope about his waist, her hand went to his forearm. "Let me go," she said.

Adamant to her request, he shook his head.

"If he's hurt or . . ." *Dead*—Lord forgive her, she had thought it. " . . . we won't be able to get him back to the farm without Ezra's help. I can tend him while you fetch Ezra."

Sympathetic, his blue eyes softened. "Alice, have you ever seen someone who's drowned?"

In the hospital, she had watched men die—too many from horrendous wounds. He had been trying to protect her. "No," she said weakly, "but no matter the circumstances, you'll need Ezra's help."

Relenting, Sam tied the rope around her waist. "I'll hold this end until you're safely down."

She kissed his cheek. "Thank you."

Grasping the rope as a lifeline, she went over the incline. Loose rocks and red clay plummeted. She halted. What if the rocks pelted Wil?

Sam waved her on. The slope gave way to a precipice. Her feet slid from under her. Hands flailing for something to grasp, she screamed. Down she went. The rope jolted to a halt. Dizzy from the drop, she dangled in midair.

Sam groaned. "Are you all right?"

She kept her eyes shut tight and clutched the rope. "No harm done."

Another groan. "I'm pulling you back up."

Don't give in to panic. *Look down.* She might locate Wil. Alice opened her eyes.

Only a few more feet, and the slope returned to a gradual grade. Leafy bushes and river birch kept her from gaining a clear view to the river. She felt the rope move—up. "Not yet, Sam. Let me finish what I set out to do."

The rope lowered—slowly and gradually. Solid ground was beneath her once more. She untied the rope and crept forward. Muck sucked her feet in the boggy earth. Water—so cold, the Rappahannock waters had recently flooded the bottomland.

She parted branches. "Wil . . ."

Still no sign. Like a sow in the mud, she wallowed through ankle-deep water. Brambles tore her skirt. A fallen sycamore spread net-like branches in the choppy river. A net . . . He could have grasped the branches and pulled himself out of the water.

"Wil, please answer."

Frantic, she searched among the web of branches. She heard a moan, and only when it echoed did she realize it was her own.

"Alice?"

It was Sam. Such fool's play to have got her hopes up. Numb and defeated, she turned.

"Alice . . ."

Her heart thumped. She froze. "Wil? Sam, fetch Ezra! Wil, where are you?"

A sluggish voice breathed her name again, and she spied a pale hand, clasping a branch. Partly submerged in a pitch-black pool, he was wedged between tree limbs and rocks.

His voice was barely audible when he spoke, " . . . thought I was dreaming."

"Wil . . ." Tears streaked unashamedly down her cheeks. She grasped his arm and tugged.

With a groan, he dragged himself from the murky pool, but he fell into the slosh of the bottomland. His skin was like ice.

She unfastened her cloak and wrapped it around him. Cradling his mud-caked body in her arms, she whispered, "Sam's gone for help. Everything shall be all right now."

"Alice . . ."

She reminded him to save his energy and hushed him.

With a rare need to talk, he wouldn't have any of it. He spoke of the war, quietly musing what had been gained by fighting. Four years of hell, but bad times weren't over. Not yet—there was too much healing for the country ahead. Then he spoke of Peopeo—not how she had died, but how she had lived. Returning to the present, he told her about the fall of Petersburg and his journey home.

He clutched her skirt, and his dark eyes met hers. "Alice, why are you wearing black?"

Alice brushed away her tears. "There's plenty of time to explain."

His icy hand fell away and made a splash as it hit the muck. Her fingers stroked through his damp hair, and he closed his eyes. To his even breathing, she hugged him tighter, whispering her love and praying that Sam wouldn't be long in returning.

Only two years before, the glistening bodies on the heights had taught her there was no glory to come from war. But if it hadn't been for the war, there would have been no smuggling supplies, tending wounded, or treating each tender moment as if it were the last. As a result, they had Emma.

The war gave life—and glory—in peculiar ways.

Historical Note

After the battle in December 1862, the city of Fredericksburg was in ruins. Most residents fled their homes and became refugees. A few brave souls returned to salvage what they could. The Army of Northern Virginia camped south of the city in winter quarters, while the Army of the Potomac settled across the river along the Rappahannock banks. Although discouraged by commanding officers, fraternizing between opposing sides was fairly common.

With the issuance of the Emancipation Proclamation, the war climate changed. At the beginning of the spring 1863 campaign, the remaining residents of Fredericksburg were forced from their homes yet again for the bloodiest year to date.

In the tangled, forbidding woods of the Wilderness, the two armies met at the Battle of Chancellorsville. Except for the amount of acreage, these woods have changed little in the ensuing 140 years.

As in *Promise & Honor*, I have taken great care to weave the historical facts with my own fictional tale. General A.P. Hill returns in his historical role. In actuality, he visited Libby Prison in January 1864, and I have incorporated his debilitating illness of uremia toward the end of his life.

Besides General Hill, the character of Elizabeth Van Lew is factual. A known spy that gathered sensitive information from the Confederate White House, she frequented Richmond prisons, often resorting to a mentally unbalanced routine as cover. The act earned her the nickname "Crazy Bet," among other names. Along with collecting intelligence, she kept a secret room ready in the Van Lew mansion for hiding escaped Union prisoners.

While attempts were common, actual prison escapes were less so. With able-bodied men in the field, prisons were understaffed. Under unusual circumstances, some prisoners walked out the main door. Sam's escape is loosely based on a failed attempt.

In the spring of 1864, the opposing armies met again in the formidable woods of the Wilderness. After a fierce fight against overwhelming numbers, General Samuel McGowan's brigade, a consistently reliable veteran unit from South Carolina, retreated in chaos. The scene between General Robert E. Lee and Wil did indeed take place between Generals Lee and McGowan. Throughout *Honor & Glory*, I have implied General McGowan's outstanding brigade. However, with the exception of those already mentioned, all of my characters are fictional. Wil is not meant to represent the real general.

During the nine-month Petersburg siege, the longest siege in U.S. history, trench warfare was a day-to-day event. Many battles and skirmishes went unrecorded. While I have taken advantage of this fact, the raid on the supply line is factual, as well as many of the events leading up to the fall of Petersburg.

In parting, I have made no effort to portray either side as right or wrong. My only aim was to show the people and the difficult decisions they faced in the name of honor and loyalty.

Best regards,
Kim Murphy

Acknowledgments

The writing of any historical novel takes tremendous research, from visiting historic sites to digging through dusty archives. I would like to thank the many individuals whose names I do not know who helped me find my way around those areas.

A special thank you goes to my editors, K.A. Corlett and Catherine Karp, and my cover designer, Mayapriya Long. My deepest appreciation also extends to Juanita Leisch, author of *Who Wore What?: Women's Wear 1861-1865*, and Doug Moore for providing photographs to make stunning cover art. Most of all, I would like to thank my family: my son, Bryan, and especially my husband, Pat; both of whom are often left wondering which century I really live in.